banana boys

(heung jiu jei)

terry woo

banana boys
(heung jiu jei)
terry woo

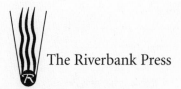

The Riverbank Press

Chinese calligraphy: Stephen Woo

Cover design: John Terauds

THE CANADA COUNCIL | LE CONSEIL DES ARTS
FOR THE ARTS | DU CANADA
SINCE 1957 | DEPUIS 1957

We acknowledge the support of
The Canada Council for the Arts
for our publishing program.

Canadian Cataloguing in Publication Data

Woo, Terry
  Banana boys

ISBN 1-896332-15-3

1. Chinese Canadians - Fiction.* I. Title.

PS8595.O5988B36 2000   C813'.6   C00-932293-0
PR9199.3.W66B36 2000

The Riverbank Press
P.O. Box 456, 31 Adelaide St. East, Toronto, Ontario, Canada M5C 2J5

Second printing
10 9 8 7 6 5 4 3

Printed and bound in Canada by Transcontinental Printing

To Gabe, Vince, Dave (Eye), Sam/Zeke, Calv, Alan, Schen, Mi, Pat, Scott, Ed, Lewis, Arvie, Gord, Pete, Sam C., Erick, Dave Bro, Larry and tens of thousands of others.

There's a place for us out there. I know it.

And if there isn't, we'll damn well make one.

"Rage, for better or worse, generates a future.
Victims are the ones who've given up on the future.
Instead, they've joined the dead. And the rest,
look at them: unless they're enraged and acting on it,
they're useless, unconscious; they're dead themselves
and they don't even know it."

– Russell Banks

"…you're not Chinese and you're not white…
what the hell are you, anyway?"

– Bernard Chang

Contents.

She is exquisitely beautiful, skin pale as the moonglow, lips red as wine and just as sweet, her hair a waterfall of black silk that blends softly with the night, taking her tresses into its fold. She is wearing an elegant set of red wedding robes done in the traditional Chinese style – conservative, but revealing enough to show her comely form, revealing herself to me because she loves me. I sense it, deeply, and am enticed. I fear, but she looks so beautiful and she loves me, I cannot resist. So I give in.

Her red silk scarf gently wraps around my abdomen, pulling me toward her pleading, outstretched arms. Wo ei ni, *she says simply,* I love you. *Her voice is melodic and tranquil, her beautiful large eyes glistening in the dark, red lips quivering in the moonlight.*

I am tired and drunk and lonely, so I do not struggle. I do not pray or make crosses with my hands, but submit passively. I feel her hot-cold embrace, sending messages of joy-terror up my spine into my wine-addled mind. Oh baby. *We kiss briefly and gently, drinking of each other. I hear the soft peal of bells in the distance – wind chimes gently ringing in the night breeze. She smells clean and perfumed.*

I am completely enraptured by her. She embraces me and leads me in a graceful, haunting dance. Across the floor, the moon, the sky. I cannot help but follow, I love her so much. Wo ei ni, *she whispers again, gently undoing my tie and unbuttoning my shirt and running her long nails across my chest.*

Glass shatters in the background. Blood is drawn. I am bleeding but I do not care. The blood is warm on my chest and seeps into my clothing, the red bleeds into the cold, fiery crimson of her robes. I am confused. I am in Love.

Her sweet scent wafts over me, overwhelming me, making me more drunk than the wine. I do not know what it is. I do not care. I am not in control, and that arouses me. My wounds are bleeding and arousing me. The pain blends into pleasure, and I cannot draw a line.

Wo ei ni, *she says again, simply, her dark eyes still reflecting her innocence and hunger. She tears into my clothing with her claws, opening more wounds and drawing more blood. She starts to kiss them, lick them, sucking gently, drawing out my life, my essence. Oh baby. I am blissful and content and drunk. It has never been this good.*

She kisses me, and her kiss, though soft and gentle, hits me like a blow to the forehead, knocking reason and fear out of me. Her hands grace over my body, drawing even more blood. Wo ei ni, she whispers, but she is much closer now and her plaintive, simple expression screams at me like a wind that does not stop.

She enters me. Suddenly, there is no sound, no pain. I have become the woman, she has become the man. She enters me, but there is no violence, no aggression, no violation. She enters me and life and vitality pours out of me in exchange for a tenderness I have never before known. Wo ei ni. It shouldn't be this way, this peaceful, but I do not know, I have always received, I have never given. I have always taken, I have always received.

Wo ei ni. *There is no pain, and it is warm, but she enters me and all else is leaving me. Her love is inside me, it makes me whole.*

Oh baby…

part 0
thanatopsis.

He's Dead, Jim.

The first thing you have to know is that I did love him. With no reservations. *Almost.*

But through my eyes, he wasn't a "normal" person, my big brother. Through my eyes, he was like a mannequin, I guess; a well-crafted, well-behaved, impeccably dressed mannequin. Smooth, handsome, well-dressed. Attractive and plastic and filled with explosives primed for detonation.

Through my eyes, he was filled with nervous, anxious, restless energy, seething beneath that plastic exterior, past the good looks, polite smile and graceful mannerisms. His actions were cool, confident, moving at a stately twenty miles per hour, his mind probably moving a thousand times that.

It frightened me. I suppose his eyes gave it away.

Definitely the eyes.

Some years ago, one afternoon, I found Rick on the porch of our modest suburban Scarborough home, tranquil amidst the car washing, the sprinklers, the hedge trimming, the screaming kids playing road hockey a few houses down. He was un-winding on the Zellers swing-chair, swinging slowly, knees flexing rhythmically, eyes glazed, smiling faintly, wearing the fast food uniform from his after-school job, replete with apron and name tag – *"Hello, my name is Richard Wong"* – and that standard ugly clip-on tie that was askew on his collar. He also was taking large hits from a 26-ouncer of vodka.

"Shirl," he said with a vacant smile, "*Mm **ho** yup hui-**ah*** (Don't go inside)."

I was only a giddy youngster back then, in Catholic plaid, my hair in pigtails, oblivious to many things.

"Why?" I asked in English, snapping my gum.

"Because you might not like it," he said. He hadn't blinked once.

I went inside, expecting a broken vase or tinfoil in the microwave or something. I stepped past the coat rack, the mirror facing the stairs, the fish tank facing the door. Everything looked okay. The vase was fine. I went into the family room. There was a fire in the fireplace. It was June.

I saw our rotary telephone, the cord wrapped tightly around the plastic receiver several times, melting beside another empty bottle of vodka. The acrid smell of toasted plastic hung in the air like the corpse of an executed man. Apparently, he had doused the telephone with the liquor and set it on fire.

"I doused the telephone with the liquor and set it on fire," he explained. "Didn't work, so's I hadda use some gasoline as well." He motioned to a plastic gas can we used for the Lawn-Boy, tucked underneath the swing chair. He giggled, tugging at his tie and missing by four inches, sliding off the swing onto the wooden floor.

I bit my lower lip, tears welling up inside. "What happened?"

"I received a call from the McCapitalistic powers that be," he said, staring at the sky, still smiling. "My employment has been terminated." He reeked of liquor. He was only sixteen.

From the porch floor, he explained the situation to me, calmly and carefully. He talked about a lot of things I didn't understand at the time – economics, the transient nature of the service sector, the exploitation of the student class by the bourgeoisie, racism in the workplace. He talked about school, its demands, the requirements to get into the university program of his choice, extra business credits, and the declining hours at his job that resulted. He talked about his supervisor, a middle-aged McCareer person who didn't understand, or really even care, as he off-handedly fired him. He talked about resisting the impulse to grab the motherfucker by the neck and slam his head into the deep fryer.

He continued to say that his termination of employment – these were his exact words, I remember – would by no means set back his "Master Plan…about money, about cars, about babes, about school, about future employment, promotion and eventual World Domination." He did this while casually unbuttoning his shirt, taking it off, pouring the rest of his vodka on the pile of clothing and trying to set it on fire with a Zippo lighter.

The confused, fearful expression on my face melted away, replaced by an empty look that crawled into my eyes as they widened several inches. The tears, flowing freely just a few seconds ago, seemed to leap back from where they came, never again to emerge. I shuffled my brother inside, away from the prying eyes of the neighbours, extinguished the smoking clothes, doused the fire in the fireplace, opened a few windows, threw away the bottles, and escorted my brother to the shower. He was still rather pleasant, still hadn't blinked once.

As I was cleaning up the porch, I noticed a bag of McTakeout by the swing chair. Underneath a few burgers, I found hundreds of dollars in small bills, wrapped up in standard cashiers' bundles. I didn't know where he got the money, and I didn't really care. I did what was expected of me. Impassively, I took the bag upstairs to Rick's room and stuffed it under his mattress, beside some other interesting items: Safety deposit box keys. Bags of capsules. A clip of bullets, but no gun.

From that day, I quietly managed affairs, cleaned up the occasional mess, always helped him if he asked, watched him skillfully maneuver out of numerous potentially messy situations, always to his own personal advantage. I observed him, expressionless, emotionless. I watched my big brother in his smooth, scheming, intelligent, hypo-manic way, build up his status and fortune and power until he finally self-destructed.

Now, he's just another slab of meat on God's cutting board. It was disturbing.

I stood there, one row back from the coffin, expressionless, emotionless. My mother was convinced that my paleness was from not eating enough. My father guessed it was because I knew something other people did not.

"You have sensed the inherent emptiness of the world," he said, eyes focused on infinity. He had just taken his daily dosage of Lithium and was calm and uselessly poignant, as always. I guess it was perceptive, but I couldn't understand why he had never been able to tune into the core of Rick's problems.

Not that Rick ever told anyone about anything, of course. Except for his little sister. Told in odd, sporadic revelations of the damned. *Why me*, I often wondered. A calculated gesture? A cry for help? Services rendered for the cheques that are putting me through school? Sadism? I don't know. I suppose keeping the secrets and managing the insanity was how I became so ex-pressionless and emotionless in the first place.

Something strange happened to Rick when he turned nine-teen.

He became convinced that he could time-shift out of his *present* consciousness into a *future* consciousness.

"Shirley," Mike said drunkenly over the phone, one night after they'd gone off to university, voice slurred but reflecting a sense of panic I was feeling myself.

"Yes?"

"It's Rick."

"Rick?"

"I think he's fucked. We're in a bar, we were just talking, and he says he's from the future or something…"

"What?"

"The future," he repeated, ignoring me. "He says he's work-ing in some company downtown, getting promoted, signing contracts, sleeping with beautiful women…"

"Have…have you guys been drinking?"

"A little. I don't know. He's fucked. I'm gonna take him home." *Click.*

I hung up, confused. That was how it started – Rick claiming that he was shifting forward in time, to future tasks, assignments, jobs, milestones, like completing his CMA exam, graduating from university with Honours, going to Taiwan for the *Chien Tan* "Love Boat" tour, completing multi-million dollar deals over a Scotch or six at a trendy downtown bistro.

At first, he would claim that he asked people like Mike to orient him – where he was, what was he doing, what the date was, what his age was, etc. – and scaring the living daylights out of them. Then got he smart and started scaring the daylights out of *me* instead.

"Shirl," he instructed me, calmly, presumably in the present, "I need you to keep track of me at certain points in my life."

"Mmm."

"Keep track of where I am, how old I am, what my status is – school, job, finances. Partners, friends. Enemies."

"Mmm."

"These time shifts never last longer than an hour or so." He continued, smiling slightly, his voice still a paragon of maddening reason. "I need all this information to find my bearings, and then I want to seek out information about my successes and mistakes, to use in the present."

"Mmm."

"Nothing as small-time as finding out stock prices, don't you worry," he said, trying to sound reassuring but sounding anything but. "That would be cheap. But you have to admit, they're an excellent thing to take advantage of."

"Mmm."

"Can you do this for me? I know it's hard to believe, but it *is* true, and I *really* need your help."

"Okay."

"You're the greatest, Shirl."

"Thanks," I said, while my heart screamed.

He only called a few times. But I kept my Promise. Except I hadn't heard from him recently. Then I thought about Richard shifting into the morgue freezer or his cremation jar or into internalized madness or wherever. I shivered, pulling my jacket tighter around my shoulders.

I looked at him there, lying his casket.

I hate him.

That's not true.

I *could* have hated him for everything, if I were capable of feeling something as visceral as hate. Maybe I almost hated myself for being unable to do anything to stop his downfall. Maybe I'd actually caused it in some way, quietly and efficiently taking in his insanity.

But seeing them beside me, mom sobbing uncontrollably and dad consoling her with tears in his own eyes, made me almost hate Rick. As much as I loved him.

People started to arrive for the funeral service: the Chans, the Ngs, the Wongs (no relation), the Yeung-Stevensons, the Brubakers. They all came up to my parents, offering condolences. Tasmin Lee, Rick's fiancée, arrived, very fashionably dressed and very distraught. She walked up with her friend Thomas in tow, tears streaming down her face, and threw herself into mom's arms, almost toppling over her (my mom is very short). A number of people I didn't recognize, presumably some of Rick's former co-workers, Hong Kong friends and ex-girlfriends, also arrived.

And then there were the Banana Boys.

Sheldon arrived first. He looked kind of out of it, fairly sad. He offered his sympathies, patted me on the head, and then sat down, staring into space.

And then came Dave. He looked distracted and irritable. He was wearing a pair of jeans with his jacket and tie, and scuffed Converse high-tops – only Dave would do that for a funeral. While he shook hands with us, I noticed he had brown paper bag shoved in his left pocket. Squinting at the coffin, he took a seat beside Sheldon and frowned.

Luke looked strange in a suit, considering I'd always seen him in leather, flannel, or Mountain Co-op gear. He made his way up to my family, squeezed my hand and looked at me, and then at his suit. Raising an eyebrow, he smiled slightly and sat down in the front row beside his sister Janice, who had arrived earlier. I almost smiled, despite the somber circumstances.

Mike must've come in just after Pastor Wong (no relation) started the service. I saw him later, hiding in one of the back rows, discreetly avoiding his parents and his sister, who were seated up front. Hands dug into the pockets of his dress pants, he noticed me looking at him. His face reddening a little, he managed a helpless shrug.

"…Richard Wong was a good boy, a strong boy, filled with direction and ambition," the pastor orated in an impassioned, accent-less voice. "He knew where he was going. Truly, his death could not have come at a sadder time, when his future looked so bright and promising." Many guests acknowledged this comment gravely, some nodding their heads. Tasmin, lower lip quivering, her lovely face streaked with tears, clutched Thomas' arm and choked.

As Pastor Wong went on, I stared at the fifth and final member of the Banana Boys. Rick was lying in a half-open oak casket, the warm April sun shining through a window, reflecting off of his perfect complexion. He was surrounded by flowers, some with white ribbons with Chinese characters scrawled in black – good luck for the afterlife, or something. The Chinese are rather big on luck. Rick's suit obscured the horrific wounds sustained by the lower half of his body, caused by the metal, broken glass and curious impalement on a statuette.

He looked as graceful and confident as he ever was in life, and at peace; this was probably because I couldn't see his eyes. I wondered if he died with his eyes open. I hate when that happens. Mom told me that in Chinese folklore, people who died unpeacefully, or with unfinished business, did so with their eyes still open. In my mind, I could see Rick in his posh downtown condo, coughing and writhing in pain, shaking with alcohol-induced convulsions until he took his last gasp. His eyes were wide open, unseeing, and he was lying among shards of glass in a pool of blood and vomit, a long translucent pyramid protruding from his bloody abdomen, the life drained out of him.

I sighed inwardly once again, feeling the tears form in my stomach, knowing that they wouldn't – *couldn't* – come out. Very few ever have in a long time. I have stayed cool and controlled and emotionless for a long, long time.

Rick is my brother. I have his blood in my veins, his flesh on my body. I don't love him. I don't hate him. I don't really feel strongly about anything. I don't think I ever have.

Pastor Wong adjusted his glasses, voice quavering with boundless Christian emotion. My thoughts drifted to the other Banana Boys. There was Luke, Dave, Sheldon, Rick and Mike. No joy, no luck in this club – they went to school together, worked like maniacs, drank a lot, complained about everything, sometimes acted like complete pigs, sometimes exhibited moments of caring and tenderness. Hit the books hard, hit the bottle even harder. Watching hockey games together, agonizing over women together, dreaming about bigger and better things. Together. Until now, I guess.

My first encounter with the Banana Boys was after they had met each other in their first semester at the University of Waterloo. Rick invited them down one weekend when mom had taken dad to this clinic in Montreal that treated bi-polars, and leaving the house in his capable hands for the weekend. He had a party, of course, along with a bunch of Rick's high school friends. The Banana Boys definitely stood out, not least because they were the only Asians there.

From that point on, whenever I encountered any of the Banana Boys, together or individually, there always seemed to be this weird bond in between them. Call it a sociology thing, or an ethnic thing, or an alcohol thing, or just wild coincidence, if you like. But it was as if they were always playing this large game of Twister, and as contorted and split and mixed up as they got, all the parts still joined up, somehow.

I usually differentiated those guys from Rick's Real Chinese Friends because the Banana Boys didn't *really* seem Chinese. Well, at least they didn't act like it, mostly. They were all CBCs, Canadian-born Chinese, "Bananas" – yellow on the outside and white on the inside. *Juk-sing.* Translated literally, the term means "hollow bamboo" in Cantonese. Hardly a flattering label, it's based on a metaphor that compares Canadian-born Chinese to a cross-section of a bamboo – hollow on one end, hollow on the other, empty through and through. In the eyes of "real" Canadians and "pure" Chinese, whatever that means, *juk-sing* have no consistent culture, no substance, no essence. They stand between two groups, not quite Canadian, and certainly not Chinese, marginal and maybe kind of messed up, belonging to and accepted by neither.

Maybe you've seen them. Many usually don't seem to…fit in, at least not well. They pronounce the "j" in words like *jook*. They eat burgers and steaks one day, and funky foods like chicken feet and pigs intestines the next. They listen to Country-Western and Heavy Metal, and despise Karaoke. They analyze and over-analyze the racial dynamics of a song lyric, a cup of coffee, or a particularly bad episode of *Kung Fu: The Legend Continues.* They cook bacon with chopsticks, and read Hong Kong magazines only for the pictures, flipping pages left to right.

Which is not to say their experiences are worse than those of most other social sub-groups. Oh no. I mean, many of them come from middle-class families, went to school, had money to spend, food to eat, clothes to wear – to certain eyes, their lives would read like one big slightly-ethnic John Hughes movie.

"…we pay our last respects to Richard," Pastor Wong continued, eyes reddening, voice trembling, "…as God claims him as His own. We all have our place. We all have our time. We may not wish it was Richard's. But it was. And we know that God will take care of him." Mom started crying again. Tasmin was already bawling uncontrollably, face smeared with make-up. I just stood and stared at Rick, somewhat depressed.

We all have our place. We all have our time.

Hollow, or not.

part 1
hi there!

Love Will Tear Us Apart.

So I'm going down the highway, heading east on the I-90 from Buffalo, feeling pretty mellow and doing about 125 clicks. I'm taking a break from work, and I'm on my way to visit my sister in Boston.

It's a nice day – the late August sun's shining, traffic is light, and upstate New York looks as brown and as unappealing as ever. I'm on my motorcycle, well beyond the state speed limit, not really understanding or caring what the equivalent is in kilometers…playing Russian Roulette with state troopers is a favourite personal pastime. The wind feels good through a gap in my leather jacket newly torn by my neighbour's dog, Wilson. The bike's handling well, and I've got the harsh sounds of *Ministry* ripping through my ears on my discman.

Life *can* be quite good.

When I was a little kid, my family used to go on trips like this all over the place. Me with my father on his Harley, my sister Janice with mom on her slightly-less powerful Honda, taking off from the urban wastes of Toronto and going wherever …Kingston, Ottawa, Montreal a few times, or up north to places with plenty of trees and fish. I remember the arguments my parents used to have – all in good fun, of course – about the advantages and disadvantages of American versus Japanese bikes, at diners and truck stops while we stuffed ourselves with greasy burgers, stale fries and sub-standard soups. I tell you, we must have been a sight to all those highway regulars – an Asian family, clad from head to toe in black leather, eating and arguing in a half-Chinese, half-English jabber.

Now, I usually travel alone. It's a lot easier that way. There's a wonderful sense of freedom in travelling alone – no worries, no responsibilities. No fights over the music, no inane small talk. It's pure ponder time. I can even sing along with the music without untowardly embarrassing myself.

My name's Luke Yeung. I'm 26 years old. I'm a full-time disc jockey at an upstart Toronto radio station that specializes in alternative industrial music. By day, I do The Morning Mosh, a refreshing and violently anarchist alternative to that Wacky-Pair-Of-Disc-Jockeys-Thing that I'm sure has worn out its welcome on airwaves across the continent. By night, I play the underground rave scene in TO, dropping a collection of funky Breaks to moon-eyed youngsters hopped up on PLUR, among other things.

I'm on vacation for a few weeks – *Zeesh better not fucking screw up my playlists!* – and on a lark, I'm going to see Janice for a few days. Janice is my little sister. We get along great. She's cool.

I come up to one of those classic Volkswagen vans – an orange anachronism with flowery curtains, Bondo spots, Dead-head stickers plastered on the side windows. I exchanged peace signs with the long-haired occupants, who were sparking one up as I passed.

Yeah, life can be good. But lately I've been having doubts. And that's not quite the norm for the Yeungster here…I've been told that I'm mellower-than-mellow, laider-than-laid-back, Gandhier-than-Gandhi. Everyone has doubts, of course, and normally I would just shrug them off as no big deal, but lately I've been thinking…just what *haven't* I been shrugging off?

Maybe I'm burning out a little.

Dave said that I'm being ridiculous. "For fuck's sake, you're only *twenty-six*! At the prime of your life, the peak of yer powers! Whattaya *mean* you're burning out? Look at Mike! *He's* burning out!"

I nodded in agreement at the time, only because I didn't want to get into another long grudge-fight with Dave. He gets pretty excitable about certain things, sometimes.

I was in the station lounge just before my vacation, leafing through a pile of new record reviews: latest *Front 242*? Great return to their roots, aggressive, clinical Belgian-industrial. Preview of the new *Chemical Brothers*? The Brothers do it again – masterful sampling amidst compelling electronic beats. *Limp*

Bizkit? Enough with the rap-metal thing, already. New *Consolidated*? Sucked rocks.

The station lounge was a great place to hang out. It's a kitschy throwback to the seventies in a clever, smug Gen-X sort of way. Velvet Elvises adorned the walls, fat ones fighting the thin ones for wall space. Incense burned. Lava lamps bubbled. A Donna Reed-style fridge stocked with freezies and Snapple hummed in the corner. The remaining wall space was plastered with a variety of Rock posters at unnatural angles, anything from the *Cocteau Twins* to *The Doors* to *Rage Against the Machine*, with a very special Bryan Adams poster serving as a dartboard. The mismatched collection of out-of-style suburban furniture was donated by the station owner's stepfather who, as a writer, felt that furniture inhibited his creative flow. He eventually found out he'd been wrong, of course, but was too embarrassed to ask for any of it back.

Anyway, in came Zeesh (short for Zahir Pardesh), the programming director of our humble station. He's a guy who positively oozes cool: long hair slicked back, silk shirt, vest, subdued tie, black jeans, well-worn black Doc Martenses. He walked up to me and dropped a large side of pork on my lap.

"Delivery," he said curtly, peering at me in an irritated sort of way through horn-rimmed glasses.

My eyes widened a notch. "What's this?"

Zeesh popped his gum. "As programming director, I authorize you not to play *House of Pork* anymore."

"And why not?" I slid the offending meat off my lap and onto a Whitney Houston record review.

He exploded. "Because there's A PILE OF THESE FUCKING THINGS IN THE OFFICE AND IT STINKS LIKE SHIT AROUND HERE! You never *listen* to me! I'm *tired* of you not ever listening to me! SubEtha Records *told* us fucked-up shit like this would happen if we played that record! *I* told you this would happen! What the *fuck* are you trying to do to us?"

"Erm…"

"…fucking *pork* all over the place! The closest I've been to the damned stuff in my entire life!!! [*Zeesh comes from a strict*

Muslim family.] Zel even found a two-pound package of *veal* on her chair, for Christ's sake!"

"Look, Zeesh," I explained patiently, "*House of Pork* is a great new Canadian band without a major deal. You know as well as I do that this station's made it by unconditionally supporting guys like this. They're good. Really good. People'll love them. How else will they make it if we don't play them?"

"I don't care if they're from my mother's village in Bangladesh! They have an insane pork cult worshipping them who're pulling shit like this all the time! Stop playing that goddamn record or I will personally *gut* you!"

"How about 'Pork Soda' by *Primus*?"

"*I MEAN IT!*" He stormed out of the room.

I shrugged and continued looking through my reviews. If this episode had happened two years ago (in fact, it sort of did, only with Kraft Dinner), I would have held my ground. Brimming with brash, karma-inducing confidence, I would have continued to play the record, defiantly drowning the station in rotting pork. I would have personally helped them with promotion and interviews and stuff, even volunteering as a roadie for gigs around the Golden Horsehoe area. And I probably would have liberated several Grade A hogs into the streets of downtown Toronto to boot.

But what did I do? I just sat there, nodding vaguely, plagued with doubts and shrugging them off, thinking about my upcoming vacation (this one).

Why was that?

Maybe I'm burning out a little. I'm getting too old for this. I'm selling out. My youth is running out. I'm saying things like "I'm getting too old for this," sometimes up to four times a day.

I have a pretty atypical family background, from what I'm told. My father was born in the early fifties, the son of a grocery store owner in Vancouver. As far as I knew, Pop had a fairly normal *Happy Days* sort of childhood – well, as normal as an Asian kid could have in Canada back then. He went to school, worked at the store, shot pool with friends, worked at the store. He owned a pair of Chucks, greased back his hair with pomade, smoked cigarettes, and worked at the store. You get the picture.

As a teenager, he became obsessed with this place called *Alishan*, a mountain of legend in Taiwan that his mother – my grandmother, who grew up there – told him about. Among other things, she told him the mountain was home to the most beautiful women in the world. That, of course, made her one of the most beautiful women in the world, but the conflict of interest evidently didn't matter much.

"During the Ming Dynasty, women from Jiangsu province were said to be the most lovely," she'd told him in Mandarin. "They were raised in the highest fashion to become personal consorts to the emperor – they were taught to write beautiful script, engage in intellectual conversation, play Chinese chess and musical instruments, and sing beautifully."

"So they were hookers?" Pop would ask, snapping his Dubble Bubble, getting a smack on the head for his insolence.

"*Aiya!* It wasn't like that at all you rude boy! These women were Royal Consorts! But… [*and I'd imagine Gram'd put up her hand as if she was directing traffic*] the women of *Alishan*, they were exquisite…at least as beautiful, if not superior. Here, on this mountain, under the big sky and the beautiful sunset, the loveliest girls made their homes and tended to their flocks…" and she'd burble on about native costumes or singing to goats or something.

But Pop didn't care about that; his imagination was already captured by this mystical Taiwanese mountain halfway around the world, loaded with fabulous babes. He was tired of being rejected by the white girls at school. He knew that someday, he would go to Taiwan and find himself a wife.

A few years later, much to the indignation of his parents, my father dropped out of university, to go on a quest across the Pacific to *Alishan*. Where he got the money, I'll never know… but eventually he ended up in Chiang's Republic of China.

When he got there, it wasn't all he'd expected. *Alishan* turned out be a cheesy tourist spot that catered to foreign students, mostly from Hong Kong and Malaysia. The traditional mountain costumes he envisioned were rented out to these students for pictures. But as disappointed as he was, he made the best of it: with a few Canadian dollars and some rudimentary Mandarin, he scammed a job teaching English to cute foreign student girls at the university. And that's where he met my mother.

In the Taiwan of the sixties, a tall English-speaking Chinese guy with foreign currency and a Canadian passport was something of a catch, so he was accosted by legions of giggling Taiwanese girls. My mom, the daughter of a retired army colonel who robbed a bank before he fled the mainland, was already fairly westernized and had money…she was also kind of a babe, so she could afford to be standoffish. That piqued Pop's interest, and wouldn't you know it, they were married within the month. He'd filled her head with visions of a Western lifestyle popularized by Hollywood movies shown at her school every weekend, and convinced her to drop out and go back to Canada with him.

They moved out east to Toronto to escape the wrath of his folks, living bohemian – a small and unfurnished apartment, motorcycle parts scattered on the floor, the sounds of *Creedence Clearwater Revival* mixing with the scent of Totally Happy Crop.

I, Lucas Alexander Yeung, was born a year later; Janice was dropped a year after that. At that point Mom and Dad slipped into some more mainstream occupations – Mom at a travel agency, Pop selling life insurance. You couldn't find more mainstream jobs than those, I suppose.

It's kind of scary how people change when they start a family. The groove gradually becomes a rut, one that's virtually impossible to escape from after a while. You become squarish, because your rent and utility payments require a certain level of responsibility. So my parents, who used to be cool, became grey and unamused…and decidedly unhappy.

What's In.	**What's Out.**
Harley-Davidson motorcycles.	Big green Impala that inhales leaded-gasoline.
Extended trips on said motorcycles.	Weekend visits to the mall, followed by dinner at Burger King.
Loud Guitar-Rock classics (no more 'Inagaddadivida'. Honey.)	Newspapers and mind-deadening insurance journals.
Totally Happy Crop.	Geraniums on the window ledge.

Fig. 1. What Price White Picket Fence?

One day in 1980, when I was ten, Pop lost it while eating a slice of unadorned toast. I think he realized that he was caught in a job he hated, and in a marriage that was increasingly dry and uninteresting. He finished his toast, gave me and Janice a peck on the forehead, and apparently said "fuck it" and got the hell out of Dodge for parts unknown.

It took two days for Mom to find out. She flipped out. I can still remember cradling Janice in our room, tears streaming down our faces as she alternately screamed and laughed outside, overturning furniture and throwing utensils at the wall for a solid hour. When it was over, she took us out for ice cream. She eventually settled into a state of perpetual bitterness.

Despite coming from a wealthy family, she refused to go back to Taiwan – that crazy Chinese face-saving thing – and elected to stick it out here, selling travel packages to edgy Taiwanese, raising us in a thoroughly dysfunctional and erratic manner.

And here I am – thoroughly dysfunctional and often erratic. Go figure.

A few hours later, I cross the New York-Mass border, idly noticing that the Berkshires really do seem dreamlike, even without the frosting. The clouds are almost cartoon-like in their perfection …dark on the bottom, fluffy and white on the top, with a lovely pinkish-tinge about them.

I smile to myself: *Dude, you are **so** relaxed.*

The sight of the mountains and the Massachusetts greenery made me think about Michael. Michael loves James Taylor… maybe I should bring him back a Taylorian souvenir from Martha's Vineyard or something.

It's kind of funny how I fell in with the Banana Boys. I met Michael in a Biology class at the University of Waterloo, and was instantly struck at how depressingly self-absorbed he was. We're all self-absorbed to some extent – personal problems, situational crises, personality quirks – but Michael is *super*-absorbent, the *Downey Jr.* of self-absorbed depression. Not that he's necessarily self-centred; just that he's so brooding and introspective that I fear one day he will collapse internally, sucking the earth and half the galaxy into a Black Hole.

A little while ago, I asked him a question about some disease, and somehow the conversation inexplicably gravitated into a deep, all-encompassing discussion about Michael's seemingly continual angst. It worries me, mostly because his situation really goes beyond a simple "*Hey pal, lighten up*". He wouldn't, of course, and after a while, I suspected he just couldn't. It's still disquieting seeing his pale, gaunt, ectomorphic self, those big dark eyes fixed on some point between here and infinity, what sort of deep, twisted thoughts, spinning like out-of-control Catherine Wheels in his head, which he duly records in his notebooks.

I asked him another innocent question a couple of winters ago, the year I dropped out of school.

"So what would you like for Christmas, Michael?"

"A remedy for my angst."

"Something a little more realistic?"

"How about a Taser gun? 65,000 volts of electricity – it completely incapacitates the victim without killing them." His eyes were large and glossy.

"How many cups of coffee have you had today, Michael?"

"Five. Why do you ask?"

"No reason."

Anyway, I met the rest of the guys through Michael at The

Bombshelter, our regular campus hangout. Dave was almost immediately obnoxious and condescending, as I recall (and, to the best of my knowledge, still is).

"Psych major, eh?" he said. "So, can you hypnotize people and make them swallow their tongues and shit like that?"

"No, that's covered in *fourth* year," I assured him, "and you'll definitely be the first to find out."

We're still all pretty good friends. Sort of. Michael and I go to the odd concert and such, and I run into Dave and Shel on and off. Not Rick, though.

More on that later…toll booth coming up.

Ah, Boston…Beantown, The Handsome Land of the Scenic Bean. It never really changes, does it? The bike's still riding smoothly, past Comm Ave., Mass Ave., Harvard Ave. I bypass Boston proper and head into Allston, a student haven and all-around fun place. There's a noticeable number of students around, driving beaters with mattresses tied to the roof, moving in, gearing up for classes at Boston U, or Boston College, a little further west on the Green Line.

I roll up to the front of my sister's flat, leather jacket daubed with bird droppings the consistency of Caramilk. A quick shower later, and we're sitting on a patio in front of Quincy Market, having a few drinks.

"So Jan," I said, snapping off my rubber band and letting my hair down, "…or should I say, 'Janice Yeung-Stevenson'? How is Lew-boy, anyway?"

"Give me a break, Luke," she smiled, sipping her rye and ginger demurely. "Lewis is just fine, thanks for asking…about as trained and obedient as he'll ever be."

"Sounds kinky."

"It is. Yesterday, he woke up extra early for no reason and brought me breakfast in bed. The dope. He sat next to me like a puppy-dog, staring with those big stupid blue eyes of his, asking if the eggs were soft-boiled enough."

"And were they?"

"They were perfect, but I still gave him a hard time." She smiled again. "He likes it rough," she said in her bad-little girl voice.

I laughed. Check one: Janice was doing fine with her nice-guy newlywed.

Janice is the greatest. She's always animated, and generally happy...and sharp as a needle, of course. Even when we were young, we always got along famously. Perhaps it was our way of making it easier for Mom after Pop took off (even though she never seemed to appreciate it), but regardless, we did everything together up to the point until I went off to school in Waterloo.

Janice had come up to visit me one weekend during third year. She came up some weekends from the University of Toronto, where she ended up in an accounting program, and generally just hung out with me – and the Banana Boys. Which was a source of interesting tension: Dave had a massive crush on her. In fact, all the guys did at some level or another, and I didn't blame them; she's a real cutie. It was only disturbing with Dave, president of the He-Man-Asian-Woman-Haters-Club (Waterloo Chapter).

"I've seen'em all, Luke," he said at the Bomber, uncharacteristically maudlin. "You know what I mean?"

"Er, 'fraid not Dave." I poured myself another beer and watched Janice sink another stripe, earning yet another curse from young Sheldon.

"Oriental girls, of course." He sighed and downed his beer in one gulp, pouring himself another one. "I mean, they're either too studious or too fobbish or too materialistic or only interested in big white guys named Steve or Darryl. And I still haven't found one yet who isn't rife with hangups."

"Except... ?" I said, already knowing the answer.

He sighed heavily again. "Except you-know-who." He made a slight motion with his head toward Janice, who was fending off yet another one of Rick's passes while Shel was measuring his next shot. I repressed the urge to make a 'stay-away-from-my-sister-man-or-I'll-beat-you-up' joke because he seemed disquietingly serious.

"I mean, she's a fair looker, to be sure," he said, lowering his voice, "but the thing that gets me is that she's the only Oriental girl I've ever met who I would describe as reasonable, together, 'with-it'. You know?"

"Mmmm," I said, poker-faced.

"And by 'with-it', I don't necessarily mean 'nice'," Dave continued, doing the annoying 'fingers-quoting' thing. "I mean, 'nice' Oriental chicks are a dime a dozen in this god-forsaken school." He scrunched up his forehead. "Nope, Janice is just plain *cool*. She's pleasant but witty, with a good head for comebacks and interesting references. She knows what she likes, what she doesn't like, she's focused, but not chip-on-the-shoulder aggressive."

"Mmmm."

"She's open and friendly, but not dippy. She's tactful, but she never lets anyone – including me – get away with copping an attitude with her. And I'm just constantly amazed at how ninety-five percent of what comes out of her mouth makes some semblance of sense, and for some odd reason…" Dave lowered his voice and almost whispered in my ear, "that really turns me on."

"Mmmm."

"She seems fun, she likes the outdoors, she gives great conversation, she played an above-average game of pool with me *[was he writing a personal at this point or what?]*, and she obviously likes the odd beer now and then. And yeah, she's pretty good looking. Did I mention that already?" Dave balled up his fists in frustration. "In my world, where Oriental women are too motherly or sisterly, too timid or bitchy, too plain or vain, too responsible or crazy, or just generally fucked up, she's a real find –" He stopped suddenly and started pounding his head lightly on the table, causing the empty pitchers to rattle.

"Um, Dave?"

"…and, of course, she's engaged. To a white guy, natch. Figures."

"Dave, what're you pounding your head on the table for *this* time?" Michael had come up behind him, carrying glasses of water for our cool-down period.

Dave's head jerked up. "Oh, you know, life, death, taxes…" Michael took some water over to Shel and Janice.

Dave leaned over. "You tell anyone about this, Luke, and I swear I will kill you in your sleep," he whispered. "Got that?"

"Mmmm." There wasn't much more I could say.

I ordered another drink, mildly observing Janice burbling about a fascinating new tax loophole her firm had discovered. Despite the sexist and racist generalizations and random bits of misogyny, Dave actually hit it rather well on the nail. Janice *was* a peach. I took such profound pleasure in hanging out with her, it seemed almost unsavoury.

"So, how's mom doing?" I asked.

Her smile faded slightly. "She's doing okay…well, as good as it gets. I talked to her a few days ago, and she didn't seem particularly responsive to anything I had to say. I think she's smoking more…her voice'd gained a notch on the rasp scale. You should give her a call sometime."

"I guess I should." I shrugged in a so-so, non-committal sort of way, knowing I wouldn't. The last thing I needed in this world was a lambasting from a psychotically bitter Mommy Dearest. Janice is the Golden Child in the family; I, unfortunately, have born the brunt of Pop skipping out. It's like she sees me as a psychic voodoo doll to get to him or something.

The shit *really* hit the fan when I dropped out of university. Most people take Psychology expecting to unlock the secrets of human nature, the intricacies of the mind, the foibles of the soul. Instead, they end up learning statistical analysis, and reading a hundred-and-one papers detailing pointless studies performed by faceless academics on the cognitive abilities of one-eyed rhesus monkeys on nights of a full moon.

Ultimately, it was the Psychology of Love course that did me in…

PSYCH 254 F,W,S The Psychology of Love 1.0 credits
Course Description: A cursory overview of Love as a psychological phenomenon. The chemical process of Love. Students will learn techniques on graphing passion vs. intimacy, and developing Taxonomies of Love. This course is taught by an aged and effete member of the faculty who quite possibly has never experienced his own subject matter, who will drone lecture after lecture about the cognitive abilities of one-eyed rhesus monkeys on nights with a full moon.

Render unto me a fucking **break.**

"Seen any good concerts lately, Jan?"

"Hah!" Janice shook her head. "I heard Sarah McLachlan did a couple of nights at The Orpheum in April, but Lewis and I couldn't make it…tax time, you know." She sighed and gave me another demure smile. "It's strange how her concerts always seem to coincide with the busiest times of my life. I'm wondering if I tortured babies in a previous life or something because I've been trying to see her in concert for five years, and I've failed every time."

I grinned. "I guess working at a radio station has its privileges. For common mortals, I'd recommend sacrificing entrails to Baal and dancing naked around a fire with your head stuck in a pig or something."

"To appease the concert-gods for better scheduling, huh?"

"Not really. But it's very relaxing."

Janice laughed, flicking back her hair and catching the eyes of two yupsters seated at the bar. *Stay away from my sister, man, or I'll beat you up…*

After a few more drinks, we toured the shops and stands around Faneuil Hall. We watched some Mentos-earnest buskers sing show tunes, and munched on some overpriced Polish sausage. Then we took off back to her place…Lewis had already set up the couch with pillows and blankets after he got off work. Nice guy, that Lewis. Nuttin' but the best for my Jan.

Woke up this morning with *Morrissey* on the brain. Looks like it's going to be a good day.

Honestly, I just don't know what I'd do without music. I'd rather be blind than deaf, given that Hobson's Choice...I'd go totally bonkers in a world of silence. Music is what carries me through life's processes, what ultimately helps me to my destinations. No journey of mine began without the right music.

Mornings are a perfect example: say you wake up when the sun hasn't risen yet, and the tune is already in your head. If it's good one, you just have to find the disc and pop it in. As the CD player groans and starts up, as you plod into the bathroom, slippers flapping, feeling like a train has run over you because of the half dozen beers you had at the club a mere six hours earlier – *you hear it. That **song.*** That song that moves something within you, energizes you, jolts the key glands in your addled brain, makes you want to strip naked and dance around and air-guitar, or at least sit down and savour the start of a new day.

Song title	Artist	Naked or Savour?
Regret	New Order	Naked
Sun Comes up, It's Tuesday Morning	Cowboy Junkies	Savour
Busy Child	The Crystal Method	Naked
Madagascar	Art of Trance	Naked
Purple Rain	Prince	Savour
Little Fluffy Clouds	The Orb	Naked
Possession	Sarah McLachlan	Savour
Political	Spirit of the West	Naked
Out of the Blue	System F	Savour
Sister Christian	Night Ranger	Naked
Sister Golden Hair	America	Savour Naked

*Fig. 2. Nudity Or Serenity? **You** Decide.*

Janice and Lewis had already left for work about an hour earlier. Lewis had left breakfast on the table, delightfully arranged in cereal-commercial fashion: croissants, orange juice and, of course, soft-boiled eggs. Jan left a note under a set of spare keys...

Breakfast, big brother. Don't say we never take care of you. There's a map on the kitchen counter. Lew says check out Cape Cod and the whales if you have the time. Have a good day, come and go as you please. The curfew around here only applies to Lewis.   J.

Mmmm…whales. Maybe tomorrow, though. I was thinking about hanging in the city today, and then hooking up with a friend who's doing graduate Psychology at Harvard (*Hauh-vuhd*). Apparently, his roommate's having a party and I'm invited and he just got these new turntables and oh, would I mind doing some DJ'ing for them? Sure, I guess, no problem.

So I spent the afternoon at Kenmore around the Fenway strip, just walking around, shopping for records, having coffee and reading Boston newspapers consisting of 90 percent American news which I didn't really care about.

Around dinner, I hopped the T up to Cambridge. As always, Harvard Square was bustling with students, buskers, beggars and really, really attractive women.

I got to Shawn's place early, so I helped him set up his decks. They were pretty good – standard Tech 1200s – but his mixer was a piece of shit, and his record collection was an atrocious assortment of dance-techno and club-anthems. Shawn was a dilettante who probably wouldn't have the patience to follow through with his hobby. I scoured the student ghetto for records, CDs, cassettes, and stereo equipment I could jury-rig into the DJ booth. Fortunately, a sketchy fellow a few houses down did – a fair selection of House and brand-name Electronica, with a smattering of Hip Hop. Along with the kick-ass Breaks purchases I'd made at Satellite Records earlier on…good enough.

Pretty soon, the pad was pulsing with music and people imbibing mass beverages. I was set up behind a table dragged from the common room, flipping vinyl, drinking a Sam Adams, jumping slightly to the Breakbeats I was throwing down. A girl I was checking out from across the room wandered over with another beer as I finished my last one off.

"Thanks," I yelled, seamlessly blending the tail end of a DJ

Stew record with a more accessible Armand Van Helden track.

"You're doing a great job," she yelled back, sidling up to me. She was great-looking; slim, medium-length blondish hair, tight ribbed top, form-fitting Gap jeans. I slipped my arm around her waist, wearing the eternal inscrutable expression on my face that said – well, nothing.

"Glad yer enjoying it. Any requests?"

She shook her head.

"My name's Luke. Yourself?"

"Colleen." We clinked bottles and danced a little at close quarters, watching some geeky MIT engineers chug to the chants of the crowd in the middle of the living room.

"Student here?" I asked, flipping the CD player to auto-pilot for a while. She nodded.

"Brandeis. My roommate is Shawn's friend. You?"

"Also Shawn's friend. Just down from Canada visiting for a while. Eh?" She grinned at the shopworn Canadian interjection, obviously thrown in for her benefit.

"Canada, huh? Whereabouts?"

"Toronto."

"Do you like Boston?"

"Looking much better now."

We ended up sticking together for the rest of the night… she seemed satisfied just hanging out, drinking beers and necking a little. I was feeling a little perverse, so I slipped in "Stairway to Heaven" by *Led Zeppelin* in the middle of the set. The song starts off slow, attracting romantic pairs to the floor, and eventually builds into a massive heavily-metallic crescendo that leaves couples confused and unsure of what to do next… *What do I do? Continue dancing slow or thrash it up?* It's always hilarious to see the people just mill around in confusion when Robert Plant starts screaming about winding down the road, Jimmy Page riffing it up. Colleen laughed when I explained.

I ended up with her phone number and a light promise for dinner and drinks the next time I was down here. Not bad, I suppose, but definitely just a casual party connection on the hook-up scale. That's the way I see sex, love, and relationships (or

Sexloverelationships, as Rick cynically calls it). Always bound by the limits of time and space – too little of the former, too much of the latter. Twentysomethings jet set, move around, shift jobs, never settle down. We can't. Coupled with AIDS and condom-commercial overkill, a hastily scrawled number and a vague promise is usually the best guys can do, at least with women who aren't loose as noodles.

I got back to Janice's apartment at around 4 am, stereo-typically taking off my shoes and tip-toeing through the door. Janice had left a Post-It note on my pillow…

So did you get lucky?   J.

Luck has nothing to do with it.

I hopped on the bike and headed for the Cape the next morning, to the sounds of *New Order* on the discman.

I savoured the clean fresh air, laced with sun and salt, as I rode…Hyannis, Martha's Vineyard, Chappaquiddick. Just breathed it all in. It was wonderful. I saw James Taylor's house, John Belushi's grave and – you guessed it – whales. Big grey ones. I took a ferry to Nantucket, trying to find the airplane terminal where they filmed *Wings*, but ended up disappointed because the insides were nothing like on the show. Isn't that always the case?

After a fun-filled week, I'm heading back to Toronto from Buffalo, via the QEW.

From the Gardiner Expressway, Toronto is a beautiful city. Definitely a city of contrasts – vibrant, corrupt, exciting, generic. I pass the ultramodern waterfront condos housing business-men and ballplayers. I pass the SkyDome and the CN Tower, well-paired, the female roundness of the dome fitting with the "phallic power of the tower," as Michael often terms it. And I pass the multitudes of venerable neon billboards hawking cameras, appliances, insurance. All very pretty and illusory.

The western portion of the expressway by the hundred-year-old Exhibition buildings is the best part; the bumps are breathtaking, especially by bike. *Woo!* Just like *The Streets of San Francisco*, only with better clothing and a cooler soundtrack.

I get off at York Street and head east via city streets. Traffic is thick but smooth, and in minutes I'm passing the picturesque Greek establishments along Danforth Ave. It's unseasonably warm for September, so the sidewalks are crowded – attractive, dark-skinned women wearing chokers and halter tops, young turks with pastel blazers and cell phones, yuppie couples eating souvlaki and drinking Molson's products on patios done up in pseudo-Acropolian motif.

I pull into my driveway at around 11 pm. My pad is a cozy space, the basement of a house on Jones Avenue in Toronto's East End. I call my pad The 808 State, in honour of the drum machine of choice, mostly because I keep the apartment constantly pulsating and thudding with hardcore or industrial or breakbeats, to the chagrin of my neighbours.

After fending off a friendly attack from Wilson, I enter the 808 State. It's a complete mess – unhung concert posters, strewn CD jewel cases and a record jackets, creating a cataloguing nightmare for any mere-mortal music collector (but I am no mere mortal in that respect). The east wall was my Wall o' Tapes, over a thousand cassettes and mixtapes accumulated over the course of twenty-odd years, and my Pile o' Vinyl, a collection of over a thousand records in Sealtest milk crates, stacked neatly and packed solid at about eye-level across the span of the room. At this point, it's overwhelmingly hellish for normal people to find a particular record from the vaguely-alphabetical bank.

The west wall houses my City o' CDs, an array of towers made from a variety of grooved woods, metals and other garbage shaped like famous vertical landmarks…my personal faves are the Empire State Building and the Tower of London (complete with Fisher-Price treasonists and enemies of the Queen hanging happily from windows). They were lovingly crafted by a drifter-slash-friend dude, in lieu of rent and some Totally Happy Crop.

There is also a setup for my 1200s, a bank of top-flight stereo equipment, a kitchenette, and a futon, with another Sealtest milk crate serving as a night table.

I dropped my jacket over the Empire State Building and hurled myself onto the futon, falling asleep almost immediately. I woke up at around 4 am after being clinically dead for five hours and cooked some eggs, and played some light jazz on the turntables (using headphones, of course, although Django Reinhardt was always so good that I'm *sure* the neighbours wouldn't have minded grooving to that sort of thing).

A nice, comfortable, relaxing morning.

The Morning Mosh starts at six.

What Were The Skies Like When You Were Young?

O h *no*…

"David! How's it going, dude?"

"Curtis. Oh, hi."

He didn't pick up on my lack of enthusiasm. I was on the way to pick up a greaseburger from one of the fine fast food establishments on Yonge St. when I ran into an old acquaintance from school: Curtis Chow, whom I have always not-so-fondly referred to as The Snake Oil Artist.

"Super-*Star!* Whutz *shakin'*, dude?"

"Curtis," I repeated, examining my fingernails critically. "Er, not much… 'dude'. Same old same old." I scanned his Young fiscal Republican getup – Italian-cut suit, tasseled loafers, Tag Heuer watch the size of an anvil – and became somewhat self-conscious about my Neo-Software Loser getup. "You seem to be doing all right."

"Can't complain," he said, smile tainted with smugness. "Business is *booming*, dude! I've just completed a contract with the Nabisco Corporation down in New Jersey – ever been to New York? It's *fabulous*, just *fabulous* – and I've just accepted a beefy contract with the State of California to develop some systems for the DMV down there. Eight beautiful months in sunny LA…in the *winter*, yet!" Like Rick, Curtis had latched onto a cushy management consulting job after graduation – something of an anathema to us software purists. And he was far, far more successful for it, evidently.

"That's nice."

"You *bet* it's nice. So, David, going anywhere for the holidays? I'm going back to Asia to do some charity work." He laughed heartily at his own joke, and I resisted the urge to vomit. "No, not really. Just flying to the Bahamas, as usual."

"Sounds delish. I'll be going to Vancouver on business. Seeing some friends out there. Drinking heavily."

"Super-*Star!* Glad to see you haven't changed." His smile hadn't changed, either. He suddenly checked his watch and deftly executed the way-too-cool-for-you-brush-off thing. "Well, you have my number [*I didn't*]…call me, dude, and we'll do lunch sometime!" Expertly turning his heel, he walked off.

"Uh, yes, you too Curtis…'dude'." I said this to his rapidly disappearing back. Returning my eyes to their proper alignment, I scrunched up my face in disgust.

"*Call me, 'dude,' and we'll do lunch sometime!*" I mimicked. "*Keep those **feet** on the ground and keep **reaching** for the stars! Semper Fi, Chip Chip **Cheerio** and all that sort of thing…*you pompous bastard." Christ. Gotta wash that snake oil off…

The name's Lowe – Dave Lowe, aka "Lowest of the Lowe". I'm twenty-five – *god, I'm old* – working as a software tester for a high-tech startup, Praxus Technologies. As in *"Praxus Makes Perfect"*.

I am also severely fucked up.

Here's the deal: I've been under a hell of a lot of pressure for the past few weeks – we ship our latest office automation software package in a few days (official codename: *Viper*…my codename: #@$#%$&!!!!). Needless to say, I've been working constantly, and eating and sleeping rather badly. You know …things to do, people to meet, coffee to drink. Couple that with a generally unsatisfying lifestyle, and woman problems (or lack of – you know the drill) and you've got the *barrel* of laughs that is my life.

In general, I'm not having a very good time. Actually, I hate all of it with a passion you cannot imagine. I can't *wait* for this albatross to ship, so I can go to Vancouver and drink myself into a coma.

I hurriedly finished my cholesterol-laden Feast of Doom, bought a pie for my co-worker Jase, and, after having a brief smoke, headed back to the office.

I've been with Praxus for about two years now, ever since I got out of university. I didn't like it much, but it paid the bills. Praxus is this smallish company of about sixty or so, all of whom

I like to refer to as Information Wage Slaves: brilliant technical people, nice guys, slightly socially-inept, who unfortunately selected software engineering as their call in life, as opposed to something more fulfilling like medicine or circus freakery.

Right now, we've got this pig of a product to ship, and the bugs are still popping out of the woodwork. It makes life extremely unhappy, especially for our two resident code-gods, Jason Lavalier (Jase) and John Van Egmond (Eggman). Nothing they can't handle, though…they're good – I mean, *really damn **good***. Praxus hired some of the smartest motherfuckers out of the best geek schools in Canada (*'scuse mah French*), people who can really Take Control Of The Machine…and Jase and Eggman were by far two of the best acquisitions, both Waterloo grads, like me.

Eggman had holed himself in his office for most of the week, but Jase was still reasonably accessible, fixing bugs from behind a pyramid of empty Jolt Cola cans. I popped my head into his office, aware of the vague sour male smell, but I decided to be tactful about it (for once).

"Delivery," I said curtly, and dropped the McPie in his guest chair, the grease immediately staining a pile of technical documentation.

Jase mumbled his thanks, face lit up by Microsoft Visual C++ running at a bajillion miles per hour.

"So, how's it going?"

He mumbled again, incoherently. I shrugged; I guess if he wasn't running around naked and tearing his hair out, the bugs were getting taken care of.

Like many other software companies, Praxus has a casual dress code and a stressful atmosphere coupled with developer's hours (ie. 11 am to anywhere after midnight, including weekends). And, of course, crushing delivery cycles, coupled with regular clothes-rending and wailing and gnashing of teeth. The office was a mishmash of machines, technical product T-shirts, *Dilbert* comics, Nerf weapons, fridges stacked with grapefruit juice and Jolt Cola. No ultra-lame fabric partitions like in other companies, thank god, but none of the offices had windows, except for Shogun's and some of the higher level managers. What better to prevent *en masse* suicides from this place.

My own space was across the hall from Jase. Despite its lack of windowage, it's a pretty good office – one thing I *don't* complain about. It's larger than most of the others because of the large number of machines for my QAing duties…and, of course, the legions of lethal radiation-emitting monitors that come with them. A solid year in this room could probably roast a pig. Greg, my manager, offered to get Shogun to buy a lead apron for me, like the ones pregnant secretaries use, but I said no. I figure that no one lives forever, and a great tan is a fair trade for slicing a few years off this carcass. That, and the extra arm I'm growing right under my chin.

My walls are plastered with posters – mostly free promotional-tech ones. I hate bare walls. Working in a room with bare walls is akin to working in an asylum, and things were damn well asylum-like enough around this place without having to deal with bare walls. Directly in front of me, I have three special posters:

- Pamela Anderson, in full bustatial form.
- Cam Neely of the Boston Bruins, retired, my favourite hockey player in the whole universe.
- Ulf Samuellson, the bio-tch who ruined Cam's career with a cheap check to the knee (the last one was riddled with wads of Bubble Yum.)

In the corner, there's a big green three-legged easy chair propped up with old MacOS manuals, stuffing bleeding out of it, and my personal pyramid of empty Coke cans.

So, after sorting through a few e-mails, I put on my favourite ball cap and got back to work, scripting my "monkeys" that crawled around the software looking for new bugs with which to torment Jase and Eggman. A day in the life.

When I was younger, I guess I wanted to be just like everyone else – you know, Brady Bunch-type normal.

But obviously, I wasn't…I couldn't be, I could never be. You're looking at a victim of the 'R'-word, beat up on a regular basis, subjected to racial taunts, general abuse, evidently because the sons of the local Hatfields thought I had slanty-eyes (*I did?*) and yellow skin (*it was?*). Case in point: do you remember that classic rhyme? *Me Chinese / Me play joke / Me go pee pee in your Coke…?* Well, imagine hearing it upwards of three times a day, often culminating in fat lips, black eyes, wounded pride.

The Dave Lowe story isn't an imperial Oriental saga involving dragons and phoenixes and ancestors long dead – if you want that shit, rent *The Joy Luck Club*. I am, as the riffraff term it, a Banana, one hundred percent white-washed. There are serious negative connotations to that, of course, but I don't fucking care – I've been out of the culture loop for so long that I can't even *fake* a good Chinese accent. Even trying, it comes out sounding like Russian or Scottish or something.

I was born in Sarnia, Ontario, in St. Joseph's Hospital. "Clouds," sung by Joni Mitchell, was playing while I was being delivered. Unlike many young Chinese boys, I don't have a Chinese name, heavy with mysticism and expectations. My dad, in hopes of making me more of a Real Canadian, named me after the competitive and emotional Leafs captain of the late sixties and early seventies, Dave Keon. Dad watched a lot of hockey and drank a lot of Labatt's products when he first moved here, as if becoming a drunk and obnoxious Leafs fan would make him a better Canadian.

Prior to that, he anglicized our family name from the weirder-looking Lo to the more anglicized Lowe, on the recommendation of one of our white neighbours. For a while in university, I wanted to change it back (*"It's my slave name"*), but Rick warned me how much havoc it would wreak on my legal and financial life.

"Not worth the time," he said over a beer, in his knowledgeable 'business law' voice. Well, add another strike to dear father's list.

"Look at it this way," said Mike. "At least you're blessed with an author's name. You know? David *Lowe*. Dave *Lowe*. It has the *flow*, you *know*? So if you ever wanted to write a book, at least you have a good name to put on the cover." He looked wistful. "Wish't I did."

"Give me a fucking break, Mike."

I grew up in a small jerkwater shithole in southwestern Ontario, the only Oriental kid in a fifty-mile radius, a *juk sing*, "*saing hau ying-mun* (mouth full of English)," as my mom was fond of saying. I'm the youngest in the family, and have two distant older sisters, Ellen and Grace. I'm afraid that they never really amounted to much – they dropped out of high school and got married to two white guys, both named Jeff. (One works on an assembly line tying barbeque tripods together in Etobicoke, and the other puts spoilers on Buick Regals up at the plant in Oshawa).

I'd be lying if I said I had a great childhood; if it wasn't the odd pummel after school every day from the local hick-kids, it was clashes with my parents. I vaguely remember the sound of laughing white boys blended in with the clatter of chopsticks, thrown down by my mother in anger on the Formica table, as the *de facto* soundtrack to my childhood.

Got home at about 10 pm…oh goody, early today, just in time for M*A*S*H reruns. I headed for the shower to refresh myself, remembering as I turned on the tap that the landlord had installed this newfangled energy-saving showerhead a few days ago, set permanently to "drool." Godammit. I need my showerhead set to "paint scour." If I don't come out bleeding, I feel gypped.

Lousy shower aside, I was lucky enough to find an apartment in the Annex when I started working in Toronto. It's a decent area around Bloor and Spadina, peppered with the University of Toronto frat houses. I live on Madison Ave., only a few blocks north of the world-famous Madison Pub (one hundred and thirty-seven taps, over twenty types of draft, *happy happy joy joy*). My place is on the second floor of an old cash house, a somewhat dingy but comfortable bachelor's apartment (accent on the *bachelor*), filled with overstuffed furniture I bought on the cheap at a moving sale two streets over. The rest of the place has been decked out in post-apocalyptic geek ever since the company went into shipping overdrive – stacks of laundry on the floor, half-eaten meals taken in a hurry, empty pop cans and beer bottles, free promotional software junk that Greg gives us to distract us from our indentured servitude (logoed pens, logoed Post-Its, logoed inflatable women, etc.).

And that's it. Welcome to Dave's Monastery: where men are men, women are absent and the beer flows like a river.

I finished my distastefully flat shower, making a note to go to Canadian Tire to get a replacement head and then kill my landlord: "*Kill my landlord. **Kill** my landlord. **Kill-Kill-Kill** my landlord…*" After changing into a T-shirt and soccer shorts, I rolled out the sofabed and turned on the TV just in time to see Hawkeye and BJ pull yet another of their crazy hijinks on Major Burns. War is, indeed, hell.

Dragged myself into the office early today – 10:30 am – with the usual payload – large Tim Horton's coffee (double-double), maple-nut doughnut, a copy of the *Sun*. Oh look: *Family Circus*. Dolly mispronounced the word "spaghetti" yet again. Tee hee. Honestly, you'd think her parents would have figured out after years of unfunny single-pane misadventures that their kids were dyslexic sub-idiots or something.

Jase was in already, grinding away at one of the nine blocks of bugs I dropped on him last night. Seeing me come in, he bounded into my office and inserted his lanky form into my armchair, grabbing paper from a nearby recycling bin and wadding the pages up into projectiles.

"Davey Dave! What's up?"

"I've just realized that the only calcium I get is when I put extra creams in my coffee," I said, frowning as I dumped them into the steaming cup.

"Maybe you'd better check for osteoporosis or something," added Jase, launching a wad and missing my Nerf basketball net.

"Jason, lad, I'm not a sixty-year-old woman, you know." I looked at the summary screen for *Viper* in our bug-tracking software. "Although I'm starting to feel like one. Dammit, Jase, I swear this goddamn project is taking a few years off of my life! As if smoking and drinking didn't do *that* enough."

"Anyway, bugs 945 to 988 are finished. I figure we're down to our last two blocks or so." Jase tossed another wadded up page with a grand Jordanesque motion. It slid across the wall into the Nerf-net.

"*Sco-ooooore*! By the way, Greg's looking for you."

"What the hell does *he* want? And since when does he leave his loft to associate with the unwashed masses?"

"Dunno." Jase brushed the hair out of his face. "Better get over there before he turfs you."

"Whatever. Thanks for the heads up." Jase tossed another wad through my net and went back to his office bellowing '*Sco-ooooore!*' down the hallway. Geez, developers are such spazoids.

Today is the day I am to meet and orient the new co-op students. I know this because Greg told me just ten minutes ago.

"You have *got* to be kidding."

"Sorry for the short notice, Dave," Greg said, pushing up his huge glasses from the bridge of his huge nose. "It was kind of up in the air for a while, but then Shogun signed them in personally yesterday. You're always bitching about manpower anyway…get them working on *Viper* or something."

"For chris*sake*, Greg! *Viper* ships in *two days*!"

"These guys are third-year Waterloo Computer Engineering students," he soothed. "They've worked for some of the best – Corel, Netscape, Microsoft – one of them even spent a year in Japan. [*Insert sarcastic awe here…what relevance this had to me or my project completely escaped me*]. Trust me, Dave, they'll be fine." Greg raised an eyebrow. "And are you saying that you *don't* need the extra manpower, then?"

That shut me up.

A while later, he shuffled two skinny, geeky-looking guys into my office, resplendent in black University of Waterloo leather jackets. "Howdy," I said curtly. "Names?"

"Andrew."

"Mark."

"Matthew…John…holy Judeo-Christian names, Batman!" I grinned despite the logistics nightmare chucked into my lap for the next few months. "Ah. That's okay. As long as yer middle names aren't Reginald and you're not Mark and Andrew the Third, or something." Mark coughed nervously.

I set them up in The Hive – an area one floor down, where all of the company's server and benchmarking machines were. I started them on cleaning up some of the higher-level bugs, and, to their credit, they were fucking brilliant. The ramp-up time was infinitesimal; by day's end, they were whole hog bug-fixing for *Viper* and developing COM Components for our next release. Miracles do happen, I suppose, if you whine hard enough.

To make a long story short, *Viper* shipped on time. I dropped a stack of freshly burned CDs on Shogun's desk thirty minutes before the noon deadline, handed Mark and Andrew over to Jase and Eggman, set my Out-Of-Office Outlook notifier, and bolted. I am now on a plane about to take off for Vancouver for a four-day Microsoft TechEd conference.

"Passengers, please fasten your seatbelts," the cabin-speaker-babe said in a sultry voice. "The plane will be leaving shortly."

I buckled my belt, yawning a little bit. I'd stayed up until 3 am, packing and e-mailing some Waterloo-Grad-Information-Wage-Slave-friends working out west, making arrangements to meet and party. Big time.

From: Dave Lowe <dlowe@Praxus.ca>
To: Vinu Malhotra <vinuma@microsoft.com>,
Derrick Kim <d4kim@microsoft.com>, Mauro
Fibonacci <flailer@real.com>
Subject: RE: Let's meet and Party. Big time.

…so I was feeling a little woozy. Nothing a few beers couldn't rectify.

The plane started its ascent, and my ears popped, so I took out a stick of gum and started chewing.

My eyes wandered across the aisle to scope out a real looker. Strange, that – the economy-class crowd was usually an unattractive and depressed-looking lot, commuters smelling of coffee and Certs breath mints, reading boring reports, getting ready to knock back scotches or tea as soon as the beverage cart makes its appearance.

She was sitting in the aisle seat right beside me, beside a fellow in the Armani with a PowerBook. Oriental, attractive, a classy news-anchorwoman air about her. A vision, I mused. Truly. Long black hair. Legs like butter. Killer business outfit – white blouse, brooch of questionable origin, red skirt and matching blazer draped on the arm of the seat. Smooth skin, a thoughtful expression on her face as she chewed on her pen and scribbled notes on a steno pad.

I grimaced slightly, and ordered a beer.

I was actually amused that the fantasy every man has before boarding a flight has happened – and was wondering what the hell to do about it. The aisle formed a natural barrier of some sort, but I was even more worried about another barrier: my low self-esteem. I took a cursory overview of myself. It wasn't as if I was terribly ugly or anything. A normal guy, I mused. Truly. Short black hair, brushed back in a reasonably neat manner. Medium build, a little on the stocky side. Somewhat well-dressed – white button-down cotton shirt, pressed charcoal jacket, khakis, black Oxford wingtips, a tie with some funky foliage. Okay, maybe the tie sucked, but at least it screamed "*I have a personality, dammit!*" compared to some of the dry zombie-corporate neckwear you get these days. Good teeth.

Ah, she probably only went out with white guys, anyway.

I used to think I was the only one out there, this messed-up westernized Chinese guy, lost in a rural wasteland of pickup trucks and big Caucasian bullies. Growing up in Sarnia, I was raised in relative isol-asian, in the Real Canadian Way, whatever the hell that meant. I mean, I preferred McDonalds burgers to *jook* (Chinese porridge), y'know? Who wouldn't?

I'm not ashamed of my race…I just don't like the problems it invariably causes. I can remember coming home for lunch in grade school, after getting trounced by two of the three Craigs in the school yard. Mom coddled me, fixed me a big steaming bowl of instant noodles and hot dogs (still a staple), and left me to watch *The Flintstones* while she screamed into the principal's office, demanding the summary execution of every Craig in the school.

That pretty much sums up the most eventful portions of my childhood. I grew up on a treadmill of persecution and protection, the youngest son of a Chinese family. I desperately tried to toughen myself up, by working early, by working out, by purposely getting into fights and other altercations, but I always had this feeling of coming up short. So as time drew on, this chip on my shoulder grew to the size of a pizza. I became abrasive, contentious, and was eventually expelled from the Lowe clan.

Still, my hometown experiences weren't entirely bad. I picked up a lot of things I still fiercely cherish. A love of classic rock and roll. An appreciation of hockey. A tasteful collection of colourful expletives. And, of course, complete and unwavering devotion to the amber nectar.

In many ways, I've become more Canadian than the average Canadian. Up until university, most of my friends were, in fact, white. I actively resisted the "Chinesey" thing until university, when I met the other Banana Boys. I was initially overwhelmed at the number of Orientals back at school, but when I met the guys, it seemed all right: it was genuinely comforting to know that there were other Chinese guys who were just as messed up as you were (if not more so).

As I recall, we were all going a little bugfuck from the workload, so our way of dealing with it would often involve congregating together at the Bomber for some drunk talk – *sweet sweet drunk talk*. We'd order bar food and a few pitchers, play some pool, get trashed, and start whining. Alcohol was a genuine release for all of us. It was cleansing, purifying. It bonded us in our collective misery, although our individual reactions varied widely. Mike, for example, would always drop out first. He'd feel guilty, or something, mutter about doing some work and stagger out, usually heading in the wrong direction.

Then Luke would usually get out next. You could tell when he was about to drop when he got all red-faced and started requesting all this weird, thrashy music and start flailing on the floor with the batcavers and raver-types.

Then Shel would conk out. That Shel, my best friend. I suppose he gets it from his hick background, as did I. We've had some pretty good drunks together. As engineering students, we'd always be participating in unofficial faculty drinking events. Too bad he dried up, the weenie.

I guess I'd go soon after. I'm by no means a small person – I'm about 5'8" (on a good day), 170 lbs, I prefer to call myself "husky" – but by half past one, I'd be ready to call it quits. By then, you could tell I was fucked by the number of swear words flying out of my mouth – bitching about school, women, family, women, money, and, of course, women.

And then there was Rick. The boy was good, I'll give him that. He was definitely lighter and thinner, a bit of a **leng**-*jei* FOB-boy (FOB = Fresh off the Boat) – slight, darkish, dressed a little too sharply, always did well with the ladies. (Whereas *my* stock of pick-up lines were from old *Simpsons* episodes: *"Marge, maybe it's the beer talking but yours is a butt that just won't quit …"*) He always managed to amaze me, because he could drink everyone under the table. I dare say he could even drink a bunch of my friends from back home under the table – even the big, lumpy, white ones.

I'd never openly admit it, but I could never keep up with Rick when it came to endurance. Just when I was about to call it quits, he'd show up with another pitcher with a wild look in his eyes.

"Come on, man! One more pitcher. Eye of the Tiger, man. *Eye of the Tiger!*"

"Well, twist my rubber arm," I'd reply, and add roughly two or three dry heaves to the morning routine.

"This is your captain speaking," crackled the cabin speakers, "if you look over to the left, you can see the city of Calgary. We'll be making our landing at Vancouver in one hour – weather at the airport is sunny, twenty-one degrees Celsius."

"Woo *hoo!*" I said aloud, irritating the crotchety old woman beside me. The last two beers didn't help, either. I ordered another Molson's Canadian, mostly just to spite her.

I glanced out the window at the stark, uninteresting plains of Alberta. TJ came from Alberta. TJ. *Tee*-Jay. Teej. My chain-smoking little flower from the wastes of the Wild Rose Country. I can see her now: in a large grassy meadow somewhere, snow-capped mountains in the background, sun radiantly reflecting off her long brown hair as she spins around, white dress on her lithe form, cigarette in one hand, a six-pack in the other. How I loved her.

I met TJ in second-year, when I was very, very drunk at the Bomber, which in itself wasn't remarkable. We kind of acci-dentally converged at the pool table. I was stumbling back from the john, rather clumsily peeling off the label on my beer. Rick had told me that tearing the label off your beer bottle and giving it to a girl meant that she had to give you a blow job.

The room suddenly went all Batman-angled and I nudged TJ heavily in the back with my elbow. She turned around, her fragrant locks grazing my partially numbed face.

"Problems, Ace?" she asked, not unkindly.

I looked at the crumpled beer label in my right hand and handed it to her, wordlessly.

She smirked, again not unkindly. "In Alberta, doing this means you're a *virgin*," she said.

And so we ended up talking – my inhibitions when it came to beautiful women were, at that point, completely annihilated. We shot some stick, drank some more. We even danced, which I usually don't do. By the end of the night, I had suspicions it was all a beer-induced dream. I mean, *me*, "Winner" firmly tattooed across my forehead, partying with a gorgeous babe? Come *on* now.

That next morning, I was fending off a killer hangover, chowing on veggie patties, Doritos and Cokes with Shel and Rick between classes. Me and Shel were in the middle of waiting for Rick outside the cafeteria. Shel was going on about some sort of lab that I had absolutely no interest in at that point, and there she was, walking into view from the Math buildings. That song I loved suddenly swelled in the recesses of alcohol-de-hydrated brain. At that moment, there was only me, TJ, and the music.

"Dave, what are you staring at?" asked Shel.

"This Is The One," I said to him simply, accidentally crushing the cup of Coke I was holding and splashing it on my Chucks.

"What?"

"Here, hold this for a sec, Shel…" I absently handed him my drink and my half-finished pattie and walked over to look at TJ from behind a tree.

Rick walked out of the caf with his food.

"Hey Shel…what's with Dave?"

"'This Is The One'," Shel repeated.

"What, again?"

I can remember the sun shining, illuminating her hair, her face, the mere sight of her almost eliminating my hangover. She was having a smoke, complaining to a friend about a hangover of her own – my kind of woman. In the sober light, I noticed that she bore a slight resemblance Jennifer Love Hewitt – the hair, the eyes, the wholesome-girl-next-door-smile…except for the fact that she drank like a fish and swore a blue streak.

She noticed me behind the tree and grinned, waving me over. "Hey hey…it's the lush from the Bomber." I was shocked that she remembered me. I jogged over and grunted a greeting.

She smiled sweetly, giving me a gentle poke in the arm. "You look like shit," she said.

Right there, I was hooked.

At most moments in my life, I can safely say that I'm both appalled and entranced by the idea of female companionship. When you think about it, the whole concept of relationships seems to be built on seemingly incompatible paradoxes and crazy extremes, wrapped in a layer of horror and emotional dismemberment.

The thing was that Teej was that she wasn't *really* a girl, in my mind. Lest you think I'm batting for the other team, the key to us getting along so well was that we were friends, and, for me, that involved treating her like I'd treat any guy I enjoyed hanging with.

And therein lies my problem. All my life, I've encountered women who were either cold and aloof, or spoiled, dippy, petulant – my mom, my sisters, my first girlfriend in high school, my ex-girlfriend Jeanette. And I got tired of it. God knows a Banana hates stereotypes, but I started believing all women were like that – unreasonable, irrational, emotional, certifiably insane. The patterns throughout my life were too strong to ignore – it sure wasn't my fault that it was, in fact, the only type of woman I've ever run into. That is, until TJ McKenna poked her hard-drinking, constantly swearing head into my life.

I always bugged her about what the initials stood for.

"Don't ask," she invariably growled, and I usually left it at that.

After a few pitchers, however, I invariably got more obnoxious about it.

"Buddy, you're getting jack *shit* out of me, so lay off," she said, softening her growl and giving me a gentle poke in the arm. "I've never told anyone, so why would I tell you?"

"Because I'm buying the next pitcher?"

"It's *your turn* to buy the next pitcher, wise-guy."

Until one day, I finally fished it out of her.

"The 'T' stands for Tiffany," she said with clear distaste in her voice. "The 'J' stands for Jane."

"Tiffany Jane McKenna."

"So there you have it."

"That's not so bad," I lied.

"Yeah, what*ever*, Dave. 'Tiffany' is the name of a phone sex bimbette. 'Jane' sounds about as exciting as a Bruins game." I let that one pass. "My parents were fucking sadists. I dropped it when I moved out here. I kinda like 'Teej' a hell of a lot better – sounds cool, hey?"

"Very cool."

"No one out here knows. So if you tell anyone, let alone tease me about this ever again, and I will hunt you down and kill you in your sleep."

"How 'bout you just rape me?"

She punched me in the arm, splashing some of my beer on the table.

"Beer crime."

"Fortunately, *you're* buying the next pitcher…"

And I did.

Teej was one of the few women I've had reasonably deep feelings for – even though we never actually went on a date, or did the nasty. Another way to look at this was that I tended to put my standards so incredibly high that there was no hope of anyone ever meeting them which, by and large, was just fine with me.

"That's such bullshit, Dave," Luke scoffed. "It's a cop out, and you know it."

"Like *you* of all people can tell me about copping out," I shot back. "*Your* whole life is a bleeding cop out."

He was right, though. It *is* a cop out, but one that prevented future emotional dismemberments. Nietzche was full of shit – whatever did not kill you made you weak, dysfunctional and scarred for life.

In any case, it's all moot now. She's practically engaged to this six-foot-one sandy-haired former right-winger for the Brandon Wheat Kings. And probably mothering the next generation of Aryan Nordic supermen in Manitoba as I speak.

I cast a furtive glance over at the vision in 11C after finishing off my third beer. Thank god the plane was carrying Canadian…nothing worse than a five-hour flight devoid of Molson's products.

I was a little tipsy and she looked so good that I actually considered breaking my regular facade of indifference and toyed around with the idea of asking her to dinner. It definitely would have been an out-of-character, unorthodox Dave-ism to do so, in any case. Since I broke up with Jeanette a couple of years ago, I have not been with woman for many moons.

I summoned up some courage, took a breath, and gave her what I thought was a mild, disarming smile.

She looked over, skipping over me completely. Not even ignoring me or anything as direct as *that*…it was as if her sights merely blipped over me, like an air-traffic control radar display blipped over a bird or something equally inconsequential. She ordered a cup of coffee from the attendant, and continued reading over her notes.

I snapped off the smile and ordered another beer.

During one of our many alcoholic forays into the human heart, me and the rest of the Boys joked about electroconvulsive shock therapy. Or *thought* we joked…Mike would typically get into these funks that were so deep, it'd frighten us (although we never admitted it).

"So you're blue," Luke said in a chipper information pamphlet voice. "So you're depressed. So you've been like this for a while, and have contemplated it all – self-help books, therapy, drugs, suicide. [*Insert uncomfortable shuffles from most of us here – with Mike, it didn't always seem that far-fetched.*] What's the solution, you may ask? Well, cheer up li'l buckaroo!" he did the inspirational fist-on-the-chin-poke to Mike, to which Mike barely responded.

"Welcome to the wonderful world of *Electroconvulsive Shock Therapy*! Yes sir, for a small hit to the provincial health care system, you too can be injected with muscle relaxants [*pause here for a brief clinking of glasses around the table*] and get wired up to a Die Hard, which will send currents through your frontal lobes, causing temporary amnesia and probable alleviation of chronic depression. Good news is that it's been statistically proven to be successful. Bad news is that there is a risk of permanent brain damage." He appraised the rapidly-emptying glasses and red faces around the table and raised an eyebrow wryly. "But what's a little brain damage among friends?"

"Sold! To the highest bidder," said Rick, raising his mug. "Where do I sign up, doc?"

"Not me, man," I intoned. "I get my fill of circuits and shit in class. I'll stick to muscle relaxants, thank you very much." I nudged Mike. "Thoughts, buddy-boy?"

"Hmmmm…" Mike cocked his head slightly. "Sounds like the perfect cure for Mental White Noise."

"Huh?"

"Mental White Noise. It's a term I've coined for that purposeless introspection that intrudes on your train of thought, when you should be thinking about school, laundry, or paying your electric bill. It happens to me a lot…I figure it may occur up to fifty thousand times a day."

"It's called daydreaming, Mike," Rick said.

"Yeah, but a lot less benevolent. Daydreaming is usually goal-oriented; Mental White Noise is directionless, keeps you from the important things in life. Daydreams are generally pleasant. Mental White Noise is controlling and obsessive and completely unavoidable." He suddenly started hitting his head on the table.

"Whoa cowboy!" I said, grabbing him.

"I *hate* Mental White Noise! I *hate* being interrupted in the middle of studying or exams with pangs of pain, heartache, for no apparent reason. I *hate* the idea of these useless thoughts draining so much of my energy…thinking about art, about race, about The Book™, women, failed relationships, relationships that could'a been, should'a been…Jesus, I wish I could just focus on what I need to focus on, without being haunted by hang-ups and lead a comfortable, noise-free life! Is that too much to ask for?" He looked at us with pleading, watery eyes.

We all fell silent, for a moment, disturbed by his honest anguish. Because it did make a hell of a lot of sense. It seemed like for the Banana Boys, with the dubious exception of Rick, Mental White Noise was an irritating and sometimes dangerous reality. Without it, our grades would probably be higher, our love lives probably better, we probably wouldn't drink as much. We also probably wouldn't be so, you know, fucked up.

"So Electroconvulsive Shock Therapy is the answer to eliminating this," said Shel.

"Yeah, either that or that goddamn Backstreet Boys song playing over and over in my head…"

"Excuse me, sir…"

My head shot up to face the stewardess, all smiles, wheeling the beverage cart.

"Would you like anything else before we land?"

I looked at her tiredly. "Electroconvulsive Shock Therapy."

She looked mildly puzzled, but her smile never wavered. "Sir…?"

"Never mind. I'll have another beer."

Same diff.

Pure And White As Ivory.

"Heart like a Gabriel, pure and white as ivory."
– The Cowboy Junkies

I was playing with Miller, my German Shepherd, in the basement, when *Ma* bellowed from upstairs.

"*Ah Shew-dun-ah! Deen wah!* (Sheldon! Phone!)"

"All right, *Ma*. I got it." I shoved Miller in the face to get him off my stomach and grabbed the ancient rotary phone.

"Ye-*ah*?"

"Yo goofball, it's me, Dave."

"Dave!" I could have sworn I smelled the fumes of multiple beers somewhere. "What do you want, moron?"

"I'm calling from the plane on one of those Aerophone-thingies."

"So?"

"The plane was delayed in Vancouver for an hour…I'll be landing at Pearson at around five-ten."

"So?"

"I'm fucking hammered."

I grinned from behind the receiver. "So?"

"So I don't think I can drive Jeepy [*Dave's dilapidated Suzuki Samurai*]. I need a ride home."

"So?"

"Sheldon, quit being an obnoxious dickhead and get down to the airport to give me a ride."

"Right. See you in about a half hour."

Dave grunted. "Terminal 2, AC 873. Yeah'm…thanks, pal. 'Preciate this." He said the last few words a little haltingly. Dave, my friend.

"No problem. Don't puke in my car."

"Whatever." *Click.*

What an idiot – drinks too much as usual, and I have to bail him out. Ah well, what are friends for? I grabbed the keys from the ceramic chicken in the hallway and yelled to my mom that I was going out.

"Drive carefully," she said, taking Miller out the back door for a walk (or rather, being dragged by Miller out the back door for a walk). She was really cute, my mom, especially when she was being walked by the dog. It was like watching a little soybean being wrenched along by a fuzzy, drooling monster.

Mike has always commented about the "epic" nature of my family story (whatever that means), but I honestly don't see it that way at all. Growing up Sheldon Kwan wasn't a particularly difficult thing.

"Well, you would if you actually *read*, Shel," he said, scribbling something in the notebook that he always carried around. "You and your family are classic *gum san.*"

"What does *gum san* mean?"

" *'Gold Mountain'*," he explained, not even looking up from his writing. "You know, the whole Chinese immigrant-thing – railroads, head tax, unfair immigration laws, the whole nine yards." He was shaking his head like I was a dumb hick or something. I guess he's sort of right. I am.

I was born and raised a Maritime boy, 'I'se the Bye That Builds the Boat' and so on. In Saint John, New Brunswick. It's small East Coast city, very blue collar, with more doughnut shops per capita than anywhere else in Canada.

I figure I grew up like any other Canadian boy. Dave doesn't believe this; he says that the fact I looked different, the fact I was Chinese, *must* have had some sort of impact.

"Why?" I asked. "I don't get it. I mean, I wasn't really treated differently than anyone else. Kell and Beau and Jay just treated me like this normal guy. I was never anything special or weird to them. I grew up doing, like, regular Caucasian activities…"

"Sheldon, you're prattling," Luke noted.

Rick snickered, nudging Dave. "What, pray tell, is a Caucasian Activity? Canasta?"

My father was originally from the West Coast, born and raised somewhere north of Vancouver, the *juk sing* son of a railroad labourer in British Columbia. *His* dad had immigrated to Canada from a village in southern China. Where exactly in China, I'm not really sure; *Ba* was always fairly tight-lipped about the old days. I figure he went through some pretty tough times, so I never pried – *Ba* is a very private person. But *yeh-yeh*, my grampa, is pretty gabby, and he never shuts up about this stuff.

Mike said that in the 1900s, there were apparently a lot of laws and regulations against Chinese people. Firstly, *yeh-yeh* had to pay a head tax of $100 (maybe $15 000 in current dollars), just to get in the country. When telling us this story (and he has, several times, sitting around the table after taking him out for *dim sum*), he often joked that he had to sell a load of gold teeth just to step into "Dis dammit country *sei gwok gah*!", pointing a toothpick at the masses of shiny gold chompers in his own mouth. We all would laugh, except for *Ba*, who would give a restrained smile, sometimes quietly mentioning that he had bought *yeh-yeh* his gold teeth years later.

Mike told me that because of these laws, there were hardly any Chinese women in Canada back then. So I still have no idea how *yeh-yeh*, the old coot, managed to snag gramma, but he did, and they got married, had seven or eight children, of which *Ba* was somewhere in the middle.

My father left the family early on, and I'm still not sure exactly when or why. He drifted across the country, working odd jobs – as a farmhand in the Okanagan Valley, an oil rigger in Alberta, mining support stuff in Sudbury, a dishwasher in Toronto. He was even part of a fire-fighting crew that was dropped by plane behind northern Ontario forest fires with little more than a backpack of water and a shovel (which was completely nuts in my opinion). I think he met my mother in Saskatchewan. I know virtually nothing about *Ma* or her side of the family, except that they don't get along because she was still a teenager when she ran off with *Ba*.

Ba ended up as an assistant mechanic at Theo's Auto Repair, a small garage in Saint John. For years, he worked pretty hard while my mom had babies, cleaned the small townhouse, and fed us pasta and potatoes. *Ba* has always had an empathy with cars that he passed on to me; I suppose that's why I became an engineer.

So the Kwans of north Saint John became a town fixture, that "nice Oriental family on Churchill Street." Even though we were kind of poor, my childhood seemed carefree. Saint John is really spread out, inserted into nooks carved into maritime forest and stone – an ideal setting for a hyperkinetic youngster to get into trouble. I made a few good friends in elementary and high school, some of whom I still stay in contact with: Kell, who's now at Penn State studying Business Administration; Beau, who I haven't spoken to since a car accident messed up his arm and some other stuff; and Jay, who is actually a pretty stupid guy and irritates me every time I see him. Kell is my best friend next to Dave; he was the one who taught me how to drink and fight, usually at the same time.

Seven years ago, my family moved to Brampton, a suburb northwest of Toronto, when my Dad got a job at GM, assembling engine blocks for trucks. Brampton is a place that everyone knows about, but only vaguely – "*Oh yeah! I pass by Brampton on the way to* <insert place name here>." Brampton is forever an "on the way to…" town; you don't actually *go* to Brampton for anything. And it sure wasn't New Brunswick.

Dave was standing at the automatic doors in the Arrivals area, red-faced from sunburn and a few too many, ears still linked to a pair of airplane headphones. He was juggling a suitcase, a brief-case, and his suitbag.

"Hiya Shelly," he greeted me with a slap on the shoulder. He threw his luggage into the back of my car, sand from his brief-case showering all over the back seat.

"Oops, sorry dude…I hightailed it to the beach right after the last meeting. Didn't even go back to the hotel to change. Stripped right there on the beach."

"So what'd you do after everyone around you went blind?"

"Har har. Man, I had a good time. Hell, I miss the West Coast already." He looked down at his hands. "Sand from English Bay still under my fingernails," he said dejectedly. And then he perked up. "Hey, I gotta gift for you." He plucked the headphones out of his ears and handed them to me.

"Boy, you're really drunk."

We drove off.

"I can't freaking believe the prices for drinks on the plane, buddy," he crabbed, "I mean, four bucks for a Canadian on the plane – *Four bucks!* For *canned* beer, yet. You'd think they'd at *least* give you bottles…the goddamn airlines gouging the hell out of…"

"Dave, you say this like I care," I grinned.

"*You* say that because you're stuck in a loser job where you never get to go anywhere," Dave said good-naturedly.

"That's where you're wrong, Dave. I actually have a job assignment up in Ottawa starting November."

Dave was surprised. "Gee. For how long, man?"

"Five months."

"I'll come up and see you, then. I'm not sure when…I have two products shipping, one in-between, one after that, maybe March. The first deadline should be pretty hellish, but the second…"

"All right Dave, you're boring me already."

"Oh, shut up, Shel." He then started telling me about the woman he'd noticed on the plane. "She was a major babe."

I chuckled. "So why would she want anything to do with *you*?"

"She *didn't*, goofball. She got picked up by this loser white guy in an expensive Italian suit."

"It must've been your latent homosexuality showing."

"Shel, why is it that whenever I see you, you're almost immediately annoying?"

I first met Dave in line at the scheduling office back in our first year at Waterloo. He was with Rick at the time, complaining loudly about his schedule. I thought he was a bit of a jerk at first; we exchanged a bit of small talk, got our schedules fixed, and then he loudly announced he had some party to go to and took off. And even though me and him would do the odd thing together, Dave was better friends with Rick, at least up until the Bad Times™. But after that, we became really good friends.

Dave is my best friend. I love him to death (but I am *not* gay). I trust him, although he doesn't entirely trust me, I think. That's okay, but I worry about why. Dave thinks he's alone in this world, which is pretty dumb, but he thinks it anyway. He lets his bitterness eat him up, without fully realizing it. He's got to understand that the reason he feels bad all the time is because he holds onto that bitterness, like it's precious or something. He's got to let it go for his own good…otherwise, he'll end up being one of those guys buying a semi-automatic gun from Zeke's Tackle Shop, climbing the CN Tower naked, indiscriminately spraying bullets into a crowd.

I pulled him aside at an engineering keg party one night, when he was going on about how life had shafted him, and looked him straight in the eye. "Dave," I said in all seriousness, head spinning from too much Red Baron, "Promise me that you'll *never* go nuts and kill people with a gun."

He squinted at me and smirked. "Are you crazy? Of course I promise."

I grasped both his shoulders unsteadily. "Okay, promise me you'll never *maim* anyone, then."

He laid a hand on my right shoulder and looked at me solemnly. "Now you know I can't do that, Shel," he said, and then burst out laughing, draining his little plastic pail of beer. I know it was a joke, but it still scares me a little

The traffic on the 401 was brisk, thick with people returning from cottage country after one last outing before the weather got too cold. It was September, but there was an Indian Summer

going on, so everyone was still in shorts and T-shirts.

"Check out the license plate on the car in front of us, dude," Dave said, pointing.

I squinted, peering past a mud smear on the windshield. "666 DEV," I read aloud.

"It's the devil's car! Satan is driving that car!"

"Satan drives a Geo?"

"Slow down here, man…radar ahead." Dave pointed to one of the police cars at the side of the road. As we passed by, he gave the finger to the cop, who only looked up briefly from his notepad. "Jesus, I hate those damn things."

"Me too."

"It's such an obvious cash grab," Dave said for about the ninetieth time. "Why the hell aren't they chasing bank robbers or rapists or real criminals, for god's sake? And when the cops stop you, they get all power-trippy, probably because they got beat up as kids and this is the only real power they've had in their pathetic, useless lives."

"Dave, do I care?"

The sign for Highway 10, Brampton came up. "Wanna stop by my place for a bite to eat?" I asked.

"Sure."

We rolled onto the suburban streets near my house. At a stoplight, I noticed a funny vibration from the car. I shifted the car to neutral.

"What'd ya do *that* for?"

"I'm not sure…the engine seems to be knocking a bit. Maybe we should pull over to check…" I suddenly stopped and stared at him. "It's *you* isn't it?"

"What is?"

"You bastard. You're bouncing your leg."

Dave looked a little embarrassed. "Um, yeah. Bad habit, I suppose." He grinned and did it some more for emphasis.

"It's a really bad habit," I said, shaking my head. "Did you know that back in China, my gramma was originally slated to marry some boy from the next village? Apparently he was a nice guy, smart, had some money, but gramma couldn't stand his habit of bouncing his leg. She ended up coming to Canada and marrying *yeh-yeh* instead."

"That's a really touching story...you should write a book." Dave thumped his chest. "But the bottom line is that the *Weekly World News* says I could lose up to thirty-five pounds a year if I bounce my leg for about an hour a day, so I'll probably keep doing it regardless."

"Yeah, you've been gaining a little weight, you fat slob."

"Shut up and drive, goofball. Those beers are making my eyeballs float. I have to take a leak."

I'm definitely no stranger to alcohol. During the later years in Saint John, Kell was virtually jamming the stuff down my throat. He had this weird predilection for Alcool Slushies – he'd buy a slushie at the Green Gables variety store and pour in half a bottle of the flavourless and odourless Everclear-like liquor with a really high alcohol content. After two of these things, you'd be retching and bruising ribs all morning, telling your mom you ate something poisonous at the school cafeteria the day before.

One summer, Kell even set up a *Dukes of Hazzard* moonshine still at his place. No joke – he ran a copper coil from a kettle on the stove down to a large clay jug, distilling Killer-Keller Juice, something that was arguably one-half alcohol. Man, I swear I lost a quarter of my brain cells that summer.

We did all sorts of crazy stuff when we drank. Once, we dragged an abandoned stove onto the main highway and watched drivers swerve around it. Another time, we walked across the lake near Jay's place – it only went up to our waists – to an island and started a fire there. The craziest thing we ever did was go to one of his artillery practices drunk (he was a sergeant in the local militia) and directed some volleys at a graveyard near the base.

"It's not like we're gonna *kill* anyone," he said, slurping happily on his Alcool Slushie.

The Banana Boys definitely have their share of drinking stories as well. Back in Waterloo, we all went out once a week on average – more if any of us had women problems. Rick had this thing called The Mode, which apparently gave him the excuse to get hammered all the time.

"I'm in The Mode," he'd say, rubbing his hands together. "You can't stop me when I'm in The Mode."

"The Mode, hmmmm?" Luke would note, amused.

"That's correct. My pockets are full, my stomach is empty, you can't stop me now. I'm *there*, man…"

"Yeah yeah," we'd all chorus, "You're in The Mode."

"Bloody well *right*, I am. I'm *in* it…I can't get out of it until I engage with the golden nectar, full force ahead."

"He's in The Mode," Mike would confirm, with mock moroseness.

"Less talk, more Mode," Rick would insist, and then we'd plunge into a traditional night of drinking, revelry and lack of memories.

I think our grades were notched down a few percent because of Rick's Mode. Except for his own, of course. I could never get how Rick could drink so much more than most of us, and *still* get stellar grades – it just didn't make sense. Mike showed me studies that proved that brain cells died when that much alcohol was ingested. He proposed an interesting alternative theory to explain it:

> Given a population of **n** brain cells, if **m** represents the number of cells killed after an alcoholic onslaught, the remaining **n – m** brain cells are tough little fuckers.

Now *that* made sense.

Much to Dave's chagrin, my interest in alcohol fizzled during my last year of university; I guess I just didn't like it much anymore. I definitely didn't miss the dry-heaving, being incapacitated for half the day after, being hungry but incapable of keeping even a Ritz cracker down. Right after graduation, Kell told me that Beau had been drinking and driving back in Saint

John, had gotten into a car accident that killed his girlfriend and fucked up his arm pretty badly. That really cooled me off.

"You *weenie!*" Dave raged.

"What's the point, anyway?" I said defensively. "Look, drinking's just a stupid thing to do. You might as well throw loons down a sewer."

He stared at me intensely. "You can't get *drunk* throwing loons down a sewer!" He stormed off in a bad mood, probably knowing that I was actually right for once.

We pulled into my driveway. I figured we'd done pretty well since Saint John, when the Kwans lived paycheque-to-paycheque in subsidized housing, a gaggle of hungry and hyperactive boys terrorizing the household.

Dave stopped dead when I opened the front door. "Come in, Dave," I said, stuffing the keys back in the ceramic chicken.

"The dog," he said, face dispassionate but voice quavering slightly. "Get the dog away from me."

"What?" Miller scrambled into the front hall and started growling at Dave.

"The *dog!* Get the dog away from me, dammit!" Miller began barking loudly, causing Dave to back away.

I slapped my forehead. "Oh, the dog. Miller! Here, Miller!" I grabbed the dog by the collar and led him to the laundry room. Miller was howling now, as if he smelled the fear Dave exuded from under the beer. I just love that mutt, but Dave hates him; he calls him "Cujo, the Instrument of Pure Evil."

"Thanks, dude," Dave said, breathing a light sigh of relief. He scanned the house. "Your mom home?"

"I think she went to buy groceries or something, so you can put down your breath mints and relax." I led him to the kitchen. "We have a leftover pizza from yesterday…"

"Peachy."

We polished off the pizza with a few Cokes. Dave told me about an odd dream he had last night. Dave had a lot of odd dreams, and he always told me about them…not that I cared. The guy will *never* learn this.

"I dreamt that CHiPs – you know, Ponch, Jon, the rest of those brown-shirted guys – invaded my apartment," he said between bites. "I had this machine gun, see, so I started shooting, until there were all these dead CHiPs cops on the floor. But Ponch wouldn't drop, so I had to give him a flying leg kick, but then he turned into a bird and flew out the window towards Saturn, which was hanging low in the sky for some strange reason."

I laughed. I obviously didn't care, but it *was* entertaining. "Okay, let's analyze this," I said in my egghead voice. "Ponch represents the object of your sexual desire, and the dream is a manifestation of your latent homosexuality…"

"That's what you said about my *last* dream, goofball."

"So it is. I'm beginning to notice a pattern here, Dave."

"Oh, shut up."

I drove Dave downtown and dropped him off at his place. On the way back, I started thinking about all the other guys. Mike and Luke, and Rick who I haven't really talked to in a while…not that anyone I know ever talks to Rick anymore. I guess I'm kind of a romantic. I miss the times when we were all together, struggling through school, getting hammered at the Bomber, generally being *together*. It was a good feeling, comfortable, you know? And now look at us, scattered to the four winds. I won't even be able to see Dave all that often when I go up to Ottawa.

"It's the nature of today's economy," Rick explained to me once, coming out of The Mode. Rick always knew a lot about money and economics and stuff. "Technology is making this a smaller world, but the concept of distance still hasn't been eliminated yet. Us twentysomethings still have to go where the potential for wealth and power is – Silicon Valley, Asia, Latin America, New York City." He smirked. "Better you don't wax sentimental on things, Sheldon…*I* certainly don't. Situations are always in flux, you know, and sentimentalism'll just weigh you down."

Hate to admit it, but he's kinda right.

I work as a gas line inspector for the local natural gas utility. It's an okay job, with plenty of nice people and easy hours, but it isn't particularly challenging: day after day, I go out to sites designated by my manager for routine maintenance and mark off everything from a standardized checklist, then sign off the work orders as they come in from the contractors. Like I said, not too hard, which is part of the reason why I'm kind of looking forward to going up to Ottawa. It'll be a nice change of scenery.

"Are you *nuts*, Shel?" Dave had scoffed back at my place, mouth full of pizza. "Lissen, dude, I've *been* up to Ottawa during the winter, when I worked for Nortel. *This* is what you have to look forward to: Arctic blasts of up to seventy kilometres an hour from Hudson's Bay, so cold your nose hairs freeze right up and lacerate your sinuses!"

"Ah, c'mon Dave, it gets pretty cold in Toronto, too." I was worried, but refused to show it.

"Ottawa in the winter is twenty times worse, trust me." Good old Dave, always there to pour sand over the bonfire as soon as it starts warming you up.

In the morning, I drove from Brampton through horrendous traffic to my first site, at Church and Queen, in downtown Toronto. I grabbed my hardhat and clipboard from a cardboard box in the back seat of the car, and walked outside to see Vic, the foreman. Vic was this butt-ugly but friendly eastern European guy with a Kill-Moose-And-Squirrel accent and bad breath.

"Sheldon!" he said, grinning and slapping my back too hard. "Good to see you! Blakeman say you go to Ottawa at end of month!"

"Yeah, that's right Vic," I said, "and it *don't* mean I'm going to ease up on the inspection reports just to make the transition easier. Get back to work, you slacker!"

He laughed, handed me a wad of pipe tags, and jumped back into the large pit dug into the street, barking something to the piping contractors. I stuffed the tags into my pocket and headed towards Burger King for a coffee and a hash brown, doffing my hardhat slightly towards an attractive brunette who was peering curiously into the pit. Women love a man in a hardhat.

Actually, a big reason I'm into going to Ottawa is I want to find a girlfriend.

Living with your parents, your social life is dry enough, never mind your love life. "At least you're saving money so that you can *spend* it on a girlfriend," my mom often says to me in Cantonese. But spend it on who, pray tell? Engineering has given me a job where women just plain don't exist.

I'm twenty-four and I've never had a real girlfriend. I think it's because I'm a shy, gawky sort of guy.

One time, I went to this Unity Jam dance at school with Mike and Rick. (Luke was busy, and Dave refused to go because "there were too many FOBs there.")

Well, there I was, obviously out of place, wearing a beer-logo T-shirt, jeans, running shoes and a sweatshirt tied around my waist. Rick was busy working the room (*work it, baby, worrrrk iiiiit...*), and I was standing with Mike, Vijay and Justin on the sidelines, sucking back beers and looking at the cute, well-dressed girls dancing in strange circled-wagon formations on the dance floor.

A new dance song started, virtually indistinguishable from the last one, and Veej began gyrating on his own patch of floor. My attention was focused on these two Oriental girls dressed in short skirts with lots of shiny sequins, and dancing close together. They noticed that I was staring, and suddenly started into a series of erotic grinding gestures with each other, licking their lips and winking at me.

I was totally caught off guard, and I felt my face get hot. I just had to look away.

Veej nudged me. "Those are *baaaad* girls," he said, grinning. "So how about it, Shelly?"

I just shook my head, face red like a idiot, and went off to get another beer.

Twenty-four and I've never really had a girlfriend. *Man.* I feel like this simple country boy, dazed by women, who all seem so mysterious, complicated and inexplicable.

The real problem is, I know who I love, and I know I can't have her.

I love my *cousin*.

"*WHAT?!?*" Dave's eyes were popping out of their sockets. "You love *WHO*? You can't do *that!*"

"Why not?" I countered (rather lamely, I thought.)

"Well…*because!*" he said, waving his arms around, "Because…well…uhhh…"

"Ye-*ah*?"

"Because you'll have kids with three heads." He said the last bit a little doubtfully. "Look, there are a lot of other chicks around here, I'll help you get one."

"But…"

"No buts, forget about her. I'll get you a mail-order bride if I have to."

What a great pal.

Mike and Luke were a little more rational. "You know, I understand that this 'three heads' stuff is a crock," Mike said. Luke was leafing through a sociology textbook, nodding his head. "It's a modern cultural-taboo thing, mostly; until recently, most Western cultures encouraged marriage between cousins. My genetics prof said that brother-sister procreation is, uh, not recommended, but between cousins, it's not as bad as society makes it out to be." Mike coughed nervously and cleared his throat. "Europe's royal families are all intermarried, and most of them turned out one-headed."

"Bad example," commented Luke, "they're all nuts. Still, Michael's generally right – she's just your first cousin, right?"

I nodded.

"Well, the textbook says that if you want a child who resembles you genetically, behaviourally, even physically, the best way to do so is to procreate with a cousin, preferably a first cousin. That maintains purity of the gene pool." Luke closed the text.

"But still…" said Mike, frowning, "Western society deems it to be, you know, in bad taste."

Luke scoffed. "*Fuck* western society, man. If young Sheldon here is smitten by his cousin, then I say damn the torpedoes and Make Love To Your Woman!"

"Shhhh!" I said, shrinking, "there are people around, you know?"

I first met Mandy, my dad's sister's youngest daughter, when I was twelve. I was actually kind of mean to her – typical boy-stuff at that age. But her family came to visit us in New Brunswick when I was seventeen and she was sixteen…and I fell in love.

We spent most of that time romping around Saint John. I showed her the most beautiful places I knew, with brooks and meadows and rocks and stuff, and I guess the setting hypnotized us so much that we actually kissed under the trees at Milledge Creek with the sun beating down, cicadas trilling softly, the creek burbling on and on. We went out for these long hikes that lasted for hours. I find that long hikes are the best way to get to know someone – after five-odd hours, their true personality is bound to come out. And Mandy was remarkable, not what I thought a girl would be like at all – she wasn't spoiled or whiny or anything. She was just a lot of fun.

Our parents never found out, and I haven't seen her since.

I really am grateful for everything I've got, all the good things that've happened to me and my family. And my friends. But sometimes I feel life super-shafted me on this one.

Actually, with the obvious exception of Rick, most of the Banana Boys have always been strangely single. I never really figured that one out. Bad experience, I guess. Like Dave was stuffed by TJ and Jeanette, Mike was royally screwed by Mina (aka Mistress Cruella), Luke blew it with his *cha* Indian girlfriend who took off for the West Coast and got married to someone else.

Dave maintains it's because we're all "screwed up," whatever that means. I don't think so; I think we're all pretty regular guys, with regular problems, regular lives.

Rick, of course, had a steady flow of girls from first year on – some really pretty ones, too. And even though I don't know where he is these days, I'm sure it's still the same way because he's so smart and good-looking (but I am *not* gay). Despite this, I worried about Rick when he was still hanging out with us. I've always had the vague sense that there was something just not...*right*. Like a phase shift or something; a sine wave slightly out of whack, but still visually perfect.

Ah well, seeing as he never hangs out with us anymore, it's probably nothing. Better to think about the people who actually care about me...as far as I know, there still is *zero* relationship-action amongst the remainder of the Banana Boys. If we shaved our heads, we'd make a pretty good troupe of Buddhist monks. Hopefully Ottawa will change that for me, at least. I bought the coffee, sat down, and began to leaf through the tags, dreaming of things to come.

Cake And Eat It Too.

New York in the fall. You can virtually see the spring in people's steps, the relief on their faces, the sheer freedom that comes with being able to wear wool suits comfortably, without having to carry a bottle of Evian everywhere you go. Fall in New York City means that all the heat and fury stored in the concrete during the summer is slowly leaching away, harmlessly, into the sky.

I walk through Times Square on the way to a client site on 48th and the Avenue of the Americas. It's 3:37 in the afternoon, so rush hour is just gearing up, effectively preventing me from grabbing a cab – total Stop-and-Go. Native New Yorkers contemptuously dismiss Times Square as a tourist trap, but I find it a cool place to be – the huge neon billboards, the bustling superstores, the massive electronic ticker tape over the Morgan Stanley building, flashing out NYSE and NASDAQ listings, taking the nation's pulse a quote at a time. It's definitely changed since the days of *Taxi Driver*. Rudy and Big Corporate took over in the early nineties and cleaned up the smarm and filth. Looks good on it.

Outsiders coming from "normal" places often find New York stressful, callous, and overwhelming. It certainly isn't the executive-produced stereotypes you see on whitebread NBC sitcoms, where people are beautifully glib and live in large apartments on a waitressing salary. Geographically, it's smaller than you'd expect – the urban/suburban sprawl of Toronto is much larger. It's the scale of things in New York that gives the illusion that it's positively massive. You can see it best in the architecture. The idea of a building in New York City mocks the wasted space above, so prevalent in Canadian cities. To the suburban mind, eight million people could conceivably be stacked neatly into finite floors of concrete boxes – provided they didn't do much other than sleep and breathe. What really defies imagination is when you think about these people coming down from those boxes (Point A, miles above sea level), cover some horizontal distance, and get to another point in another box (Point B, also miles above sea level). What passes for streets are these conduits wedged uncomfortably between monumental super-structures, tributes to a Big God. In New York, the lives of the termites in these ineffectual little pipes would really seem – ineffectual. The City was definitely built to scales that would give a wide-eyed Canadian boy a minor coronary if he thought about it long enough. Then again, I'm not your ordinary wide-eyed Canadian boy.

Here's my card –

Richard Wong, B.Math, CMC, CNC, MCSE
Associate Consultant

Jones Lavoie
International

Jones and Lavoie International
40 Bay Street, Suite 1000
Toronto, Ontario, M6A 2K2

416.555.1000 x666
rwong@joneslavoie.com

Fig. 3. Call me, we'll do lunch sometime.

Jones and Lavoie is a management consulting firm that provides services like business process reengineering, corporate headhunting and organizational streamlining (read: *The Axe*) to medium-to-large enterprises and governments around the world. I'm based in the Toronto branch, finishing up a four-month assignment in New York City, well on my way to World Domination.

Mike, ever the writer, came up with a flattering description of me when I called him to pick me up after nine-odd drinks at a local "townie" bar back in Waterloo.

"You're a total slickster," he said, eyeing me down another scotch. "A smooth-talking silver-tongued devil, a social chameleon. In a snap, you have the ability to sense what people are like, and you're able to blend perfectly into their vision of normality, leaving an indelible impression in your wake." I shrugged, pouring another couple of shots from the bottle, so he continued.

"But you know what gets me about you? You have this positively uncanny skill for *enveloping* people…by talking to someone, anyone, you can actually make that person feel totally unique, like he or she was the most important person in the world, their problems completely relevant and significant. You're *good*…really, *really* good, and you know it. You virtually exude positive, healthy confidence – an '*I am the purveyor of your deepest desires*' type of confidence, without getting all chipper and Mentos-like. That makes people want to lay gold and silver roses at your feet – and women want to sleep with you." He paused, and then suddenly whipped out his notebook and started writing all of it down.

"I hate you, you know that?" he said, scribbling so hard in his book that the glasses on the table rattled.

Hmmm – not too bad. He'd be quite the successful writer if he wasn't so neurotic.

I am not relaying this to you just to be narcissistic. I want you to understand that these sorts of things constitute mere tools, which are part of my workshop. The purpose: to make as much money as humanly possible. I bypassed the positions of Analyst and Junior Consultant in record time; the New York assignment caps a contract that brings in a gross of $456,000 (that's about 700K in Northern Pesos), with commitments totaling three times that over the course of two years – *hoo-AH*. And when I get back to Toronto, welcome to full-fledged Consultant status – which I intend to reject after a year or so to start my own practice, taking as many of my clients with me as I can. (The legalities haven't been hammered out yet – remind me to get a lawyer to take care of that when I get back to Toronto.) I certainly appreciate money in a way that makes most people kind of antsy around me if I talked about it, a *Shining*-quality obsession, not very pleasant. From the power it represents, to basic economic qualities it possesses, even the most superficial aspects of it physically – the look, the smell, the texture – I can safely say that *I LOVE MONEY*. And she, apparently, likes me. In high school, I was voted "Person Most Likely to be Thrown in a Minimum Security Prison for Embezzlement and Shanked by a former Stockbroker." Brother, they didn't know the *half* of it.

I stopped in at the new Starbucks in the building's lobby, and then caught a high-speed elevator to the 56th floor. While Maxi-musMedia.com was one of our smaller clients, it nonetheless had already exceeded its potential by over two-thousand per-cent over the course of the year. As a result, their revenues had quintupled, pointing towards a lucrative IPO. It had also caused the company to balloon, their finances spinning out of control. I was called in to "batten down the hatches," to control their date with destiny, as it were. I walked into the foyer, nodding a pleasant hello to Denise, their drop-dead gorgeous receptionist who was inexplicably plagued with insecurities. I was precisely twelve minutes early for my appointment. Just enough time to effectively hit on her.

"Morning, Denise." I offered her some of my muffin.

"Good morning, Rick. Thanks." She tore off a tiny bit from the cap and brushed her beautiful auburn hair back, giving me a dazzling smile. Getting her to call me 'Rick' (down from the stodgy 'Richard' and the positively strangulating 'Mr. Wong') took three weeks of gentle and seemingly innocuous coaxing. It took another week for small talk, and one more to achieve the reasonably personal conversations that we have these days. Hey, I had to occupy myself with *something* while waiting for my clients.

"Max is talking to Randy right now…you can wait in his office if you'd like."

"Hmmm...I think I'll wait out here." I permitted myself a cough and a charming grin. "If you don't mind, of course."

"Of course not!" she said quickly, and we talked a little bit about her latest date with a shmoe from Queens. "New York men are such jerks," she said, shaking her lovely head in despair.

Hmmm...I can be "Not-New-York-Men"...

MaximusMedia.com had just settled into their digs three weeks ago, a vast improvement from their old space out in Battery Park City. I was greeted with calming green carpets, brightly painted walls, framed Monet prints and product posters, cappuccino machines, and a trophy case gleaming with freshly-minted industry awards. And more humming machines and displays than you'd find on *Battlestar Galactica*, which assuaged my fears about the company not having the technical oomph to back up their goals, at least superficially. The CEO, a pleasantly brilliant yet remarkably homely nerd by the name of Max Singh, wisely decided he needed a Chief Financial Officer after the last quarter.

"I'm a geek," he said to me the other day, sunlight glinting off his non-shine-free glasses through the windows of his spartan office, "and I know squat about money – I went to *Caltech*, for freak's sake." He gave a high-pitched, throaty giggle. "Me and Randy've been looking after the financials for a while, and we were doing an okay job, but he's getting irritated and would rather get back to programming and such, so we need some sort of Monsieur Moneybags who really knows the green stuff to keep the finances cool and rock the IPO."

I nodded, ignoring Max's sad attempt at high-powered business-speke, and immediately thought of three candidates – one, a former client, brilliant with corporate finances, who was ever-so-disgruntled with his current employer.

Within a week, after consultation with Elissa back in TO, some drinks and directed soul-searching at a small bar in New Jersey, I got him to sign with Max, without even breaking a sweat. I spent the next three days tying up loose ends on the thick business plan I laid out for them. When all was said and done – final purchases lodged, last cheque signed, low-impact industrial espionage conducted by yours truly – we wrapped up the project and Max celebrated by taking me and a few other MaxMed employees to Peter Luger's Steak House out in Brooklyn for some quality slabs of meat.

Denise was there, too.

The dessert was just marvellous. Hoo-*AH*.

My last few days in New York were spent cleaning out my desk, organizing the move back to TO, and making arrangements for a small vacation in New Orleans with Tasmin. After FedExing a few cheques and documents for Shirley to take care of, I took a cab to the Metronome in Chelsea to meet some friends for a night of partying. Metronome is a peculiar creature in the pantheon of bars and clubs in New York – clean, spacious, cubic metres of wasted space overhead, fixtures that are strictly ornamental, not just exposed plumbing passed off as "character-laden." My biggest culture shock was that all the bars and clubs in New York City closed at four in the morning, with many more after-hours clubs to select from. When I first got to The City, I went out with a few co-workers from the Toronto office, and they were completely strung out by 2 am. That's the way Torontonian biorhythms function – last call at a quarter to two, kicked out at a quarter after, a bite to eat at half-past two, and finally passing out at three in the morning, a Taco Bell soft taco hanging out of your mouth. It took about a week in Manhattan with Jake and Iain and Kerrigan and the rest of the New York Rage Collective to get over that. And now I positively *thrive* on the night. And why shouldn't I? That's when vampires come out.

In the morning, I set out to execute my other significant task: breaking it off with these two girls I've been involved with for the last three and a half months. They're both rather nice – a blonde cellist from Barnard, and a Taiwanese girl from an upper-middle class Long Island suburb – but evidently, they took the relationships more seriously than I did. I don't like it when that happens, but it's an occupational hazard. In the end, Sheryl accepted it in stride, but Lisa took it rather hard. Not much I could do about it. Tasmin was waiting for me back in

Toronto, along with my plans for setting up a private practice. Cruel to be kind, in the right measure.

Ever since my Biz-Math days in the wastes of Waterloo Ho-Down Central, I'd always wanted to go to New York City. It was so obviously the center of it all, the nucleus of a pulsating mass of money and power. Perhaps a lot of this need was based on the media-induced misconception (I watched *Wall Street* about two dozen times). I mean, which would *you* believe is the real New York: *Seinfeld* or *Taxi Driver*? *Friends* or *Kids*? I suppose I didn't really care. It's merely a function of the type of person you are. Do you see the glass as half full or half empty? I pour my own glass. The truth is that I've always felt uncomfortable in Canada. Actually, a better word would be bored. Canadians bleat about being superior to Americans, but the truth is you've got this population of overeducated, unmotivated, government-coddled whiners, with minuscule drive and competitive spirit. They've been pampered from cradle to grave in so many ways, raised in an environment that isn't commerce-friendly. Middle of the road, highly-taxed, self-deprecating, mediocre. The archetypal nation of losers. Which will make it easier for people like me to own it in a few years.

Tasmin is flying down from Toronto to LaGuardia at 6:16 tonight, and we take AA Flight 745 to New Orleans tomorrow. Why New Orleans? I've been everywhere else. Steve Langlois from the Toronto office had told me about it at the end of a conference call last week.

"Three words, Rick: *Cool-as-Shit*. Rue Bourbon in the French Quarter will just blow yer mind – completely devoted to sex, booze, and quasi-legal debauchery. A buck a beer, and you can even take'm out from the bars and walk around, drinking 'em outside. And the babes, man, *fuck!* There's something uncanny about that city – incredibly attractive women all over the place. I wasn't entirely sure if they were tourists, locals or…you know. But they were *definitely* lookers, so what the fuck?"

"Sounds good, Steve – I was thinking about going there with Tasmin."

"Hold off on that noble notion, man. New Orleans isn't great place to take your fiancée. It *is* a great place to go with a bunch of drunken-bastard buddies, though."

"Thanks for the advice, Steve…see you in eight days."

"Cool, Rick. Bring me back a sixer of Blackened Voodoo brew. Man, I miss that stuff." *Click.*

Before I was able to get out the door to pick up Tasmin, Dr. Eng, my psychiatrist in New York, phoned about renewing my perscription. "I've summarized your progress, and prepared a detailed statement with the necessary dosages for your doctor in Toronto," he said, oozing Hippocratic concern.

"Thanks, Doc."

"Call me when you get back to Canada. Let me know how you're doing."

I see a psychiatrist not because I'm crazy, but because I want to be Superman.

Before you imagine a cuckoo flying out of my forehead, allow me to explain…

Everything comes down to one thing in this world: *chemistry.* It's the lowest common denominator in human behaviour; it's the reason why things happen, why we make things happen. Most people are born with the chemistry to lead normal lives, right on the bell curve. Others are not so lucky, and require treatment or augmentation. Still others naturally have the chemistry required to play the game of World Domination. Although I counted myself in the latter category, I *did* discover limitations. Back in university, I found myself starting to burn out. The constant studying, partying, fucking, and near-total lack of sleep caught up with me, and I did not like it. I was a mere mortal, subject to the wear and tear, stresses and strains that destroyed lesser men. Others had a variety of ways to deal with it; some exercised obsessively, some binged occasionally, or all the time. Some went into therapy. Some hung themselves in their closets. So I decided to enact a radical plan – augment my already superior neurochemistry beyond the bounds of normal human performance. Enter Pyloxodin™, the Wonder Drug – not your average picker-upper, but a new breed of pharmaceutical that not only eliminated depression safely and permanently, it enhanced performance and increased key personality traits deemed beneficial in the world economy – confidence, independence, self-esteem – with few side-effects. I wanted to run at 110 percent efficiency – 210 percent if at all possible. So enter Part Two of my cunning plan: pleading to some sort of insanity in order to obtain the right prescription.

Convincing a psychiatrist that I was clinically depressed when I clearly am not is something of a feat. As with all things in life, it required a decent acting job. In addition to citing my father as a genetic anomaly, I also found myself rehashing these silly cultural issues tossed around by the Banana Boys. Frustration, alienation, rage, guilt, cultural conflict, suicidal thoughts – I almost emulated Mike. It took an enormous amount of patience, but I eventually coaxed a prescription from the system. Slow but steady progress led to the dosages I take today. Some may say that I'm playing a dangerous game, but they don't understand. It's all about control. Joy, pain, love, hate, lust, sadness, the sheer desire to succeed and conquer – all of these things ultimately can be mastered when you take control of the chemical reactions underlying them.

I brought Tasmin back the the hotel, and after ripping off her clothes and fucking her brains out, we went out to dinner.

Tasmin is a classic top-of-the-line Hong Kong girl – pale, slim, long black hair, big brown doe-ish eyes, unblemished Shiseido-buffed skin. In terms of looks, she was model-quality; in terms of personality, she was also model-quality. Years of pampering by her father, who owns a lucrative chain of restaurants in Toronto, has left her with a battery of expensive tastes and outlandish fashions bordering on *haute couture*, a legion of male FOB admirers and that odd predilection for stationery and Sanrio paraphenalia that completes the FOB-chick archetype. She is high-maintenance, but also high-return. The cost of doing business.

"*Ah-**Reech**-utt-ah*," she pouted in Cantonese, "Why do we have to go to New Orleans, anyway? It doesn't sound all that interesting."

"Just to take a look around," I replied, also in Cantonese. "It's good to expand your horizons, correct? You're doing me a huge favour, honey, by coming – I love you." I gave her a peck on the cheek, and she giggled. It took me a little while to get back into FOB-speke, but once I'm in it, I am most definitely in it. Hong Kong girls, especially the beautiful ones, tend to be bossy and controlling. They run relationships using "unspoken needs" – their men are supposed to automatically guess what they need, what they want, and respond – instantly, or else. It tends to make the man obsequious and toadyish – a far cry from the overbearing patriarchal stereotype Asian guys are supposed to have – especially if the girl is, in fact, model-quality. I know for a fact that many Banana Boys I know wouldn't be able to handle this, completely incapable of sensing "unspoken needs." (Dave, for example, wouldn't last two rounds with a Hong Kong girl – he'd be hit with the "insensitive guy" rap in seconds.) Myself, I can do the Perfect-HK-FOB-Boy thing. It's cake, just a matter of practice, submerging natural Banana tendencies, and manipulation of every good-looking FOB girl I could lock my crosshairs onto. I learned to become a cloud, an organic interface that envelopes my prey, connecting with her at each and every one of her pertinent pressure points. I'm sensitive to her every whim; I respond to her needs, simultaneously altering them to fit my own. The physical aspect of this task is challenging; I need to be able to appropriately adjust expressions, speech patterns, behaviour, habits, and provide her with everything she wants physically and emotionally. Or at least manipulate her into believing that she received it. I'm able to submerge the target so completely in the illusion of perfection that I can extract virtually anything I want from her. In exchange for that illusion, she wholeheartedly gives me her love. It is unilateral, admittedly, but isn't that better than no love at all? And, of course, the cash that comes along with it doesn't hurt, either.

I got back to my Harbourfront condo after having dropped Tasmin off in Unionville for some family function, which I got out of saying that I had to take care of some work. She said to pick her up again at midnight.

"Posh" is the perfect way to describe my apartment. It's cloaked in distinct neo-yuppie flair – framed Nagel prints, nice consumer electronics like a large-screen TV, DVD, and a Karaoke-laserdisc machine (Tasmin loves to Karaoke; I hate it). Leather furniture in light oyster tones that perfectly matches the broadloom. Framed glamour shots of Tasmin, strategically placed to confirm the contract (at least visually). Spacious kitchen, an even more spacious bedroom, with an excellent view of Lake Ontario. Few children, no pets. Since I could count on Shirley to look after the place, I hadn't needed to sublet it. The pad is virtually unchanged since I left it in June, aside from the neat stack of mail and the Pyloxodin™ package Shirley picked up for me last week.

Yawning, I throw my jacket on the glass coffee table in front of the TV. Goddamn, I need a drink. We'd gotten back from New Orleans a little early to meet Tasmin's family for *dim sum* at her father's newly-opened restaurant out in Mississauga. The whole morning, Tasmin's little brother and sister bounced around the restaurant like hyperkinetic pinballs. Tasmin's mom burbled non-stop about her problems, her friends' problems, her friends' friends' problems. And her father, forever pressuring us to get married, and me to start up my Toronto practice right away. It took a full hour to explain to him the situation with my clients (remind me to get that damn lawyer ASAP). And then the afternoon shopping with Tasmin, who hadn't shut up about the heat and the humidity in New Orleans since we got back: *Calgon, take me away.* I poured myself a Canadian Club on the rocks. A double…triple? Didn't matter, I needed it. Certain things used to bother me a lot – I usually just let it backwash with a few drinks and a dose or two, and it doesn't bother me as much anymore.

"Nothing a few beers can't take care of," Dave used to say. Fuck, man, I *love* drinking. I've loved it ever since I started drinking with Lance and Kevin in grade school. I don't drink because I'm depressed, or because I want to forget, or even because I like being drunk. I drink because I love drinking. It's just so – pleasurable. You know? *So many brain cells…so little time.* I looked at the clock – *shit, 10:22 pm already.* Not too bright drinking before I had to pick up Tasmin, but what the hell. Oh, and I missed my dosage yet again. Absently, I tore open the prescription bag from the counter, unscrewed the bottle, and poured out double the regular dosage of triangular orange tablets, washing them down with some quality Canadian whiskey. I decided to call my mom. Good filial son.

"*Wei?*" she said, sound of dishes being washed in the background.

"Mom? It's me, Rick," I said in Cantonese.

"Rick! *Deem gai nei moh **dah** bei ngoh-ah, dai tau **ha**?* (Why haven't you called me, you shrimp head?)"

"Been a little busy."

"Too busy to call your family," she scolded.

"Sorry mom, how's Dad?" I ask, smoothly switching the subject.

"Daddy's sleeping. He just went to the doctor today." I nodded from behind the phone. The father unit's Lithium treatments make him sleepy; he usually hibernated for a while after every doctor's appointment.

"And Shirley?"

"Fine. She says third-year university is hard. You should talk to her more often, otherwise you two will become alienated when I die…" Sounds of rustling as the receiver changes hands. "Hi, Rick." An almost imperceptible pause. "Today is Tuesday October 5th…"

(In English, now) "Not necessary, Shirl. How goes?"

"Fine. I picked up your mail and paid off your bills – your cheques are under the phone. I watered your plants. I wrote down your messages and left the notes beside your…um, package."

"Thanks, sis. How's school going? Got a boyfriend yet?"

"It's fine. School's hard. My organics prof is a jerk. No boyfriend." All matter-of-factly, without a trace of emotion. That's Shirl, I guess.

"No fear. By the way, I cut a cheque before going down south – have you received it?"

"Yes, Rick, I did. Thank you. How was New Orleans?"

"It was all right. The city is very…uninhibited."

We talked a little more, and after a final round of scolding from mom, I hung up.

As millions of little neurotransmitters filtered slowly through my brain, I let myself relax a little. Being Richard Wong, Superstar, is hard work. But it was worth it. The old Rick was a loser and an idiot. The old Rick came from a middle class family that lives in marginally-middle-class suburban Scarborough. He was born in Hong Kong; the family moved to Canada a year later. That didn't make him a pure *juk sing*. It made him better. The old Rick was inordinately influenced by his family. Their hardships shaped him, molded him, eventually cut him off from them, although they were unaware that this happened. And that was for the best. Case in point: The father, a very weak man. In contrast, the mother is strong, shrewd, action-oriented, but emotionally dead from having to take care of everybody, most of all the father. The two escaped China after the big-C Communists took over and met in post-war Hong Kong, mom a street-wise girl with ten brothers and sisters; the father, a handsome wimp. A long time ago, the mother had fallen in love with the father and took him under her wing (to her own mother's deep chagrin) and kept him from getting killed on the streets of Hong Kong. The father, you see, was incompetent and insane. The father barely survived there, eking out an existence with a useless hodgepodge of odd jobs, studies, and failed business ventures. No, I think the occupation which best suited the father was that of poet – but times were reportedly tough in post-war Hong Kong, and the demand for poetry was understandably at an all-time low. If he'd been born a few dynasties earlier, I think he would have made a fine scholar-bureaucrat; but in that era, he was deadweight. The father did not have the Confucian stoicism of his generation. My grandfather, however, a cavalry captain from an army that got their asses kicked by the Japanese, had it in spades; he punished the father for this perceived weakness.

My grandfather was a northerner, Mandarin, a harsh man, highly disciplined. The mother told Rick about him, about how one time in the middle of the night, a thief was caught prowling outside in the bushes of the officer's mansion the family lived in. My grandfather took his long Chinese cavalry sword and killed the thief with a sharp thrust in one of the murder holes on the outside walls. There was another time when the grandfather caught some of his men gambling in the barracks while on duty. He shot one of them, just like that. To say this man was a martinet was like saying Godzilla ate leaves and changed colour while sleeping on a branch. Rick understood the grandfather to be the ultimate killing machine. Rick understood why grandfather would have reacted none too kindly to his Number-One son being a Nancy-boy poet as opposed to a soldier, a warrior. He understood the determination *to "whup that bo-ah into shape"* (or whatever the Mandarin equivalent at the time was). He imagined that the father obeyed everything the son-of-a-bitch said, whether it was to run laps, kill a sick dog with a bayonet, kneel on broken glass for immunity to pain, or stand for hours in the mansion compound in horse position. Without dinner. In the rain. Naked. Rick imagined that hate or anger could have never entered the father's mind because proper Confucian programming would never allow it. Sons obeyed their father, and that was the undisputed law. He imagined how fear, extreme fear, mind-numbing fear, took its place, and lodged into the father's tender, impressionable brain, completely screwing up his mental plumbing. He imagined the father, then a scrawny teenage boy, high-tailing it south alone as the big-C Communists overran Shanghai and slaughtered the minority of soldiers remaining loyal to the Nationalists, killing the grandfather and pretty much the rest of the family. He imagined the father ending up some-how in the streets of Hong Kong, confused, broke, unable to speak Cantonese, and very hungry.

The mother told Rick all this when he was younger, when he still felt some sympathy for the father. As a child, Rick had wondered why the father looked so blue, why he would stare off into space, sometimes bursting into tears. Years later, however, when the father was later diagnosed with a bi-polar disorder, it became irrelevant. Inconsequential. Rick understands that the mother loves the father unit. Very much. Which is why she still takes care of him, with patience and determination. Although very small and seemingly fragile, the mother sometimes makes Godzilla seem like a leaf-eating branch-sleeping colour-changer. She never talks about the father in any way but good, but I do know that the father's weakness is real, and this weak-ness formed very strong roots for my strength. Despite the mother's love, I believe that the shame was ultimately carried with the father – of not being a good son, of not protecting his family, of being *gau si*, dog shit, a "useless-son-of-a-bitch" who ran away, not a man because he loved poetry and not war.

Irrelevant.

Today, the father is "retired", and the mother works as an accountant at some garment company in Scarborough, splitting duty with me in putting Shirley through school.

Glanced at the clock again after my third drink – 11:29 pm. Time to pick up Tasmin. I threw on my jacket, fished my car keys out of my pocket and headed toward the elevators, tip-toeing so as not to disturb Mrs. Brubaker. Nice woman, Mrs. B.

She was always able to sense if I had been drinking.

I have a slick car: a pitch-black BMW 325is Coupe, spoilers galore, dangly gold Chinese charms on the rearview mirror, personalized license plates (RIC 888, Of course). I got it with the help of student loans back in school – it set me back in terms of payments, but it's a necessary building block towards World Domination.

Growing up, I picked up a lot of things I liked quite easily – pool, sports, girls – and bypassed a lot of things I didn't – chores, studying, piano lessons (the latter was forced on me by my mom, and I endured it for a few years just to get her off my back.) I was also – *dare I say it?* – suave and debonair, a killer, a silver-tongued devil if I needed to be. One of the first snags in the road to World Domination occurred in late grade school. Scarborough at that time was an admixture of Chinese and Vietnamese, and I was often picked on by these Vietnamese kids. At first, Mom tried to bail me out, but she was always so busy with the father and her job and Shirley that I eventually had to take matters into my own hands. So I quickly forged an alliance with these two big black guys, Lance and Kevin, and we kicked some serious Vietnamese ass one evening behind the Dragon Centre. Blood on the parking lot, cash in the pocket. I can still remember going out with the money we extorted from them and getting really, really drunk. I've always been able to acquire money, easily and efficiently. It's part of understanding its value, well before my peers did – how to make it work for you, the probability and risk in obtaining it, opportunity costs, marginal utility. While the other kids were blowing their allowances on video games or hockey cards, I engaged in getting them to blow their money on other things – entertainment, recreational pharmaceuticals, personal safety (Lance and Kevin helped me out with that) or various games of chance, like poker, pool, and blackjack. To make money, you must first *have* it – my starting capital was Mom's emergency stash, which I'd enterprisingly found at the back of her closet.

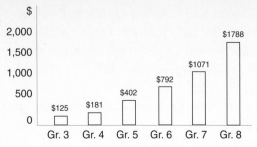

Fig. 4. *Everything Counts in Large Amounts.*

High school was a little different – I needed to focus to do well enough to get into the Waterloo Math-Biz Coop program, with a side of keg parties, *The Smiths*, and having sex with cheerleaders.

I arrived at the Golden Harvest Seafood Restaurant at 11:57 pm. Tasmin's father greeted me with a wave and a vague smile, seated at the head of a table like an old Chinese warlord presiding over the festivities. I sat beside a clot of extended family and poured some tea for them. Even though I just wanted to grab Tasmin and get laid, I stayed for about a half-an-hour, chatting politely with some aunties and uncles before liberating her. Respectful Chinese sons-in-law always had innumerable aunties and uncles. These days, I suppose I'm indistinguishable from any other HK FOB boy. Obviously, I wasn't always a FOB – I was a bonafide Banana entering my first year of Waterloo. It feels like another life, or rather, a blind spot, a backslide, a useless mash of drinking and neurosis. I'd known Mike as a family friend for a while, but it was actually Dave who I met up with first and hung out with, most of that time. I was Luke's roommate one term, and I frequently got Mike to take me home when I was too wasted to drive. Only halfway through university, it started getting to me – "it" being their hang-ups. The Banana Boys were an unusually depressed, bitter and clueless group, and even I couldn't succeed in extracting any significant value from them. In fact, I've rarely run into *juk sing* whom I could consider reasonable and well-adjusted. At the same time, the FOBs I noticed had their shit together. In grade school and high school, I never thought that deeply about it all that much; like most *juk sing*, I thought they were too ethnic, outlandish, kind of snobby: "*We're from Hong Kong, we have loads of money, we drive nice cars, we don't really care what you think of us – have a nice day.*" But the thing that most attracted to me to their otherwise alien culture was their respect for money. Money has always been a massive part of traditional Chinese culture. Money is given out during the Lunar New Year, replica-money is burned for use in the afterlife. Names are invoked to welcome wealth to a business, symbols and statues are devoted to collecting prosperity, like one collected baseball cards. But the FOBs, the new Hong Kongers, they take this worship and devotion to new heights, from games to cars to clothing to real estate. They definitely have the right idea. I eventually re-evaluated my position, and realized that the FOBs had *exactly* what I wanted. I observed closely, and imitated. I asked the right questions, emulated the right moves. I worked on thinking in Cantonese, mastering the language, altering my social patterns and behaviour. I practised with Hong Kong girlfriends I picked up at school, learning a lot from them, right down to the hair, the clothes, the diet, the music. I even picked up *Ka-ra-o-ke*, though I still loathe it. I eventually became what Mike had described me as – the perfect social chameleon. By graduation, no one could tell me from a real FOB; no one even remotely could sense my Banana background. I even impressed myself. And what did I gain? New opportunities, new money, new paths to World Domination. Becoming the perfect FOB-boy paid off handsomely – my mom stopped bothering me, I made a number of fashionable and moneyed friends, I gained employment advantages, connections, large lines of credit, and beautiful, ivory-skinned Chinese girlfriends.

And what did I lose? The Banana Boys. I didn't really think much of it – I was just tired of it all.

The meal ended a little after two. After saying goodbye to the clan, Tasmin and I headed back to the apartment. In the car, I permitted myself a slight smile of satisfaction.

At a certain point in all our lives, there will be a fork in the road. What you cannot do is just stand there, wailing and gnashing your teeth and rending your clothes and scream, *"Why me, God?"* I chose the road going East. Because I have goals, you see? Targets, milestones. Revenue projections. I'm going somewhere. I have no time for the anger, the whining, the angst, the shticks, the idiosyncrasies. The fucked perspectives, the difficulty with dealing with things. I was tired because I knew that all of these faces were mere concoctions to hide their own insubstantial fears and insecurities. Whether they knew it or not was moot – the fact is that they are all pathetic screw-ups.

I choose to reject my birthright, the hollowness of *juk sing*, of being bamboo, this 'Banana-hood'.

*I'm **going** somewhere.*

I am driving a slick black BMW with a mid-to-high-range cellular phone quietly purring beside me, and a mid-to-high-range Chinese girlfriend also quietly purring beside me. What can I say? I *win*.

My Brain Hurts.

> Both tricyclics and MAOI's (Monoamine Oxidase Inhibitors)
> increase the availability of monoamine neurotransmitters
> at synapses, prompting theorists to propose various…

God, I'm tired.

I think I've read the same sentence five or six times already.

Flip flip flip…

…Forty-two pages to go.

Sigh.

I glance at the clock on my desk. I can't believe it's already 8 pm. On a Friday night. *Pret*-ty sad. My office mate, Todd, went home hours ago. The building feels dark and empty.

Might as well pack it up.

About a year ago, Luke had warned me that grad life is markedly different than undergrad life. He's right. It seems that all the good stuff about being a student (friends, partying, social interaction, promiscuity, having a life, etc.) is completely absent in the world of the grad student. I guess that leaves only the unpleasant stuff, like studying long after everyone else has left, whilst entertaining suicidal thoughts.

Yesterday, my supervising prof reprimanded me for the lack of results in my work. It was pretty mild as far as tongue-lashings go, but it propelled me into a downward spiral of doubt, uncertainty, and clouds of useless regret about why I'm here. I suppose I've got to endure. Just one year left. Just one year left. But this place is sucking the soul right out of me. I can feel it bleeding through my pores into the ether, never again to be reclaimed.

I step outside the University of Toronto Biology building and walk north toward Bloor St. It's a rainy fall evening, still kind of warm. The tires of taxis and limos are singing on the pavement, newly sealed by a September shower. Young'uns in phat pants and fun fur are heading for a party down on College St. A group of girls in short skirts are hopping a cab for a night out. One of them looks like my ex-girlfriend. An old couple dodders by – the woman is clutching an exorbitantly expensive flower from one of the street vendors ($5, plus GST). Very sweet.

I feel so empty.

Maybe a fourth cup of coffee will cheer me up.

I step into the Bloor and Spadina Ave. outlet of the Second Cup, my Second Home, located a few blocks from the university science buildings. It's a corporate-type coffee place, but I like it all the same; in stark contrast to the grey concrete outside, it's usually warm and cheery (albeit artificially). The aroma of freshly-brewed flavoured coffees smacks me in the face as I walk in. To non-caffeine addicts, that alone is usually enough to wake them up. Unfortunately, I'm an addict. That's what my ex-girlfriend kept calling me. She used to chastise me for the amount of coffee I drank. She used to chastise me for everything I did.

Ingrid was there, setting up the dishwasher for another load. "Hey," she said, smiling, automatically grabbing a regular-sized mug and hovering over a pot of freshly-brewed Irish Cream Classic. "Irish Cream?"

I smiled wearily. "You've got it."

"A buck fifty." I pulled out some change and my nearly-shredded coffee card, yawning.

"Well *you* look tired," she said sympathetically.

"I am. I have this major assignment next week, so I've been putting in some extra hours." I looked at her and squinted. "Gee, you've been here since the morning. A nice girl like you should be going out, you know, to par-*tay* and such."

Ingrid laughed, brushing back her hair and tying it up with a black scrunchie. "Overtime," she said. "Rent's coming up, and I've got this little deficit. You're lucky you're going to school. Real life just plain sucks."

"Yes, very lucky," I said, smiling faintly. Ingrid was my

favourite Certified Coffee Agent at the Second Cup, not only because she was good-looking, but also because she was friendly and open – you didn't really find that a lot in downtown Toronto. Funny thing is, we have never formally introduced ourselves. I wouldn't know her name if she wasn't wearing her official Certified Coffee Agent name tag.

```
c:>finger mchao@neuro.utoronto.ca
Name: Michael C.C. Chao
Masters Student (MSc)
Dept: Science (Neurochemistry)
University of Toronto
Rm 308, Ramesay Wright Building
```

There's not much more than that...it's as boring and unpleasant as it reads on the computer screen of my antique PC.

I find the best way to gauge the status of any particular person at any particular time is to draw a BrainChart™: pie charts drawn of your brain at specific moment in your life, reflecting what exactly is on your mind.

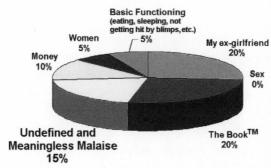

Fig. 5. Mike's BrainChart™ (as of Sept 21st)

I first came up with the idea of BrainCharts™ back at Waterloo, much to the collective derision of the Banana Boys. "Mike, how the *hell* do you get to sleep at nights thinking like this?" they asked (more or less in unison).

"Dude, you have to relax," said Luke, "and enjoy life more. Quantifying stuff like this'll only make your life miserable, like." Mission accomplished.

I'd originally intended to enter medical school when I finished my undergraduate Science degree at the University of Waterloo …not that I was actually interested in being a doctor. That's moot, I suppose: I didn't do well at all on the MCAT entry exam, and in the aftermath no med school would touch me with a ten-foot pole. So I was encouraged (ie. pressured) by my folks to do graduate studies at the hometown university, and try again later.

I'm twenty-five, going on ninety-three. At least that's what it feels like. Most of my friends are working at these amazing jobs, preparing for amazing careers, many are engaged or married. Raising families, buying RRSPs and sport-utility vehicles. Me, I'm single, still living with my parents, and floating in purgatory. It's like Dave said to me on his twenty-fifth birthday: "Once you've turned twenty-five, man, it's just *over* – no *seriously!* Think of it as a milestone, or more appropriately, a grindstone hanging around your neck. Yeppers, the big two-five…you're a quarter of a century old, a third of the way through your life. And halfway to hell. Cheers."

After my cup, I enter the St. George subway station and plug some *Blue Rodeo* into my Walkman. I look around the station, moderately busy, mostly filled with young people. I just don't understand. *They say there are a million stories in the naked city.* In a corner, there is a guy smiling and joking with a girl; across the platform, there is a couple holding hands; exiting the train, a shiny, happy group of guys and gals on various Missions from God. I am surrounded by multitudes of people who are living, laughing, falling in and out of love, and yet I feel incapable of doing the same.

Passion is what drives these lustful, clumsy shells of ours. Passion in love, politics, sport, art – these are the things that keep us going, that keep us driving towards the ideal – impossible, yes. But it keeps us going. To lack passion is to lack essence. And boy, do I ever lack essence.

Well, that's not entirely true. What I really want to do, I guess, is write. It's one of the few things that makes me *feel* something during these empty, lonely times. For the past five years or so, I've been scribbling away at a vague literary entity I refer to as The Book™. So far, I have a basic conception of what it's going to be about, but what I really have is a legion of disjointed ideas scratched down on anything that happened to be convenient, collecting dust in this Campbell's Soup box at home. If you were to look inside, you'd find a mix mash of steno notebooks, notepads, loose-leaf pages, computer printouts, old receipts, ticket stubs, business cards, beer labels, cocktail napkins, even a piece of leather (long story behind *that* one). For a long time, I've hoped to take this box and convert it into a novel of epic proportions, but life rarely works out the way you want it to. I haven't had the chance to just do it – to sit down, write, submit it to a publisher, get it published, and retire rich and famous to an island in the Caribbean. Pre-med programs are not particularly conducive to creative pursuits, graduate studies even less so. On Luke's suggestion, I've even considered hybrid-ing my love of writing with my current field of study, but I've been put off with visions of writing, say, obscure papers, or workplace health-and-safety pamphlets, or dry and personality-free science articles targeting other angst-ridden graduate students.

What it comes down to, I think, is lack of focus: "*Ho doh geem, moh bah lei* (Too many knives, none of them sharp)," my mom is always fond of saying. Meaning that the thing that propelled me through grade school and high school – excelling at all things equally well, like math, geography, writing, art, bean-bag counting, nap time – was no help to me now. Mediocrity is kind of funny that way, isn't it?

But I stuck with it – that Chinese "guilt" thing, you know. Guilt has always played an inordinately large role in the Chinese Canadian family. Parents, in addition to doling it out, also feel guilty themselves when their kids screw up – "*What could we have done differently?*" – regardless of whether they had anything to do with it or not. I know that my failure to get into med school and move out of the house like a normal, fully-matured offspring was something of an embarrassment to them. But they put on the face and carried on. As did I. It's the Chinese

Way. While Western kids seem to accept the sacrifices made by their parents gracefully, the question in many Banana brains is, "*Man, they've given me so much, there's no way I can ever repay them.*" Which is why my failures and personal desires were such awful gaping wounds in my life: I am not repaying them very well.

In a culture that values professional success, social status and loads of money, writing is a craft that is disparaged because it isn't conducive to these goals in the modern economy. Maybe a few centuries ago when the written word of the poet-scholar was considered sacred, even holy by the Chinese. But alas, with modern Chinese families, writing is ranked a few leagues below the prototypical emblems of Asian success. There were times I wondered why I was cursed with an interest in something as useless and unproductive as writing. Why couldn't I have been cursed with an interest in quantum physics or fixing eyeballs or balancing ledgers or something? It would've made life so much easier.

My ex-girlfriend, unsympathetic as always, used to scoff at the conundrum. "Grow up, Mike. This suffering artist attitude isn't going to get you anywhere. You need to focus on the important stuff and treat your writing as a hobby. What's the big deal, anyway?"

Hah, as if it were that easy – typical Mina thinking. You can't shrug off your passion just like that. You just *can't*.

So when all was said and done, I ended up with a Bachelor of Sciences specializing in nothing in particular, thousands of dollars in accrued student loans, and no med school to show for it. Oh yes, and a box of old looseleaf sheets, some fresh, some yellowed from time and neglect.

And an unobtained dream.

I suppose my greatest fear is of not doing anything at all – to leave it all behind, my life, my Passion, the only feeling I have. Becoming my Campbell's Soup box – broken pieces of prose, poignant, useless, as disjointed as the way I feel. To me, that would be the greatest tragedy, and it is a fear that colours my dreams at night, and shades my days in these sterile hallways, grey and meaningless.

❊

It usually takes a half hour to take the subway up to Finch, the northern-most station on the Yonge line. After that, another twenty minutes by bus across a dull suburban plain, and then a five-minute walk home. I repeat all of this in reverse in the morning, and then reverse it again the following evening. It never ends.

I saw Shirley on tonight's train, probably coming back from evening classes. I see her only occasionally – she transfers to a Scarborough-bound bus at York Mills station. Sometimes we nod to each other, sometimes we ignore each other. Sometimes I pretend I'm asleep. Sometimes she does.

Tonight, we just nodded, and buried ourselves in our respective textbooks. It's just as well. We rarely talk, and when we do, the subject of Rick never comes up. We used to talk about Rick more when I was still in university about his…issues. These days, I guess it's moot – he's probably doing amazingly well in his world of mega-finance. Rick always does amazingly well in everything.

When I got home, mom and dad were watching a Chinese soap opera on tape, borrowed from my uncle. Tape 79 out of a hundred billion – that's the way it is with Chinese soap operas. My younger sister, Jen, was out, probably with her new boyfriend.

"*Ah bao*," mom called from the family room in Cantonese, "get an orange from the kitchen and peel it for yourself."

"Yes'm."

Unlike Rick, I had what you would call an unremarkable childhood. I did well in school, played the piano (which I hated), went to Chinese classes (which I also hated) on Saturday mornings instead of watching Wonder Twin powers activate. My dad came to Canada in the sixties for a PhD and a job, and we've lived in Thornhill, a suburb north of Toronto, pretty much all of my life. I'm a *juk sing*, born and raised, growing up a middle-class, suburban Canadian under the shelter of corporate health, dental, accident insurance plans. Dad's a chemist for a major pharmaceutical company, a quarter-century man, gold-watch and all. Mom is a classy woman with a degree in Chinese literature

Banana Boys • 93

– not too useful over here, except for quoting ancient Chinese proverbs whenever she yells at me.

When I was riding high in high school and the first-year of university, my mom would talk about me in such glowing terms, to my relatives and my friends. "It's like I've built and fashioned a model," she used to say, "and every so often I have to step back and look at it proudly, inviting everyone else to do the same."

Yeah, I thought, *often at the cost of making the children miserable.* The Chinese have this thing called *mien ji* (face); it gives parents prestige if their kids perform well in school, work, or anything else. If unchecked, the "face game" can spiral into a somewhat sadistic pastime for Chinese mothers, who mercilessly compare the accomplishments of their "fashioned models," showing-off to friends, one-upping neighbours, cowing their children, stealing their childhoods. At age eight, for example, I was dragged kicking and screaming to piano lessons (*piano lesions*, as I later referred to them), presumably because every other Chinese parent in the community made their kids do the same thing. To cajole me into playing, my mom told me this story of the piano store owner's son (who, as I recall, was walking out of the store carrying a huge bag of hockey equipment) when we went there to purchase the Great Oak Satan.

"Don't wanna play," I sulked like the ungrateful brat I was.

And then she explained to me about how the son had resisted taking piano lessons, and now that he was too old he regretted it. The classic ethnic guilt trip which, as was revealed to me a few years ago, was also a bald-faced lie.

So I folded like a cheap road map. Every Thursday night, instead of watching *Cosby*, *Cheers* and *Family Ties*, I was brought to the musty old house of my musty old piano teacher, Mrs. Blatchford, to do Minuets and Scherzos and other boring stuff from composers long dead and buried.

Even worse was the practising. God, I hated the practising. I hated being stuck in front of the Oak Satan every day at 4 pm, sighing as I gazed longingly outside at the sun, the sky, most of my Canadian friends playing baseball or road hockey or somesuch.

But the absolute worst was when my family had guests over. "Oh *Mi*-koh! [*faking surprise as I slinked past the living room*] Come sit down and say hello to uncle and auntie! Say [*faking spontaneity*] I have an idea! Why don't you play something on the piano?" And all the guests would then look at you like ferrets marking a field mouse for dinner.

And you'd groan like the ungrateful *juk sing* that you were, but you'd do it under the threat of a knuckle in the head. So you'd play and your parents' "face" points would be jacked up by a few hundred or so. All the other guests would clap politely, secretly planning to slap their kids in leg irons when they got back home. And the wheel would turn once again. It seemed like a particularly vicious game of Keep Up With the Joneses, or, in my specific case, the Wongs: *"Ah, Rick has played piano for six years…he skipped a grade and took two Conservatory exams in six months…has won awards…recorded albums…will play at Carnegie Hall/Wembley Stadium/the Kremlin next Tuesday."* **Argh.**

When I reached age fifteen, I was given the choice to continue, or quit. I dropped the goddamn thing like a searing hot potato. And to this day, my mom insists that they were making me play the piano because it disciplined me, helped me develop my memory, as well as my leadership skills. (And not only that, it was supposed to improve my slapshot, make me immune to rickets and make my breath fresh and minty.)

A number of years later, I picked up the guitar. I loved it – and I still do – because *I* picked it up and started playing it, unforced, uncajoled. My mom is pretty fond of saying "Ah, you can only play the guitar so well because of the musical background piano lessons gave you." I usually snort in response, but deep down, I suppose she's right.

The next day, I stopped by to talk to Professor Allenberg, my thesis supervisor. He's a biology professor specializing in the neurochemical basis of human emotion. That seems really interesting, doesn't it? I mean, who wouldn't want to find out the physical basis of things as crazy as love, hate, depression and sexual attraction? But when you get down to the nitty-gritty, it's just a lot of statistics and messing around with frozen monkey membranes. Definitely not as glamourous as you'd suspect.

Prof. Allenberg is all right as a prof – he's pretty smart, and he treats me fairly…when he's not bawling me out, that is. But he's also kind of – unorthodox. Okay, he's kind of weird and nutty. The classic Nutty Professor. He left this note on his door:

> *"Todd, Michael – I'll be away from the office from yesterday until Tuesday of last week. Please water my geraniums. Stay away from fried foods. Thx, Allenberg."*

Graduate students have a reputation of being abused by their supervisors. This wasn't really the case with Prof. Allenberg…except for when he paired me with my office mate, Todd Brudner. Todd's actually not that bad a guy, but we had what you'd call a "defining moment" right at the beginning of our relationship that more or less set the tone for "*Hi…Bye.*"

On the first day I started at U of T, I went downstairs with him to the caf for some lunch and we exchanged the usual introductory niceties.

"I did my undergrad at the University of Waterloo," I said.

"Waterloo, eh?" He nodded his head with interest. "Good engineering school."

I smiled slightly. "So I've heard. A couple of friends of mine were there for that."

"And were they Oriental as well?"

Whammo.

A shot. A scream. A pirate ship appears on the horizon. A pause, while the impossible possibility of flinging coffee in his face then running amok with an assault rifle briefly passed through my mind, and then the impractical idea of spending the next two years with him hating me in the cramped grad office smacks it into left field.

"*Y-e-e-e-e-s,*" I managed. "Erm…why do you ask?"

"Oh. Well, my cousin is in engineering, and he's noticed a lot of Orientals there. He's taken to calling the place 'The Chinese Pavilion.'" He laughed innocently.

I gave a strained – *very strained* – smile. "Nice of him to notice. Well, as long as he doesn't, you know, bring in a bunch of skinheads to beat 'em up and stuff…"

Todd snorted into his Coke. "Not likely. He's Jewish."

After that, I just avoided him. I just didn't need the headaches, you know?

Today, Todd wasn't here either. I guess he must have seen the note first and then took off to see his girlfriend or something. If there's credit to be given , it's the fact that Todd is able to do as little work as possible and still remain acceptable to Prof. Allenberg. Too bad I can't get away with the same thing without being castrated, but that's the way the cookie *crrrrrumbles*.

From: Dave Lowe <dlowe@Praxus.ca>
To: "Malaise Guy" <mchao@neuro.utoronto.ca>
Subject: Man-Stuff.

Meat. Beer. Bawdy jokes. My place, 6pm Thursday. Just got a new Coleman and a pile of marinated steaks, ready to roar. Price of admission: a twelver of Canadian. Be there or be vaguely quadrilateral. Davey Dave.

"Yo Mike," Dave said, busting Kramer-style into my office in the late afternoon.

"Hi Dave…be with you in a second, I have to finish this paragraph." I turned back to my monitor. "The beer's in the freezer, under the petrie dishes."

"Hope you didn't put any freaky shit on top of it. I'd hate to unleash an epidemic or something." He took out the twelver and scanned the office. "Boy, is this place ever boring as… *Ooooh!* Molecular model set! May I?"

"Be my guest."

He plunked the beers down on the floor, sat down at Todd's desk and started plugging carbon, nitrogen and hydrogen atoms together.

"So, Mikey, whater'ya working on?"

"Paper due next week on the effects of a new anti-depressant on the mating patterns of rabbits. It's shaping up okay. I'm just penning up the bibliography before I can…"

"Say Mike," Dave interrupted, "I'll give you ten bucks if you can name this molecule." He held up a byzantine monstrosity of free atoms and broken bonds that wasn't even remotely possible in this universe.

"I don't know."

"Buddy, I'll *tell* you what it is! It's the cure for AIDS! I've found it! I've found it! After years and years and years of blood, sweat and research…"

I shook my head, grinning wearily. "Dave, this molecule is completely impossible. I mean, you have nitrogen there, oxygen here, a quadruple bond crossing a double bond here…it can't exist. Trust me."

"But it'll help millions of people! It'll win a Nobel Prize! It can't be an impossibility! It *can't*, damn you!" He looked at me and then the molecule, and dropped it in one of my drawers, slamming it shut. "O*kay*, I'm bored. Log off and let's get on with the meat and beers."

We drove Jeepy to his place on Madison Ave., underneath the shimmering cicadas on a freakishly hot September afternoon…a pleasant change from all the rain we'd been having. It reminded me a lot of California.

He invited me to sit out on his smallish balcony overlooking the Delta Kappa frat house, and handed me a glass from his freezer.

"Chilled glasses," I remarked, impressed. "How thoughtful."

"Don't flatter yourself, Mike," he said, setting down a Tupperware bowl of marinated steaks. "You know I *love* chilled beer glasses. *God*, how I love them." He tossed me a Canadian from the case, which I poured into my glass. It accepted its loving amber kiss with a frosted sigh. "Cheers, Big Ears."

"Down it goes, Big Nose." *Gulp.* I give off a contented hum. "Thanks for having me out, Dave."

"Hey, no prob." He primed the grill generously with lighter fluid and started Q-ing with a flourish. "So how's life as a grad-school serf, bubbie?"

"Yeah, as if you care."

"Dude, I *care*!" Dave pretended to be hurt. "I *care*, man! *Look* at the sensitive man! He *cares*! I tell you I gain sexual gratification from your academic success!"

"Yeah, it was good for me too, Dave. Smoke, hon?" He laughed, and we clinked glasses.

"So have you, like, created any genetically engineered deviants yet?"

"No Dave, I don't know any girls you'd be interested in."

"Yee-*OWCH*! Good one Mike…I can smell the burning carcass from over here. Or is that just the steaks?" Dave flipped over a slab of meat on the grill. "Nope, not the steaks. This is beautiful, innit?"

"Very nice."

I met Dave in first-year, when we were both holed up in the horrible Waterloo student residences. Every day at dinner, we would sit at the same table with the rest of the East Quad guys, sucking back Tang and eating lasagna recycled from yesterday's chili, which suspiciously resembled the lasagna served a few days before.

We were both geeks in school. We'd always have "geek conversations" about the stupidest things. My favourite: a discussion on physics and Italian food when the dorm served spaghetti, yet again.

"Spaghetti, yet again," grunted Dave.

I grimaced at the industrial-sized portion of baked pasta tangles, gloved in an unhappy looking sheath of cheese and sauce. "You kind of wish they, you know, would develop an antidote for this. Anti-pasta or something."

"That's anti*pasto*," corrected Mauro, my next-door neighbour.

"What *is* antipasto anyway?" Dave asked.

"It's like olives and pickles and stuff, served before the main course."

"Oh yeah? Is that anything like matter and anti-matter?" A shrug passed around the table. "What I want to know is this: what *would* you get if you mixed pasta with anti-pasto?"

"An explosion of unimaginable proportions?" I offered.

"Yes. Yes! I can see it." Dave switched into his Carl Sagan voice. *"Mixing pasta and anti-pasto – terrible, horrible, catastrophic...matter and time are torn apart in a massive cataclysm... annihilation, mass destruction, everyone becomes Italian..."*

"It must not be, Dave. We must prevent this." And after eating, we destroyed the leftover pasta on our plates by pouring Jello and Coke all over it. The unspoken policy on residence food was this: what you don't finish, you destroy for fear of it reappearing in front of you another day in some other morphed form.

As he lifted yet another Canadian to his dry lips, I briefly imagined Dave with a puffy white hat and a novelty apron from the It Store: *World's Greatest Dad*. I chuckled.

"Something funny, jerk-off?" he said, not unkindly.

"No. I mean, yes. For a minute there, I just pictured you as a perfect suburban father, barbequing mounds of burgers and hot dogs for your three-point-two kids, feeding scraps to Rover, driving a wood-panelled station wagon..."

He laughed loudly. "Ha ha ha! Ha ha...aha ha ha ha...*no*." Bemused, he took another large swig of beer. "No father. No kids. No Rover."

"And why not, pray tell?"

"I hate dogs. Seriously, though, I'm not marriage material."

"Why do you say that?"

"I figured something out a long time ago," he said impassively flipping a T-bone within a wall of sizzling flame, "that we are all merely functions of our parents. You know…

$$x(Dave) = y(Dad) * z(Mom).$$

"The strengths of your parents beget your strengths; their weaknesses are your weaknesses. And, by default of genetics, they become your children's, as well. There's really not much more to it." He frowned. "Child rearing was definitely *not* one of my folks' strengths. And I'll be damned if I subject some innocent rugrat to lousy parenting by genetic default."

"Genetics doesn't work that way, Dave."

" 'Course it does," he smiled crookedly. "Well, maybe not. Let's just put it this way – I don't need the grief."

"Well, I still think you'd look good in a puffy hat," I remarked.

After barbecuing the steaks, we sat around to wait for Shel. He was supposed to come by a little after six-thirty, but we were still waiting at seven.

"So where is he?" I asked.

"Dunno. Maybe he became the Star Child from *2001* or something. In any case, the steaks are getting cold and I'm going to eat them."

"Fiend!"

"Indeed." He forked a beautifully-marbled slab for me, and we started eating. They were really excellent.

I met Shel through Dave and, curiously enough, Rick, even though I knew him through his family. Luke joined the group shortly afterward. We had some pretty fun times, but to me, it was a little more than that. They made me realize some things about *juk sings* in general – about our issues, concerns, about the seeming prosperity of our respective positions in life, but our seeming obliviousness to all of it. That could be it – obliviousness. The Essence of Banana.

That's the way it was. Something was…*there.* Something

that bugged us, nagged at us, kept us all slightly off-kilter. It was like an undefined burden of some sort, kind of hard to describe. The burden of being a good driver. A hard drinker. A good hockey player. A bad student. Someone who didn't do computers. Someone who didn't do laundry. Someone who could pronounce their L's and R's properly. Those who are smart enough to be aware of it (or stupid enough; depends on how you look at it, really) might try to ignore it. Scorn it, maybe: *"I've got my place, my friends – I don't care." "It's someone else's problem…I don't care." "It's not me…I'm cool…I don't care."* Or they might over-compensate for it by going to the extremes, to the point of being annoying and neurotic. But it always came back to us in one way or another, like that darned cat. Every time someone slipped up, we all paid for it. Somehow. Somewhere.

Like I said, it's kind of difficult to describe cleanly. Because eventually, things like family, money, education, privilege, come into it and then the explanation starts sounding kind of stupid and petty. In fact, I found that trying to articulate it to certain (i.e. Caucasian) people was about as useful as trying to nail marmalade to the wall. But past the mundanity, the hodgepodge of sports, pop-culture sound-bytes, gripes about work and women, *Simpsons* quotes, alcoholic experiences, I still sensed something there – something I resolved to explore, perhaps in The Book™. That is, if I ever got a chance to write the damned thing.

After the meal, Dave started going on about – *what else?* – women, as we polished off a few more beers from the twelver, basking in the simmer of a beautiful Indian summer evening.

"Ever notice how young girls are, you know, looking more developed these days?"

"Er, what exactly do you mean, 'developed'?" I asked, accepting another chilled glass, struggling to down my last one. Only my third beer, and I was already buzzing.

"It's hard to say. All right, say girls from high school." Dave curved his hands in a vague wavy motion and then dropped them, grimacing. "Okay, jail-bait, that's what I'm talking about. You look on the streets, and it's really getting hard to tell, because chicks these days are looking so…so…"

"Right, right, 'developed.'"

"Exactly." Dave popped open his sixth beer of the night and continued. "I mean physically...*shit*, man, there are some *babes* out there, you know? And the way they dress and stuff, you can't really tell if they're eighteen or sixteen or even younger, sometimes...unless they open their mouths and the air gets let out of their heads." I shook my head at that one. Dave was a pig, but sometimes he was a *funny* pig.

"It's crazy, man, just crazy. Guys just need to be more careful for fear of landing in the slammer."

"Fifteen'll get you twenty..." I said, grinning.

"Good one." He tapped his forehead with his index finger, rolling his eyes upward in mock-thought. "So what do you think it is, Mike? Something in the water? In the air, maybe?"

I pondered this for a split second, and then looked at the gristle on my plate. "It might be the meat," I said. "I mean, meat these days is pumped full of hormones to make it richer, larger, better marbled, right? I don't know much about this, but back at Waterloo, a friend of mine in Agricultural Studies told me that most of these growth hormones are female."

"No shit? Like estrogen?"

"Yeah, sort of. In any case, if you're a girl weaned on meat like this, it may follow that you'll tend to be more, er, 'developed' at a younger age. More hormones in your system could mean being taller, having larger breasts, more adult features at a younger age."

Dave nodded. "Makes sense, dude. So what about guys?"

I sipped my beer thoughtfully. "Not so sure," I said, shrugging. "I'd guess that boys could be, you know, 'less developed' because of an increase of female hormones in their system."

Dave looked at me and then at his steak. He shrugged and continued eating.

"If I had breasts, I guess I'd never have to leave the house," he mumbled, mouth full. "Power, sister."

I had a good time at Dave's. Call him bitter, sarcastic, sexually-frustrated, but he can certainly Q a mean steak.

I suppose I had good times with most of the guys, actually, but it's not like we got together all that much anymore. We were all just too busy, you know? Dave with his development cycles, Luke with his music and aimless wanderings, Shel's going to Ottawa, and Rick. Rick, presumably in his high-powered world of finance, corporate politics, pharmaceutical enhancement, and plans for World Domination. *Presumably.* I haven't talked to that guy in ages.

We all had work to do, our own separate lives to deal with. That's the way it should be, I suppose. All very normal, very right.

But I'm empty and aching, and I don't know why.

So I'm sitting in the dark, in my newly renovated basement, looking at Charisse, my guitar. There is a single lamp from the track lighting on the ceiling trained on the case, lying open on the ground. Its beam is trained on her burnished oak top and brass strings, casting radiant reflections onto the stucco ceiling above. Dust motes dance in the beam of light, betraying her loneliness. And my own.

Another long day at school. Another day of cranking through books, adjusting the freezers, playing with the petrie dishes, scribbling notes, playing Free-Cell and Hearts on the antique PC in my office. Another subway and bus ride, coming home to a meal of rice and beef and tomatoes and reruns of *Cheers*. I am feeling particularly depressed tonight. So what else is new?

I love my guitar. And she loves me. I am now writing this simple line in my songbook: "... *To my one true love, my guitar.*" Sometimes I think that I reserve my deepest feelings for inanimate objects (like my guitar, my coffee, The Book™) because I am incapable of expressing emotion toward anything else.

She left me about a year and a half ago on the twenty-third of January. Mina, my ex-girlfriend. One month after our second anniversary, a week after my birthday, a month before Valentines Day, three months before final exams. She cheated on me with this other bastard, cried a few crocodile tears, and then she just left me.

"Look at it this way," Luke said kindly. I was moping about back at school, trying hard to continue, failing miserably. "Now you can concentrate on the things you love – your guitar, your coffee, The Book™. And hanging with us. Yeah, I know, she was one of those things…but I firmly believe Love is a finite resource, and she really wasn't worth your time and energy if she could do *that* to you." He patted me on the shoulder rather awkwardly.

I nodded, nearly comatose. Heartache does that to you. "Things you love. Things you can truly trust. Things that won't betray you. Things that won't plunge their hand into your chest and rip out your still-beating heart and eat it right in front of you."

"Er, yeah. Right."

To my one true love, my guitar.

I stare at you, your lovely, shapely form, in the dark. How long has it been, my love? I cannot say, it's so hard to tell. I've tried, my love, I've tried. Just last month, do you remember? I've tried to love you and play you like all those other nights. We were happy together, then…happy at being sad.

And so I tried again, but it didn't sound right. It just didn't flow. It sounded trite, somehow, contrived, sickly. The songs were too dated, too old. Today is alternative-dance-techno, we have no real place here anymore. We've lost our refuge. I didn't want to make a mockery of both of us, my love, so I stopped. You may have cried, but I was unable to hear you.

My love, my love. Don't cry. Maybe later, maybe when it's all over, I'll pick up the pieces and try again with all of my heart. If I don't kill myself first.

"*Mi-koh! Ah Mi-koh ah!*" Mom yelled suddenly, above the din of the HKTVB serial in the family room. "*Sik chang!* Eat your oranges!"

And so I leave you once again, my love. For sliced oranges.

part 2
neurosis.

My Favourite Weapon Is The Look In Your Eyes.

*It's the Morning Mosh, Luke Yeung here at 6 am. How the **hell** are y'all this fine minus-five degree morning? Don't y'all just **looove** this damn country? It's time for wild sub-zero fun as old man winter heaps those chilling arctic winds to make our days better and brighter once again…a sort of payback for the kick-ass Indian Summer we had, from a very, very, **very** vengeful and bitter old guy. Kind of reminds me of an ex-girlfriend…so put on those bala-klavas and start sacrificing those goats to Ma Nature for spring sunshine and roses…here's some* Throbbing Gristle *to warm you up on your way to work. Keep it tuned to Morning Mosh window and keep venting your anger with the Yeungster until 10 am."* I flipped off the mike and grabbed my thermos of JetFuel™ java, smiling tiredly at the thumbs-up sign from Scab in the producer's booth.

"Dude, you are *so* relaxed," he commented over the mike.

Woke up this morning with *Throbbing Gristle* on the brain, which set a perverse tone for the rest of the day. *Gristle* was a pioneer in the industrial music movement in the early eighties, with a great motto – "Entertainment Through Pain" – and their music showed it; bizarre, pulsating rhythms and unidentifiable sounds coupled with 'interesting' vocals. There's really no other way to describe it. Their concert practices paint the best picture: Scab, who's also from the UK, told me that they experimented with sub-sonics and disturbing graphic images on large screens during live performances, designed to make the audience nauseous.

I look outside at the dry, bitter cold coating the corner of Queen and Bathurst. Hellishly cold, and it's only mid-November…it's as if fall just evaporated overnight, replaced by the brutal howlings of a frosty lunatic. My bike is in the shop, so I had to take the transit straight from the club. Last night was pretty cool – I had a DJ gig over at *Detox 00*, a new club on Richmond St. West. Clubs like this are popping up like toaster strudels all over the city, giving less-famous locals like myself a little more exposure. I was fortunate enough to snag the "early" slot from 10 pm to 11:30 (parties usually start at nine or ten), spinning some Breaks under the moniker of "DJ Lucky Luke" to a sparse but enthusiastic crowd. Still, six-odd hours of DJing and nocturnal jumping and pumping did little for my vigour.

After the Mosh was over, I dragged myself into the lounge and crashed for two hours, waking up to a vision of Zeesh in a ridiculously outlandish outfit. "Hey Zeesh…you look like Herb Tarlek," I remarked, snapping my hair back up with a rubber band.

Zeesh smirked. "Watch it, man."

"No no, I mean that as a *total* compliment." Zeesh was decked out in a tweed jacket, complete with elbow patches, a denim vest with an KMFDM T-shirt underneath, German military pants and a brand-new pair of Doc Martenses. You can always tell a new pair of Docs from a mile away. At the station, Docs are the standard-issue footwear, so whenever someone buys them (and some of us go through the things like hotel towels), we all go on high ribbing alert: *"Hey man, nice Docs!" "Nice Docs, man." "Those are really, really nice Docs."*

"Hey Zeesh," called Zel from her office. "Nice Docs."

Zeesh grinned like a kid with a new Big Wheel. "They are, aren't they? I also got this jacket for nine bucks at that thrift shop at Gerrard and Parliament. It's 100 per cent Scottish wool – *'If it's no' Sco'ish, it's* **crrrrrrrapppp!***' "*– He did the catwalk a little, earning wolf whistles from Scab and Lehanna, our newscaster. He winked, and stepped into Zel's office.

Pretty, but useless, I thought. I looked down at my own get-up: black *Ministry* concert t-shirt, BR khakis, plaid flannel tied around my waist and, of course, Docs. Poster Boy for 1992. Just last week, I was walking up Yonge St. wearing the same T-shirt and I was approached by a Christian fundamentalist-type of an unidentified denomination, complete with tie, pamphlets, and glazed expression on raptured face. After plying me with a bit of smalltalk, he pointed to my shirt and asked me what Ministry I belonged to.

"Well brother, I worship Satan, Our Dark Lord," I replied, crossing my eyes and giving him the devil sign.

He then proceeded to scream "*SINNER! SINNER REPENT!*" several times, following me for a block before I disappeared into the Wellesley subway station.

Confucius once said that to gauge the state of ethics and morality within a society, all you have to do is listen to the music – specifically, to a mere five chords of a popular song. If they are in harmony, then moral standards are high; peace and goodness reign over the land. If not, then the society has degenerated into effete immorality.

Listening to our station would have given Confucius a reason to forget society and go back to generating pithy sayings for fortune cookies. CMSH was one of the most blatantly evil-sounding stations on the airwaves.

"People don't want to listen to mild or normal music in the morning," Zel had explained to me when I signed on to do the show about a year ago, "they want to be beaten over the head, Taser-ed awake with aggressive music. *That's* what makes people feel alive, ready to face the apocalyptic reality which is modern Toronto."

I looked out at the apocalyptic reality that was the corner of Queen and Bathurst – the hot dog vendors, coffee shops and restaurants – and wondered which type of amphetamine Zel was on at the moment.

"Okay…"

"It's *not* okay, godammit!" She stood up dramatically, sending papers fluttering everywhere. "Lucas, my love, I envision something *special* for the Morning Mosh. Something that *gives* till it hurts! Something that *gives* the people of this hellhole pit the proper attitude to face authoritarian bosses, annoying secretaries, back-stabbing colleagues, rude waiters and waitresses, blood-sucking tow truck drivers, and the rest of the scum and slime which infest this sewer we call Tee-*Oh*." She drew out the last syllable with almost evangelical fervency. "You got that?"

"Sure. I guess I…"

"*No!*" She interrupted, jabbing her finger into my forehead and sending some bangle flying loose. "*No* guess! *Never* guess! This is the way it *is*, you spoiled suburban demon-child! Don't you *see*? Can't you *see*? We are the messengers of mind-lacerating *fury*! We are the jumper cables into the *Id* of this city! We are the psychic can-opener to the can of seething anger, aggression and bad motherfucking *whoop-ass*! It screams and claws from the insides of our skulls, crying to be let loose on a world that has had it easy for far too long! *Got that*???"

I raised my hand in a crisp *heil* and snapped to attention, rubbing my forehead with the other hand.

"That's the spirit! Now work out tomorrow's playlist with Zeesh and have it on my desk by 4 pm today or I'll have your eyes for breakfast."

I guess it helped that I grew up with this sort of music; it's the soundtrack of my angry and postured childhood. But these days, I treat alternative-industrial as little more than bread and butter. My current passion is electronic music – not the commercial-quality electronica they play in Gap ads, but the hard, hits-you-in-the-face, grabs-you-by-the-balls-but-leaves-you-surprisingly-happy stuff they play at raves. It's refreshing to've found music that makes you feel good for a change after years of Alcoholics Anonymous lyrics sung by depressed British people. Raving has taught me that music doesn't have to make you miserable, suicidal, or aggressive. (The Yellow Butterflies also help.)

I love all kinds of music – Jazz with coffee and breakfast, Blues after a bad relationship, and, of course, the alternative-industrial fare that now pays the bills. Truth be told, I even like music I don't really like all that much. But Breakbeats – *man, oh man*. Breaks quintessentially define the contemporary beat culture, a merging of the white and the black, a masterful blend of sped-up Hip Hop, Techno and big, fat Acid wobbles, without the rapping and the attitude. There's just something about hearing a break drop that grabs me by the nuts and will not let go, screaming *YOU MUST MOVE!* And I'm only too happy to comply. Unlike House (danceable but pedestrian) or Jungle (intricate but aggressive) or Happy Hardcore (too many fourteen year-olds tweaked up on jib), Breaks doesn't follow a four-four beat pattern. It features a certain syncopation rooted in Hip Hop – 1 2 33 4 or 1 2 (3)3 4 – that makes it slick, funky, and facilitates a whole lot of bad-ass nut-grabbing.

But it does make it a little harder to mix. No choice in that matter, though – if you love the music, the only way to get closer to it is to play it. It's kinda hard to describe how cool it is…when you're up there, facing the throng of sketchy, quasi-happy screaming youth, hovering over your set of 1200's and a Vestax, the music gripping you in an hypnotic flow, compelling you to groove along to hyperkinetic sounds, inescapable rhythms, high on the attention and self-awareness, all at no less than 120 beats per minute.

Despite my innate distrust of authority figures, and occasional crises like PorkGate (as it's now being called), Zeesh and I get along pretty well. His position as station manager injects a bit of anal-retentiveness into his personality, but he's still a pretty cool guy.

As a "business expense," we sometimes go to the underground-bordering-on-abnormal dance clubs around King St. West. The culture at these clubs is interesting. For one thing, people don't dance with other people; they dance with the wall. You never try to pick up girls who dance with the wall, because they're saying something to you: *"Get the **fuck** outta my face you testosterone-charged inbred, it's the **wall** I want."*

Normal beings would find the ambience inside these places exaggeratedly dark and grotesque. The dress code is strictly Goth: black on black. The walls pulse with beats that are distinctly uneven, unharmonious, and slightly disorienting. What little ambient light there is in the venue is absorbed by the walls, the clothing, the black nail polish and lipstick.

Now, Dave thinks my music is weird, but compared to Zeesh, my taste was downright Top 40. Last week, Zeesh and I went down to *The Tar Pit* to see a concert held by two spindly gay German men wearing black turtlenecks and purple Doc Marten combat boots. One played a snare drum and the other banged out cheesy, repetitive synth chords on a Moog X-25, singing in an impossibly monotone voice…

> *Waste your youth*
> **Pah**-*ty…***Pah**-*ty*
> *Drink a lot and vomit*
> *Waste your youth*
> *What are you wearing, Mädchen?*

"Well, at least it's not commercial," said Zeesh. "Like that homeboy-Hip Hop stuff you like."

"Breaks is not Hip Hop, Zeesh."

"Whatever."

"The problem is that you refuse to acknowledge that electronic music is the wave of the future, man," I argued. "Even metal and industrial groups are integrating turntablism into their act. Totally uninspired. Modern alternative music is in an uninspired rut I doubt it'll ever get out of."

"That's your meal-ticket you're criticizing there," observed Zeesh lightly.

"When was the last inspired alternative rock album produced?"

We answered in unison: *"Stone Roses, Self-Titled Album, 1989."*

"You got it."

"Uninspired, possibly," said Zeesh, refilling his pipe and puffing contentedly, "but there are always exceptions."

I rolled my eyes as Dieter started to *danse on sprocket*. In the world of industrial music, the line between what's innovative and what's merely preposterous was definitely a thin one.

After a cup of mediocre coffee over at the doughnut shop across from the station, I went home to grab a bite before the *Cowboy Junkies* concert at Massey Hall, the first of three sold-out shows. I managed to snag some tickets for Michael and myself from Scab, who had "a source."

I slammed the door to the 808 State to avoid Wilson, only to find Seth, the drifter-slash-friend-dude, in the kitchen. He was at the Formica table, crafting a new building for my City o' CDs. I half-expected Seth to show up when the weather started getting cold; he stays anywhere from two weeks to Groundhog Day.

"Was in northern Ontario for a bit, playing some bars and growing some green," he explained, mouth full of tacks, "and spent some down-time fishing and stuff."

"Your whole life is 'down-time'," I observed.

"Funny, Mister Rat Race. Do you have a spare key? I had to pick your lock to get in…get yourself a better lock, man, you can't trust anyone these days." He motioned to his handiwork, still in disjointed pieces. "In a few months, it'll be the Leaning Tower of Pisa, room for forty CDs. What do you think?"

"Looks pretty cool."

"DING DING DING DING DING! 4:20, light'em up." Seth dropped his tools and we proceeded to have some Totally Happy Crop.

Seth is this long-haired wannabe rocker with no real musical talent: "*The image is great for the babes,*" he confided to anyone who cared to listen. He was always "between gigs" with some phantom grunge group that apparently didn't do Toronto "for political reasons." Seth is okay, though the archetype was getting a little tired – you can't throw a stick down Queen St. without hitting a pod of Mr. Sensitive Ponytail musician-types, talking about their latest indie release over a latte, or their upcoming gig at The Horseshoe. Still, he didn't eat much, and he had some interesting and useful skills, and decent connections for quality Totally Happy Crop. To a guy who goes broke Tuesdays and alternate Wednesdays, that's like finding gold bars.

After dinner, Seth took off to some party, and I headed for the Eaton's Centre to meet Michael at 7 pm. A wayward gust from southern Ohio had warmed the air up considerably, making the walk more palatable. Michael was waiting patiently by the bank of TD Green Machine ATMs, inside the mall's main entrance, reading a copy of *Now* magazine.

"Hey there, Michael," I said, proffering a ticket. "Pretty lousy seats, though…behind a pillar."

Michael stuck out his lower lip. "Pity. I'd have loved a clear space between me and Margo to proclaim my eternal, undying love."

"Stay away from her, man. She's mine." The beautiful and sultry lead singer of the *Cowboy Junkies* owned the eternal love of millions.

"Zeesh was telling me that he actually met Margo, playing a smallish club down in Texas somewhere," I said as we made our way up Yonge St. towards Sam's to shop for CDs. "Dude, you'd never be able to even get *close* to her up here. He even got to hug her."

"Arrgh!"

"Yeah, the lucky bastard."

Today, it was "Buy Three, Get One Free" at HMV for some reason or another, which was either good or bad luck, depending on what angle you held my bankbook up at. We made a sharp right before we hit the tacky swirling neon records of Sam's, and came out of the store with a teetering stack each. New one by *Sloan. Orbital's* latest. Continuous DJ mixes from John Kelley and DJ Hardware. Some *Pure, Deep Forest, KISS* (believe it or not, I was a huge *KISS* fan way back when), *The Sundays*, some independent discs I heard good things about from Lehanna at the station. Some discounted Bluenotes jazz samplers, the soundtrack to the latest gritty-teen comedy drama from the WB Network, and…

"Pat Boone?" Mike said incredulously.

"It was half price."

"Good God. You're an addict. Dave has a billion useless CDs with old software on them – you should get him to give them to you and save some cash." He was right; a banner day for the Yeungster's finances it was not. But *fuck* man, I *love* new CDs. I am addicted to them, controlled by them, slave to their will. I love the way they shine, the way the sunlight reflects off your walls when you wiggle them around. I love the shapes, the lines, the detailed artwork on top. I would have *sex* with new CDs if I could, but I find I don't mention that to people, often.

Massey Hall was thronged with people waiting to get inside. Michael shelled out for two shirts and a program to the hucksters out front (nice, but I already had a zillion-and-one black concert T-shirts, so I didn't get one). And then we were treated to an incredible show. And Margo, of course.

Margo...*MAR-GOOOOOO!* She's a beautiful person, plain and simple. She makes you believe she is singing for you and you alone. It's like there's this connection between you and her, one that can't be broken by anything, any one, in the entire universe. Her words are for *you*. Her message for *you*. Hearing her sing about wedding rings and lonely people and finding Mr. Right is just so good that it almost hurt the soul.

At one point, I glanced over at Michael, completely enthralled, a tear in his eye. Out of all the guys, Michael is the best to see concerts with. He just *gets* it. And he's refreshingly multi-dimensional, unlike Dave who only likes death-metal, Shel who only likes *The Violent Femmes*, or Rick who liked *Depeche Mode* (and Canto-Pop, presumably).

He's also suprisingly talented; I've had the pleasure of listening to Michael sing and play the guitar a few times, in talent shows held by the Bomber. He was pretty good – his voice isn't as rich and powerful like a soul vocalist, but it's steady, solid, and tuneful. Kind of makes you wonder why, between The Book™ and his guitar, he's become an indentured graduate sharecropper.

After the concert, we ambled down to Queen St. for some drinks. To the amusement of some of the other concert goers, we feigned plaintive, obsessive puppy lust like a couple of love-struck idiots.

"*Margo...MAR-GOOOOOO!*" we bellowed.

"My *God*, I love her."

"So do I."

"I love her more than *you* do."

"No way, man, impossible. I love her times *two*."

"I love her times *four*."

"Times a *hundred*."

"Times *infinity*."

"*Double* that and that's how much I love her."

"Stay away from her, man. She's mine."

"Margo…*MAR-GOOOOOO!*"

"I want to have your baby, Margo!"

"Margo, I want to choose your china patterns!"

"I want you to meet my fish!"

We both laughed uproariously as we entered *The Bishop and the Belcher*, an English pub near Spadina Ave. Smoke, fried food, attractive women, and a few pints of Rickards Red – the ideal way to follow up a T.O. concert. Michael was remarking about a record review I'd written in *Now* for a rock group called *Sub-Idiot*. My review…

> *Group:* Sub-Idiot
> *Album:* Surgical Instruments
> *Rating:* 0 (out of five)
> *Let's start by quoting one of their songs: "Ahhh…FUCK! FUCK FUCK FUCK FUCK FUCK you fucking ARGHHH FUCK FUCK FUCK!"*
> *Yeah! Them's good song words! Everything rhymes with fuck! Yeah!*
> *– Luke Yeung*

"Liked that one, did you?" I smiled over the rim of my pint glass.

"How much did they pay you for that so-called review, anyway?"

"A hundred dollars."

"Good God. That's money for nothing, and chicks for free."

"All right, Michael, the beer's on me then, so it's money well spent."

As with most nights with Mr. Rickards, our conversation degenerated as the blood alcohol level rose. Michael, unfortunately, was not a happy drunk.

"Went to see the career counsellor today," he said, hunching forward against the table. "She looked a lot like my ex-girl-friend."

"Dude, you gotta get off this Mistress Cruella thing."

"After what she did to me?"

"Infidelity happens all the time, dude. Just happened on *General Hospital* this afternoon."

"Went to see the career counsellor today," he said, avoiding my attempt at humour. "She told me that a Masters degree wouldn't matter all that much on med school applications, or even in terms of a full-time job."

"Well, it makes sense, I guess," I commented. "Grad school is supposed to be for people who are, you know, *into* their work. And apparently for people with normal levels of self-loathing."

"I know, I know." He sighed, noticing the look of exaspe-ration crawling onto my face. "I'm angsting. Another day, another depressing helix, a downward spiral into a personal hell of my own making. Hoo-*AH*."

"Cripes, dude – just shut up and write The Book™."

"Come on, Luke. It's not that easy." He noted another exas-perated expression and furrowed his brow. "Okay, okay it *is* that easy," he amended, "for *you* maybe. But not for me. It's my parents. They're so hell bent that I get into med school that it would crush them if I gave up on it."

"You just *think* it would crush them."

Michael's personal albatross is The Book™. It's not that the concept is flawed or anything like that; it's just that I doubt his ability to focus. Grief is decent lighter fluid for creative pursuits, but eventually obsession corrupts grief and turns it into a sick-ness, a disease. Self-absorption has a funny way of warping one's perception of reality, and it dulls focus faster than any-thing I can think of.

And that's what it really comes down to for Michael: he needs to write the damn Book™. He knows what he wants; he just needs to do it. Take Michael's Book Idea Repository, for example. All these little pieces of paper in a Campbell's Soup box, flashes of brilliance with zero order, just *sitting* there. And, as far as I can tell, he keeps adding more – but that's the problem. He has no focus, he'll never be able to sort through six-odd years of psychobabble and psychoscribblings. Looking at that box makes me shiver, wondering about years of failed spring cleanings back at the 808 State.

"You know what my folks think of my writing," said Michael, betraying a little frustration, "They *don't*. '*Paging Doctor Michael Chao*'…'*Shall I prep you for surgery, Doctor Chao?*'…'*Doctor Chao, we're losing him!*' *That's* what they want to hear." He made an ineffectual motion with his left hand and took another drink. "Ah, who'm I fooling. It's me, it's all me. I'm a hopeless loser, I just don't have the guts to do it."

"Step One, Doctor Chao: get out of school."

"I wish I could. I hate it, but at least it provides structure in my life, right?"

"So does a cage. Dude, as long as you're within this structure, you'll never be happy."

"Unhappy, yes. Uncomfortable, no."

"You look pretty uncomfortable from where I'm standing, comfort boy."

Impulsively, he fished out his stack of CDs. "*Miles Davis, The Crystal Method, Cowboy Junkies* – all courtesy of the Get Mike To Med School Fund. I'm getting bought off by chump change that merely sustains, never fulfills. Lord help me, I like having my pants down and grabbing my ankles, in a perverse sort of way."

I snorted.

"I'm glad one of us finds it funny." He sighed again. "The world of writing is a jungle, man. For every success, there are ten miserable failures who end up bitter and disillusioned in the gutter."

"You're *already* bitter and disillusioned."

"But I'm not in the gutter," he said, shaking his head. "And as long as I stay in school, my family, OSAP, and the XYZ Corporation pays for all of it. Curse or blessing, you decide."

Blessing, you spoiled child, I thought, but of course Michael already knew this.

"You ever hear that story about the bear in the zoo?" I offered. He shook his head. "Okay, there's this bear, you see. He's always growling and moaning, every single day, and one time the zookeeper walks in and asks, *'Yo bear…why are you growling and moaning all the time?'*"

"Because he's caged up?"

"Because he has this small tack stuck on his butt," I countered. "So the zookeeper asks, *'Why don't you, you know, just pull it out?'* And then the bear replies: *'Because this way, at least I know where the tack* **is.***'*"

"Very profound."

"Ain't it, though?"

"I *know* all this," he said in obvious frustration, rapping his hand against the handles of his chair, "and yet I'm still so…so *miserable.* I'm weak. Lazy. Indoctrinated with a philosophy of inaction, sucking back the mere pittance of comfort, not having the guts to go for it."

"I couldn't have put it better myself, Dr. Analysis. I'll say it again: just shut up and write The Book™."

"I can't. And I just don't understand why. What's wrong with me, anyway? I think I must be crazy or something. God, I need a Prozac milkshake."

"Michael," I said, trying to remove the contempt from my voice, "You *know* he idea of anti-depressants is such bullshit. I mean, what the hell is 'normal', anyway? It's merely an externally generated notion, likely generated from sexist, patriarchal and ethnocentric societal norms, that *you* yourself allow to affect *you*."

"*Mmmm*," Michael mocked in a dreamy Homer Simpson voice, "*Sexist Patriarchy*."

"People aren't like that," I continued, ignoring him. "People get cranky and depressed…that's the way it is, and it's the way it should be. Forget Chemical Utopia. Drink more beer."

We did, but it didn't stop the Downward Spiral.

"What kind of depth do I truly have, anyway?" he continued, sinking deeper into the stinking quagmire. "Have I ever seen the true face of horror? Have I ever seen death or destruction or pestilence or seas of blood or looked into the gaping jaws of hell, screaming for God or whoever to save me from a fate worse than death? No?" He drained his beer. "Then I haven't got a bloody leg to stand on, have I?"

I said nothing.

"Then why does it *hurt* so goddamn much?" he asked.

So we sat in relative silence, Michael stewing in his self-absorbed juices, me thinking of something, *anything*, uplifting to say.

"Michael," I offered, "Maybe you need to become a Buddhist or something. Get enlightenment and everlasting peace in your soul."

"I don't want to shave my head," he replied, face on the table.

"You know what I mean."

"From what I know about Buddhism," he said, lifting his head and smiling crookedly, "it's a pretty depressing religion."

"Just hear me out. The Buddhists have what they call the The Four Noble Truths:

> *1. Life is painful.*
> *2. Pain comes from desire.*
> *3. To extinguish pain you must extinguish all desire.*
> *4. To extinguish all desire, you have to follow bizarre ascetic rules, shave your head, and wear more orange than a candy raver.*

I listed these off in my Asian guru voice. *"But the frogurt is also cuuursed!"*

Michael grinned despite himself. *"That's bad.* So what's the cure, Master Luke? Meditation? Psychotherapy? Large-calibre ammunition?"

"Anti-Buddhism."

"Is that like Christian Science?"

1. Life sure beats Death.
2. But Life can also Suck. When it does, the pain isn't per-
manent — it'll go away, eventually.
3. To extinguish the pain, wait it out and try to keep your
mind off of things. Pick up juggling or crochet or something.
4. Never, ever drink a lot when you're really depressed.

Michael scratched his head. "And where'd you pick up these stone tablets?"

"Well, I was actually in a bar with Dave and Shel."

"Go figure. How'd those guys react to this?"

"Dave kind of liked them, except for the last one. Shel didn't really understand."

"Sounds like responses one would expect…"

"Pay attention to that number three. Think about it, dude – or not. Maybe you should *stop* thinking for a while…take a vacation or something. It's really not all bad. It'll all come together in due time. Okay?"

Michael scratched his head again, and then nodded.

"Okay."

We got out of the bar at around 1:30 am or thereabouts, so I invited Michael, who was slightly buzzed, to crash at my place. I'd figured that Seth would get lucky or something tonight, and wouldn't be coming back to the 808 State.

Lying awake on my futon, a pang unexpectedly hit me. I suddenly started thinking about the most serious mistake I'd ever made, and suddenly felt a pain I'd been shrugging off for a long time.

"You just can't avoid that pang of pain," Michael explained back at the Belcher. "It just happens sometimes. It starts off with a small shiver, small spasms, like miniature fishhooks dragging across your heart." He started breathing a little heavier, a mild look of discomfort creeping across his face, worrying me a little.

"It's hard to explain," he said. "Regrets for things that have transpired, for directions taken, for possibilities forsaken and long gone but not forgotten. It usually happens when I'm off guard, maybe when the moment seems too sharp, too perfect: a cup of coffee, a crisp winter day, a good book, comfortable hum in the background, soulful song on the walkman – a beer with a good friend." I was touched.

"It's so very strange," he continued, voice curiously higher as if he was on helium, eyes wandering out the window to Queen St., "but the pain almost feels…*good* sometimes. *Too* good. You miss it when it is not there; you hate it when it's there. It's like being overwhelmed by a massive attack of something. Nostalgia." He sighed, his eyes were large and watery. *"The good and the bad cascades over each other like milk over a mountain of chocolate, the sweetness and pain caressing your spine like an ethereal lover, calling to you from across a river, a valley, and you can't…you won't…"* He suddenly snapped out of it, and emptied the pitcher. "And then, like a flash, as fast as it was here, it is once again gone. Excuse me," he said to the passing waitress, "another pitcher, please."

There was no denying that Michael could be eloquent. *Paging Doctor Chao: Your book has been published and it's a great success. Congratulations, my friend.*

4 am. The time when all-night parties start rocking, the headliners start spinning, the White Diamonds or Green Roughnecks start kicking in. And here, in the 808 State, Michael is snoring under my kitchen table, and moonlight is glinting off of my Wall O' Tapes.

And at that point, I felt nauseous. I got up to get a glass of water.

I suppose I'm carrying a lot of useless baggage around – more than one would suspect. It's so easy for certain people to forget the bad things in life. Like Rick, for example. I learned a lot about his arguably amoral philosophies on life the year I roomed with him in university. He never seemed to have any issues – no guilt or sorrow or pain or regret – because his memory has be trained to be so conveniently selective, his attention span a deficit of emotion. Especially when it came to Sexloverelationships. He had women over all the time – different ones, disposable ones – and he certainly wasn't playing Scrabble with them.

"Well, you just have to be pragmatic about it," he told me once while munching Lucky Charms at five in the morning in little more than his boxers. I'd just gotten back from DJing a house party, and was eyeing him nervously as he picked out all the marshmallows while Sarah or Sandra or whomever was sleeping in his room. Rick himself never, ever seemed to sleep – by the end of the term, I was thinking that he was a vampire, tempting me to fill my room with garlic and crosses.

"Er, pragmatic."

"Yeah. Think about it, Luke. Baggage weighs you down. Learn to travel light. The past outlives its usefulness once it's ceased to be the present. Keeping it inside makes you seem deep and substantial, but that's a crock – what you really are is fucked."

I guess I'm fucked.

Her name was Sonja.

Two years ago, right after dropping out of university, I started off as an intern at the radio station, then a fledgling underground operation with a listenership of eight. The job involved connecting Cable A to Jack B, picking up new CDs, buying pizza and cleaning up – which I did until Zel discovered that I DJed a bit and had a pretty good radio voice. She started me off on a couple of graveyard slots a week.

I met Sonja during my initial Adventures In Late Night DJing. I was spinning a *Siouxee* track in the middle of the two-to-six slot one morning when suddenly I had this haunting feeling that I was horribly alone. So, on impulse, I offered $100 to the next caller who phoned in. And guess what?

Total silence. Now *that* was the definition of True Loneliness.

It was a catharsis, though. True loneliness yields true freedom, a perverse sort of liberation. It was the complete opposite of claustrophobia – here I was, with the broadcasting power of enough watts that said "Here I am!" to a virtual space which spanned streets, buildings, frequencies, different atmospheric levels. In my cramped DJ booth in a shabby building on Bathurst St., I found myself suddenly with galaxies of space in which I was totally, unabashedly free.

So I started deviating from the station list and played stuff I wanted to hear. I felt like some *Joy Division* one moment, some *Siouxee* at another. If it felt right putting on a Jazz record, I just did it. I'd bought a few Breaks and Trance CDs, so I tried my best to do a continuous DJ mix with the station's lousy equipment, ending off with some ambient techno, including my fave song of all time – 'A Huge and Ever Growing Pulsating Brain That Rules From the Centre of the Ultraworld' by *The Orb* (with a play time of 18:52, the name is not the only thing that was long about it.) Some *Stone Roses, Roxy Music, Dead Kennedys, Rush* (Zeesh would have gutted me for that alone), *English Beat* and, of course, the *Cowboy Junkies*. I even played 'Crazy' by Patsy Cline, shedding a tear on nostalgia I could not have possibly experienced first hand.

By 5:30 am, I was exhausted and drenched with sweat. The booth was strewn with CDs, tapes, LPs, jewel cases and sleeves, Blue Butterflies. And she called me. She said she'd been listening all night, while tending a doughnut shop on Gerrard St. Sonja not only loved every single song I played, she loved "the *pattern* I played it in, the *spaces* I created, the *story* it told to her." She was "enslaved by the soundscape I'd lovingly crafted from the heart." Her words. Beautiful words. I was hooked on the spot. Even if she was an *X-Files* alien, I thought I had found my soulmate.

She wanted to claim the $100, but only on condition that I let her take me out to dinner with it. (As a side note, I tried it out again a month or so later, but by then the station had unfortunately gained a little in popularity – I lost my $100, this time to a 21-year old security guard with a nightstick fetish.)

Sonja turned out to be nineteen, Indian, very attractive, and partial to belly hoops, black leather and House music *(five out of six isn't bad)*. Although she was the daughter of Brahmin, she'd rebelled at a young age, shaving her head and running away from her native Calgary with a blond biker named Aaron, who left her for dead in a crackhouse at Sherbourne and Dundas St. She picked herself up, and ended up working odd jobs around the city, doing community college part-time.

So we went to dinner. Two hours later, we were in my room making passionate love. It was undeniable – the chemistry was precisely sub-atomic, electrical, setting off quarks and leptons in both our bodies and minds, pulsating with a wild energy I had never felt before. And have never felt since.

Love is such a funny thing. It's not a controlled substance, something you can regulate like turntables or mixers or THC-levels. It's not something you ultimately have mastery over, and can choose to subdue. Love has that extra variable multiplied by a degree of magnitude because there's another person involved. When it works, there's such intensity, like an invisible bond between body and mind, life and death, television and remote control.

*It worked. It was **working**.*

And then I ended it. For no particular reason.

Obviously, I choked.

I don't believe that there exists an Ideal Woman out there. She is a spectre that no person could ever live up to. It's a pretty callous thing to do to prospective partners, callous and cruel. People who hold onto this ideal, this perfect template in their minds, will ultimately doom themselves and their relationships, because, inevitably, they'll just end up "settling" for someone. And I ask you, how fair *is* that? Better to approach people as just that – people. You know, good ones, bad ones. Compatible ones, incompatible ones.

Still, just between you and me…she was The Ideal Woman. For me. Just something that inserts a jarring note into the symphony of Luke Yeung's apparent life of leisure and relaxation. No one, as they say, is perfect.

Joy.

"2 years is just too long to go without it."
— Ad for brake maintenance

The key to success, Dave," said Greg in his tremulous, nasal voice, "…is a good drive." He wound up and took a mighty swing, destroying yet another framed Ansel Adams print with a golf ball.

I was sitting in a plush Swedish office chair in my boss' office, glumly staring out at the hustle and bustle going on down on Bay – office drones going to lunch, joggers spewing vapour breath, hot dog vendors hawking nitrate sticks of death, buskers doing the music-thing for shivering and decidedly disinterested passersby.

I swiveled around to look at Greg teeing up for another shot, and tapped my finger impatiently on his model of The Millennium Falcon. After getting off a disastrously long first pass of testing the alpha version of *Jaguar* – v2.0 of our office automation software – I wasn't in the mood for Greg's little office habits.

"So, about this piece of *shit* you call software…"

"Hey, watch it, bub," he warned mildly, pointing at the software specification lying on the blotter with his driver, "that 'piece of shit' is going to buy me a new Porsche. How are Mark and Andrew working out, by the way?"

"Fine, actually." I said, frowning slightly. "No complaints. Yet. So, about this piece of…"

"Are you *sure* the bug count is over five hundred?"

"No. I just made that part up. Of *course* I'm sure." I shook my head. To be questioned by a freak who destroys a thousand dollars worth of office decor a year with bad drives. There is no justice.

Still, I have to admit it; Gregory S. State was a bloody genius, well worth the office carnage to Praxus Technologies. Convinced by Shogun to drop out of the University of Waterloo at age six-teen – *he was in university at age sixteen!* – Greg had been solely responsible for generating about a quarter of all the code at the company before he got promoted to project manager two years ago – just a little after he became a millionaire and stopped coding altogether. (There's a sign in that, somewhere.) Currently, he's in charge of products that account for over a third of Praxus' annual revenue. Which is not to say his golf shot was any good. It wasn't.

Greg pulled a handkerchief emblazoned with Keroppi and blew his nose. An eccentric as well, Greg was. He sported an expensive silk vest over a denim shirt, with a garish orange-and-red tie. His long hair was slicked back, revealing the vaguely unattractive features of his face.

"Well, my fine feathered test-meister, if it's infeasible, what do you suggest?"

"Look, man, *you're* the project manager for this. *You* tell *me*. All I know is that the product is way too saturated with features, and that means bugs. Do your job and cut some of the crap out, or beta'll never happen."

He set down his driver and walked over to his computer, called up the test build of *Jaguar*, and began to expertly refute every single sample bug contained in my report, fingers ablur on the keyboard, graphics reflecting off of his huge glasses.

"Shogun is bullish on being able to support the Classification and Routing business objects, Dave. Oh, and the scripting interface. And we have to keep in mind the SDK, fax support, COM-CORBA bridge support, the component packs we need to come out with next year…"

"Why not add Molecular Deconstruction and the ability to Travel Through Time?"

"Dave, you *know* that's in version 2.1. Seriously, though, if you want to nix all of that stuff, you're going to have to come with me to explain why, like."

"Are you nuts? Shogun'd have my head on a stake surrounded by worshipping pygmies faster than you could say *hara kiri*!" Shogun was the company nickname for our glorious CEO, another brilliant techno-rogue. He was heavily into some sort of Japanese management style, hence the name. Frequently, meetings with Shogun took place while he was practising with his katana, trimming bonsais, or catching flies with chopsticks or something equally as outlandish.

"I don't understand," Greg said noncommittally.

"You know that Shogun hates me. He'd turf me on the spot."

"You're being silly, Dave. Your job is safe…Shogun is strictly neutral about you."

My frown turned into a pained expression.

With a final elaborate keystroke, he swiveled over to me and handed back my report. "Well, you'd better get to work," he said. "This is a lot of stuff to cover in a week."

"Thanks." I grabbed the report and headed outside for a badly needed smoke, miffed. *And every meeting with/His so-called superior/Is another humiliating kick in the crotch…*

Computers were always cake to me, but I was merely lukewarm about the things, unlike ninety-five percent of the people at this company. Which is why I ended up testing software instead of developing it, I suppose. Back at school, I had a bizarre habit of breaking software just by looking at it, which naturally put a serious hamper on most of my grades. Ironic that it turned into my bread and butter in real life.

It all started off pretty typically: being press-ganged into Engineering school by the folks. I guess I'd originally agreed to go into engineering because of its perceived purity, of idea, of task at hand. A secure, creative, non-political profession. Engineers *made* things, you see – they didn't hinder or destroy things like politicians, lawyers or middle-managers did.

But by the end of my first year in Engineering, I found that it just wasn't the case. Outrageous fees. Useless courses. Outdated standards. Vicious politics. Orwellian bureaucracy. Faculty filled with these holier-than-thou academics who had serious God complexes and lorded over you like you were scum. Some others weren't that bad…that is, if they could actually teach. But they couldn't.

Socially, the engineering class I belonged to was also a big fat zero. Aside from Veen and the rest of the Brown Crowd, most of my class were either overly competitive assholes or people as stimulating as day-old olive loaf. There was Squid Row, the name I gave to the first row of most of our classes, stacked with FOBs replete with cellular phones, cutesy Sanrio pencil cases, hair greased and griddled, oval faces framed by oval designer glasses making them look like *X-Files* aliens, and spoke more Assembly language than English. Behind them sat overweight, unshaven, long-haired Japanime-loving guys who hardly showered…and spoke more Assembly language than English.

And, of course, the women. Or lack thereof. Seven out of the eighty people in the class were women and, strangely enough, they constituted about a third of the class' collective weight. They were all married to other classmates by fourth year. In engineering, if you found a woman, you didn't let go for fear of not being able to find another one.

By the summer's end, I was pretty much ready to drop out, which I couldn't exactly do, being a good Chinese boy and all. It's an easy pit to fall into, as Mike and Shel'll tell you: Asian parents are single-mindedly psychotic about getting you into a "respectable" profession at a "respectable" school, in order to give you a "respectable" career. So I had to form some sort of attitude to get me through. I developed this eerie ability to focus, to concentrate all my negative emotions at specific times when needed, to get me through the hurdles. A ferocity that often shocked and scared many people, that could cut through meaningless and boring classes like Thermodynamics or Differential Equations like a Vorpal Sword +3 *(+2 hit points)*.

To replenish all that energy, I did what any other red-blooded, overworked, undersexed engineer did: I drank. I can remember saying 'fuck it' and going to the Bomber to drink heavily – almost every night. I can remember in the middle of my last set of finals suddenly kneeling down in a washroom stall and begging god to end it all (much to the shock and discomfort of the patron beside me.)

But god spared my worthless hide, and I barely graduated, taking away this pearl of wisdom from my disheartening and generally unenjoyable academic experience: everything in this world is as stupid and sullied and superficial as everything else, so why bother? That's why I eventually submitted to a lower-level technical drone job in the field of Information Technology, I guess. It wasn't all I ever dreamed of, but it had a certain level of technical purity. The cash was enough to lead the fabulously decadent lifestyle you see me in now – Hamburger Helper on Wednesdays, instant noodles and hot dogs on Fridays.

But, of course – *no guts, no glory*. Jobs like mine eerily resembled the position of Starfleet Engineer – you spend most of your time like Geordi LaForge, running around checking transfer conduits, crawling around Jeffries tubes, setting up Tachyon beams, performing Level-1 Diagnostics. No fame, no babes, no cool-coloured uniforms. Just Level-1 Diagnostics.

From: TJ McKenna <tjmckenna@statscan.ca>
To: Dave Lowe <dlowe@praxus.ca>
Subject: How's my favourite lush?

Hey there Pal – long time no email. How goes? Things are great here in Winnipeg. I know you think there's jack shit to do out here, but it sure fucking beats Toronto. People are waaay friendlier out west, Toronto people are total *jerks*...

So this is what bliss reads like. Job going well. Taking a masters part-time. Replaced the old K-car with an old Toyota. Quit smoking for good. Still happily administering blow jobs to the neo-Aryan Wheat King she'd been going out with for years...

Sigh. How I loved her.

The thing is, I guess I fell in some semblance of "love" with Teej, somewhere back there. And I put "love" in quotes because I've always had doubts about what "love" really was, even in the traditional sense of the word. I don't think I've ever really felt "true love" for anyone, not even TJ, and I don't think I ever will. (I mean, if "love" meant wanting to go out, shoot pool, drink lots of beer and then ripping off her clothes where she stood and jumping her right there, then I suppose I was in "love" with her …in the traditional sense of the word. But, I suspect it wasn't.)

Beyond wondering about the usual reasons why things didn't work out (ie. was I too ugly, too fat, too Oriental, not Oriental enough, not forward enough, always broke, etc.), I often wondered if it was because I was too nice. What a revolting thought. Part of me wonders if she thought she was…*what?* Perhaps actually doing me a *favour* by not getting romantically involved. That she didn't want to see me hurt. Huh. Go figure.

It's really all imponderable hypothesis – water under the bridge, as useless as air. Aside from the odd e-mail, I have virtually no contact with her. But she still enters my mind, visions of her, possibilities still tweak my heart. And even though I've more or less given up on her, every so often, I'd still wonder…if only a little. I miss the tensions and the sensations, but I also feel relieved that we left it at a genial point – something that was, well, not great, but not all that bad. It's the first and only "relationship" with a woman I've had that was like that. And overall, I guess it felt rather good. Especially considering the Bad Times™.

But I wonder what that says about me as relationship material in general?

As Teej would say: "Jack *shit*."

Just then, Jase stuck his head into my office, and I snapped my head up, nearly giving myself whiplash (*Worker's Comp? Probably not.*)

"C'mon in."

"Yo Dave," he said, brushing his greasy bangs back and pushing his glasses up. He flipped a juggling pin around with his left hand. "I'm just waiting for Build 1673 to compile."

"Mmmm."

"You goofing off again?"

"Mmmm."

"You look kind of bummed, man."

"Mmmm."

"Juggle time?"

"Juggle time."

We went out in the hall, moved about six feet apart and started tossing around the four pins, much to the irritation of a passing sales guy.

My thoughts drifted to yesterday evening. I'd gotten off a little early and went to the local Loblaws to grab some Kraft Dinner and Campbell's Soup to keep me alive for the next week. Just past the Warholian display of Chicken Noodle and Yankee Bean, an old Chinese lady with a small boy in tow was asking a young, ball cap wearing, gum-chewing white punk to direct her to some *bok choy*.

"What the hell is *bok choy*?" he asked brusquely, rolling his eyes. (Florida Panthers jersey under his apron, San Jose Sharks cap on his head. *Whatta fucking **loser**.*)

"*Bok choy*," the lady explained. "*Chi-nesu we-ge-ta-boh*." The little boy beside her started sucking his thumb.

"I'm *soll-ee*, what is that?" sneered the punk. I found myself pretending to examine the nutritional information on a can of Manhattan Clam Chowder very closely, but actually straining to hear the asshole. "I no understand? *We-ge-ta-boh, we-ge-ta-boh*."

"*Bok choy*," she insisted.

"Me love you long time? GI Numbah One? Give boom boom?"

Jesus fucking christ, I thought, *where the **fuck** did they get this inbred from? My home town?*

"Excuse me," I interrupted, pulling the lady aside. "*Bok Choy hei…hei…*" I snapped my finger a few times and tapped the noggin, trying to remember the word for 'left'. "*Joh! Joh, bok choy hei **joh**, hei goh doh.*" (Inside, I was wincing. *Boy, did my Cantonese ever suck.*)

The lady thanked me about three times, and scurried off, little kid in tow.

I turned to the punk. "Having fun harassing old ladies, eh?"

He cracked his gum and squinted at me. "So? What business is it of yours?"

I half-closed my eyelids. "It's my business 'cause I'm choosing to make it my business."

"Yeah, whatever." He laughed.

"Just cool it, okay?"

"Ah, fuck off, buddy."

I stuck my index finger into his face. "Listen, you stupid cracker, if I ever catch you mocking Chinese people like that again, I'm gonna rip your fucking arms off and stuff them down your throat. You understand – 'buddy'?"

"Fuck you!" he shot back. *Good one, Hatfield.*

We stood chest to chest, attracting the attention of some passersby. A few moments passed. I leaned over a little, getting really close to him and started talking to him slowly, menacingly, in a very low voice. "Look, son," I said with strained pleasantness, "Let me tell you something, because I don't think you understand. I can speak, read and write English better than you, you got that, white boy? I am intellectually and physically superior to you in every way. You are *shit* compared to me. Complete and utter *shit*. Do you understand? Now why don't you go back to your *loser* job and your *loser* life, and just remember what I said." I turned abruptly and walked away, grabbing my foodstuffs, completely on auto-pilot.

Once outside the store, I set down my groceries and leaned against the wall, taking a few sharp breaths in the cold fall air. My heart was still racing a little, and my sight was slightly blurred.

> **Racial Incident Log. Incident:** #894
> **Date:** November 7th
> **Notes:** Fair comeback. Decent but unclever use of swear words. Kind of makes you seem insecure, by mentioning proficiency with the English language. Felt queasy and uncomfortable afterwards, but suppressed desire to inflict physical violence.
> **Grade:** B-
> **Comments:** Good job, soldier! For that you get a Coke.

So, I'm a hard marker.

It must seem sort of strange to evaluate racial incidents this way, like the *Rainman* catalogued incidents of personal injury (*"File under 'R' for 'Racist Assholes and Other Scum' "*). But I do.

You would too if you ran into this garbage constantly, like I did in grade school: believe me, I've heard enough cries of "Chink!" and "Slope!" to last me several lifetimes. It still burns me up how this sort of shit can happen when all you're doing is picking up hot dogs, Kraft Dinner, and a lousy head of *bok choy.*

Don't get me wrong – it's not like I'm a particularly big fan of the FOBs myself. I do my share of ragging on them, and I tend to get annoyed with their loud speech patterns, their egregious displays of money, their snickers and looks of contempt toward my own lousy Cantonese. But one thing's for sure, dammit – *I'm the only one **allowed** to rag on 'em.* Others need not apply. The Chinese criticize their own kind more harshly than any other culture; it's a built-in form of self-monitoring. But if a goddamn cake-boy does it, well, that's just racism, plain and simple, and watch out: I'll be the first to rise up in their defense. In spades.

Heading home in Jeepy afterwards, I glanced over at my groceries. Nary a grain of rice or drop of soy sauce in sight, which only accentuated my pain and confusion. I am just a messed-up Banana Boy, floundering about in a messed up world.

I think I've only told Shel about my filing system; he looked at me like my head was about to turn around *Exorcist*-style.

"Dave, how the *hell* do you get to sleep at nights thinking this way?" he asked…

BWAP!

"Shit!"

"You okay, Dave?" Jase scrambled over, pulling out a dirty handkerchief to stanch my nose, bloodied by a pin taken in the face. Deep thought and juggling didn't mix all too well, evidently.

"Um, yeah, Jase," I said, gingerly dabbing my nose with the repellent cloth and quickly returning it to him. "It's nothing. I think your build's finished." Jase immediately gathered up his pins and zipped back into his office, presumably to type in the six-hundred-odd code-optimization ideas that seeped into his large brain during the five-minute juggle.

From: Vinu Malhotra <vinuma@microsoft.com>
To: Dave Lowe <dlowe@Praxus.ca>
Subject: The Official MIT Nerd Test (fwd)

I clocked it at 31%. Tell me how you did.
Veen.

The Official MIT Nerd Test...Score one point for each
YES. Total score is % nerdity. Good luck.
1. Have you ever used a computer?
2. Have you ever programmed a computer?
3. Have you ever built a computer?
4. Ever done #2 for money?
    ...
12. Do you own a Rubik's Cube?
13. Do you know how to solve it?
14. Have you ever designed a multistep chemical
    synthesis?
15. Is your weight less than your IQ?
16. Do you know Maxwell's Equations?
17. Do you have them on a T-Shirt?
18. Done #2 for money?
    ...
47. Have you ever played D&D?
48. Have you ever read The Hitchhikers Guide
    to the Galaxy?
49. Do you know Schrödinger's Equation?
50. Done #2 for money?
    ...
80. Do you know more than three
    programming languages?
81. Can you name more than ten
    Star Trek episodes?
82. Are you socially inept?
83. Have you ever used the word "asymptotic"?
84. Do you have greasy hair?
85. Are you unaware of it?
    ...
93. Do you own a CRC?
94. Do you own a CRT?
95. Do you own an HP?
96. Do you know how to use it?
97. Do you know the Latin name for a fruit fly?
98. Have you ever interpolated?
99. Have you ever extrapolated?
100. Have you ever reached sexual climax
    doing #2?

RANK	CLASSIFICATION
1-20	Normal person.
21-40	Pretty sad.
40-60	Get a life!
61-80	Inhuman levels of geekiness. Alert! Alert!
81-100	Gene-pool threat. Recommend: Sterilization.

"Yo, Jase, what'd you get?"

"Thirty-nine."

"Andrew?"

"Thirty-seven. Mark got forty-five."

"*Forty-five*? Jesus, I work with *nerds*!" I presented them a hard copy of the test. "I'm pleased to say that I clocked the Nerd Test at twenty-five. Pay homage, pay homage."

"You're so cool, boss," chorused Mark and Andrew.

To remedy our collective geekiness, I suggested that we all go to The Madison Pub for dinner and drinks after work. That night, the Maddy was bustling with the U of T frat-boy crowd, but Rod managed to spot me from behind the bar.

"Howdy Dave," Rod yelled, tapping an unidentified keg.

"Hey Rod. How the hell did you spot me in the crowd?"

He looked appraisingly at my cap. "The most disreputable ball cap I've ever seen."

"Hey! Them's fightin' words, Roddy!" I said, secretly pleased. My Bosox cap is my signature, my *50-Mission Cap* (after the *Tragically Hip* song). I never leave home without it. It's dirty, sweat-stained, and so worked in that it would collapse like a raw egg if laid on any hard and reasonably flat surface.

"So dinner or drinks?"

"How 'bout both?" It was great having Norm status at a bar. "By the way, what are you tapping?"

"Something new, could be of profound interest to you, my friend – 'Sam Adams Honey Porter.'" Rod switched into his beer-commercial voice. "*Roasted malt and honey for a full, round flavour to this dark robust porter.*"

"Woo *hoo*! Sign me up for a pitcher at our table," I said, Jase and Mark and Andrew nodding enthusiastically. "And one for these guys, too."

"Two pitchers. Will do. It'll be a few minutes, though,

before the tapping's done."

Ah, there's nothing more awe inspiring than the cracking open of a fresh new keg. We sat down, and I grinned like a little kid on Christmas day when Rod brought over chilled glasses along with the pitchers.

Raising my glass, my spine tingled in anticipation of the liquid gold splashing the back of my parched throat, carbonation sizzling down my esophagus and eventually settling down for a smooth flow down to my stomach. After two more, when the sensations failed to weaken, I pondered something that was mildly alarming: I figured if anyone were to ask me if I'd give up beer or sex at this point, I'd be lying if I said I'd give up beer. But you can't very well give up something that you haven't had in quite a while, I'm guessing. In the words of one Robert Plant, *"It's been a long time, been a long time, been a long lonely, lonely, lonely, lonely, lonely time..."*

"Ah, beer!" I announced melodramatically, doling out generous rations of Honey Porter, "my one weakness, my Achilles' heel, if you will. After a hard day's work, there is nothing, absolutely nothing, like a cold one. Or several, for that matter." Jase and Mark and Andrew agreed, and we all proceeded to get trashed.

"So's the way I sees it," I explained to Mark and Andrew's rapidly reddening faces, "I figure developing a drinking problem's not only inevitable from where we all come from – it's a bodily defense mechanism."

"Got that right," said Jase. "If you're in a tech school in the middle of nowhere, you can pretty much kiss sobriety goodbye. Waterloo ain't a school where people drink for social reasons – we're talking about a school where suicide was an equal option to counseling." He paused, deflating a little. "There was a guy who killed himself in my quad, you know. And a few of my classmates just flipped out and left."

"No way!" chorused Mark and Andrew in unison.

"Way," I said, enjoying the opportunity to play mentor to a couple of young whelps. "You're just starting out, but you'll see how that goddamn place'll exact several pounds of flesh from you in sheer stress. And booze is a bonafide way to regain those precious calories. There was even a school of thought at the time that swore by the benefits of alcohol-induced clarity for subjects like Thermodynamics, Quantum Physics and Advanced Algorithms…"

"You know what they say, Dave," said Jase, '*After a few beer, it all comes clear*'." Me and Jase clinked glasses again at that one.

"Or, at least it won't matter as much," added Andrew.

It felt kind of weird, leading the pups down a stray path towards their destruction, but I chalked it up to environmental influence. I come from a small town full of people whose greatest ambition was to drink every weekend and get their face on a hockey card. Back in Mayberry North, the idea of a good time was loading your dad's Chevy pickup with two-fours of Labatt 50 at sundown, driving to a field, leaving your headlights on and getting fucked up. Eh, who *said* Canada was devoid of culture?

We ended up having far more beer than food, and at about ten-nish, the four of us staggered out to the subway, completely hammered, intent on getting back to the office and playing *Quake's* latest offering, networked on a number of machines in The Hive. *Quake* is this cool virtual slice 'em and dice 'em game where you run around in a twisted virtual-scape, picking up big mother guns, blowing away cyberdemons, armoured spiders and flying skulls. And, of course, each other – although Jase, Mark and Andrew were much more adept at getting frags (player kills) than I was.

My virtual self rounded a corner, passing yet another one of my carcasses lying in front of the door. "Oh god! Flying Skulls!" I moaned.

"Flying *flaming* skulls," Jase corrected, reloading his virtual shotgun.

I winced as my virtual self crumpled in a bleeding mess. "I hate flying flaming skulls."

Jase grunted while gunning down another flying flaming skull. Just then, Andrew came running around the corner with a plasma rifle, raining hot death on Jason's humble form.

"My *Lord* that hurt."

"Easy frags coming up," Mark and Andrew chimed, swooping in on the common place where Jase was being rebirthed and setting up a crossfire to catch his freshly born virtual self.

Working at Praxus was like being in a dream. Time had no meaning. Life was work and work was life – they both melded into one large globular mass. The place was wide and free – free soft drinks, free food some nights, e-mail and networked *Quake* – you honestly never had to leave, and that was exactly the way Shogun and Co. wanted it. We're all one big happy bleeding family, we are.

Not that you needed any other family, working at Praxus. Just last night, Eggman's wife brought his daughter in because she had to work late at the hospital.

"Haven't seen her awake in a while," he said as she grabbed his glasses. "My daughter, not my wife. Lately, I've been coming home when she's been put to bed."

"Cute kid," I said, giving her a pack of Yum swiped off of Jase's desk.

"Oh, she's not old enough to chew gum yet, Dave. She can't even talk. Here, I'll show you." He hefted his daughter up and looked at her. "Darlene? Darlene, hon?" He tickled her chin, eliciting gurgles of pleasure. "Can you talk yet? Hmmm? Say something, dear. Can you say 'Object Model'? Can you say '64-Bit'? Can you say 'Daddy's a Geek?'"

I laughed. "Eggman, you're cracking. Go home; the next block of bugs won't be ready until after midnight, anyway."

"Okay. I'll just finish number 645 and I'll take off. Quality time, honey, come on…" he said, smooching Darlene on the cheek and twirling her into his office, shutting the door with his foot.

I looked at his closed door, shaking my head. Far be it for me to say anything about Quality Time when it comes to family and such, but a place is chewing up too much of your life when the only place you can see your kids was in the hallways of work. Software companies have a curious way of doing things like that. Not that I know anything about kids, of course. I'm probably the furthest thing from marriage material you can get.

At about three in the morning, hung over and tired of looking at the mountains of my virtual corpses around the Quake-scape, I tore myself away from the machine and bid my farewells. Jase and Markandandrew (my, how *Lord of the Flies*...they were starting to blur, becoming inseparable in my mind) were still going strong, the Quake-scape eerily reflected in their glasses, about 80-some frags each. I stumbled into the washroom to wash my sticky hands, and reeled down to the empty parking garage rather unevenly, to get Jeepy.

I have this jeep. His name is Jeepy – a 1988 battered blue-grey Suzuki Samurai, with rust spots strategically placed all over his left side. The back window is cracked, and, like the good little engineer I am, I fixed it up with duct tape. I fix everything with duct tape (and alcohol).

Luke once told me some disturbing statistics about Samurais; about how a sharp 90-degree turn can flip them over because of their high centre of gravity. I didn't care. Jeepy would never do that to me, because Jeepy loves me.

I opened the door, scratching the already scratched finish with my keys. The floor and the seats are covered with unfolded maps, cassette tapes, empty cigarette packs and Froot Loop boxes, and bags of McWaste, bundled but not disposed of. On the rear-view mirror, there is a two-year old Little Tree air freshener that had long expired.

Jeepy and me belong together. He even has a personalized license plate. It says JEEPY. The Banana Boys thoughtfully got it for me one birthday a long, long time ago.

I paused before inserting my key. Driving home drunk: bad idea. Ah, what the fuck. I'd already been killed eighty-odd times, anyway.

I'm not an alcoholic, you know. I have very strict criteria for alcoholism. Really I do. And it works.

- You drink to excess alone.
- You drink until your piss turns clear.

Whoops.

I'm trying to fall asleep, but the room keeps spinning this one direction.

And I'm thinking about this funny thing called Love. It's something I think about a lot, presumably because it's so important to me, and probably because I'm a big fucking idiot. But whenever I *do* think about it, I always end up with the same conclusion: "*Whoever cares the least, wins the most.*"

Love, you see, greets you with bliss and passion. It gives you happiness. Contentment. But it inevitably turns sour: how can it not, in a world full of emotional perils and modern neurotic complications? You try to leave it, but it grabs you by the buttocks and wrestles you to the ground, biting your ears off. You give it, Love, a knee to the groin, but it one-ups you and grabs your crotch and starts yanking sharply upwards, causing you to collapse in an agonized pile at the bottom of the barroom floor.

You moan helplessly as Love proceeds to spit on you and give you a few kicks to the abdomen, followed by a one-two combination, finishing off with a brutal suplex that sends you out the window, straight into the street gutter.

Love is important to me, but I don't much like Love. Love makes you weak, susceptible to stupid ideas like spending money on roses and not beer. Love fills your head with much nonsense and imponderable hypothesis, so much that you lose track of more important things like work, hockey and *Seinfield*.

Love relegates your brain functioning to "less than optimal." Love is the equivalent of handing your heart over on a silver platter with a large steak knife and saying, "*Here, bon appetit!*"

I think Love is best summed up by a Meryn Cadell song, wise beyond its time:

> *Being in love really sucks,*
> *Being in love really sucks,*
> *A kiss, a hug, a couple of fucks,*
> *Being in love really sucks.*

But whatever the case, you'll always run full force into it, Love, like a crash test dummy into a concrete wall with big ugly metal spikes protruding from it...

She is outside Queens Park, buying a magazine at the corner kiosk. It's summer. Even though it is hot and sunny, and you are wearing a T-shirt and shorts, she is decked out in black: black shoes, black jeans, black leather jacket, black halter-top-thingie underneath. Even the scrunchie tying back her long black hair is guess-what.

She is not stunningly beautiful, but there's something about her – Looks that don't kill/But wound for life. *She is a no-nonsense type, you guess correctly, very low capacity for bullshit. So, for some totally unexplained reason, you decide to chuck aside your carefully cultivated indifference and introduce yourself.*

*You nervously walk up to her, and she looks up questioningly. She is rather attractive up close, poised, somewhat sure of herself. So you strike up a conversation – it goes quite well, considering. A few great dates, nights shooting pool, spins on her bike on hot, moonburnt summer evenings. "Zowie," you think to yourself, "She seems to have it together – looks, intelligence, apparent stability, coolness. Woo **hoo**, let the good times roll." She has enough similarities to make her appealing, she has enough differences to make her intriguing. She is soft as cream, yet hard as nails. You're hooked.*

And after a while, the nightmare begins.

*The problems start with differences in ethnicity. We may look vaguely similar to the untrained eye, but we were as different as guns and butter – I don't care what anyone else says, Koreans and Chinese are **different**, goddammit! And the differences are disastrous – cultural attitudes, superiority/inferiority issues, outrageous* *biases, neo-Christian dogma, sexual positions, all crashing together in a Pan-Asian Cultural Demolition Derby.*

Oh, and don't get me started on the "Asian woman" thing. What the fuck is it with Asian women and Asian men? What is this war in the heart of nature? She's a real beaut: a pathological, borderline-auto-racist feminist who laid it all on the men, and I mean all – sexism, patriarchy, reduced economic opportunity, both world wars and the fact that we sold her great-grandmother for a goat a few centuries ago in a village north of Taegu. Couple this with a notoriously stubborn male ego (ie. mine), and there you go: Taepo-Dong Missiles launched up the wazoo.

Finally, throw in the white ex-boyfriend factor, whose Harley was always parked outside her place, along with condoms you didn't contribute to, toss in a dash of "So what?" and a nip of "What the fuck business is it of yours?", and pretty soon, you lose your cool and she's running over you with her bike outside of your own home, leaving you for dead on the pavement.

"Whoever cares the least, wins the most."

I was suckered into caring. I just didn't check if Miss Jeanette Park had jumped into the same pit with me, the pit of unwavering love and slavish devotion, and I paid for it.

Am I bitter about this?

Treacherous snake-woman. I hope your stubborn, curmudgeonly leather-clad soul rots in the deepest, darkest, foulest corner of Dante's Easy-Bake…

You got your answer. Now let's change the subject.

In the middle of the night, I got up to get a Tylenol and some water for my honey porter-induced headache. I stopped thinking about Jeanette and started thinking about The Ideal Woman. Publicly, I will scoff at the idea, citing examples like Teej (unobtainable) or Jeanette (pre*post*erous) or even Daphne (for*get* it) as proof of its folly. Mike has this theory about The One I generally agree with – that is, there is no The One, and that the concept creates standards no one can live up to.

But I can't avoid it. The idea of The One is so tantalizing it drips like warm honey on my bitter tongue.

In my mind, I see a willowy Asian woman: long black hair, pale complexion, large expressive brown eyes, perhaps like the ones on Japanime heroines. She has a smallish nose, and a smallish mouth, which generously gives smallish smiles.

She's neatly dressed, yet very casual bordering on slobhood at home. She's intelligent and quiet, but never afraid to speak her mind when she feels she's right, calling me on my copped attitudes with a firm stare and a wry sense of humour.

She's reasonable and serious, but she can also relax and cut loose once in a while. She's might be in a "responsible" field like accounting or optometry, but she has a full appreciation of the finer things in life, to counterbalance my artless lack of culture.

She likes reading, she treasures her time alone, but she also loves spending time with me, just goofing off – lying in the park in the summer, driving for takeout late at night, making snide comments at the latest fall offerings by the Fox Network. She likes good coffee and good music, some of which we would argue about in a good-natured sort of way. She likes the occasional beer; when she does drink, she laughs a lot and turns red.

She likes to try new things, like going out for Ethiopian or Romanian, or giving that new neo-Uiguric-Etruscan place a shot. She makes a great Caesar salad, but otherwise, she can't cook worth beans – she pawns off all the cooking duties on me.

So I lie in my bed in a state of half-sleep, thinking about her: leaning against a fence rail by the waterfront on a sunny day, wind lightly tossing her dark tresses, my jean jacket draped over her slender shoulders. She's smiling very slightly, for no other reason than the fact that she's just enjoying herself.

I drift closer to wakefulness now, wanting to meet her, to have her, vowing that I would ultimately search for her and win her over. I am awake, resolving that I *will* be ready on the chance that I meet her someday, at a restaurant or in a bookstore, or in a coffee shop somewhere. I will be ready to express my feelings to her.

I toss my covers aside, going over to my dresser for a pen

and paper to write down a perfect script to follow when the time comes, when I will eventually encounter my Ideal Woman.

Then it occurs to me that she might be Janice Yeung, so I go back to bed.

At 11:30, I lurch back into work. Jase is still there playing Quake, glasses askew, desk having spawned a dozen more empty Jolt cans. "Coke is for wussies," he says.

"Jolt can *kill*, Jase," I'd reply. "I mean, twice the caffeine. I don't do that shit, man. And don't go feeding that shit to my co-ops."

Seeing me enter my office, he pokes his head in. "Looks dead, sounds dead…"

"Can't talk, need coffee."

"I was just about to get another Jolt. How do you want it?"

"Cold, black and bitter. Like my heart."

"On second thought, I think I'll let you get that yourself…"

"Had a lot on my mind last night," I muttered. I logged on and start reading my e-mail.

"By the way, Greg came by and was asking for you again."

"Again?"

"Yup."

I shook my head. "Either he needs my input more than I suspect, or he's developing a crush on me."

"I don't know the full story," said Jase, scratching his sparse beard, "but it sounds like there's a fire to be put out." He got up from the chair, walked over and patted me on the head. "And it sounds like you're the fire extinguisher."

Joy.

Megaton Punch.

"You can go to the four corners of the earth looking for love,
but until you give up, you'll never find it."

My supervisor had me return the Norcan-mobile a week before I took off for Ottawa, so I had to bum some rides off a senior engineer from the office. He lives only a few blocks away from me, so it wasn't a big deal.

Murray Stancik is a pretty nice guy – he reminds me a lot of the people back in Saint John, brusque but friendly. He's forty-three, still an associate foreman at the company, unmarried, balding, pleasantly overweight, and a chronic chain smoker, as evidenced by the small mountains of butts located at the unlikeliest of places in his car.

"I tell you, Sheldon m'boy," he said in a booming, friendly tone as our car made its way east on the 401, the freeway that spans Toronto, and most of Southern Ontario, "you're moving up in the world. Hell, Blakeman at the office just *loves* you, thinks you're a fuckin' genius – says one day you'll own the whole goddamn utility." He laughed.

I grinned and shook my head in a so-so sort of way. "I'm pretty grateful that the boss is letting me go up to Ottawa."

"Ottawa's okay, but T.O.'s the place where it happens. Son, this city is alive, full of stories, you know. When I was your age, I got a job doing repairs on the 401. This highway *alone* has its share of stories – every single fixture, every guard rail, every offramp."

"Like what?"

"Like one of the off-ramps east of Etobicoke – can't remember which one, exactly. Anyway, during the tail end of some repairs my crew was doing, this snazzy-looking red sports car crashed into a semi, and the cops asked me and the guys to help clean up. The man and the woman in the car were killed, but the thing was that the guy – who'd been driving – was missing his freaking *dick*!"

"No way! Cut off by something?"

"Damn right it was," Murray said, smirking. "The woman was lying dead on his lap. Guess what they found his dick inside of?"

I blushed slightly, and coughed.

"Yeah yeah, I know. But *fuck*, Sheldon, what a way to go!" He barked a coarse, hearty laugh and lit up another cigarette. That made three for a forty-minute drive downtown.

The last day on the job was supposed to be pretty routine, but Vic and the rest of the crew started it off on a great note by presenting me with a large bottle of Crown Royal, to be mixed with coffees all around (during work hours, of course). Mid-morning, we polished off the whiskey and booked from work, ending up at a pub on Adelaide St. for many beers and several rounds of foosball. I was probably going to see everyone again in a few months, but we celebrated anyway. Those guys would celebrate my Confirmation if it meant beer and foosball, I swear to God.

That night, I went out with Dave, Luke and Mike for some farewell snacks at the Duke of Wellington, around Davenport and Bloor St. I didn't do that much drinking because I was kind of tired from the afternoon.

"I thought you didn't drink anymore, Shel," said Luke, amused.

I shrugged. "The crew drank most of the Crown Royal, anyway."

"So have you found a place up in Ottawa yet?" asked Mike, mouth full of Duke wings.

"Yeah. I'm taking a friend's room that he was renting during Co-op up there. It's on Stewart St. – you know, where all the Waterloo students are. I think it's pretty close to the Market, but I'm not too sure. I think I'll be living with an Electrical who's working at Corel or something. I didn't want roommates, but it's really hard getting a place on such short notice…"

"Shel…" noted Luke.

"Oh. I'm prattling. Sorry." I capped my hand on top of my glass as Dave tried to pour me another Rickards Red.

"Wiener," he muttered.

Luke and Mike took off from the Duke early because they had stuff to do in the morning. So did me and Dave, but we stuck around drinking, anyway.

"I'm gonna miss you, Dave," I said, sincerely.

"Jesus, Shel, you're the worlds biggest *sap.*"

After much cajoling from Dave, I buckled under and we got really drunk. And, of course, we started talking about women. All our conversations were either about school, work, or women. Three pitchers later, we were hip deep in substantial philosophical analysis.

"I like large, firm breasts," he said, cupping his hands expressively and almost knocking his beer over. Dave, like Captain Kirk, liked to emphasize his orations with pertinent hand gestures.

"You're such a pig!" I took another large gulp. "You know, I don't mind small firm ones. Daphne has small firm ones." Daphne Chan was this awesome Chinese girl we'd both known back in Waterloo. She was gorgeous, intelligent, and was secretly aspiring to be an anchorwoman for some major news network.

"Daphne's a dog, man," Dave said, scowling.

"Shit man, you're cut off!"

"She's a dipstick, and her breasts are, like, way too small." He continued bouncing his cupped hands around, eliciting nasty looks from the girls sitting next to us. He then clenched them tightly and grinned. "Well, okay, small firm ones are all right, but they're usually attached to Oriental girls like Daphne, and that spells trouble, dude."

"Fuck off, Dave! You like Oriental girls as much as I do.

You're just bitter."

"Yeah, I guess." He downed the rest of his beer and refilled it, spilling some on the table. He frowned hazedly. "I have a theory about that."

"About what?"

"About Sexloverelationships. You know, the dynamics between men and women in general. From a Banana Boy perspective."

"And you've come up with a tidy little theory to sum it all up," I said skeptically.

"Damn straight."

"So?"

"'Scuse me, darlin'?" Dave tapped the waitress on the shoulder. "Do you have a piece of paper I could borrow...?"

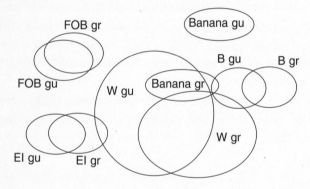

Fig. 6. Those Wacky Racial Dynamics.

I goggled. "Wow. You've been doing some serious research."

"The Experiment of Life."

"So what is this...?"

"Venn diagram."

"Holy cow," I said in half-disbelief. "You're such a geek." I picked up the chart. "I don't understand any of this."

"Well, if you examine the intersections between various circles, you'll clearly see the relationships between men and women based on race. For example, you'll notice how White Girls quite naturally intersect with White guys. There are smaller intersections with Black Guys, and other guys, but they are, in fact, smaller."

"And Asian guys? White Girls don't intersect with Asian Guys?"

"Nope. To them, we're too geeky, and quite possibly all gay." I shook my head and he continued, pointing his pen over to the largest circle.

"Now you'll see that White guys'll intersect with anything. They're at the top of the sociological ladder, so of course they do. White guys are all fucking sluts. Notice how a large portion of them intersect with Asian Women. We can call these guys 'losers'."

"Erm…"

"'Yellow Fever' and all that. You know, the type who goes over to Japan or Taiwan to teach English at all-girls-schools because he can't score with white chicks over here." He pointed his pen over to a set of different circles. "Now, over here, we have Black Girls and Black Guys. Two words when it comes to Black Girls: *Denzel Washington*. Black Men tend to favour yer typical African-American mates, but a large subset like white chicks – you know, that Jungle Fever thing. And quite a few as you can see have a craving for the yellowness, but you can't say anything about that, because that'd be racist and you'd get your ass kicked. Same thing with some Asian girls because they like big dick, evidently."

"Wait a minute…"

"You can see that East Indian Guys and Girls prefer each other. Girls tend to look for a nice young *raj* to settle down with. Guys typically want an Indian girl who runs through fields, arms raised, singing, like in those movies you see on Channel 47." I vaguely noticed that the girls beside us were staring as Dave went on, loudly regaling the intricacies of his chart. One of them, the Oriental one, even had a clenched fist, and she was shaking slightly.

"And now we get to the good shit – the Orientals. Okay, look at the circles representing FOBS – mostly HK FOBS, but you can stack in Taiwanese and Koreans in there, too. They're an island unto themselves. The chicks want a guy with a nice car and loads of money, and Banana Boys usually don't have the right stuff to score with these bitches. The guys just want a good looking squeeze to match the upholstery in their souped-up Integra."

"Dave…"

"Oh yeah, and Banana Girls. If they don't study a bajillion hours a day, they'll go for white guys, black guys, Jewish guys, Indian guys (both kinds), purple guys, all guys – except for you-know-what's." He saw my expression, so he elaborated. "Truth hurts, don't it? The more liberalized, aggressive Ai-zhun-wim-men o' the nineties wouldn't give the average Banana Boy the time of day. We remind 'em too much of fathers, brothers, evil patriarchs, and kamikaze pilots. Whew, I need a drink."

At this point, I noticed that we'd gone through a pitcher and a half during his demo, and that we were both extremely drunk. I was also flabbergasted. I mean, what exactly can you say when someone comes up to you and quite casually pours a bag of cow manure on your lap?

"And, um…this?" I slurred weakly. I pointed to the lone circle in the corner.

"That," he said, with finality, "represents us. The Banana Boys o' the world. We got…well, uh…we got cats. Dogs. Potted plants. Shuffleboard." He smiled crookedly. "It's funny because it's true."

A long pause.

"You…you're *serious* about this, aren't you…?" I began.

"Of course not."

"This is the biggest load of *bullshit* that I've ever…"

"You're absolutely right," Dave said, clapping me on the shoulder and missing. "It *is* bullshit – of that there is no doubt. It's obvious that personal inadequacies force me to overcompensate with unfounded generalizations. But there are patterns out there, you know? Patterns that are a little difficult for a decent, level-headed dude like me to ignore." He smiled rather strangely, cleared his throat a little and announced the next bit rather loudly. "It seems like all the reasonable women in this world are all taken…and what we're left with are the ones who're psychotic or pathological. Or both."

I scratched my chin, and tried to focus the beer goggles on the now-beer-stained chart. *Bullshit.* All of it. *Or was it?* At that particular moment, with all the alcohol and the longing, the bad experiences with women from the past and my general rotten luck for over twenty years, I felt that glaring, nagging kernel of truth in there. Somewhere.

The girls beside us got up to leave, spitting out the word "asshole" at Dave, to which he raised his glass good-naturedly.

"Dave," I said unevenly, feeling slightly nauseous. "This is all very, very wrong."

"Shelly," Dave gurgled within the depths of his sozzled brain, about to shut down on me, "I'd *love* to find an attractive, intelligent, relatively westernized and unattached Chinese girl with no attitude and minimal hangups over things. God *knows* I would. But I'm too far gone. Deadweight. It's over for me. Leave me behind and save yourself, Shel."

We then got kicked out of the Duke after I threw up all over the table.

There was always this strange relationship between Dave and alcohol. With him, drinking seemed like a perverted grail-quest or something.

"I don't like alcohol within itself," he'd say. "That would be stupid. I like alcohol as a *means to an end*. It's the bonding agent, the truth maker. Things are shared under the influence. Friendships made because you're on the same level, you've degenerated to the same level. I can't explain it. There's brotherhood being made here, with many pitchers of beer."

I sort of agreed at the time, but sometimes I'd think that it was too much. I'd be afraid that Dave was giving something that's just an inert substance more credit than it really deserves. Alcohol as a bonding agent? Friendships made? That's a load of garbage. Bonds and friends are made because of the people, not because of some fermented barley and hops. Alcohol is not a holy liquid. It's just a stupid substance that makes you drunk, makes you spin out of control, kills your brain cells. It crashes cars, fucks up your arm and…kills girlfriends.

I'm afraid that he's losing himself in something stupid.

"Dave," I urged after being at the Bomber for the third day in a row, "I think you've been drinking too much."

"What? Yeah? I suppose I have."

"You're a bad role model for the youngsters here, Dave," said Luke in mock disapproval, "glorifying drinking the way you do."

Dave laughed heartily, spilling some beer on me for the nth time. "Luke Luke Luke, you silly bastard!" He laid a fatherly hand on Luke's shoulder.

"I don't *glorify* drinking. I *romanticize* it."

We all laughed at that, but I still worried.

Even more so with his race thing. I'd imagine seeing the world through Dave's Race-Coloured Glasses wasn't too conducive to happiness and peace of mind. But I guess that wasn't too much of a surprise, considering the rough childhood he'd had. But still, you can take something too far, you know? The Venn diagram was seriously fucked up, but he also had this "system" for evaluating racist events or something, which was also seriously fucked up. I can remember snorting in disbelief when he told me about it. It was just so...*weird.*

"What's so weird about it?" he asked neutrally.

"Dave, how the *hell* do you get to sleep at nights thinking this way?"

But arguing about it with him wouldn't have changed anything. *Ma* has always said that although you can change things about yourself, you can never change your basic character. I suppose all the beatings that Dave endured when he was younger were cauterized into his basic character, and for that, I guess I kind of feel sorry for him. I can see it now, when he's about seventy-five years old, languishing at a nursing home somewhere:

> **Dave's Racial Incident Log.**
> **Racial Incident:** #100000000
> **Date:** November 7th, 2050
> **Notes:** Fair comeback; ran over toes with wheelchair and beat the living crap out of whitey with cane. Felt queasy and uncomfortable; had to take a Pepto afterward.
> **Grade:** B-

The big thing for him, these days, was the whole Asian Girl/ White Guy thing. Maybe he has a point. But overall I just can't see how it's anybody's business who somebody is dating or chooses to marry, or why anyone else should care. If two people can find even a little bit of happiness in this cold world, I say good for them.

I met my supervisor on my first day at the Ottawa office. Mr. McFadden is this curmudgeonly old Scottish guy who has a few months left before he retires to his cabin in northern Ontario. He speaks with a thick accent and hates Americans.

"Yeh might've noticed that Ottawa's in th' middle o' no-where comin' up here from Toronto," he drawled in his brogue, driving west on the Queensway on our way out to Nepean to see a few of the sites I'd be in charge of. "It's not only because of political reasons th' capital was located here. Th' capital was moved north from Kingston for fear of invasion by the Yanks. Did yeh know that up 'til 1925, we still had cannons pointed south towards th' state o' New York?"

I shook my head.

"Ottawa was an excellent place in terms o' military defen-sibility – it was inland, th' hills around here blocked cannon fire, and th' swampy land and shite all around would make an infantry invasion extremely difficult…th' French were seriously bogged down in this area during the French-English War. But on th' same note, that's why this damn city is a civil engineerin' nightmare, 'specially in terms of developin' access routes for vehicles and resources like gas lines." He pulled up into the site. "And that's th' type o' stuff you'll be strugglin' with here."

The job turned out to be significantly more challenging than what I was doing in Toronto. Not only doing inspections, but a good amount of design engineering as well – actually using a small amount of stuff I'd studied in school – *who'd a thunk it*?

It was a bit of a surprise because I never thought school was all that useful or interesting. None of us did – the Banana Boys, I mean – and the time we logged at the Bomber definitely showed it. "Engineering is hardly a place where you take courses to 'find your inner self'," Mike had said, and he was dead right.

I'm sure my attitude was kind of warped by Dave. He keeps saying that Engineering has stunted our social growth, largely because of the skewed man-woman ratio. "We didn't have a chance to experience, you know, normal situations in our formative years – and the women there didn't either. Not that it matters – women do *not* go into a technical-sausage-factory-program like Engineering for an MRS degree. Most've them are here because they have something to prove, and as a result, they're all messed up and have these bags of chips on their shoulders."

"Oink oink, Dave," said Luke.

"Bite me, Stick."

I kind of dragged myself through the university years, getting below-average grades, eventually graduating with third-class honours. But regardless of the unglamourous reality that was engineering school, I was fervently determined to be one, largely because *Ba* wanted to be one…but never got the chance. *Ba*'s hopes were crushed when his parents refused to send him to university: the Kwan family resources were apparently tied up in *Yeh-yeh's* Number One son, who's now a successful heart specialist in Florida, and never even talks to the old man anymore.

Becoming a mechanic was the closest *Ba* ever got to being an engineer. I can remember when I was about ten years old, on a hot summer day, Mom had to take my younger brother Kevin to the hospital because of chicken pox so she dropped me off at the garage. Dad set me up playing with his toolbox, and within a half-hour, I'd taken apart the entire box.

He just chuckled, obviously loving and treasuring me, *his* Number One Son, and clapped his greasy baseball cap onto my head, heading outside to the pop machine to get a Coke.

And I felt proud, seeing him there in the sun, leaning against the wall in his blue overalls which were smeared with grease. He was crossing his work-booted feet and idly flipping a wrench while drinking that Coke. That's when I thought to myself that he was the epitome of manhood: *"From that day on, I'm going to walk like him, **be** like him, in every way."*

Being up here in Ottawa, in charge of systems responsible for delivering natural gas to over a half-million homes, I know I've done him proud.

On the bus to work every day, I pass by this Catholic high school. Even as the weather got colder, I noticed that the girls still wore those little kilts. Not that I minded all that much.

I grew up a good Catholic boy. *Ba* was never really religious (he used sermon time to catch up on sleep), but *Ma* definitely was – it might have been her upbringing. Every single Sunday for ten years, she'd hustled us to St. Alphonsus', even setting me up as an altar boy. I can remember being under intense pressure every time I went up to put the silver candelabra-type thing into the mount on the altar. The mount was really small, you see, and I always ended up juggling the thing for at least a minute, sometimes dropping it with a loud clang, before I could slide it in, usually to her profound embarrassment. It was a heck lot of pressure for an eight-year old.

She also enrolled me and Kevin (with a little bit of resistance from my father) at the local Catholic elementary school. So I became indoctrinated in the Catholic way pretty early on, and by the time I became interested in girls, that wasn't necessarily a good thing. A lot of the girls were kind of, uh, *repressed* at my school, and I found myself coughing nervously and chanting the *Kyrie Eleison* under my breath whenever they got all sassy. (I'm not sure if it was the Catholic liturgy or just *Mr. Mister*.)

Oh yeah, and those kilts. I had a thing for those short little kilts. An interesting thing girls at my school would do was cheat using their kilts…they'd write answers on their thighs, and lift them up underneath the desk during tests. It was virtually foolproof, especially if they were in a class taught by a male teacher;

there's no way they could be caught without the cops getting involved.

A message was waiting at my desk when I got in. It was Justin, a classmate from Civil Engineering. There were a number of them in Ottawa, mostly doing highway or traffic stuff with Transport Canada.

"Good to have you up here, Shelly. Me and Vijay are heading over to *Stoney's* in The Market after work. You in?"

"Sounds great." My first foray in The Quest™.

At the bar, while Justin was macking out with his Lawrence Fishburne-Malcolm X good looks, I reverted back to shy chicken-shit – back to the wall, checking out girls, peeling labels off bottles, goofy expression on my face. I did see some girls I liked, but it just didn't seem right…you know, just "picking up" at a bar like that. It never does.

There was a really pretty Asian girl in the middle of the dance floor who was completely decked out. I didn't do anything about it, of course, except note that the whole thing reminded me of how Dave and Daphne always duked it out when the engineers went out as a group back in Waterloo. We'd sometimes all go to Fed Hall and drink Molson's Dry – back to the wall, checking out girls, peeling labels off bottles, goofy expressions on our faces. Except Dave, of course. He was just bitter.

"Shit, man," he growled, squinting at Daphne, "she always goes the whole nine yards for these places, doesn't she?"

I grinned. "Yeah, and you being gay prevents you from, like, enjoying it, right?"

Dave rolled his eyes. "She's just a *cock*-tease. The makeup, the cutoff-bare midriff tops, the short skirt, the Fuck Me boots, the crowd of guys around her drooling a pool. That 'naughty schoolgirl' look countered by a solid dose of Look-But-Don't-Touch…*fuck*, man!" He shook his hand like he'd touched a hot potato. "The lyrics of *Paint It Black* are going through my brain."

"Come off it, Dave. You *know* you'd do her until her eyes changed colour if she gave you half the chance."

"God forbid."

"Well, I think she looks hot."

"It's not that, Shelly. It's *attitude*, you know? She strings guys along like toys. Guys flock around her like pathetic southern suitors around *Miz* Scarlett O'Hara."

"So?"

He grimaced and took another pull from his bottle. "Take it from a vet of the Love Wars. That kind takes you off guard, she'll ooze all over you like syrup, sweet as sugar, taking you for all you're worth. You and Mike, like all other typical Nice Guys, have been strung along for years."

As if on cue, Mike loped up to us, bringing a couple of fresh beers, also staring at Daphne.

"The girl's a total fuck machine," Mike said, uncharacteristically.

Dave nudged me knowingly. "Strung along for years. Pathetic young whelps."

When the song was over, she came over to us and draped herself all over a tall blond guy wearing a purple Wilfred Laurier jacket. I saw her looking out the corner of her eye at Dave, maybe trying to get a reaction out of him. It worked; he was doing a slow burn.

"Daphne, you really think you're hot shit, don't you?"

"I'm sorry, Dave, what was that?" said Daphne, smiling sweetly and batting her eyes.

"Think again if you think you're going to fool me with that routine."

"I wouldn't give you the time of day, Dave, so fuck off."

"Oh yes, I know your type," Dave continued. "Into adventure, Bad Boys for the longest time. Meanwhile I'm back at home studying like mad. While I was programming my VIC-20, you were out with a leather-clad slab of meat named Bart who smoked, drove a Camaro and was covered in gold-chains and bad cologne."

"His name was Daniel, Dave, and he surfed," smiled Daphne.

"Pretty soon," Dave said prophetically, "It's all going to run out, you know. One day you'll be sucking white dick, and then the ol' biological clock'll start to tick, and the next second you'll be scouring the earth for a Nice Guy to settle down with, to sink your teeth into, but by then it'll be too late – your looks are gone, and you're just fucked."

"Fuck you, Dave."

"Some things are better left unsaid, I know."

"God, you're such an asshole."

"So nice of you to categorize me anatomically, baby cakes." Dave shook his head, a little too violently. "I'm here to tell you no *way*, sister. This is one Nice Guy immune to your devil-charms."

"Dave, *sugar*, don't flatter yourself." She said 'sugar' like one would say 'leper' or 'pond scum' or something. She moved in closer with a slight smile, playfully cocking her head to one side, stroking Dave's forearm, arousing me. "Davey," she said in a bad-little-girl voice, "you might as well face the truth; you're just *dying* to fuck me – and you never *will*. You're a bitter and repressed loser who's just holding deuces, while I'm holding all the Aces."

Dave looked angry, but he kept his cool...well, sort of. "Deuces can be wild, honey lamb," he said quietly, "and in my case, I may be wild enough to scale this building with a high-powered rifle and ruin your cute little outfit. For starters."

Daphne gave him and then me a withering glare, and went back to the blond Laurier guy.

"Game, set, match?" wondered Dave aloud.

Probably not.

Back at Stoney's, I gave up and went home. I came to grips a long time ago with the fact that girls like the one on the dance floor, or Daphne, or anyone one else with "devil-charm," would never truly go for wide-eyed-puppy-dog-types like me. Oddly enough, though, I thought Daphne and Dave'd make a good pair, of sorts. If they didn't murder each other within the first week or so.

I enrolled in a Mandarin language course at the University of Ottawa.

Every Tuesday and Thursday, I went down to the U of O for

evening classes. It was about a fifteen-minute walk from my place on Stewart St., which got progressively tougher as the harsh Ottawa winter came on with force. I can't say I really enjoyed spending two-hours learning phonetics – *bo po mo fo, de te ne le, etc.* – and it wasn't all that useful, either. My family spoke Cantonese. I would've preferred taking that, if it was available – it'd be nice to know what my folks were talking about three-quarters of the time. Oh well.

The class was half FOB ("Probably looking to learn how to say *Don't run over me with a tank* for when they get back home," Dave would say callously) and half Caucasian guys who, curiously enough, seemed to be on the same Quest™ as I was.

I did meet an okay-looking girl…her name was Annie, and she was in Business over at Carleton. But she was from Hong Kong, and we had absolutely nothing in common, so it never went anywhere. It kind of died out during our second date, when the communication lines broke down entirely. I suppose only understanding 25 per cent of what the other person said isn't conducive to a healthy relationship. I almost blamed *Ma* for not teaching me more Cantonese, but then I remembered actively resisting going to Chinese school back in New Brunswick because I didn't want to miss *Schoolhouse Rock* on early Saturday mornings. So I guess me and Lolly Adverb are at fault, ultimately.

I also became extremely attracted to this McDonald's counter girl.

Karen N. (as her name tag read) was this really cute blonde cashier at the Rideau St. McDonald's, a place I sometimes went to before work for my much-needed hash brown and coffee. She had very nice hair, only partially obscured by her visor, and the fact that she still looked good in the shapeless uniform definitely said something about her figure. But beyond that, she was a complete unknown – our conversations were limited to "That's forty-seven cents change, come again."

But, as wiser men say, spare change is not enough to build a relationship. Plus, it's kind of tacky asking a girl out over a fast-food counter. Don't you think?

As kind of a last ditch, I went to the Laundromat.

You *know* you're getting desperate when you subscribe to *that* myth, brainwashed by those Levis commercials – read: there *are* no gaggles of model-quality men and women who do laundry at the Laundromat. There just aren't. Most are pretty average students who brought textbooks along and studied (something I could never do back at school because the white noise would put me to sleep within fifteen minutes). Or, if you like doing laundry in the middle of the morning, you run into some pretty bizarre people – mostly pale, skinny guys who twitch nervously as they count their change or fold their underwear.

As I captured a laundry cart and started sorting my whites and my colours, I wondered what exactly you could say to a beautiful girl while doing your laundry? *"Change for a loonie?" "How do you work this lint thingie?" "Interesting choice of fabric softener. Baby." "Niiiice unmentionables."* Sounds kind of lame. Well, no lamer than I felt.

That night, I was thinking about how badly The Quest™ was going over a ham sandwich and reruns of *Magnum PI* when Vijay called. He invited me to a Waterloo Engineering reunion party in Orleans, northeast of Ottawa – mostly Electrical Engineers.

"You can't spell 'GEEK' without Double-E," Veej said, "but they're Boatracing up there, so that means all you can drink! Woo *hoo*!"

I looked at my sandwich and Tom Selleck, and opted in. Fuck The Quest™. I'm drinking myself into a stupor out of sheer frustration.

I went to the party ready to get into The Mode, but I made the mistake of starting off with a shot of Goldschläger, a cinnamon schnapps with real 24-karat gold flakes. It was disgusting – it felt like someone had put a bunch of those little Valentine heart-candies in my mouth and crammed them down with a broomstick. After that, the beer didn't go down too well, so I ended up drinking Coke and watching the other engineers get hammered Boatracing. Boatracing was a Waterloo engineering rite of passage – involving drinking many beers in rapid succession from two eight-ounce glasses (and repeatedly throwing up afterward).

By midnight, Veej and Justin were totally wasted from four rounds of Boatracing and Justin ended up falling down the stairs on his head. I rushed over to pick him up.

"You okay?" I asked, picking up his glasses. He nodded, unfazed.

Alice, another classmate who'd come down from her job in Montreal, gave me a peck on the cheek. "Thanks, Shelly."

"Think we should call the hospital or something?"

"No, that's okay. I'll take care of him. Time to go home, Justin, hon." Justin, leaning against the banister, started stumbling for the door. Alice smiled wickedly. "And in this condition, I can have my way with him, you know what I mean?" I nodded, not really knowing.

The whole thing blew over at around two in the morning and as the only sober person in the house, I was elected to drive everyone home using Veej's minivan. At the time of the last drunken drop-off, I was feeling pretty lousy. Nice Guys do, in fact, Finish Last.

"Nice guys not only finish last," Rick once said, "they don't even get off the bench to play the game. I'm telling you, Shel, to be able to get in there, you have to learn to be something of an asshole."

"Huh? What do you mean?"

"Let's be frank: at this stage, girls aren't interested in Nice Guys. No freaking way. They're into excitement, danger, risk – pissing off their mommies and daddies. So give it to them. Give into your selfish desires and make it happen, regardless of what the other person wants. It's the Me generation, after all. Stop being so concerned about other people, and concentrate on getting what *you* want."

There was also a nagging kernel of truth in there. Somewhere. But in my heart, I know I can't do this. And I don't think the other guys can, either. Luke couldn't. Mike couldn't. And despite all his macho posturing, Dave couldn't. At the core, we were just Nice Guys – it's just our basic character.

And as a result, we finish last. And are left only with a mini-van full of vomit to show for it.

Driving the van back, I started thinking about what women looked for in a man, and all I could come up with was the word "exceptional." Like in terms of a skill or a quality. Mike could sing, play the guitar and write. Luke could DJ and dance, and he knew everything about rock music. Dave knew computers and he could juggle. Rick dressed well and was drop-dead handsome (But I am *not* gay). Me? What *did* I have? I looked deeply into myself for an exceptional quality that would help out in The Quest™.

There was nothing.

"Well, you're a decent sort of fellow," offered Luke. "You know, superior Catholic morals and such, especially among us heathen."

Nothing.

"Well," Mike started slowly, "you're, um, you're obviously intelligent. You know a lot about, you know, bridges and concrete and…and…" Then he suddenly brightened. "You love animals. Like your dog. I've never known anyone so exceptionally affectionate towards his dog."

Nothing.

"Give me a freaking *break*, Shel," Dave smirked, familiar frown forming on the edges of his brow, "You're worried about *this*? This is the type of neurotic, useless shit chicks worry about

…if someone dislikes you, just say 'Screw 'em'…"

Oh shut up Dave.

Nothing.

Only Rick had something interesting to offer. I had no idea what it meant, but it seemed like something interesting.

"The key, Shel," he said one night at the Bomber, bloodshot eyes pulsating eerily with every move, "is proper branding."

"Branding?" I asked, puzzled.

"So you think you're unexceptional. Well, you're right. But so what? Corporations have made millions marketing nondescript products and turning them into something someone talks about all the time. I mean, what was coffee until Starbucks branded it into Starbucks Coffee? It's still just a lousy cup of coffee, but they sure sell a hell of lot of it." He tapped me on the shoulder. "What we gotta do is make you the Starbucks of men – something women pick up along with their bagel and a twelve-pack of condoms on the way to the office. Like me." He nodded imperceptibly to a girl watching him by the pool table, and then walked off with her without even saying goodbye.

Hmmm.

A twelve pack of…?

Nothing.

The common thread, unfortunately, was *this*: I was a friendly, likable, decent Nice Guy.

And this was *not* what I wanted to hear!

Women are not looking for Nice Guys. They all say they are for some strange reason, and some may actually believe it. But the majority are looking for the exceptional. Good and bad. Guys on the extreme – basketball star or bad-boy biker; rock musician or wife-beating drug-addict. "To be sugar-daddied or to mother," Mike said resignedly, and I sadly had to agree.

The end of The Quest™ came, strangely enough, when I decided to give it up. Whoever made up the rules to life sure had a weird sense of humour.

After returning the van, I took the bus home to my place. The weather had turned decidedly shitty: it snowed heavily, then it rained, then freezing rain, and then it snowed again – I almost slipped and cracked my head open as I got off the bus. Add that to being on the verge of resigning myself to celibacy for life, so you couldn't say that I was in a very good mood when I saw her.

A girl was kind of just sitting cross-legged in the middle of the sidewalk, clutching a pot or something tightly to her stomach. She looked about thirteen in the weak glare of the streetlight, and she looked completely miserable. So I slid over to offer help.

"Is everything okay?"

"Help," she whimpered.

"What's wrong?"

"I need to get over to Daly Ave.," she said, motioning her head westward, "and I can't walk without falling every step." It wasn't hard to see why…the road hadn't been cleared well, and the sidewalk was a bank of snow coated with a thick sheet of ice. Kathy didn't look heavy enough to even make a dent in it.

That was her name, Kathy. She was a small elf of a woman, very cute, wearing an oversized Gore-Tex jacket with these little ineffectual boots with zero traction – not that it would have made a difference with her weight. It was hard to make her out in the dark, but she was small, wide-eyed, and really, *really* cute, as far as I could tell.

I took the rice cooker, dented from several falls, and with my heavy steel-tipped CSA-approved Civil Engineering work boots, I crunched into the ice-glazed snow and made a path she could follow. "Just like King Wenceslaus, on the Feast of Stephen," she said, beaming up at me.

So I went five blocks out of my way at a snail's pace that December night…a very Nice Guy thing to do. And when I got there, she insisted that I stay for a cup of tea, plus some other stuff.

She turned out to be twenty-one, thank goodness.

The Happy Land Of Gameshows.

Fall End of Quarter is a seriously stressful time on Bay Street. During these few days before the quarter expires, you've got people on every floor of every building toiling over tools of their trade – computers, cheques, cell phones, signed and unsigned contracts – for the express purpose of coming up with numbers that will convince shareholders that they are pulling in far more money than they actually are. You know it's that time in Toronto when even though the weather has turned chillier, the temperature inside is at least twelve degrees higher, with salespeople rolling up the sleeves of their dress shirts, their jackets slung over chairs in a frantic effort to make (or make up) these numbers. I'm putting the finishing touches on my own report for the firm's senior partners. Quite frankly, it's a work of art: names, numbers and billable hours so proper and enticing that they should be framed in solid gold and silver. I tap in the final keystrokes, hit Save and lean back in my all-leather ergonomic chair, looking down at myself. Hmm. Not a single wrinkle or perspiration stain on my dark grey Italian suit. Cake.

The offices of Jones and Lavoie Toronto carefully package something distinctly unhealthy about the modern Western economic model. Actually, the entire practice of management consulting does: behind the high-quality redwood and brass fixtures, the tastefully framed pictures and antiques, behind the smiles of the beautiful receptionists, the young and industrious-looking employees who could just as easily be featured on A&F and J. Crew catalogues, lies the idea that profit can be made by telling people how stupid they are. We swoop into corporations and government agencies like well-dressed vultures, and, in exchange for fat contracts, we scrutinize their strategies, people, processes, technology, and usually recommend cuts – deep cuts, sporadic cuts, cuts disguised as repositioning, restructuring, rebranding, or "synergistic focus on core competencies." We don't actually *produce* anything, other than thick reports that recommend deep cuts – that's one up on lawyers. But not by much. JLI reports are thickly-bound warrants of fiscal Darwinism, each page obscuring the odour of fear and misery with a nice font and power phrases like "synergistic focus on core competencies." We are the purveyors of bad news, hidden behind technical details, the professional tone obscuring the screams of the common wretch.

I have my numbers, though, so I didn't care all that much.

I don't make work my life like the way most young professionals do. I don't need to. I find work to be easy. I always have. The hours are long, but as long as the results are there at End of Quarter, your actual *presence* isn't required. A meeting here, a phone call there, properly distributed e-mail, faxes, some tech-speke and branding: *"You **like** this juicemaker. You **want** this juicemaker. You would sell your **kidneys** for this juicemaker…"* And your presence is virtually established – even if you're not there. It's all about maintaining credibility. Opportunities in the field are increasing hyperspatially with each mega-merger, each IPO, each e-Business Interaction. New clients are practically kicking down the doors of the senior partners. Every client I sign on makes me contacts, some of which, with the right flesh-pressing and proper legal advice will one day become mine.

> *Pinky: What are we going to do tomorrow night, Brain?*
> *The Brain: Same thing we do every night, Pinky…*
> *try to take over the world!*

The Toronto office itself makes an interesting sociological study in modern dysfunction. The marriage rate was 18 out of 63 – a dismal 22.2 per cent, with two divorces in the works. This is great news to the partners: the firm is particularly fond of career-minded singles, driven to work by the difficulty of maintaining permanent relationships. The backbone of the firm is an unsolid marriage.

The elegant office décor belies high-levels of stress and

clashing egos, not to mention deviant personal practices. Mike Lau, for example, is a bodybuilder who is an expert in data warehousing systems design – with approximately five years left to live thanks to steroid abuse. Steve Langlois is a genial Blue Jays fan and a monster at financing technology IPOs…and a practising sado-masochist. Elissa Jaeger is a blonde bombshell who is a whiz at executive corporate headhunting…she hated men and had a frightening predilection for handguns. And, of course, there's myself. The slickster Rickster, master technology consultant and deal-closer extraordinaire.

And behind that lay…*what*?

I can't seem to remember.

I must be doing a damn good job, then. Carry on, MacDuff.

The next day, all of the consultants were called to a general meeting by one of the senior partners. Mike Lau and I swung downstairs to grab a coffee before heading to the conference room. Mike ('Dr. Steroid') is a fairly bright guy who just graduated from Western's business school. He's also a jock-meso-morph-juice monkey whose only goal outside of partnership in the firm is to go to rave parties and get laid as much as possible. On the way back upstairs, he was regaling to me the wonders of this new protein supplement he was trying out.

"It's the best, man, the fucking *shit*!" he exclaimed. "With it, I figure I'll get my body fat down to four per cent in no time. Then the bitches'll really get it. Parties every week at Fluid, Granite, Systems Soundbar…Twat City, my friend, Twat City!"

Crude, but effective. Too bad he was going to die due to his dangerously low body fat and consistent drug use – heart failure, found underneath Nautilus setup, benching over three-hundred pounds. (How'd I know this? Time machine.)

To say that Jones and Lavoie meetings are stressful is a complete understatement…I'm certain these little get-togethers are choreographed by the Marquis de Sade.

"End of Quarter," suggested senior partner John Forsyth icily, "means *End of Quarter*. The *quarter* has *ended*, you see… meaning the contracts you were working on should have been signed, sealed and fucking delivered to us at twelve midnight. It is no good *after* twelve, as that is *start* of quarter. I need not remind you that if we do not make our numbers, our credibility suffers, we do not get paid as we should, and some of you will be out on the street engineering business processes at your local fast food restaurant." John never minced words when it came to revenues. John never minced words with anything, actually… he was the anti-Anthony Robbins of motivation. But he got results. Today's raking-over-the-coals wasn't of concern to me, of course; my numbers fucking rocked. Mike, however, wasn't so lucky: he was told to report to Human Resources after the group flaying.

Another partner stepped up and proceeded to tear strips out of us because of a major contract lost with MCI-Worldcom, and he also announced the suspicious "retirement" of a senior partner in Accounting. But, on a lighter note, I was promoted to Senior Consultant. I accepted gracefully and elevated the task of getting a lawyer to the top of my list, right above finishing my New York post-mortem and right below making a phone call to Tasmin's father.

I got home at 9:06 pm. The few phone calls I made germinated into hour-long deal discussions. Goddamn, I needed a drink. A few vodka tonics later, I picked up the paper bag with the Pyloxodin™ prescription Shirley picked up for me. She thoughtfully tied some mail to it from the folkses home with a rubber band – *snap*. Included in the junk mail was a menu for The Noble House, an expensive but well-worth-it delivery service. I picked up the phone and ordered; Tasmin wasn't coming over tonight to cook. Not your typical Egg Foo Yung or sweet-and-sour nonsense, of course. Tender steak in a black bean sauce. Scallops, shrimp and fresh greens. Some rice. I could have easily made rice myself in the cooker, but I was too busy mixing a drink. The great thing about the influx of Hong Kong Chinese has been the stratospheric elevation of the quality and authenticity of Chinese food in Toronto. Some of the best chefs from the former crown colony abandoned ship over the past few years and set up shop in TO, much to my pleasure. I've been drinking a lot more since I came back from New York. Work stress, I suppose. Enhanced performance invites more work, and people have different ways of dealing with it – working out, hating men, shooting guns, unsavoury sexual practices. Myself? I fix drinks. I find it re-laxing. Ordinarily. Unfortunately, the drinks tasted watered down – Shirley, I suspected, trying to manage me a little. I grabbed a fresh bottle from the bar and made a triple to wash down a dose-and-a-half of the pills. I then called Tasmin and made a dinner and shopping date with her tomorrow at the Eaton Centre. The shopping was her idea – hazards of high-maintenance. After dinner and a few more drinks, I went to bed. Big gold card day tomorrow.

Geez. Youngsters these days. They certainly suck.

I should've known that the little trolls came out to the malls in force on Saturday. Looking at them, I wondered how the hell people got off saying that Hong Kong FOBs are the foreigners. Kids are so fucking cool these days, aren't they? Check out the fashions. Guys wearing wide-barreled pants, oversized ball caps angled gangsta-style. Shirts and jackets proudly displaying three different team logos at the same time. Skateboards and ghetto blasters, wearing sneers shaped by tongue-piercing and crystal meth. And the girls were even worse. Fuzzy phat pants with plastic chains that drag on the ground. Cheap plastic barrettes on their greasy heads, oversized dress shirts and ties obscuring their flat and undeveloped chests. Ridiculous cartoon purses and knapsacks, pacifiers on beaded chains around their necks. It was a regression to a childhood that never could've happened anywhere except a daycare centre gone very, very insane. Tasmin and I waded through the wolfpack in the main entrance of the

Eaton Centre at the corner of Yonge and Dundas. Tasmin wanted to go to Club Monaco first for some casual wear. FOB chicks love Club Monaco. And then downstairs, through the old Eaton's, and back upstairs to the various upscale boutiques on the second floor of the mall. As Tasmin was trying on a dinner dress, I found myself thinking of Dave. I can remember back at school when Dave and I would plant ourselves in front of the television *à la* Beavis-and-Butthead, with a case of beer and sharpened wits.

"Where's *ER* based again?" Dave once asked, popping open another beer.

"Chicago."

"Well, the show makes Chicago look like the most incompetently run city in the world. I mean, how many car accidents and construction disasters can happen in one day in one city?"

"No Asians, either," I remarked. "Who ever heard of a hospital devoid of Asian doctors? It's culturally impossible. Our parental units would never stand for it."

"*Mike's* parental units would never stand for it."

"*Next!*" Dave flicked the remote and tuned into a series about a cyborg-detective who solved urban crimes. "Now look at *this* crap," Dave once said in disgust. "This is just plain insulting. I mean, who does the director think we are, anyway? A bunch of mindless explosion-loving Gen-X idiots?"

I smiled. "Survey *says…* !"

"No Orientals, either…and the show's based in *San Francisco*, for chrissake. I give this show a definite thumbs down."

I popped open two more beers. "I think we should rate movies based on how many beers you need to enjoy them on. Zero beers would be a totally engrossing, brilliant show."

Dave nodded, flicking a cap over his shoulder and pinging the doorknob dead on. "Except we should grade it out of more than just four…say, oh, how about twenty beers."

"Make it a two-four, and you've got a deal. For example: 'This movie required consumption of a two-four; spending half the flick in the washroom and pissing on the urinal cakes at the side of the toilet bowl was better entertainment than the movie itself.'"

"*Next!*"

We reserved a special place in our hearts for game shows. Personally, I liked *Wheel of Fortune*: "*Vanna's a total babe, man.*" Dave liked *Jeopardy* because he liked showing off his scads of useless knowledge.

"*Wheel of Fortune* is just this lame game of hangman," he scoffed. "Not to mention you get to *keep* all the prizes you win. In Jeopardy, you have to have the highest total to win it all; anything lower and you burn. A lot like life. Hold on – *Final Jeopardy.*"

"*…Ectopolias Migratoras, the Latin name for this now-extinct bird,*" Alex Trebek said from the TV. "*Contestants, good luck.*"

"The Dodo," shrugged Dave, "Maybe. I don't know jack about birds."

"No way," I argued. "*Migratoras* means migratory or something. Dodo's just sit there doing, like, nothing."

"Much like we're doing right now."

A mousy, buttoned-down paralegal named Irving got the right answer (the Passenger Pigeon).

"He's Asian, of course," I said, raising my bottle. "Intellectually superior; socially challenged."

"He's a *freak*," said Dave decisively, "a total *freak*. What sort of *freak* knows something like that? Only a *freak* would have the right answer for that question. He's an alien."

"He's not of this world."

"He is evil."

"He is of the devil."

"He will be the death of us all." Dave smiled a Davish-crooked smile and grabbed another beer.

What a fucking waste of time.

"*Ah Reech-ut, ah,*" Tasmin said, breaking me out of my reverie. "*Ho-mm ho tei?* (Do I look good?)"

I nodded. "Stunning," I said in Cantonese. "Just like Vanna White."

"Who?"

"Never mind."

After shopping, I decided to drop by to see how the folks were doing.

"Hi mom," I said, coming through the garage door.

"Richard! You dumb boy!" she scolded in Cantonese, but obviously pleased. "I'm glad you come home."

Tasmin said 'hi', stooping down to hug my mother. (My mother is very short).

"Are you both staying for dinner? If you are, we should all go out. Twenty-five per cent discount at Magic Wok restaurant," she said ingenuously.

I looked over at Tasmin. "*Ho-ah, lau mai-ah* (Sure, we'll stay)."

Physically, both my sister and I inherited the father's northern stature and features (and, apparently, his good looks), but we were most definitely raised as my Cantonese mother's kids: *Nurture versus Nature.* Both Shirl and I were taught Cantonese, not Mandarin, learned her likes and dislikes, and were ultimately guided by her morals and social mores (well, most of them, anyway). Aside from the prerequisite genetic material he provided, the father had virtually no hand in raising us. Knowing Cantonese is useful in dealing with Hong Kong Chinese (and, of course, their money), but it's not particularly pleasant to listen to. I describe a lot of my mom's speech as "scolding", although that's not technically true; the Cantonese *lingua*, with nine different tones and pervasiveness of crude slang, only makes it sound like scolding. Luke once said it sounded like a person gargling while getting their throat ripped out.

"Sometimes I wish my mom could speak to me in Mandarin," Shel once said, back at school. "It's so much more a pleasant language, don't you think?" Dave and Mike nodded knowingly; being yelled at in Cantonese was something we all experienced at one time or another.

"You got it," approved Mike. "The way I see it is this: Mandarin is to French as Cantonese is to German. It's that phonetic upswing, the lilt, that makes Mandarin a much more elegant language, much like French…Cantonese by contrast is harsh and guttural, like a hammer through a watermelon. Being able to speak Cantonese *gently* is a feat. It involves meticulous avoidance of slang. It involves discipline of your tonality... something my mom certainly doesn't have. That's why I've always encouraged her to yell at me in Mandarin instead of Cantonese." He suddenly looked thoughtful. "Did you know that there's a Chinese dialect where essentially the same word – *ngoh* – is repeated six times and it translates into 'The Russian in the Grass is Trying to Stab Me'...*Ngoh ngoh ngoh ngoh ngoh ngoh.* Cool, eh?"

Yet another useless tidbit from en-Mike-clopaedia Britannica. A waste of a fine analytical mind, I believe.

Tasmin went into the kitchen to talk to mom, and I went to the family room. The father was sleeping on the couch and Shirley was doing her organics homework to an episode of *Seinfeld*. "Hi Rick," she said, not looking up from her homework.

"Hiya Shirl." I instinctively reached for my wallet. I always have these vague feelings of guilt around Shirley for some reason, and I guess I compensate by pushing money at her all the time.

"How goes?"

"Fine." No expression.

"Good." An awkward pause. "How's school?"

"Fine." Another pause. It was starting to sound like a Hemingway novel. "I saw Mike on the subway today."

"Really." *Why would she mention that?* "Er, how's dad?"

"Fine."

I looked at the father impassively, snoring softly, his lanky form draped across the whole of the couch. Wasted from Lithium. I suppose I love the father, but I do not respect him for his weakness. That's a good thing, though. Where he is weak, what he lacks, I am strong, I have gained – in spades. He is deficient, and I am proficient. It's like a large genetic zero-sum game, stockpiling the necessary tools for World Domination.

I forgot to take my pills again. Damn. As methodical as I am with the job, my methodology for following prescriptions is pathetically inconsistent. If I were on birth control, I'd be mother to a Greek-Italian family by now.

Lying in my bedroom with Tasmin slumbering on my chest, I began gauging my status in life. Oddly enough, I came up a little short – I *never* come up short. I am feeling uncertain about a few things, and I don't really know why. Which is kind of strange, because I take anti-depressants to *reduce* uncertainty. In my line of work, I'm paid to reduce the risk of my clients, and that's impossible to do unless you reduce uncertainties within *yourself*. A recent magazine article in *Toronto Life* recently raised an interesting issue about these sorts of drugs: are they a pharmaceutical plot to ultimately control us? Its case was based on the reasons why the drugs are used, and typical results – both of which pointed to greater adherence to western-styled capitalistic societal values. And while for me, these values – productivity, energy, personal confidence – were beneficial, it made you kind of wonder if it was simply meant to be this way. Or rather, it *didn't* make you wonder – 'wondering' was the disease of losers like the Banana Boys. The article pithily referred to Pyloxodin™ and like meds as "mental penis implants for women," alluding to the phallocentrism of its results. I thought this was *apropos* of the Jones and Lavoie environment, where more than a few female consultants in the firm subscribed to it. Myself, I saw it as a useful tool to make my billable hours at work go through the roof. (The latter culminated in a longish glass pyramid trophy that looked suspiciously like an American Music Award, a mere year of service under my belt. It now stands proudly on my coffee table.)

Realistically, I have no time to dwell on the past. That's why I sever the past as soon as it has used up its value to me. This is largely the reason why I eventually broke it off with the Banana Boys. We were in a rut. I moved on to better things. My definition of "fun" drifted beyond going to the bar and bitching about things. My definition of "value" determined that the relationships there wouldn't get me what I wanted. It certainly wasn't as if the Banana Boys provided a bastion of stability. The tangled web between the Banana Boys were notoriously fragmented and inconsistent. It seemed like all Banana-type relationships were like that…a microcosm for Asian and Asian American politics. We fought about as much as we had good times together, and to me there was something wrong with that. Contrary to what Mike wanted you to believe, the so-called Banana Boy Brotherhood Ethic was one of the weakest I know of. Shriners, Freemasons, Engineers and Harvard Alums had stronger bonding mechanisms. Banana's rarely acknowledged each other's existence, and when we did, the sniping and back-stabbing and incessant questioning was ridiculous. We were a ragtag collection of militants, intellectuals, mama's boys, capitalists, whitewashed sellouts. Why bother even trying? I have no use for a "pile of sand."

I remember one time, when my emotions got the better of me, I made these views clear. Bad mistake. Luke and Dave and Mike were bickering about race (what else was new?) at the Bomber after a set of midterms. It all started when Luke was busting Dave's chops for ragging on someone who cut his Jeepy off in the Davis Centre parking lot.

"Dumb FOB," Dave spat, "They've gotta be the most irritating people on earth. Bloody BMW-driving-Marlboro-smoking-obnoxious-rich kids. Solomon or Ferdinand or whoever he was even had those dangly gold charms on the rear-view and stupid stuffed animals in the back. You give a FOB a nice set of wheels and they think they're King of the Road."

"Ignorant stereotypes," dismissed Luke with an I'm-A-Superior-Liberal wave.

"It's not just the parking spot," insisted Dave testily, "it's the attitude that comes along with the money, the nice cars, the cell phones. They think they're so much better than we are."

"Bullshit," scoffed Luke. "You're just critical because you look like them. You're afraid white people'll identify you as such."

"That's a load of *crap*…"

"Never mind them…I hate those Chinese Christians," added Shel. "They always make you feel guilty about not going to church and stuff."

"When was the last time you were in church, Shel?" asked Mike.

"I'd rather not say."

"Stereotypes," Luke repeated. "Personally, I'm more irritated about these hardcore Asian American activist-types. Every time a movie or a sitcom or a Taco Bell commercial comes on without an Asian presence, they get all wound up and make it out to be the biggest crime since Martin Luther King was shot."

"Now who's stereotyping?" sniped Dave.

"Shut up, Banana Boy."

"Guys," said Mike, "I think conveying these notions is a complete waste of time. I mean, we're all Chinese, right? We're all Asian. We're brothers. Sticking together is vitally important for our political solidarity…"

"There *is* no political solidarity," I interjected quietly.

"What?" said Mike, distracted. Both Dave and Luke stopped breathing down each other's necks for a second and looked at me. I usually ignored these sorts of conversations whenever they came about, either by drinking more, or trying to hook up, or, frequently, both.

"I said there is no political solidarity."

"Of course there is… ," began Mike.

"No, there isn't. None. Zero. Zilch. You guys just have to get it though your brainwashed heads. Asians have *no* political solidarity. We are the most divisive species on earth…what'd you say earlier, Mike? *A Pile of Sand.* Thus quoth the great Sun Yat-Sen, father of Chinese Republicanism or whatever the hell he was the father of."

Mike furrowed his brow. "I think you're taking it out of context…"

"Am I? Just check it out. Most of us have been trained to be passive, helpless, deferential. Others have been mentally enslaved, stupid little puppy dogs, so as to dump on their own kind, not to mention themselves. Others are bitter, whiny losers." Dave frowned. "Still others have been trained to quietly go about doing their math homework or programming or some such drone-level Information Wage Slave-tasks."

"Now wait a minute…"

"Open your eyes," I continued, fuelled by the alcohol. "The

FOBs don't give a shit about anything but money. The Chinese Christians are too busy racking up the brownie points for Jesus. And the whitewashed are so comfortable with their accepted role as 'The Cool Asian Who Isn't Like All The Others' they'll continue to plant their lips firmly on white ass." Luke looked a little unsettled. "And Dave here'll try to convince you our own women have turned against us. The Vietnamese hate the Chinese, the Koreans hate the Japanese, the Cambodians hate the Vietnamese and so on and so forth. Even the so-called Asian American Activists are a bunch of irrelevant elitists who are busy turning on so-called 'sellouts' – they're as bad as the rest of 'em. And the rest of us have our brains so balled up on sports and money and school and Sexloverelationships that we just don't give a flying fuck anymore."

That instigated a babble of protests, to which I kind of tuned out. I'd said too much already. Because it doesn't really matter. I've understood this from the very beginning. Asians are the visible minority that will never be a single, unified group in this country. We have no common interest or experience, unlike the Blacks or the Jews or the Québecois, who'll always get what they want because they are smart and we remain stupidly divisive. We have no marketable demographic, so we will continue to be ignored. Our standard of living is so high it doesn't make any difference anyway.

So thinking about it obsessively, talking about it, continuously whining about it and ourselves like Mike and Dave and Luke and sometimes Shel did, wasn't going to change this. It was all just useless cultural baggage.

So I stopped trying. I became a FOB.

And I'm much happier this way. *Honest.*

I look over Tasmin and check my clock. 2:49 am. I can't sleep.

I tap the touch light on the night table. At its minimum setting, it illuminates my room in a ghostly glare. Shadows dance on the walls, across my CD collection. Across my library of tax guides and books on investments and mutual funds. Across stuffed animals from my current girlfriend, my ex, my ex-ex, and my ex-cubed.

Tasmin shifts uneasily and pouts in her sleep. I stroke her hair until her frown is erased, and she settles back into a peaceful slumber. I pick up a Post-It note beside the package I asked Shirl to get me…

> *Richard Wong, Age 26*
> *Toronto (was in New York City)*
> *Jones and Lavoie International*
> *Notes: Just got promotion at firm.*
> *- S.*

Reliability. That's Shirley.

About a week later, I was walking to my car with Tasmin after a night out. We had been out with some friends at a bar up in Richmond Hill – some sushi, a few drinks, Karaoke. *Ka-ra-ok-e.* Those lush, velvety, smoke-filled interiors, filled with brass fixtures, attractive waitresses, Armani Exchange-clad Chinese posses. Videos featuring attractive Japanese girls holding hands and laughing in a garden. A skinny Chinese guy wearing what must be easily a thousand dollars worth of clothing belting out such adult-contemporary classics as "Careless Whisper" and "Right Here Waiting" as if he'd practiced it for weeks (which he probably had).

On the way from the bar to the parking lot, two suburban crackers were heckling us, one of them making stupid monkey-like martial arts type sounds. We ignored them, like we usually did, so the cracker in the Bulls ball cap spoke up.

"Yo, Charlie!" he jeered. Typical suburban brat – expensive baseball cap with matching Starter jacket, oversized Romero jeans hung low on skinny hips, arrogant WASP sneer on his face. "Charlie! Got twenty bucks?"

"'Course he does," said the other one, wobbling, probably drunk. "Prolly has a *hundred* bucks."

"*Ah-**Reet**-chut…wah **meht** yeh-ah*? (What are they saying?)" asked Tasmin, looking worried. Unlike me, she couldn't switch from Cantonese to English too quickly, especially after a night out with the FOB-crowd.

"*Moh **yeh**…mm-**gwan** ngoh-deh si* (Nothing…none of our business)," I replied curtly. "Just forget it." We went past them, perhaps more slowly than we should have.

"Nice girlfriend," said Bulls cap. "Hey, baby? Wannee lickee my dickee? Eh, chickee?" They both laughed.

I turned to Tasmin, who was beginning to comprehend.

"Want to return to the car?" I asked, not really asking as I tossed her the keys. She nodded and hurried away.

I spun around to face the boy, tie flapping over my left shoulder. "Now that's not very nice," I said, smiling very slightly, very dangerously.

"Fuck you, Chinaman. I was talking to the bitch."

I moved a little closer. "So why don't you talk to *me*?" My knee shot up and caught him in the kidney area, and he went down like a bag of charcoal briquettes.

"Talk to *me*," I said pleasantly, balling up my fist and punching him in the face a few times. I looked over to his pal, who was leaning against the wall, unsure of what to do. Probably never encountered a FOB who actually responded to their jibes before.

I turned back to my bloody bag of charcoal and took off his ball cap, grabbing him by his hockey hair and lifting his face closer to mine.

"Talk to *me*," I repeated pleasantly. "Say '*I like Chinese*'. *Say* it, boy. *Say* it." He only groaned, so I whacked his jugular, sending some bloody spit onto my Banana Republic jacket.

"*Say* it, kid. Say it for *me*."

He mumbled something from his rapidly swelling lips.

Close enough. "Say it again: '*I like Chinese*'."

Mumble mumble mumble.

"'*I like Chinese. I like Chinese*'."

Mumble mumble mumble mumble mumble.

I threw his head down on the pavement and walked past his buddy to my car.

Tasmin hugged me tightly when I got in, nearly cutting off my circulation. Shit, is there anything I do that doesn't turn her on? I wiped some blood off my fist and jacket, and we drove back to my place.

It didn't happen all that often, this type of stuff. To me. To non-Bananas. We stick to our own kind and worry about Fobby things. Important things, like business, money, cars. We have no use for anything else, you see. We have goals. Targets, milestones. Revenue projections.

Banana's seem to always look for trouble like this, or at least it always found them. FOBs have their own world, the whites have theirs, and they very rarely intersect. Bananas are the intersection – messed up, hypersensitized, marginalized, somewhere in between – and we all know that most car crashes occur at intersections. However, I am becoming unnecessarily deep and analytical. I am thinking too much about the whole episode. All I want to do is go home and fix a drink, have sex and go to sleep.

Who Possesses Your Soul?

*T*he bus passes buildings that hide the true terror the city holds. My mind drifts past the charade and shines the harsh light of truth on the sickness of this city. Past restaurants and massage parlours that hold enslaved Slavic women paying off illegal immigration debts. Past offices holding angry and borderline-suicidal investment bankers and technical writers, working at a desk holding unpaid bills, a bottle of pills, and a small-calibre handgun. Past basement clubs where fourteen-year-old children are convulsing under the influence of ketamine and crystal meth, their hollow eyes searching and blotched spindly arms reaching for something they can no longer truly grasp. Past side streets where police beat and perform intensive cavity searches on young black men, or shoot them when they tire of the inconvenience. Past tenements filled with battered women and raped schoolgirls, lying in the stairwell, tartans torn and stained with virgin blood. Past dumpsters filled with drug needles and infant corpses, bloated and unidentifiable, left by mothers high on crack and low on funds. One apartment holds the bodies of a senior couple, bludgeoned to death by a 14-year-old paperboy overdosed on Sega and Mutant Ninja Turtles for a string of pearls and $70 cash.

There is little love left in this city. I feel it being leached from this place like metal leaches heat, like jade leaches gold.

We pass by a Health Canada safe sex billboard featuring a group of racially-diverse and fresh-faced virginal teens. The Asian girl looks like my ex-girlfriend, only not as pretty. Beside her grinning visage, there is a catchy slogan: "No Glove, No Love." Except someone had crossed out "No Glove" with a large spray-painted X. The subtlety did not escape me. They know. But somehow, that does not make me glad…only sadder.

Because the magic is dead. The wonder is gone. The only magic and wonder left are in Robertson Davies' novels. We live alone in a stark, impure world without anything to propel us further forward *as a species. We are doomed to die screaming and flailing in a cess-pool of horror generated by ourselves. We are solely to blame…*

The squeal of the bus' brakes jars me awake. The air shimmers briefly, and reverts from X-ray negative back to a semblance of normal. But I know it's still there. It will always be there.

Todd wasn't in yet when I got in the office, so I played with the Internet for a little while. I started reading Usenet. Bad move. I usually subscribed my newsreader to the cultural discussion newsgroups, largely because I am an idiot: the content was offensive, musings of maladjusted misanthropes, absolutely no socially redeeming features. Like *can.community.asian*, a newsgroup that technically dealt with issues involving Asian Canadian cultural issues, but often ends up as a forum for white supremacists, neo-Cons, and white guys looking for a nice Oriental girl for massages and home cooked meals.

```
From: Jack McGraw <jmcgraw@ottawa.freenet.ca>
To: can.community.asian
Subject: Crap posted by some socialist jackass

Some liberal jackass <gtam@mech3.uvic.ca> said:
>McAngus you racist bastard, immigrants are
>people too, you know. They want the same things
>out of life as you and your inbred ancestors did.
>So just lay off and leave them alone, you stupid
>son of a
<<more liberal crap from previous poster deleted>>
It's so typical of you socialist clones to be spouting
this Politically-correct *bullshit* when you know
*full and well* that this country is falling to pieces
because of all the fucking immigration. Racism is
just a convenient word for you socialists to
describe anyone with a sense of self-sufficiency
and fair-play. If having reasonable neo-conservative
views makes me a racist, then I say just send all
the chinks back to the eastern cesspools and opium
dens from whence they came. J/M
*****************************************************
The goal of socialism is to make everyone equally poor
*****************************************************
```

You're born here. You're raised here. You raise a family, earn the respect of your friends and colleagues. You work hard, play fair, shoot straight, pay your taxes – you're a normal, productive member of Canadian society. And yet with a lone word from a single prejudiced freak, you are immediately degraded, grouped in with a fictional bunch of slant-eyed, yellow-skinned heathen *Chi-nee* who kowtow, do laundry and serve *chow mein*.

It **hurts**.

I **hate** it.

You think, *"It's so **unfair**."* You think, *"What's the point of it all?"* You think, *"Screw you guys, I'm going home."* Except that you *are* home. All that blood, sweat, tears, anthems, and you're *still* treated like garbage by garbage.

I want to do something about it. I'm compelled to, commanded. I guess I'm not the type just to sit back and fade into the background, hoping no one notices me, leaving it as somebody else's problem, when there's so much wrong. Someone has to do something. Someone has to care. But a great many people in the world have spent their lives devoted to righting these injustices. They care, labour mightily, speak eloquently, and die, most likely disappointed at how little things have actually changed. It's tough.

So I post back, knowing the ultimate futility that is the Internet. But the thing that gets me most about it is that morality or responsibility is definitely not required to contribute. The disease is obscured before everyone and their mother had a modem and a web browser; it was there, just harder to see. It eats further into the Canadian psyche than people gave it credit for. "Fair play." "Real Canadians." "The True North Strong and Free." Fucking *bullshit*.

Mina and I fought about it. All the time.

"Who *cares*?" she said, visibly upset because I was visibly upset. "You're getting worked up over *nothing*!"

"*I* care," I insisted. "And it's *not* nothing. They're attacking you, too."

"Did they mention me?"

"Uh, no, but…"

"God, Mike, you're so fucked up."

Dave, a reformed net news junkie way before I caught the bug, was a little kinder. He tried to put it in perspective for me.

"Nature of the Beast, boyo," he said non-committally. "Internet's cheap, efficient and relatively unregulated. It's a platform that virtually invites extremists of all sorts – previously isolated freaks and misfits – to communicate with each other. Internet allows 'em to grow in strength and collectively bathe in their foaming and diseased dogma, completely shielded." He shrugged his shoulders impassively. "Shit man, cyberspace is *full* of dickless wonders who know very well that they can say whatever they bloody well want, and be free of any physical ramifications like a bullet in the head."

"So what can we do about this?" I asked rather plaintively.

"Nothing," Dave replied grimly, doing the three-fingered salute on his own machine after it froze up. He shook his head in frustration.

"Ah, the wonders of modern technology."

Another substandard review from Allenberg today. Shoot me now or wait 'till I get home? *Shoot him now! Shoot him now! He does **not** have to shoot you now. He does **so** have to shoot me now! SO SHOOT ME NOW!*

BLAM*!*

*You'rrrrrre **deth**-picable...*

Could it be that my persistent glumness is attributable to biological factors? Being a student (albeit a reluctant one) of the natural sciences, I've often thought about the possibility. I've often noticed that my moods are significantly altered by changes in the weather, for example. Maybe that gland in the back of my head that's light sensitive was enlarged or mutated or something. God knows I'd be dangling from the rafters if I was living in Vancouver.

Genetically, there may also be another link. Both my parents seem all right, discounting the regular psychoses about education and lunging for the bill at restaurants that I attributed to the foibles of Chinese culture. But then there was my grandfather.

My grandfather on my father's side is an interesting fellow, to say the least. I hesitate to call him crazy…well, okay, he's crazy as a loon, although he's never been officially diagnosed as such. I sometimes visit him at the old folks' home at Mount Pleasant in midtown, because my mom said that I should. (Who was I to object? Good filial grandson.)

"I believe he's taking a nap now," the nurse at reception said, calling up his schedule on her computer. "He's also medicated, so he may be a little disoriented. But you may go in, if you like." Hesitantly, I walked into his room, where he was napping in a chair facing the Mount Pleasant Cemetery outside.

"*Yeh-yeh*?" I asked quietly in Cantonese. He stirred a little and looked at me passively.

"*Yeh-yeh*?" Another look.

"*Mi-koh*," he said, recognition flooding his eyes.

"Yes, it's me. *Nei **deem**-ah?* (How are you doing?)"

"*Mi-koh*," he said again. I nodded.

"*Mi-koh*," he said one more time, and then he lapsed into a senile passivity. I guess I don't blame him; there were times when I wished I could do the same. It's been a rough day.

According to my mom, dad's side of the family has always been a little strange. Dad hardly talked about it, but my mom told me something really bizarre. Apparently, *yeh-yeh's* father, my great-grandfather, was part of the resistance movement against the Manchu Dynasty in China near the beginning of the 20th Century. At the beginning of the 1911 Chinese Revolution, when the Republican Nationalists revolted against their Manchu overlords, the revolutionaries passed messages hidden in mooncakes, a special Chinese dessert made of flour, eggs and lotus seed paste, traditionally eaten during the Mid-Autumn Festival. That year, many of these special mooncakes contained messages – meeting places, times, key contacts – central to the revolution.

According to my mom, great-grandfather *ate* his message, thus earning a nickname, which was the Chinese equivalent of

"You Eeeediot!"

Yeh-yeh's own mental condition was evidently triggered by his experiences in Nanking when the Japanese took over. Few details available here, but the results were obvious – he's always been a few cards short of a deck.

Another interesting cultural tidbit: a few weeks ago, amidst an apoplectic fit, he claimed that the Chaos were direct descendants from the great Chinese pirate general, Koxinga. That's right, Koxinga: hero of the Ming, enemy of the Ching, demonized by the Dutch, great pillager of Taiwan, three hundred-odd years ago. I passed it off as delusional meanderings for a while, but he seemed rather convinced. There's something about stark, raving insanity that makes things more compelling, if not outright believable.

After unsuccessfully trying to communicate with him for another ten minutes, I gave up and headed home. I'll stop by again next week. I walked back to the subway station, opening my umbrella to shield me from the grey blatter that just began to fall. Hm. It's always raining somewhere…except in California.

You know, I don't think I particularly like the idea of having some sort of great ancestry behind me. It's not like my present status as a malaise-ridden grad student was doing such a mighty heritage proud. There's also the matter of not being particularly the conquering personality type. Emotionally castrated, perpetually empty and spineless, I couldn't even bring myself to follow the courage of my own convictions, not in terms of school, The Book™, nothing. The great Koxinga may have bellowed heartily from the bow of the lead Junk of his huge fleet, laughing as he invited rain and lightning to strike him down where he stood, on his way to sack villages and trading posts and rape Dutch women. Mike Chao just sighs heavily, cursing at the rain, waiting for the lights to change while huddling miserably under a three-dollar umbrella. Epic stuff.

The Book™ is arguably the most important thing in my life. But it, too, is subject to the foibles of mood.

On some days, I felt pretty darned good about it; I might be reading a few odd passages and thinking that they were really good, that I was actually a good writer, that it was eventually going to get done. Hey, it *had* to get done, right? There was no way around it. But on other days, like today, I'd be plagued with innumerable self-doubts. I'd ultimately feel that it was point-less, futile. I'd feel that I didn't have the time or the energy for anything like this. Here I am, sitting on enough material in my Campbell's Soup box for several novels, and I don't even have time to write a matchbook cover, and even if I did, it'd be fruit-less because who's going to be interested in the garbage that I have to say, anyway?

Not that anyone else was fired up by the The Book™. Even among the Banana Boys. Their general reaction to The Book™ was fairly disappointing.

"Sounds like *Generation X*," said Luke, poker-faced.

"Sounds like *The Joy Luck Club*," said Dave, rolling his eyes in contempt.

"Sounds pretty narrow in terms of audience – not enough mass consumer appeal," said Rick.

"What about me? Am I in The Book™?" asked Shel excitedly.

"Mike, do you know what you need for the guaranteed success of The Book™?" said Luke once, biting into a falafel. I shook my head.

"A death sentence imposed on you by Islamic clerics."

"Brilliant, man," said Dave, downing his beer. "I heard there's a sale going on for those – there's a two-for-one down at the Wal-Mart, and you get a State of Kansas Jello Mold as a bonus…" Everyone laughed at that. That's when I got the feeling no one was taking this all that seriously.

Not that I blamed them. Whenever anyone asked me what The Book™ was specifically about, I ended up giving unsatis-factory and relatively evasive answers. Because it wasn't really *about* anything.

"It's kind of hard to describe," I explained, not entirely sure of the proper terminology to use. "You can't really classify it as Sci-Fi or Mystery or under any other traditional genre, because plot is kind of irrelevant to what I'm trying to accomplish. Rather, I'm more interested in capturing the thoughts and the attitudes of certain people." I flailed my arms around expressively, as if that would clear things up. It didn't. "Like you guys, for example – how you think, how you feel. The actual events that occur in The Book™ are relatively mundane, but I want to show that from a certain perspective, the mundane can be a pretty noble thing."

"So, basically, your book is one big *Seinfeld* episode," said Rick. "Except Seinfeld is Chinese. And so is George. And Kramer."

"How about Elaine?" Shel asked.

"She's pretty cool, don't you think?"

"Yeah, I love Elaine."

Help, I thought.

Sometimes entertaining repartee would arise from talking about The Book™. Nothing serious, of course – *never serious* – but interestingly inane nonetheless.

"So have you, like, figured out names for your characters yet?" asked Shel conversationally.

"Um, not yet…"

"Well you've *got* to have a character in there named Elvis," interrupted Dave loudly, " 'cause he's The King. 'Elvis X. Chang'. Yeah." He sat back, with a vaguely pleased look on his face. "It pays homage to one of the most influential men in music history, you see? And gives you a token minority at the same time. Two in one."

"Well, if you're talking about the cultural mosaic thing," offered Luke, "you've *got* to put in a Native American."

"Um…"

"Yup. Definitely so. I mean, look at the success of *Dances With Wolves*? Definitely a Native American. 'Jiminez Running Bear'. Kind of throws in the Latino-Native-American angle, don't you think?"

"That's the stupidest thing I've ever heard," argued Dave. "Elvis X. Chang is much cooler."

"Jiminez Running Bear," insisted Luke.

"Elvis X. Chang."

"Jiminez Running Bear!"

"Elvis!"

"May the dark spirit of Tatanka crush your soul."

"Fuck off, Luke."

"I kind of like Japanese names myself," said Shel unhelpfully. "Like Yamashita or Mitsubishi or something."

Oh God, I thought.

I can't say that my parents take The Book™ all that seriously, either. Dad thinks I should just concentrate on getting into med school. Mom calls The Book™ "*siu gou jei*," which literally means "small baby tale" in Cantonese. Not a book, or a novel…just a small baby tale. It might be the foibles of language – God knows there are enough of *those* in Chinese-English translation – but the addition of that "*–jei*" ("baby") at the end kind of trivializes it. It makes the task that much more insignificant. As if learning how to fix brains was that much more important. That's what we have alcohol for.

The sun broke over the buildings in a red mist this morning, spilling from the wound like blood hungrily seeking space beyond the flesh. My mind is full of blood today because I read a story in the paper about a mother willfully feeding crack to her baby. I do not know what a crack baby looked like, but I imagined there was much blood. I imagined the crack baby wailing, eyes bloodshot and bleeding from the sockets, bony little fingers grasping for something, gasping for air as his mother leaves him to be arraigned.

I shake my head and gaze once again into the mist, wondering what was wrong with me for thinking this way. Why must my thoughts be filled with blood? Because I am a sick and dysfunctional person. Because I am possibly insane. I fear this despite having certifiable medical analyses which say that I am not, that my depression is merely a product of adjustment problems, 'adolescent funk', as it were.

Only I am no longer an adolescent. So I believe that I am insane.

And I wonder why I was ever made, why God had the twisted sense of humour to put this mind and this heart in this body in this world. And I try to think rationally, but the fear and anger in me oozes from my pores, bleaching me white. My heart palpitates, my hands grow sweaty as my brain works steadily trying to derail me, each lobe taking turns stabbing at my heart. My body hates me; the organs are at war with each other. I grow constipated and malnourished. Every nerve ending in my body twitches with the sensation that they are feeding on each other...

The phone suddenly rings, jarring me from my Mental White Noise. *Poof.* Gone. The pain of the moment that I just felt feels merely foolish now.

"Um, hello?"

"Hi, Michael."

"Oh, hi Luke." An awkward pause. "What's up?"

It turns out Luke's friend was opening up a new dance club on Richmond St., and Luke had tickets. "It's going to be pretty cool," he said. "You could crash at my place afterwards, if ya need to – Seth probably won't be in tonight."

"How about Dave?"

"He says he 'hates all that weird-assed dancey shit.' Thus quoth the raven. So how about it?"

"Sure." Maybe it'll jerk me out of the state I've been in. "What's the plan?"

"Come on over to the 808 State at around seven and we'll take off from here. I need to stop by *Eastern Bloc* before we get to the club. I've had this damned Breaks song in my head all day, and if I don't get hold of it, I swear I'll run amok."

"Right. 7 pm, your place. See ya."

"Ciao." *Click.*

I got to the 808 State a little later than expected, in part because Allenberg had me conduct a few extra experiments, but also because I spent ten minutes trying to get past Wilson, the neighbour's dog.

A wild-eyed Luke threw open the door. "You're *late!*"

"Sorry. Allenberg had me doing..."

"I don't *care*, goddammit!" He grabbed his leather jacket and his headphones, and hauled me out into the hallway, waving his arms around. "The store closes at *seven-thirty* today! I need to get that record or else!"

"All right, all right, we'll catch a cab or something. I'll spring for it."

We got to the store with minutes to spare, and Luke ended up getting what he needed – a limited pressing of a Robb G track, remixed by the Boston Bruins. He still had his head-phones on, bopping to the beat, ten minutes after we paid for the disc and left the store. The junkie just got his fix.

> *"Blemishes are hid by night and every fault forgiven;*
> *darkness makes any woman fair."*
> - Ovid, *Ars Amatoria*, I.

Hell was the name of Luke's friend's nightclub. I'd heard the ads for its grand opening a few weeks ago: *"Friday Nights, just **Go To Hell!**"* The layout was quite impressive – a faithful Dantean motif, twisted forms of what were presumably the damned behind translucent walls. Many sections of the club had plaster imi-tations of craggy brimstone, and there were actual thin pillars of flame that flared up behind protective railings every time a new song started, giving the whole place a predictably evil look.

The music was largely unremarkable – Hip Hop, R&B, with a strong strain of Disco. It was a disturbing trend I noticed lately, the shockingly tasteless revival of Disco – *what is **with** that*? I guess it has a good beat, but the connotations it brought up are atrocious – scratchy polyester clothes, bad haircuts, cheesy pick-up lines, execrably bad taste.

Luke agreed. "These days, the term Innovative Dance Music means dredging up some banal and obscure song from the seventies and remixing it with Hip Hop or House beats – the Puff Daddy Syndrome. I mean, if I hated that song then, what on earth would make a producer believe that I would appreciate an updated Hip Hop version?"

"How about your Breaks, then?"

"Breaks is *not* Hip Hop, Michael. Say that again and I cap your ass, bitch."

Not that I talked much with Luke tonight. Sweat flying off his forehead, he was moshing with everyone and no one in particular, flailing madly to some updated *KC and the Sunshine Band*. I was standing by the wall with a beer, as usual, just observing. I was feeling kind of perverse, so I bought a pack of cigarettes from the machine out in the foyer; after half the pack, my mouth felt like shit.

I felt like a fish out of water. It was a mistake to have come; I spent most of the evening stuck to the same wall, sucking back bottles of Molson Dry, getting shoved around by juicy, shirtless muscle-heads, trying not to gawk at the waitresses, decked out in red leotards, horns and spiked heels. That's me, cursed with a shyness that is criminally vulgar...

> *"There's a club if you've got to go*
> *You could find somebody – who really loves you.*
> *So you go and you stand on your own,*
> *And you leave on your own*
> *And you go home and you cry and you want to die."*

Nothing clears the dance floor faster than a slow song, and it got crowded near my patch of wall, so I gave up and went outside.

It was about midnight on a cold fall night on Queen St. The usual crowd was out – bikers milled around the entrance of *The Black Bull*, stylish young yuppies crowded a blues bar playing live music, the odd couple stopped to listen to a street saxophonist. I reached into my coat pocket and pulled out the pack of Players I'd plowed into. Only three left. I wanted another one, but my throat hurt too much. I was feeling violent and destructive.

From the Pizza Pizza across the street emerged a very pretty Asian girl. She looked like my ex-girlfriend. She was with a guy – a wimpy Caucasian guy wearing glasses and a jean jacket. They were holding hands and sharing a steaming slice of pizza, giggling. I sighed, leaning against the wall, replaying all the horror stories and failures of my past love life, getting too deeply into it, feeling little pinpricks of moisture forming at the base of my eyeballs, but I'm too tired and too drunk to cry.

Within minutes, I was back inside double-fisting a pair of Buds; within a half-hour of closing time, I was staggering down an alleyway, vomiting behind some boxes and wishing I was dead. My tolerance has been pretty low since I left university. I sat down heavily after my second heave and my mind floated above the steel fire escapes into the starry sky above and straight into the past.

Lost. Lonely. Drunk, stupid and borderline-suicidal.

All night, I have been quietly and drunkenly observing people, anthropological rituals of mating and courtship, exchanges of affection or lust, between happy, young, energized creatures. By 11 pm, I am debating whether or not to join in; ten minutes later, I'm beating my head against the pillar, ultimately knowing that I am incapable or unwilling to do so. Like a lab rat that's been shocked too many times, I've learned helplessness.

After regaining my composure, I wandered back to the main entrance of the club. People were filing out, hailing cabs, buying bratwursts from a street-meat vendor. Luke was outside, chatting with a cute redhead. I walked up to him and faked sobriety.

"Luke, I think I'll head home now."

He looked at me with concern. "You all right, dude? Really, you can crash at my place." From his body language, however, it was obvious that he was rooting for the other team.

"No, I remember I have something to do tomorrow morning for my folks," I lied. "So I'll catch you later. Remember to pick up your record at the coat check."

"Thanks for reminding me, dude."

I left him in the capable arms of the young lady. He's taken care of for the night.

On my way to the Osgoode subway station, I regressed into a drunken, pathetic stupor. I hadn't had this much to drink in a long time. I felt sick, like acids and poisons had been injected into me, setting my intestines on fire, consuming my heart, my brain and leaving only a gaping hole to cool in the sombre wind.

My eyes grew heavy, lidded with nausea. There was a druggy-buzz clouding my line of sight. I felt so bizarrely out of control that I didn't know what to do. Mental White Noise was inundating my mind. Cars came by and I whispered to them, I begged them: *Kill me. Please. Kill me. Please kill me…*

It was like being in Love, only less painful.

I stumbled onto the last subway train north for the night, the only person in the car. By force of drunken momentum, I tripped into the car, grabbed one of the poles in the middle for standing passengers and spun around it, eventually sitting down on the floor.

Infidelity. The infidel. Mina, my ex, aka Mistress Cruella. And I have not gotten over it. *I could not.*

I'm sure better men have survived that sort of thing, simply moved on, the negative experience not even rating a blip on their psychological radar screen. But I am not better men. I am Michael Chao.

My most vivid memory of that sorry time was, surprisingly, not when she admitted it; it was the alcoholic therapy that came afterwards, the Tequila Brain-Death Night prescribed by the rest of the guys. Luke and Dave had caught wind of my troubles and Dave, ever helpful, came over to my dorm room with three bottles of Tequila Sauza. Rick and Shel had a night class, and joined us later.

"Store was closed, so we couldn't get lemon or salt," said Luke.

"Because *bonehead* here just *had* to stop by the record store to pick up a load of weird-assed music," fumed Dave. They started arguing, as usual, as I looked forlornly on.

Suddenly, the two looked away from each other and turned to me simultaneously. "Aw, man, I'm sorry," they groaned in unison. Then we hit the damned tequila, sans lemon and salt. Here's to good friends.

Shel and Rick dropped by after the first bottle, and we raged for another hour or so. Halfway through the last one, I stumbled out into the street with Dave and Shel in tow. Luke had passed out on my bed, and Rick was finishing off the last bottle or two by himself.

The air suddenly shimmered and blurred, and I lurched into the blue recycling bins at the edge of the curb, cutting my forehead. Tears were streaming down my face, but I was silent, almost serene. Perfect Moment.

And then I let out an immediate howl of pain that scorched my ears and broke my larynx, echoing into the cool night air.

Dave grabbed me and held me close. Shel stared at us like a zombie.

That was nearly two years ago.

After grabbing a twenty-dollar cab ride home from Finch station, I staggered through the back door of my home, disabling the burglar alarm. My parents, my sister were asleep. I crawled into the downstairs washroom and threw up for the last time. Dun-coloured glop all over the side of the bowl. Yet another job for the Toilet Duck, I guess.

Sigh.

Here's a secret: Mina was not *truly* the root of my loss of will and passion, drained out of me like so much as oil from a sinking supertanker. Or maybe it was like a tumour being re-moved from an infected brain. Do you know what they do to tumours? Current methods of treatment are actually fairly primitive. Your brain is much like an undercooked egg – not particularly solid, much of it. To remove the tumour, surgeons either cook the tumour and pick it out like a scab, frying thou-sands of healthy neurons nearby, or vacu-suck it out, also taking along thousands of other healthy neurons.

Either way, it involves a sort of lobotomy. I feel in many ways that I have undergone such a procedure, that the emotional disaster with Mina ("*the tumour*") has taken much of my brain, also taking my will and passion by accident. *Gee, that sounds cool, doesn't it?*

The guys used to joke around about Electroconvulsive Shock therapy as a cure for my excessive negative thinking. Only now, I do not think it was a joke. I think it actually happened. It really happened. I am convinced now that the old Mike Chao was eliminated by Electroconvulsive Shock therapy, fried out of my mind by a single, intense episode.

A week after she admitted to cheating on me, she sought me out in the hallways of the CPH "just to talk". *Jesus Christ Almighty, what the fuck **was** it with women? They screw you over in the most unreasonable way, and then they want to **talk** about it…*

"I did it because you're so unhappy all the time," she said.

"I just can't take this anymore," she said.

"You drove me to this, I'm sorry," she said.

I shook my head violently. "Uh uh, *no!* Let's get this straight – there's *no* fucking way you're going to turn it around and pin this on *me!* *You* hurt *me*, you got that? After giving you my heart, you turn around and *eat* it, you…you fucking *bitch!*" I yelled. Back then, I never believed in strong, silently suffering hero types, so I yelled. I yelled, I yelled, I yelled some more.

Shocked, and used to me being quiet and docile, Mina started to cry. "I didn't *drive* you to this! I didn't, God damn you! *You* cheated on *me*! *You* betrayed *me*, because you're a spineless slut!" It was obvious I was attracting some serious bystander attention, but I kept yelling anyway. Stopping would have meant dealing with an awkward silence punctuated by her sobs.

"I can't believe I was *stupid* enough to consider marrying you! But you were too selfish and scared to deal with me! I've never been anything but good to you, and you fuck me over! And now you have the *nerve* to want me to feel bad about 'driving' you to cheat on me! Well, *fuck you!* FUCK YOU!"

She was wailing now. Some asshole that fancied himself peacemaker and protector of all weak and frail women came over and shoved me. "Calm down, buddy," he grunted, "she's feeling bad enough…"

"I have a better idea, 'buddy'! Why don't you mind your own fucking business?" I suggested, waving my fist inches from his face. Before that, I'd never threatened another human being. "You don't have a *clue* what she did to me – not a fucking *clue*! So go back to yer *damn* horse and yer *damn* shining armour and leave me the fuck alone!" I stomped off towards a washroom, tears of rage streaking my flushed face. I felt dizzy. I had never expended that much vitriol at a single time in my entire life. Bawling someone out required a spectacular amount of air.

I walked away from that day feeling like every vital fluid had been leeched out. And whatever she did not take, my anger had burned up in a single disastrous atmosphere re-entry. I felt raped, emotionally raped, my innermost emotions and hopes and fears violated, betrayed. But that's silly, isn't it? Society dictates that men cannot be raped or violated. I once had this radical feminist sociology teacher who ranted that men could never be raped, could never understand the feeling of being raped. Men only *perpetrate* in this society, you see; we are never victims, because of some stupid infrastructure our forefathers set up a long time ago, that has reduced us from being people to conveniently stereotyped unit groups with no individual value.

After it was all said and done, the emptiness pervaded me. I felt helpless, hopeless, completely unshielded and vulnerable to every foible life and love could possibly throw.

I guess the reason why I cannot approach Love at the same levels I approached it before is because experience has taught me that it's the only emotion with the one, true key to your soul. I know it sounds kind of corny, but it is true.

The fact is this: releasing that key unlocked something so beautiful it was terrible, so powerful it was horrible. Love manifests itself in so many extremes – happiness, sadness, desire, anger, depression, rage. I am scared of the person that *was* me – he was so intense, so extreme, that it was frightening beyond reason. The person I am now looks at the person I was, and I do not like him. It's not that I particularly like the person I am right *now*, but I'm telling you that *he* was ten thousand times worse – passionate, ignorant, undisciplined, immature. Vulnerable.

So I decided I had to be stereotypically inscrutable. The Inscrutable Chinaman, The Silence of Generations. Lock it all up. Never let anyone else inside, that deep, forever. Do you understand? *Never.* I swore it, I swore it on my pain. The pain almost became sacred to me, holy, tender. The pain served to remind me that as empty as I was, I can only truly be filled with myself, with things of value that I can honestly call my own. Not a woman. Never a woman. Cruelty is a woman's gift. She brings it to me like a bleeding flower which cuts my hands, my heart, my soul. Her clean, pure face beams into mine, only to reveal fangs that will devour all that is precious within me. The fickle hunger that is only a woman's. The unfaithfulness that is theirs to give, with change.

But of course this isn't the answer. I am still very sick. I know this. And I honestly wonder if I'll ever get better. It seems, sometimes, that I never will. I just want to give up. God, I wish I could just step on a bus bound for nowhere in particular, fall asleep for a long, long time, and end up somewhere else where no one knows me, no one cares, with nothing but time to work it out.

part 3
hysteresis.

Welcome To Slavery.

Shit!" exclaimed Lehanna, slapping the monitor of our PC outside the studio.

"Luke," Scab said over the mike as a *Frontline Assembly* song roared to an end, "Lehanna's having a serious problem with the PC – she can't get at the newswire service." Lehanna bellowed in rage in the background, overturning her chair and stomping around in a serious huff.

"*...and that was* Frontline Assembly," I announced, giving Scab the OK sign through the booth glass. "*The time is 7 am on the Morning Mosh, and now for the news. Lehanna's unavailable because she's...she's, ah...taking a shit. So yours truly'll be giving you the news this hour...yeah.*"

I scratched my head. "*Um, yeah. Okay...news – absolutely nothing happened yesterday. Traffic? Nope, no traffic, weather? None o' that either.* **Okay!** *On to the important stuff, more music – here's, uh – ummm...here's some* Rage Against the Machine. *Which is exactly what our staff'll be doing all this hour...*" I slapped the off switch, and Scab gave me a weak thumbs up. Behind him, Lehanna and Zeesh were not looking particularly pleased.

"What?" I inquired.

"'*Taking a **shit**'?*" said Lehanna, extremely ticked. "For God's sake, Luke, you could have said I was *drunk* or something..."

"Luke, what the *fuck* was that?" demanded Zeesh.

"Reflex, Zeesh, sorry, okay?"

"All right, Lehanna, you've got a half hour to get copies of the *Star* and *Now* from the corner store, and that's our news, okay?"

Lehanna took off like a shot, still grumbling.

He turned to me. "Luke, that was pretty stupid, you know."

"Reflex," I repeated. "Look, I'll make it up to you. I have a friend who knows this computer stuff. I'll get him to fix the machine by 8 am – 8:30, max. Okay?"

Zeesh shook his head and left the booth.

Ah, fuck him.

I set up an extra-long remix of a *Skinny Puppy* song, and then called Dave at home. As I recalled, he usually he didn't get up until 10 am or so.

"Hello?"

"Dave, it's me, Luke."

"*Hello?*"

"I need your help, man. Bad."

"Yeah, whatever, Stick. What the fuck is it, anyway? Only got four hours of sleep…"

"Can you come down here and check our computer? It's down, and we can't get at our newswire service."

"Shit, Luke, call the 1-800 number!"

"I've got a pair of tickets to see *Def Leppard* at Maple Leaf Gardens next week with yer name on 'em."

There was a short pause at Dave's end.

"I'll be over in ten." *Click.*

Dave arrived at the station dressed really poorly – checked Umbro soccer shorts, a ski jacket atop a threadbare T-shirt, dirty ball cap, and a scowl that could have melted zinc. "The concert seats'd better be damn good ones, Stick," he warned. "Any coffee?"

I tossed him my thermos of JetFuel™ java as he sat down in front of the dead terminal, shaking the fresh January snow off of his jacket.

Within five minutes, the machine was up and running, much to Lehanna's elation, who squealed and gave him a huge kiss. Shocked, Dave recoiled, and Lehanna ran into the DJ booth with fresh printouts in time for the 7:30 news.

"The monitor plug fell out," Dave explained.

I looked at him incredulously. "That's it?"

"Yup. The rubber's split at the end of the plug. Does she move the monitor around a lot?"

"Yeah…she likes different views of the office every so often."

Dave rolled his eyes. "Pretty stupid. I ended up jury rigging the thing back on with duct tape." I smiled. Dave was the consummate engineer; he always used duct tape to solve his problems. And alcohol. "Simple problem – it's so *like* you artsy-types to miss it. Now where are the tickets?" Dave stuck out his hand.

"I'll get them to your office by noon today – I still have to wrangle them off of a friend who works at the Q." Dave frowned. "Don't worry, man, I swear I'll get them to you. Buy you lunch, too."

"Swiss Chalet?" he said, softening his expression.

"Anything you want. Look, I gotta get back on the air. Thanks again, man." I went back into the booth, giving Dave the thumbs up sign. He shrugged and left.

Dave and I have gotten into a lot of fights since we've known each other, culminating in the Mother-Of-All-Arguments during what he calls his Bad Times™. But we've weathered them, and we're still friends.

In many ways, we're polar opposites. He's a techie; I'm an artsy. He drinks beer; I drink "girl-drinks." He's a chauvinist; I'm a feminist. And he likes classic rock, of all things. A while ago, I heard these intensely cerebral lyrics when I brought the bike to the shop, and I immediately thought of Dave in high-school: hockey hair, wearing one of those black metal shirts with short white sleeves, cigarette pack stuck up the right shoulder, drinking Labatt 50 in the back of a pickup truck…

> *Infamous butcher, Angel of Death*
> *Monarch to the Kingdom of the Dead!*
> *Sadistic surgeon of demise, Satan of the noblest blood,*
> *Surgery without anesthesia*
> *The way that I want you to die!*

I ended up sending him a copy of the lyrics via e-mail, earning three middle fingers on a scale of five.

Dave hates my music. "Christ man, there's nothing I hate more than that yoyoyo-homeboy Hip Hop garbage you love so much."

"Breaks is not Hip Hop, Dave."

"Whatever. It's almost as bad as that industrial-alternative stuff you play at your station. I mean, how the *hell* can you listen to that shit?" He says the last bit emphatically, as if he were at a diesel fuel buffet or something. "What are you, a masochist? Why don't you listen to something, like, you know, normal?"

"Dave, I hardly think that the crap you listen to is considered 'normal'."

"Them's fightin' words, Stick."

Dave thinks I listen to harsh, violent, unforgiving music to punish myself, to make up for my sense of effete insufficiency. He thinks I listen to it because it is powerful and compelling ... and I am not. Interesting theory. Maybe it holds some credence.

Over the years, we've sort of developed a 'Jo-Blair'-type relationship, you know, from *The Facts of Life* – contentious and abrasive on the outside, with odd moments of tenderness. He's a pretty good friend, but I can't resist bugging him about certain things, because the reactions I get from him are just too rich.

For example, Dave is almost militantly lowbrow. And I tease him about that, because I don't believe he's half the hick he wants us to believe he is. A perfect Dave-ism: he likes to joke that he's an "orangeneck," meaning an Asian redneck with yellow skin. Get it?

The largest source of tension between us is his rampant homophobia and blatant misogyny, especially against Asian women. I strongly suspect that this anger stems from the fact that he's just sexually frustrated.

"Luke, you can't deny that there are whole whacks of these pathetic white-boys who have a fetish for Orientals, and that *sucks*," he spat at me over a few drinks about a week ago.

"That's ridiculous. What's it to you, anyway?"

"It's an attraction based on racist myth and misconception, and that impacts all of us as yellows in this country. You know,

Jungle Fever and all that stuff. White people don't go out with the *person*, they go out with the *culture*, or rather their misconceptions of the culture. And things aren't helped when these stupid little China Girls pander to this sort of thinking."

"*I* think you're just jealous."

"*You'd* be jealous too, if you didn't only fuck Indian women."

"Watch it, caveman." I tried another tack. "Why any self-respecting guy would waste two seconds of time on any woman so stupid that they would date someone specifically because of their race is *completely* beyond my comprehension. Anyone can date whomever they damn well please, and your whining isn't going to change anything. Everyone has the free will to make a *choice*…"

"Oh yeah…a *choice*," Dave said sarcastically. "These Asian chicks are making a well-informed, non-biased *choice* – a vibrant, powerful *choice*, as a vibrant, powerful Woman o' the New Millenium. It's the choice of a new generation, throwing off the shackles of evil-Chinese-guy patriarchy – whether it's actually there or not."

"Sarcasm's the lowest form of humour, Dave."

"Yes, but it's the only form you'll understand. It just pisses me off when these chicks are obviously camouflaging their own racism and ignorance with a progressive veneer." He batted his eyes and mocked viciously. "*Yoo hoooo! Look at meeeee. Look at the powerful Asian chick! I AM a powerful individual, I AM choice and freedom incarnate! I CHOOSE to embrace the inherent goodness of the white guy …*"

"For God's sake, Dave, keep your voice down."

"*…and I CHOOSE to reject the evil inherent in that bad, bad culture!*" He downed his beer in disgust. "Never mind if that so-called 'vibrant, powerful' choice is fundamentally flawed with prejudice within itself – hey, it's *cause célèbre*, it sells books, it's 'Oriental Girl Power, Spice Up Your Life!'"

"Asian, Dave – use the term 'Asian'. It's more politically correct."

"*Fuck* politically correct, we're Canadians. Quick, Stick, how many Oriental girls do you see with white guys? Like, a lot? How many of us guys do you see with white girls? Like none?"

"That's pure bullshit, Dave," I said. "You're just being an idiot. *I've* gone out with more Caucasian women than Asian women, for goodness sake."

"Virtually none," he amended, "But you're a statistical freak. Beyond that, the disparity is blatantly obvious, too, unless you're blind or fanatically PC."

"Shallowness isn't the proprietary domain of women, you know. Not even close. There are plenty of Asian dudes who only go for Caucasian girls…"

"You're absolutely correct," he replied. "Oriental guys who only go for white girls are even *worse*. Especially the ones who *can*. They're the types who say, '*Yep, Asian guys are losers, but I'm not, and I can get white chicks, so I'm waaay better than alla youse*.' But the fact remains that our kind gets a raw deal all over. We're these asexual computer geeks or evil criminals or house-boys with no allure because the media, society as a whole, paints us that way. Asian women are so balled up with these images of blond frat-boys as the masculine ideal when they're young that they grow up to snub their own kind in favour of guys named Brock Landers or Chest Rockwell."

"Ah. Right," I said with half-closed eyes, "Asian women are so weak-willed and weak-minded that they can easily be pro-grammed by society to be self-loathing, cultureless twinkies who only lust after white guys and despise Asian men. Whereas Asian men, of course, are not so weak-willed…"

"Give me a fucking break, Mr. Liberal-Sensitive-Ponytail. We're *all* weak-willed and weak-minded in a certain way. Every single human bean on this god-forsaken planet – we're *all* pro-grammed by *something* to some degree. Check out how you yourself get this glassy, crazed look in your eyes when you're spouting your feminist dogma, slavishly arguing for the honour of women everywhere. It's pure possession. The only escape from this is beer."

"God, you're a moron."

"Cheers, Stick."

It was times like those I had to remind myself that there are many good things about him. To be fair, there are. He was honourable, for example – if he incurred a debt, emotional or financial, Dave'd pay you back, or die trying. He'll stick out his neck to help his friends, like he did this morning. He's down-to-earth, in the trenches – if he sees someone suffering unjustly, he'll get his hands dirty to alleviate that injustice. Okay, he was an all-around decent fellow, moronic male machismo aside.

After the *Mosh*, I called Seth and asked him to pick up Dave's concert tickets from my friend at the Q and deliver them to the station.

He woke me up in the lounge. "Johnny said that it'd cost you some tix to the upcoming *Nine Inch Nails* concert," he said, passing me the envelope.

"No probs, we're getting some comps tomorrow. Thanks, dude." *Zeesh is going to kill me.*

"No sweat. DING DING DING DING DING! Time to light'em up." I closed the lounge door and put a towel on the floor to cover the crack.

The January freeze sobered me up as I walked to Dave's office. I found him yawning, still drinking from the thermos of JetFuel™ he'd snarfed from me.

"The tickets for the thermos, you scammer."

"With pleasure. I don't go for this fancy shmancy artsy-guy coffee." The exchange was made, and we headed into the bitter cold up Yonge St. to the rotisserie chicken restaurant.

"Looks like Shel's found hisself a girlie," Dave grunted, lighting a cigarette after sitting down. He offered me one. "Death Stick, Stick?"

"Thanks." I accepted the death stick and sat back, blowing a few rings. "Well good for him. So when's the happy date?"

"I asked him the same thing, and he just hemmed and hawed," shrugged Dave. "But I'm sure it's coming – our last phone conversation was alarmingly peppered with '*Kathy says…*' and other such puppydog nonsense."

"Whipped?"

"*Pistol*-whipped is more like it." Dave gestured with his cigarette in frustration. "It seems like everybody around me is getting hitched and/or whipped in one way or another. One day we're staggering drunk out of the Bomber and pissing outside East Quad, the next moment they're morphed into these repulsive husband types with zero-capacity for the important things in life. Like beer."

"And whining," I added, grinning. Dave made a face, but let it pass. "I know what you mean. Well, take heart, my friend …Michael and myself aren't hooked up yet."

"That's hardly any consolation. Mike's guaranteed to end up in a suburban family lifestyle someday, and you're obviously gay."

I had to laugh at that one.

Dave sighed ruefully. "Love Bites."

"Love Bleeds," I joined in.

A pause.

"*It's bringing me to my knees!*" we both bellowed, much to the shock of the patrons in the restaurant.

"What a great song," approved Dave, chuckling.

The thing I found surprising about Dave was that he was curiously timid when it came to women. Back at school, you would always see him hunched at a table with his beer, strangely averting his gaze from the dance floor, or at a dance club with Michael, hugging the wall with their backs, clutching a longneck by the neck, looking with a combination of lust and uncertainty.

"'*Marge, you know how bashful I am,*'" Dave would say sarcastically in his Homer Simpson-voice. "'*I can't even say the word 'titmouse' without giggling like a schoolgirl…tee hee hee!*'"

Not that he could hope for any success the way he's been dressing lately. The last few times I've seen him, he's been something of a mess. He'd lost his ugly Umbro shorts, thank goodness, only to replace them with a torn pair of Gap jeans. Plaid work shirt, tails hanging out. Favourite ball cap, worked in like anything, of course, jammed on his head. Stubble from not having shaved for two days. And he was slightly overweight to top it all off…'Jo-Blair' we may act like, but we actually resembled Laurel and Hardy.

"Yeah, I know," he acknowledged. "Part of it's work; part of it's apathy. I've even taken to wearing (*ugh*) track pants lately, because I've been a little out of shape, and it kind of hurts my gut when I wear my 'cool' pairs of slacks and jeans. It's exactly like that classic line from *Seinfeld* – '*Wearing track pants is like telling the world: 'Look, I give up, so I might as well be comfortable'.*'"

"You give up?"

"Yeah. I guess that's a sad attitude, but there it is. I'm at an age where chicks are either going to like me – or they're not. If they do, I'll be aware of it; if they don't, well, that's okay too and pass the pork rinds." The food came, and we started eating.

"Look, man, I just don't care anymore," he said, pouring sauce over his fries. "No, that's a lie. I *do* care, but I just can't be bothered with it anymore. And *that's* the truth."

"Spoken like a true person who hasn't gotten any for two years."

"Fuck off, Luke."

Actually, it seemed that all of the guys had this penchant for unworkable relationships – except for Rick, of course, but it's common knowledge that he treated relationships with little substantiality, anyway. The rest of us all seemed to bumble along, cluelessly searching, *nookin' po nub in aw de wong paces*, getting stung, getting hurt, getting drunk.

Personally, I don't particularly think it's a bad thing being single, but it does have repercussions. Dave continually gives me flak about it, and I believe Sheldon suspects that I'm gay.

"Zoinks, Dave, get this through your terminally pickled skull," I said, washing my hand in the little finger-bowls they gave out, "not everyone wants a significant other."

"Oh, get off your high horse. *Everyone* wants a girlfriend, even you, Stick. You're just rationalizing like the rest of us." His comments actually irritated me – it was one of the few hot buttons that Dave was able to push.

The truth (*and it is, dammit*) is that I believe it's vitally important to be alone. At certain times, at least. Being alone is therapeutic…cleansing, purifying, if you will. Life is so much less complicated when you're alone. Things are clearer. I believe that if you're unable to deal with being alone, then you can't possibly deal with being *together*. That makes sense, doesn't it? One ultimately has to have satisfaction with the self, bride-stripped-bare of all connections and relationships, before truly benefiting from the presence of a significant other.

It follows that I am still alone because I still haven't come to grips with Sonja. Fine, fine. "*Do as I say; Not as I Do*".

Our station's frequency is located dangerously close to a polka station. We've petitioned the CRTC to get it changed, but to no avail. So, say if you had your walkman set to CMSH, and it was jogged around in your knapsack or something, you might turn it on one day and find yourself listening to *Hermann Schweitzberg and his Barrel Buddies*. More than one listener had called in to say that our alternative-experimental format had gone too far.

"This situation," said Zel after today's *Mosh*, "is unacceptable."

"Well, Zel, there isn't all that much we can do."

"Polka is *evil*. It is *Satanic*. It is *Satan's* music, don't you see? Distilled straight from the testicles of Satan himself."

"*Eugh.*" I recoiled slightly. "Well, I'm not exactly sure what we can…"

"*You'll* stop it, won't you Luke? You'll exorcise this abomination from my presence? Won't you Luke? Luke, you *must*. You are my firstborn, heir to the throne. Destroy this evil and purge the earth."

"Sure, Zel, all right," I sighed. She went back into her office and started screaming at the wall. I'm *really* getting too old for this.

Outside, Zeesh was on the newly-fixed PC, typing up some sort of official-looking letter with his index fingers. "What's up?" I asked.

He grunted. "Some league of blue-haired little old ladies is taking us to court because *The Morning Mosh* and its evil DJ [he glared at me meaningfully] apparently swore a lot on the air and was promoting satanic practices involving pigs and pork and such." Zeesh had been running on a short fuse against me lately, mostly because the long national nightmare of PorkGate still hadn't died off. The Johnny Fever-type situation wasn't going to up my standings with him much.

"*And stop playing that damned* Pork *record!*" he bellowed after me as I left for the day.

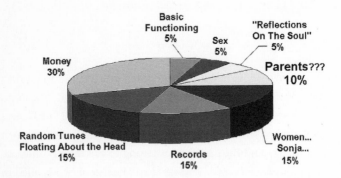

Fig. 7. Luke's BrainChart™ (as of Jan 17th)

Today, I received a letter from Sonja. She's in Edmonton working as a dental assistant, and apparently engaged. (How…nice.) But not to a nice *raj* – her fiancé sounded as WASP as WASP can be. She wants me to go out to attend her wedding in July. I have mixed feelings about this.

"About her fiancé being a WASP?" Michael asked incredulously over the phone.

"No, of course not," I said, irritation creeping into my voice. "About going to the wedding."

"Oh."

"Well," I said after a slight pause, "Maybe a *little*…"

"I am very surprised," Michael said tonelessly. "You're always ragging on Dave and me for our sexist views about interracial dating and such."

That was true. But then my mind flashed to our final words about a year ago, before she took off for parts out west.

"That's, um, a lot of condoms," I commented dispassionately, helping her load the last milk crate of personal items into her Bug.

She smiled lightly. "They'll get used." That stung me a little, but I deserved it. It was, after all, entirely my fault.

"By whom?"

She shrugged. "I really don't know."

"Maybe you'll find a nice *raj* out there. Have a nice Indian ceremony or something. Ganesh has been subdued."

She chuckled, despite it all. "Maybe. Maybe not." She batted her long eyelashes in a way that made me want to kidnap her and keep her forever. "It'd probably be easier that way, you know, with my parents out there. Knowing them, they probably have a list of arranged possibilities the length of my arm."

"I'm sure it'll all work out…" We kissed for the last time, and then she was off.

"…*my Love*."

Apparently, a significant portion of The Book™ deals with sexism against Asian men in Western society. It's a topic that I've argued about with both Dave and Michael many times, but not with a hell of a lot of enthusiasm.

"Think about it, Luke," Michael said. "Our image is really, really poor out there. In fact, it couldn't suck any worse. The archetype for the Asian male is weak, unmasculine, unappealing, morally corrupt, and generally ignored – geez, why *else* do you never see Asian guys in movies or TV shows, despite there being a half a billion of us on this planet? And if you ever see them, they're in these ridiculously brain-dead stereotypical Chinaman roles like martial artists, mathematicians or Yakuza gangsters."

"That's not true."

"No? Name one leading Asian male actor in a Hollywood movie this year?"

"Jackie Chan."

"Martial Artist."

"Okay, Chow Yun-Fat."

"Yakuza gangster."

"He's a *good* guy."

"Yakuza-*like* then. Where are the normal schlubs, you know, like us? The doctors, the engineers, the Hip Hop DJs." I let it pass. Mike shook his head in frustration. "We're not *there*. We're *nowhere*. And the result is marginalization of our kind – learned helplessness. We learn to accept our lot in life as the invisible, hard-working minority, good only for programming computers or delivering flounder. That's the *truth*."

No, it *wasn't*. I'll **tell** you the truth.

We are at the apex of the male-dominated civilization, and *that's* the truth. Life is a cakewalk for men, especially compared to the lot that women have faced over thousands of years. No media roles? *Wah*. Can't get a date? *Boo hoo*. Culturally emasculated? *What good is a penis, anyway?* It's so special interest, it boggles the mind that people as smart as Mike or Dave would even *consider* worrying about it.

The marginalization that Michael may write about and Dave constantly complains about is, quite frankly, trivial compared to the fundamental lack of safety and respect women face, even in this enlightened Age of Aquarius. Let's take this hypothetical situation as an example:

Scenario 1

Stimulus: A female student comes home from a hard day of classes, sits down, has a glass of orange juice. The house is empty. The phone rings. She picks it up. "Hello?" A man's voice.

Stimulus: "You don't know me, but I know you well. I've been watching you. I fantasize about you. I am thinking of you now. You are in front of me. You are taking off your clothes…"

Response: Shock. Panic. A cold sweat. A scream. The more desensitized may manage a weak croak, or the false bravado of a "fuck you," but it's not real.

Response: She slams the receiver on its hook. It shakes. She shakes. Raw, naked fear. Frustration. Violation.

Scenario 2

Stimulus: A male student comes home from a hard day of classes, sits down, has a glass of orange juice (all right, a beer). The house is empty. The phone rings. He picks it up. "Hello?" A woman's voice.

Stimulus: "You don't know me, but I know you well. I've been watching you. I fantasize about you. I am thinking of you now. You are in front of me. You are taking off your clothes…"

Response: "Oh, yeah, really?" "What else?" "Who is this?"
"Tell me more. Baby." "Where are you? Can I come
over?" "Are you free for dinner tonight?"
Response: Interest, curiosity. Arousal? An anecdote for
the boys at the bar later that night. The lucky *dog*.

Fig. 8. Men Suck.

"Michael," I countered, "we live in a patriarchal society, with patriarchal norms, patriarchal expectations. You cannot combat sexism against men unless sexism in general is addressed – and *surprise*, most of it is still directed at women." He was silent, so I continued. "Just look around, dude – the structures are laid out in a society where women's actions, their thoughts, the way they dress even, are still largely prescribed through assumptions and stereotypes, and enforced through fear and violence. Sexual harassment. Glass ceilings. Spousal abuse. Seven raped women in Scarborough. Two dead girls in St. Catharines. Fourteen dead engineers in Montreal. Dead solely because of their gender. Good God."

Would you let your younger sister walk home alone late at night in this city? Even if it was just a half-hour away? Fifteen minutes? I'd sooner cut my throat than let Janice do it. And that angers me. It burns me up. To the fucking bone. So don't tell me Asian guys have it bad in this world. The fact is, we have it far too good.

Woke up this morning with *Xanadu* on the brain. Looks like it's going to be a bad day.

Song title	Artist	Naked or Savour?
Xanadu	Olivia Newton-John	Neither

Fig. 9. Neither.

Shuffling off my futon, I popped on some *U2* to erase the evil from my head, and pretty soon I'm air-guitaring to classic Edge-riffs, savouring Bono's painful, angst-filled vocals. The song was so soulful, so mellow, the pain so thick in his voice that it made my back teeth ache just hearing it. *Perfect.* Before my electronic music kick, I can remember going to *U2* concerts all the time, back when their shows could still be held at Massey Hall – they'd have their trademark white flag flying on top. It was a religious experience. At the end of the concert, they'd wind up playing "40," and the crowd would chant along with them, and for hours and hours afterward in the neighbouring streets, bars, subway cars…*How long/To sing this song?/How long/To sing this song…?*

I liked *U2* best when they were incessantly questioning in their music, yearning for truth. There's something beautiful about yearning. It's the recognition of imperfection. It implies a quest for some sort of meaning. In yearning, the present itself may not be beautiful, but the process yields something far more precious and enduring. I guess that sums up Michael. It's his yearning that shines through his constant depression, somehow saving him, preventing him from being merely a loser.

"Thanks, I think," he said, scratching his head. "You know, my high school English teacher once said that all tragic figures in literature, like Hamlet or Macbeth, had to have some sort of redeeming quality, something noble about them, like yearning; otherwise, they would merely be idiots. Not that I think I'm noble or anything," he added hastily.

"But you're certainly self-effacing," I said. "Grab some pride, Michael. You're a great guy." That made him smile, if only a little.

I thought about Rick, whose yearnings I never fully understood, except that he probably hid it in his hell-bent-for-leather quest for material success. And his drinking. I think it was his antithesis for the Golden-Boy-Chipper routine he gave out 95 percent of the time. The drinking was the one thing that worried me the most. I mean, Dave has always made a big deal about loving alcohol and all that, but there was still a fathomable level of control: somehow, you just *knew* that. With Rick, I was never as certain.

One time, we left an Oktoberfest celebration early, from a beer hall somewhere downtown. Waterloo has the largest Oktoberfest outside of Germany, and the Banana Boys were usually there in force, representing approximately three-quarters the Asian contingent among the football players, drunk girls from Nova Scotia, old people in lederhosen. Michael and I were walking Rick back to our apartment because he had downed a whole pitcher of beer under a minute and then did the funky chicken dance while taking off his clothes. We were kicked out for that, of course.

"Raw deal," he slurred, putting his clothes back on in the parking lot. "I was just about to arrange a threesome with these girls, like."

"They were pretty sweet," Michael offered wistfully, hands jammed in his pockets.

"Yes, they were. And the Oktoberfest Nazis had to flex their muscle, mess it all up." He spoke calmly but suddenly, in a fit of drunken rage, he put his fist through the window of an unsuspecting Geo. Michael and I gaped at him in utter shock as he proceeded to rummage in the broken glass for a ring that had come off, despite all the blood spurting from an ugly looking wound.

A silence flitted across the parking lot.

"Nice," I said, simply.

"Yeah, like a shot of pepper spray in the face is nice!" Michael gibbered. "Jesus *Christ*, Luke, how can you deadpan something like this...?"

"It's just my way, okay?" I snapped, losing it for a nano-second but immediately gaining it back. "Okay. This is not good, not good."

"I need a Band-Aid," Rick said plaintively.

We ended up securing Rick's wound with my flannel and hailing a cab to the hospital.

"I think I cut an artery." Rick looked at me serenely, the epitome of drunken logic. "I vaguely remember something about living for fifteen minutes after you cut an artery. What time is it?"

"Time to shut up," I suggested.

About three minutes from death, he was sewn up. Cost: one cut artery, one cut vein, a few nerves, and a cast for two months

– making him the darling of more than a few women, I might add. And my eternal fear that he was going to eventually kill himself with his drinking one day.

Hardware, my favourite trance DJ hands-down, was headlining at a rave thrown by one of the better production companies in the city. I don't really go to raves all that often anymore, unless I'm actually playing, but I *had* to see Hardware, and the locals lineup included some personal Breaks faves – Marty McFly, Big League Chu, Robb G, D-Monic. Filing into the west-end warehouse venue, I observe the usual rave crowd with disinterest: hordes of ballcap, phat-pants and suede-shoe wearing sub-brats, ready to get seriously fucked up on non-alphabetic substances. Sketchy kids. The scene sure has changed: *"It used to be about the music, man."*

I went with Seth to the party, who handed me a pair of earplugs in the lineup outside. I rejected them – wouldn't have done any good, anyway. My hearing is already practically obliterated. The last I checked, my hearing was pegged at no lower than 90 decibels, about six points higher than the average, and rising as fast as Dave's cholesterol levels. The concerts of my youth were catching up to me. By the age of 65, they'll have to wheel in bagpipes and land mines to get my attention, I think.

Big League was spectacular, throwing down a set of Breaks so hard and funky, I almost threw my back out. Next, Hardware came up to spin. And he put on an incredible set. Breaks is my current passion, but Trance will always be my first love. It's what I started with; it's become fundamental to the spirit. It detaches you from your surroundings, transporting you to another place, one completely different than the mechanical drudge of the real world outside. Looking around, it seems like people styling to Trance often reach their arms upward, as if they're trying to drink in a vastness that didn't physically exist in the typically crowded warehouse environment. That's the beauty of Trance music…it creates an illusion of space above you, a sort of intersection between heaven and earth.

Hardware definitely put a million percent into his sets, and after a mere four tracks, the dance floor was a roiling mass of chemically-happy youth, a maelstrom of glowsticks, water bottles, sweat, Blue Butterflies. In the middle of the anthemic buildup in "Out of the Blue", I suddenly stopped and looked around at the madness, blinking, feeling a lump develop in my stomach that burst out in form of a sob. Seth and the sub-brats around me were too preoccupied swaying and screaming in approval to notice.

I didn't really understand it. It was crazy, wonderful, dream-like, like always…but there was the pain inside of me.

I tried to figure out what had happened as I rode the subway home in the early morning, ears ringing. It was atypical, to say the least. I don't think it was about Sonja. But it may have been about my parents.

It's been, what, sixteen years? Since he left us? Two years since I've talked to mom, ever since I dropped out of hell – I mean *school*. Me downtown, her uptown. The rare, terse phone call now and then, usually orchestrated by Janice. Like a credit card with a late, late due date, it kind of catches up to you after a while. "*Buy now, pay later.*" So when I got back to the 808 State at around 9:30 am, I called her. Just Out Of The Blue, after two years.

"*Wei?*"

"Hi, mom."

"Yes? Luke, is that you?" She sounded mildly surprised.

Only mildly? "Er, yeah. How are you?"

"Fine, *bao*. What's up?"

I smiled slightly from behind the receiver. 'What's up' was a purely Western term I got her using years ago. "Um, not much. Work and all that." I took a deep breath. "I was wondering if you'd like to have dinner sometime this week? Like Thursday or something?"

"Yes, *bao*, that's fine. Where would you like to meet?"

"Um, how about *Hsin Sei Gai*?" It was the only Chinese restaurant I could remember. "What say I pick you up at six?"

"On your motorcycle?" she asked, suddenly disapproving. "*Ni ji dao…*"

"No no, I'll borrow a car!" I snapped back irritably. Sigh. *She'd ridden a bike for years.* "So six, okay mom?"

"*Hao*," she said shortly. "Don't be late." She promptly hung up, leaving me hanging onto my receiver, regretting the whole matter ever-so-slightly.

So I'm sitting here at the Chinese restaurant, sipping on one of those little cups of tea, looking across the table at my mom, who's smoking a Viscount Mild. Still a very pretty woman, my mother – thin, well-dressed, lustrous black hair. A little puffy around the eyes. Still had her own eyebrows, though, unlike many other Chinese women her age who had them tattooed on.

"How are things at the travel agency?" I asked.

"Busy," she replied simply, in English, taking another drag at her Death Stick. "How is the radio station?"

"So-so. Not bad." I bobbed my head a little.

We sat and looked at each other awkwardly. Fortunately, the waiter came by, so we ordered some dishes and a few bowls of rice.

"Well. *[Insert a contrived cough here]* I saw Janice a while ago."

"I know. She told me about it."

"Uh, yeah. She seems to be doing fine with Lewis…her job's good…"

"I know. She calls once a week," she said. *Like a good, responsible daughter*, she implied. I gritted my teeth behind the teacup.

We sat and looked at each other. The waiter came by with the rice.

"So…"

"Why did you ask me to dinner?"

"Erm…" I fumbled with my words. Weird how mom was

the only person who made me do that. "Erm, I guess I just wanted to see you. That's all. It's been a long time."

She nodded, lighting up another damn cigarette.

"Any problems with all this, *Ma*?" She just looked at me, so I went on, starting to get a little pissed off. "Want to vent on me a little, for old times sake?"

"You sound like your father," she said in English, looking at me through half-closed eyes.

"And this, of course, is a bad thing."

She nodded. "It is. You know that. It wouldn't be as bad if it just stopped there," she said, switching to Mandarin, "but it doesn't. Character never changes. Only attitudes do."

Argh. Homilies. "I didn't really want to get into your personal problems tonight, mom."

"What do you expect?" she shot back. A familiar old bitterness crawled back into her voice. "I didn't create these problems. Your father did. *You* did. I'm Chinese – I remember things. Sixteen years is not a long time. Two years is not, either. You both disappointed me."

"Get over it, mom."

Her eyes narrowed into two cyanide-filled syringes. "*Huang-un fu yi...*I can see you're just the same. That doesn't change. You could have been different, *but...*" I braced myself, expecting her to fire the old 'dropping out of school' salvo. It didn't happen.

"Forget it," she said. "Just forget it. You're just your father, basic character. Irresponsible. All impulse, no consideration. Always running. No future." She stubbed her cigarette in the ashtray and got up. "I'm asking the waiter to wrap the meal up. Take it home and have it for lunch tomorrow. I'm not hungry."

*Damn. Who **says** getting yelled at in Mandarin was better than Cantonese?* "Aw, Jesus Christ, mom, will you sit down and just eat?"

"No."

Severe Tire Damage.

I'm sitting here with Jase (who's stupidly but proudly wearing his Montreal Canadiens jersey), and Markandandrew in the cheap seats at the Air Canada Centre, knocking back a few and screaming like idiots along with 16,000 other Leafs fans as Tie Domi proceeds to knock the block off of an unlucky Blackhawk.

"Now *that's* hockey," I bellow for the tenth time.

"Looks like a bar brawl to me," pipes up Mark.

"You only say that because you lack perspective," I say pleasantly. "Marcus me lad, let me tell you something about this great game of ours." I motion to the spirited fracas on the ice. "Fighting is an integral part of this game, a bonafide component, if you will. When fighting happens in football or baseball, or golf or bowling, the people involved get fined and suspended. Only in hockey can grown men go at it like modern gladiators, fists flying and blood bouncing off the ice…and merely be penalized with a few minutes in the box." I sweep my hand to include the legion of fans around us in the cheap seats, spilling their clutched beers, howling for Blackhawk blood. "And you can see that the crowd is getting into it without killing each other. I'd like to see this much emotion without fatalities at an English soccer game."

"*Football*, Dave, the English play *football*." Jase takes off his glasses and polishes them with his jersey. "And blood doesn't 'bounce' off of ice. It just sticks there."

"Yeah, whatever."

The fight ends, with the referee assessing a load of penalties for both teams. Stuff is thrown on the ice and chants of "BULL-SHIT! BULL-SHIT!" echo through the arena as the announcer tells us that the Leaf goaltender has been thrown out of the game for instigation. Raw deal: *I mean, just because he charged the Hawk centreman and tried to butcher him with his stick doesn't* *necessarily mean he **instigated**…*

While the cleaning crews remove the garbage from the ice, the arena dispatched two blimps emblazoned with the Maple Leafs logo to the other side of the rink, floating above the crowd and dropping prizes.

"Now *that*," I say, pointing emphatically, "that's *not* hockey. I mean, this great game is being completely bastardized by cutesey promotional crap like that."

"I think it's cool," says Jase, downing the rest of his light beer.

"It's *stupid*, that's what it is. It's a travesty. Same with all those lasers and fog they put on at the beginning of the game – it's just shameless Hollywood commercialism. This game is turning into a goddamn marketing circus. I mean, what is this, basketball?" I look over to the blimps, floating back to home base. "Besides, those things aren't dropping free stuff on *us*."

"So they aren't."

"Wonder why that could be… ?"

"It's because you're Oriental," confides Jase, jokingly.

"Yeah. Racist blimps."

The Leafs ended up losing to the Blackhawks 4–2, dropping their record to a lousy 15–20–2. We wandered outside to the controlled chaos. Some of the more zealous fans were bitching about the loss, but high-fiving each other because of the big fight. The Leafers sucked, and badly, but on the bright side they had a sociopath for a goaltender.

"*Our Goalie Can Beat Up Your Goalie*" proclaimed one sign, and I stuck my thumb up in appreciation. "Good game, eh fellas?" I crowed. Markandandrew, eternally in their black Waterloo leather jackets, nodded enthusiastically, but Jase was skeptical.

"It was okay, Dave," he said. "But the Leafs are going against the Canadiens tomorrow. If Mon-sewer Goaltender tries that garbage with the Habs, he'll be freshly killed." Jase was a fourth-generation anglicized francophone who couldn't speak the language but still loved the French teams.

"Ah, you're just bitter that Les Habs suck almost as badly as the Leafs do."

"Bite me, Dave."

We followed the crowd up Bay St., and after grabbing some street meat, we headed toward King St. to snarl up traffic, in drunken yet orderly Canadian fashion. Jase and me started up an immortal Stompin' Tom Connors song, and we were joined by a few other guys, wailing off-key…

> Oh! The good old hockey game!
> Is the best game you could name!
> And the best game you could name!
> Is the good old hockey game!

And, of course, it *is*.

Like in any other Canadian town, hockey is a popular kids pastime in Sarnia, ranking right up there with ball tag, hockey cards, fishing in the "crik," drinking until you black out. Every weekend, the local arena is filled with parents, clutching their coffee and cigarettes, watching their kids play from six in the morning to six at night.

Playing hockey was admittedly more my dad's idea than mine – what better way to stamp me as A Real Canadian? And the fact I was able to play it actually surprised me, considering the great expense required to start a kid up in the sport. Just think about it: for baseball, all you need is a glove; for basketball, a ball, maybe a pair of discounted Nikes. In contrast, hockey tips the scales at a few hundred bucks for pads, gloves, skates, helmets, protective equipment for your happy little guy, down there.

I started playing at age eight, at the Atom level. At that age, I kept up with the rest of the kids; as time drew on, I noticed that the Caucasian kids just got bigger and bigger. By the time I was fifteen, I was getting killed out there by six-foot-tall redwoods with lots of padding and little remorse. It was a vicious pattern: take my shift, get killed. Take my shift, get killed.

I played for another year or so, until I broke a finger fielding a slap shot, which more or less retired me to the Armchair League. I still miss it, though; the rank smell of the change room, rocking on the blue line during the national anthem, shaking hands with the other team after (*G'game…g'game…g'game*).

The Coke dad would buy me afterward.

My point? I think playing hockey, probably more than anything, has defined my Canadianness – more than my parents, my schooling, my friends, my music, my drinking.

Well, maybe not the drinking…

We stopped at a bar on Richmond St. *Sportsline* came on at 11:30, showing highlights of the fisticuffs and running the usual post-game interviews, the standard template we can all mouth by heart: "*Yeah, well all we can do is just go out there…just give it 100 per cent…practise a lot more…play as part of the team…try our best…let's just take it one day at a time…*" Athlete interviews are the most boring things you could listen to in the world; the bigger the star, the more boring the interview.

They switched to basketball highlights next, showing unattractive scenes of a Laker spitting into a bucket. "I think the amount of spitting is directly proportional to how well you play," I argued. "The more you spit, the better you are. It's like Samson's hair, only with spit."

"Bullshit, Dave."

"No, really."

"Speaking of which, do you know what they put in chewing tobacco?" piped up Andrew. I shook my head.

"Can you believe fibreglass?"

"*Fibreglass?*"

"Yeah." He scratched his pimply chin. "Apparently, the idea is for the fibreglass to cut several hundred extremely tiny wounds in your mouth so you can absorb the nicotine faster."

"No shit?" said Jase, refilling his mug.

"No shit. That's why it's supposed to be a zillion times more addictive than smoking." Andrew paused and looked at me as I pulled out a Death Stick. I paused mid-light.

"Hey kid, watch the hyperbole. And don't get preachy with me unless you want me to cut several hundred extremely small wounds in your mouth." *Puff puff.*

"Yes, boss."

Sitting there, drinking beers and smoking cigarettes and watching hockey highlights gave me a serious feeling of *déjà vu*.

Teej and I would always get together to watch the Calgary-Edmonton match-ups whenever they were on. She originally came from a hicktown in Alberta, somewhere between the two, some place called Red Lake or Dog's Jaw or Great Deer's Jaw or something. I can never remember.

I teased Teej about the Flames a lot. I called them The Calgary National Theatre Company because of the tendency of their players to take dives for cheap penalties.

"Oh look," I said, pointing to Joe Johnson's sprawled form on the ice after a blatant dive. "Looks like Joey Jo Jo's trying out for the latest role in *Hamlet*."

"Ah, shut up, Dave." She looked wistfully at Johnson's chiselled visage, contorted in mock pain as he limped melodramatically back to the bench. "You know, I went to high school with that guy."

"Oh yeah?" I said, interest perking up.

"Mmmm hmmm. He was yer typical overly good-looking dumb jock. I even had a crush on him at one point. A lot of girls did." I stuck my finger down my throat to fake a gag, eliciting a laugh from her.

"Yeah, exactly! When he heard he was drafted by the Flames, he went out immediately to buy a Porsche or something. Crashed it the first night he had it out."

"*Lew-hew-hew-zer!*"

"Kind of, don't you think? But at least he drove a Porsche. What piece of shit do you drive again, Dave?"

I, of course, failed to score with her yet again that night.

When I got home, I called Shel in Ottawa. I had some free time coming up, and wanted to make a trip up there to see the goof.

"So Dave, when are you coming up?"

"Well, *Jaguar* ships in about a week, so I'm still in total hell-crunch mode. I was thinking a few days after that, depending on how the roads are. The highway up there gets pretty hairy in the winter, you know."

"Super-*great*! It'll be great to see you, buddy. I love you, man! But I'm not gay."

"You're a *loser*, that's what you are. See ya, pal."

I hung up the phone, feeling warm. Great guy, that Shel. Condescension aside, you might be surprised that I often wish that I was more like him, in certain ways. Shel is – how can I put this? – he's a goofball, a complete and total goofball. He has this freshness, this naiveté, this improbable innocence about him. A simple lad, he's not particularly hung up on things, and as a result, seemed a little happier than the rest of the Banana Boys. Far be it for me to say that he's unintelligent, but sometimes he seems so refreshingly free of complexes and Mental White Noise that it's alternately endearing and annoying.

This is classic Shel: one time, we were invited to this wine and cheese by a friend of mine.

"Dave, what do I bring to these things?"

"Well, Sheldon," I said humourlessly, "it's called a 'Wine and Cheese'. You can bring some wine, or maybe some cheese."

He looked at me funny for a second, and slowly said, "All right. I'll see you there."

That night, he arrived with a package of Kraft Singles. To this day, I'm not sure if he was just yanking my chain.

Sheldon's my best friend in the whole world, the only person I can trust (not that I really trust anyone; bad relationships and *The X-Files*, you know). During the Bad Times™ – breaking up with Jeanette, the rest of my family, and most of the Banana Boys – he was the only person who stuck by me. Completely, through thick and thin. Rick certainly didn't, and although Luke and Mike are still my friends these days, they kind of wavered a bit, too. But not Shel. Not one iota did he budge. And for that, I owe him my current sanity, and a debt of honour.

I suppose that's a function of him being a genuinely friendly guy. Out of all of us, he's the one who clocks in the most smiles, a genuine aura of frank friendliness. But the thing I envy about him most is his ability to be romantic. When it comes to matters of the heart, it seems like he runs his life like one of those black-and-white pictures you see on prints and postcards and such – man on a train station platform, firmly grasping his love, joyous embrace, laughter, wine, roses.

"You ever notice the moon, Dave?" he said to me once, wasted from an engineering Batch party.

"What kind of question is *that*?"

"The moon," he continued softly, "is constant. Isn't it? It doesn't matter where you are – north, south, east or west, it's always there, looking after you, in all its golden beauty."

"Are you making a pass at me or something?"

" Shut up, Dave!" He suddenly looked thoughtful. "If I ever have a girlfriend who parts from me," he said earnestly, "I'll tell her that I'll look at the moon, and wherever she is, I'll think of her, because she's under the same moon. The moon will be our connection."

"Anyone ever tell you that you're the biggest *sap* in all of mankind?"

I guess I heap my fair share of derision on Shel for being a romantic fool. But the truth is that I want very badly to Love the way he can. I'm jealous of the fact that he is able to have healthy romantic relationships, that he is able to *want* them. Whereas I, Mister Fucked-Up-In-Love, am destined only to have temporary and dysfunctional ones, coloured by politics, alcohol and mildly unpleasant mood swings.

Mike called next to ask about some computer problems.

"Shit, Mike, call the 1-800 number."

"I would, but I'm in the middle of this flame war with McAngus, and I have to get this insult in."

"You're wasting your time on that stuff," I said derisively, "Dude, you gotta realize that the Usenet's contribution to this world is far outweighed by the quirks of those who are stupid and offensive. Guys like McAngus are only demonstrating their neuroses and general insecurity bordering on the pathetic."

"Hey, that sounds like a *classic* flame. Can you repeat that? I have to get it down."

"Jesus, Mike, get away from the Usenet and take up rac-quetball or something."

Now Mike is the cerebral opposite of Shel. I guess he's got a good head on his shoulders…except for when he's smashing it into a wall somewhere for whatever reason: academic problems, racial injustice, or a relationship which read like a *Matchbox 20* song. Our five-year history with that guy has been filled with these tortured discussions about how miserable he is, how dis-satisfied he is, even some frank talks about suicide. And although Mistress Cruella *did* fuck him over pretty severely, he still hasn't dealt with it satisfactorily. (I don't care what anyone else thinks: nothing quite holds a candle to getting run over by a half-ton Harley-Davidson. Once you've had that happen to you, everything else becomes cake.)

I've never gotten why Mike gets so worked up about things the way he only can. As a scientist, he should know that basic physics dictates that Entropy will get us all in the end. Every-thing – I mean *everything* – will turn into a meaningless turmoil of matter and energy sooner or later, so it just doesn't matter. You may be happy one moment and not feel the grip of self-preservation that nature put in our brains – Love sometimes does that – but in the absolute end, it'll just be Game Over, and even those who are able to extract something "meaningful" from this soup will be history.

Ah, but I suppose Mike isn't really a scientist. He's an *artiste*, so he needs to feel angst in order to create. The chump.

"So what do you think of my theory?" I asked the guys one night at the Bomber.

"I think you need a Prozac the size of a baseball," observed Luke.

"Har har, Stick."

With Mike, sometimes I want to just grab him by the lapels and slap some sense into him…*Mike, dude, you are a total loser. Anyone who lets life beat them rather than trying to win probably deserves it, and is certainly destined for it. You're obviously ad-dicted to being abused, and you certainly invite it wearing your scarlet letter 'V' for victim that any moron with half an eye can see a mile away. I mean Jesus, how bad can it really be? What makes you so special that you deserve to lie awake nights and pray that you don't wake up? Just deal with the fact that women are insane and inherently evil.*

It ultimately comes down to this: when you approach the end of your days, do you really want to remember this one insecure and psychotic female as the decisive pivot of your existence who had you beat in the game of life, making you suffer in pathetic misery for the rest of your days? Only losers who take life so seriously have the capacity for the uncanny misery you display. Get over it, dude.

Then again, there is no way I could do this without flipping the harsh light of micro-analysis on myself. What can I say? I suck.

"Yo, Dave!" Jase bellowed from his office. "Ya gotta come on over and check this out."

I saved the last bug in our tracking system and slapped on my screensaver, showering my screen with flying toasters.

"Problems with the last build?"

"No. Look at this." Jase pointed to a domain listing of Internet addresses purchased and reserved by Procter and Gamble.

"Good grief…!"

P&G	(FLU-DOM)	FLU.COM
P&G	(FOLGERS-DOM)	FOLGERS.COM
P&G	(GUMS-DOM)	GUMS.COM
P&G	(ANTIPERSPIRANT-DOM)	ANTIPERSPIRANT.COM
P&G	(PIMPLES-DOM)	PIMPLES.COM
P&G	(BADBREATH-DOM)	BADBREATH.COM
P&G	(UNDERARM-DOM)	UNDERARM.COM
P&G	(DANDRUFF-DOM)	DANDRUFF.COM
P&G	(DIARRHEA-DOM)	DIARRHEA.COM

"Kind of gross, isn't it?" Jase wadded up a piece of paper, tossing it at his Nerf basketball net. "I mean, how'd you like to send e-mail from *davelowe@dandruff.com*?"

"I hear you. Try sealing a major business deal over e-mail with a domain like *diarrhea.com*. Forward a copy of this to me, will ya? Some friends'll get a kick out of it."

"Will do." He clicked a mouse button and leaned back in his chair. "Wanna see the Kraft domain listing as well?"

"Not right now. If I don't get this thing finished by this afternoon, Greg will kill me and rape my dead body."

"You really have a way with words, Dave, do you know that?

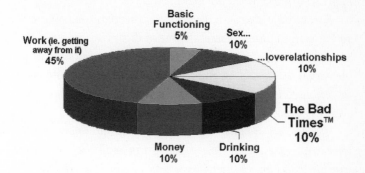

Fig. 9. Dave's BrainChart™ (as of Feb 12th)

So once again, I'm leaving the office at 1 am, fingers numb from typing, eyes completely shot from CRT rays. *Jaguar* is shipping in two weeks, and things are getting out of control, par for the course. As I pass the kitchen, I see Markanandrew, filling their nylon UW knapsacks with Cokes and Dr. Peppers from the fridge like squirrels readying their winter stores.

"Hey," I bark.

They freeze and turn around. I walk up to them, glowering. "Juice," I say.

I open the other fridge and with a well-practised swiping motion, I drop about ten cans of apple and orange juice into my own bag. "Drink juice at home. Cokes and Jolts only for grind time. Got that? Drink juice, and you'll live longer and happier."

"Yes, boss."

For good measure, I also snag a roll of toilet paper for each of us. You can never get enough toilet paper.

It was past 1:30 when I got home. I emptied my loot on the floor and collapsed onto my sofabed into a fitful sleep.

I am wandering this sterile, well-lit room full of cute and extra-

ordinarily fat little babies, sucking their thumbs, playing with their feet. A loud movie-trailer voice is booming from unseen speakers, listing numbers from one to one-hundred. Red-hooded surgeons are taking these babies off one by one to a red-lit room at my right, double-doors swinging every time another one is carted off. I got scared, worried. There are only two babies left. Where are they taking them? What are they about to do to them?

I woke up with a start. Feeling unsettled, I turned on the TV and flipped channels. There was one of those cheesy, late-night, locally produced commercials – you know, the ones featuring the actual dealer, acting ability nil. This one for a motorcycle dealership in Etobicoke. I dozed off again, leaving him to squawk away in his cowboy hat and gorilla suit…

It's a sultry summer night, mid-August, full moon, the air thick with pine, the highways still warm with the day's heat. Jeanette had come up from Toronto one evening and we went out riding, on some back roads north of the school, just for the hell of it. I am gently holding her slim, taut form, gripping her leather jacket, letting the sound of the engine melt into the background and feeling one with her, my Love. But honestly, it was the music that did it. We were both joined to my old, battered walkman, clearly falling apart as evidenced by the elastic band wrapped around it so my Pink Floyd tape wouldn't fall out. The mellow tones of "Comfortably Numb" was drifting into our shared space, above the motor, and that was precisely, exactly the way I felt at that moment, the moment that the future would knight as 'pure perfection'.

Mike often talks about these Perfect Moments in life, how at a single point in time, everything – your position, your actions, your environment, the food you're eating, coffee you're drinking, music you're listening to – are just perfect. I guess that was mine. And it is why I find it too difficult to let it go.

Perfection is really just an indicator that things are going to get worse, much like disaster is an indication that things are probably going to get better. And nothing could be any worse than the Bad Times™.

Bad Time #	Date	Description
1	Sept 4	I start school. God, I hate this place.
2	Oct 17	I get nuked in mid-terms.
3	Dec 15	I get nuked in finals.
4	Jan 23	Mike gets fucked over by Mina (aka Mistress Cruella). Tequila Brain Death Night follows.
5	Feb 14	I find a different brand of condom at Jeanette's place. Huge fight follows.
6	Feb 26	Drinking with Shel and Rick. I talk with Jeanette. Huge fight follows. She runs me over with her bike.
7	Mar 16	Incendiary words exchanged with the family. Huge fight follows. Old man clops me on the chops, the old bastard.
8	Mar 22	Drinking with the guys. Huge fight follows – the Mother-of-All-Arguments. Rick ditches us. Banana Boys unofficially dissolved.
9	Apr 14	I get nuked in finals. Almost (*almost!*) don't graduate.
10	May/June	I find myself lying drunk, with a huge gash on my leg, behind a warehouse in Bolton, unsure of how I get there. *Alcohol – the cause of, and solution to, life's problems.*

Fig. 10. Itinerary of the Damned.

Nine months of problems and crises, layering and cascading on top of each other like a sick and perverted lasagna of angst. I drank a hell of a lot more than I ever do now (hard to believe, I know), and through the blur of bitterness and Rickards Red, hardly a day passed when I didn't ponder my worthless existence and think about blowing my fucking brains out. Things got so bad and so out of control that the weaker, more vulnerable emotions started coming out. So I forcibly concealed these emotions, and that left only the angry and abrasive ones. I was afraid – really, *really* afraid – but I preferred to be hated rather than pitied.

And man, was I ever hated. I managed to alienate most of the Banana Boys back then, Rick and Luke and Mike…except for Shel. Good old Shel.

These days, I'm much better now. Sounds kind of hack-neyed, but time does heal all wounds…well, most of 'em, anyway. I don't think I'll ever achieve true perfection, just like I'll never truly let go of all the bitterness. But the Bad Times™ have taught me that you just have learn to *joh yun* – you know, be a normal person, around other normal people. Honey, there just ain't no other way.

The only sore point from all of this is Rick. He not only disappeared from my life, he left all of us. And that still makes me angry, because I love those guys to death. They're good people, Luke, Shel and Mike – they all made the effort, thought I was worth the effort, and I fully appreciated it.

But not Rick.

Ah, screw 'im. His loss.

In the end, the Bad Times™ taught me a valuable lesson about people as a whole. People are multi-dimensional func-tions with underlying variables you could not possibly fathom. When the variables change, the entire function changes, and the graph you're looking at becomes totally different. Nothing – and no one – is reliable in this world. To believe that is to put yourself at a severe disadvantage.

In the delirium of half-sleep, more things from the subconscious float up and addle the pate – battlefields, bears, dentists, meat cleavers, fruit-bats, breakfast cereals…

I shake my head. This is fucked up shit, man. I climb out of bed, plodding to the kitchen. I pour some water from my Brita and drink, eyeing the Formica kitchen counter uneasily. *Les folks* had wall-to-wall Formica at the restaurant, a shabby little Chinese-Canadian restaurant in Sarnia on the Golden Mile – you know, take-out, sweet-and-sour-whatever, fried something-or-other. Stuff bonafide Chinese wouldn't be caught dead eating.

The restaurant sits in a sixties-style strip plaza, beside a wholesale carpet outlet and a large hand holding a rotating pizza that had long stopped rotating. In the entrance sat a sixties-style cash register atop a glass display case filled with chocolate bars, chewing gum and breath mints. Behind it was *Choi Sun Yeh*, a little statue of a Chinese god smoking something that looked suspiciously like a crack pipe. *Choi* was apparently the treasurer of the gods, bringer of good luck and prosperity to my folkses greasy spoon.

Inside, there was room enough to seat about forty, although we set out place settings for forty-six. There was a smallish bar featuring a small selection of beers and liquor. The decor was classic Neo-Chinese-Mish-Mash – hanging lanterns, wood tables, plastic phoenixes and dragons, framed pictures of the Great Wall and some unnamed pagodas. The tables all featured those little steel napkin dispensers and paper placemats with the twelve animals of the Chinese Zodiac, complete with simplistically mystical explanations. All these combined to give the dining room a cheesy feel that undoubtedly most patrons took to be uniquely Chinese.

In the back, there was a table with a primitive adding machine, and a box holding a fortune in American coins, wrapped in neat little packets by me and my mom. Beyond that – the kitchen, with cooking tools, large fryers and stoves, an industrial-sized sink filled with steel pots and pans, and racks of Corelle plates, sporting plain western-styled trim that clashed badly with the Neo-Chinese-Mish-Mash.

This was home for one-third of my life. I bused tables, laid out clean placemats, peeled shrimp and washed dishes in exchange for pocket money, which I usually blew on baseball cards and Donkey Kong. I hated the place, but it did provide the family with a reasonable living, pandering to Caucasians who knew as much about real Chinese cuisine as I did (which was nothing at all).

Before the Great Schism between me and my family, I'd hop in Jeepy and go back home to Sarnia once a month. After the Friday computer lab, I'd put on my well-worn Red Sox cap, pop on a pair of fake Ray Bans and head west. It's an unbelievably dull three-hour drive from Waterloo to Sarnia, past all those little hick towns with funny names…Drumbo. Ingersoll. Innerkip. Camlachie. I'd bring snacks for the ride; one of my favourites was a box of Froot Loops. I'd munch on them, dry, all the way home.

My mother is a real piece of work – excitable, immature, high-strung. Undeniably Chinese. She always nagged me, had a comment or criticism about everything. If you didn't listen to what she was saying, or do what she wanted you to, or if things didn't go her way, she'd start stamping her little foot and wailing until you couldn't help but start yelling back.

My sisters were always able to let things wash with my mom. "You just have to know how to handle her, Dave," Grace would advise me (me and Ellen never got along.) "Makes no difference to you, anyway. Just let her babble until it's all out, and then do your own thing. Works for me."

But I could never let it slide. Mom was a nag-tactician, her techniques for getting under my skin honed to perfection. She extracted past sins like an oral surgeon extracted wisdom teeth (whether they were still there or not). It wasn't just annoying; it drove me fucking nuts. And my response was usually typical *juk sing* insolence, **gwei jok fung** – my mom always yelled at me for my *sei leut see jui* ("damned lawyers mouth," which pretty much constituted every response I gave her, regardless of who was actually right).

The Big One was dropped sometime in fourth year, during a long weekend. Mom was nagging Grace about dating Jeff. "Why don't you find a Chinese boy," she squealed in Cantonese (never mind that a Real Chinese Boy was harder to find in Sarnia than a sober hick.) Grace just stood by passively, taking it, but I was doing a serious slow burn until I couldn't take it any more and I had to open my big mouth.

"Mom, will you just shut up? Grace should be able to go out with whoever she wants. Stop interfering with our love lives, will you?"

That startled her. I hurt her, and regretted it immediately, but then her mouth turned into a thin, hard line. She turned on her heel and marched upstairs, returning with a box.

"Okay," she said in English, "I'll stop interfere with your love life. You take this back. It has nothing to do with me." She dropped the box on the ground. Inside were mementos of my first relationship in high school – some stuffed animals, pictures, other knick-knacks. I recalled the tearful day I neatly packed up these things after a painful break up, my mom comforting me and kindly shuttling the stuff away into her closet.

*I saw **red**.*

"What *is* this? What the *fuck* is this?!" I yelled.

"You ask me to keep this," she said primly, "and I give it back. *Mm-**gwan** ngoh si* (none of my business), I don't want to interfere with you."

I couldn't believe what she was doing. It was cruel. It re-opened wounds. But I couldn't articulate that reasonably at that point. I was livid.

Ground zero…buh-bye.

"*YOU GODDAMN BITCH!*" I screamed. My mom and Grace jumped a foot. "*JUST WHO THE FUCK IS THE CHILD HERE? YOU OR ME?*"

Dad, who normally stayed neutral during our altercations, came roaring out of the family room like a Polaris missile fresh out of the silo.

Ground zero…buh-bye.

"*WHERE THE **HELL** DO YOU GET OFF TALKING TO YOUR MOTHER LIKE THAT?*" he roared, the vein in his forehead bulging like an alien trying to rip out of his flesh. "*YOU'VE GONE TOO FAR! THIS IS YOUR GODDAMN MOTHER! DO YOU UNDERSTAND?*"

"*Jesus*, Dad, do you know what she *did*?"

"*IT DOESN'T MATTER! SHE'S YOUR MOTHER! YOU WILL NOT TALK TO HER LIKE THAT. UNDERSTAND?*"

"FUCK THAT!"

"SHUT UP!"

Blammo.

A beefy hand to the chops. Me on the ground, tears in my eyes. Dad standing over me, quivering. Mom and Grace, whimpering and clutching his large arms ineffectually, trying to hold him back.

At that moment, I couldn't see straight. I was so angry I could've killed all of them, right there. My teeth gritted slowly. My fists balled up into tightly packed bundles of dynamite. Return salvo, armed and ready.

Ground zero…buh-bye.

"You motherfucking *bastard*…you *hit* me. YOU – HIT – ME!"

Dad was shaking violently, speechless, so I continued. "You've never hit me! EVER! That's fucking *it*, I am getting the *hell* out of this! Mom, *fuck you!* Dad, *fuck you!* FUCK ALL OF YOU! Goddamn ethnic shit – christ, I still can't believe you HIT me! You fucking lay another hand on me and I call the goddamn cops, you hear me you old lunatic?"

"*LISTEN HERE, YOU…*"

"*FUCK YOU, OLD MAN! I'M THROUGH. DO YOU HEAR? THROUGH! SAY GOODBYE TO YOUR ONLY SON, AND HELLO TO A LIFE OF RETIRED LONELINESS, YOU STUPID GODDAMN MOTHERFUCKERS!*" I ran out of the house, tears still clouding my vision, started Jeepy and tore off.

That was it. One moment of anger. One stupid move on his part. A bunch of stupid words on my part. Finito, kaput.

When I got back to Waterloo, I grimly proceeded to sever all ties from my former family. Changed my phone number. Discarded any and all family-related paraphernalia. A curt explanation to the guys – "*Me and the family on the outs – one word from any of youse and I will slit your fucking throats.*" The insane, psychotic focus that served me so well in my academics – the concentration of pure hatred into a finely-tuned arrow that ultimately shot me through four boring years of school – came into full action, and I never looked back.

Mom tried to come down to smooth things over, but I

rebuffed her. I even broke my lease and moved, leaving no forwarding address, no phone number. She couldn't really find me after that. Only a few more months anyway, 'till I graduated – do the damned school, get the damned degree and bolt to a full-time job in that big ol' damned city of Toronto. Get lost in a sea of people, and what's done is done. Clean and simple.

A lie, of course. You just can't cut family like that. But I sure as hell tried, and I'm still trying. And lying here, alone in my bed at 5 am, staring at the stucco on the ceiling, I am apparently not succeeding.

Love, Wine, Roses.

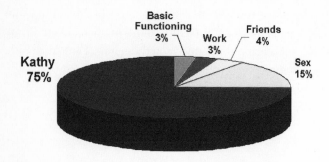

Fig. 11. Shel's BrainChart™ (as of Feb 12th)

Monday morning. I woke up at six-thirty in minus-twenty-degree weather, minus thirty with the wind chill. I know it's the middle of February, but this…this is just *crazy*.

I gave Kathy, who doesn't have classes until 9:30, a little kiss on the cheek and walked into the washroom, yawning hugely. Stepping into the shower was like stepping onto a solid block of ice – *holy jeez*! Why can't they make heaters for bathtubs, like they do for engine blocks? They can send a man to the moon…

After a breakfast of bagels and peanut butter, and leaving a rose beside Kathy's slumbering form (I bought the rose secretly last night, when we went out for dinner), I put on my ski jacket and work boots and trudged out into the Arctic blast to the bus stop. The office wouldn't let me keep the truck after work hours. You can't have it all, I guess.

I've been going out with Kathy for about three months and now, between her and work, time has just flown like the wind. We went up to Montreal a week ago. Even though it was two hours away, I could only remember ten minutes of the bus trip because we smooched the whole time. "*La Fuerza del Amor* (The Force of Love)," Luke called it.

I am deliriously happy, but there is one thing nagging at me. It sounds kind of dumb, but I'm worried about how Dave is taking all of this. Dave's my best friend, and I know he wants me to be happy. But I feel strangely guilty, because I've completed the The Quest™…and he still hasn't.

"Who is this chick?" he asked over the phone, a few days after I'd met her.

"Kathy. She's supergreat."

"Does she drink?"

"Oh no. She's a Music major at the U of O. She studies really hard at school, like."

Dave clucked his tongue a little. "She's not one of these girls who writes her notes with big bubbly letters, is she? The type who draws hearts all over her books and highlights things and uses four-different colour pens? Yecch!"

"No, Dave. She plays the piano. I think she used to play the violin, too. Kathy says she wants to go to Europe next summer to see all sorts of churches and cathedrals, where great composers like Bach and Chopin played. Or something. She's really neat-o. Kathy says…"

"Is she Oriental?" he interrupted.

"Huh? Yeah. Yeah, she is."

"Chinese?"

"Yup."

"Is she Banana or FOB, or somewhere in between?"

"In between, I guess. She was born in Hong Kong, and moved here when she was really young. Like Rick," I added, regretting it as soon as it came out of my mouth.

Dave just grunted. "Whatever. So did you do her yet?"

"*Dave!*"

"Just kidding. She sounds nice."

"She's super nice. So Dave, when are you coming up?"

"Well, *Jaguar* ships in about a week, so I'm still in total hell-crunch mode. I was thinking a few days after that, depending on how the roads are. The highway up there gets pretty hairy in the winter, you know."

Kathy knows all about Dave. I've told her everything about

us…things we've been through, drinking stories, the Bad Times™. How much I love that guy. Now she thinks we're gay lovers.

On the way to work, I gaze out the bus window at a Beer Store parking lot. Ha ha, the snow on the ground's carved with circular tire tracks made by some drunken locals doing donuts with their pickups last night. It reminds me of a bunch of New Brunswick winters with Kell and Beau in *his* pickup.

Mr. McFadden didn't even let me take off my coat before barking at me and my partner Sean to head out to a site. "Kwan! Hickey! Gloucester!" Mr. McFadden only said two or three words to me a day unless he was complaining about Americans.

"Figures that the junior inspectors get all the shitty jobs," Sean growled, cranking the truck heater up to maximum. Gloucester is an outlying suburb of Ottawa; the site is also outdoors, guaranteed to expose us to the brutal elements. "I should'a stayed in Windsor. Now I know how I got this transfer so easily – no experienced line inspector in his right mind would volunteer to do duty up in this freezing hellhole during the winter."

"Live and learn," I grinned, shifting gears. I was still warm from being with Kathy.

The office assigned us pagers for work, so I pulled this trick on Sean yesterday: I dialed his pager number and gave the message service the number to a gay chat line. Needless to say, he was looking for me this morning.

"Rabid dogs will eat your flesh, you bastard," he snarled. Well, the other guys in the office thought it was pretty funny. *I* thought it was hilarious when Dave pulled it on me during my last co-op job. Luke didn't, though.

"Not funny," he said, clearly offended. "You're both stupid, moronic, insensitive gay-bashing louts. Do us all a favour and lose the homophobic crap, okay? I mean, what *is* it with you guys?"

"Hiding something, Stick?" smirked Dave.

"What are *you* hiding? You and Shel have this predilection for homophobic jokes – always teasing each other, calling each other gay. It's odd." Luke looked at me intensely. "Maybe it's a subconscious manifestation of something…"

"Puh-*leeze*, Luke," Dave said, eyes rolling.

"They're only jokes, Luke," I said, slightly mystified. "We don't mean anything by it."

And we don't. Saint John, as I mentioned before, is a pretty blue-collar town…and Kell and Beau and the rest of the guys back there were definitely blue-collar. These kinds of jokes were pretty standard, along with comments about your mother and farm animals. But they never meant anything. I mean, my first year roommate in university was gay, and that didn't bother me at all.

"That's one of the lamest excuses I've ever heard," Luke said primly. "Every single derogatory comment you make has the net effect of degrading a human being, just like you. Any way you slice it, you're nothing but a *bigot.*"

That hurt. Maybe he's right. But we really, really don't mean anything by it. Honest. I guess the jokes are substitutes for terms of endearment. You know, the whole male-bonding cajoling thing. It's naggingly suspicious to say things like "I love you" to your best guy friend without adding an ironic trailer like "man" at the end of it (like those Bud Light Commercials: *"I love you, man!"*) Even if you really mean it. And even then, you have to reply with, "You're such a fag!" and punch him in the arm or something.

I guess it's not too politically correct, but it's a guy thing. Guys are weird. Well, no weirder than women.

After a day of braving the Gloucester cold, I headed home at around 5 pm. It was already dark. I opened the door to the house and hit a solid wall of chemicals.

"What the… ?"

It was kind of cute: Kathy had decided to coat my other pair of work boots with waterproofing solvents. But by the second coat, she was so dizzy she'd practically passed out.

"Gee, Kath, why didn't you do all this outside?" I opened a window, but then closed it again after the room temperature dropped to minus nine in ten seconds,

"Are you crazy, Shel? It's *freezing* outside!"

I picked up the spray can and read the label aloud. "WARN-ING: *Should be applied in well-ventilated areas.*" I smiled, patting her on the head. "I guess that goes double for you – you're so small, a single hit has double the effect. It probably takes the poison three seconds to completely circulate."

"Oh Shel, shut up." I laughed and kissed her on the forehead. That's something every Canadian goes through yearly, I guess…freebasing waterproof solvents.

While Kath recovered on the couch, I went into the kitchen to fix us some dinner. Hmm, no food. I hadn't gone grocery shopping for a while, but it was just too cold to trek out to one of the restaurants on Rideau St. So I ordered some pizza.

Passed by the Catholic school again. *I can't believe this* – it's so cold, and they're still wearing those little kilts. This time, I averted my eyes. I have a girlfriend now, you know.

That evening, I received a call from Luke. He called inconveniently after I'd, uh, retired with Kathy for the night.

"So how's it going with your woman?" he asked.

"Great, great," I whispered, cradling the receiver with my chin. Kathy was sleeping beside me. "She's sleeping right now…"

"Oho." I could almost hear Luke's eyebrow arching in interest. "Being true to your religious principles, are we now?"

I coughed.

"Dude, I have a solution for you. Just convert. Then you can do the nasty all you want."

"Convert? Convert to what?"

"I tried to get Mike to become an Anti-Buddhist, but he didn't go for it. How about Agnostic?"

"Er, what's that?"

"Agnostic: you worship the god Agnos. No, just kidding. Agnostics aren't too sure about the existence of a god, and generally prefer not to think about it."

"Nice direct approach," I commented.

"Isn't it though? So how about it? Might provide you with some useful leeway at this moment…"

"I don't think so, Luke…" I said, gingerly sliding my arm from under Kathy's head and shaking off the pins and needles. "All those years being an altar boy kind of drums the Catholicism in you, you know?"

"Hey, I didn't know you were an altar boy." He chuckled. "So did you ever, you know, get *violated* by a bishop or anything…?"

"Cripes, Luke!"

"Oop, sorry man. Did I step over a line?"

I shrugged. "Well, I guess not. Almost every single person I've told that to has made a comment like that. Dave never shuts up about it."

"Well, what did you expect?" he argued. "I mean, the frequency of that sort of thing happening is, you know, a little high for a holier-than-thou-type field like *that*. I mean, the worst scandal a church should go through is bingo fraud…"

"Ah, Luke, can we talk about this later?"

"Oh. Sorry about that. So have fun, nudge nudge, wink wink, say no more, say no more." *Click.*

It's funny, but my being Catholic has always been a source of teasing from Luke. He teases me about a lot, it seems. It kinda bugs me, actually.

The cold February days zipped by, turning into cold March days. Thoughts of what would happen when my Ottawa assignment was up in early April crossed my mind, and probably Kathy's, too, but we didn't talk about it. Once, she started to, but I put my finger on her lips.

"Shhhh" I said gently. "Kath, I don't want to talk about the future. I don't care about reality, I don't care about being practical. I just want to enjoy *now*." She nodded, and then we kissed for about the millionth time.

Dave called today. "Shipping hell is *over*!" he crowed exuberantly. "*Jaguar* is *dead* and *buried* – break out the whips and the Crisco."

"That's sick. So when are you thinking of coming up, then, Dave?"

"The day after tomorrow – prolly stay for four days. And boy, be prepared to drink!" He then paused. "Oh. Right. I forgot. You don't drink anymore. Wiener."

"I'll have one if it'll make you feel better, Dave."

"Stop it! You're giving me warm fuzzies. By the way, man, how's the music up in Ottawa these days? I want to know if I need to bring a load of cassettes in Jeepy. There's nothing worse than a five-hour drive with lousy Luke-style music all the way."

"I'd be ecstatic if there was Luke-style music," I said, sighing. "The radio is terrible here. There are a lot of soldier-boy-types around the CFBs here, and all they like is classic rock or country. It's complete radio tundra."

I could almost hear Dave grimace from behind the phone. "Hey, watch it! I like classic rock. I prefer it to the faggety alternative music everyone is playing here – even the classic rock station is getting into that stuff these days. But you can always do what I do when I get tired of the radio."

"Jerk off?"

"Har har. I listen to *Berlitz Learn to Speak*-whatever tapes! I just started on German yesterday…'*Der ist ein Bratwurst in meine Lederhosen*; There is a sausage in my pants.'" He laughed at his own joke. "So how's your chickee-bay-bee?"

"Super great. Me and Kathy get along really well."

"Christ, I knew it. You're whipped like anything."

"Shut up, Dave."

"Whipped, whipped, whipped. I hope you at least lost your virginity in the whole deal."

"Shut *up*, Dave."

"I guess you have." He paused thoughtfully. "You know, I think I'm regaining mine. Do I get to meet her?"

"Actually, she's back in Sudbury this weekend – it's Spring Break for all the Arts students. She'll be gone until the sixteenth. It looks like you're gonna miss her by three days. That's too bad, I guess."

"What's the matter, goofball? Too embarrassed to introduce her?" He chortled. "Afraid I'll tell her, you know, the truth about you and your attraction to farm animals?"

"Dave, you *know* I only have eyes for you. What time are you going to show up?"

"Seven-ish. And make sure you pick up a two-four of Canadian."

"Okay. Catch you later."

After I hung up, I called Kathy. We talked until two in the morning. Dave's right; I'm whipped.

The roads turned into death-traps overnight because of a storm, but Dave insisted on coming up, despite catching a nasty cold, too. "No one's going to deny me some richly deserved R&R," he said, blowing his nose over the phone. "And besides, it's the only time I can get off, before we start up on the next goddamn project."

"Yo Goofball," he wheezed as I opened the door.

"Dave! How was the drive?"

"Shitty," he moaned, pounding the snow off of his jacket. "I was trapped behind this little ol' lady from Pasedena going about forty clicks all the way up the highway." He launched into a spasm of coughing.

"Gosh, you sound awful."

"No shit. Gad, man, I had to park two blocks away because of the snow mountains piled up by the plows…there's like *zero* parking action in front of your house. And me in my weakened condition! Ah well, nothing a few beers can't cure." He threw his duffle bag into the living room, spraying fresh snow all over the floor. "Oops. So how far is it to the Market from here, anyway?"

"It's a fifteen-minute walk," I said, causing Dave to gag.

"Maybe we should chill out here for a bit. Everything's open until two, anyway. Want some coffee or something?"

"Would maim for one, thanks." He dropped himself onto the couch in the living room and turned on the TV as I went into the kitchen.

"Here you go," I said, proffering him a steaming cup. He sniffed it and frowned.

"This ain't Columbian, Shel."

"I thought you might want something for your cold," I said, holding up a packet scrawled with Chinese. "It's some sort of Chinese remedy. Kathy gave me a box of this stuff when I had a cold a few weeks ago." I pretended to read the characters on the back. *"Pour into cup and mix with hot water – good for sound mind, healthy body, cures latent homosexuality…"*

"Chyeah *right*, man!" Dave smirked. "You read Chinese as well as I do, which is, like, not at all."

"Can't pull the wool over your eyes, Dave."

"Damn straight. Thanks for the brew." We watched a rerun of *Star Trek: The Next Generation*, punctuated by his sniffs, slurps and coughs. Wesley was watching a tape of his dead father on the holodeck. "What I'm wondering is *this*: why the hell aren't the holodecks on the Enterprise always burgeoning with young adolescent boys? I know *I'd* be there all the time. And I'm not an adolescent."

"Proud of that, eh, Dave?"

"Not particularly."

About an hour later, we headed toward the Market. It was a snowy night in Downtown Ottawa…packs of drunken techno-geeks from the neighbouring industrial sweatshops of Kanata and Nepean sprinkled the various bars and clubs, their belches, *Simpson's* quotes and assorted drunken geek-speke muffled by the falling snow.

We went over to Mexicali Rosa's and started talking over a rapidly dwindling pitcher, mostly from Dave's doing. I was just keeping him company. That Dave. Through sickness and health, it would take a monster truck to drag him away from his beer.

I looked at my watch. "Where the heck is the waitress?"

"No idea, man. Maybe she doesn't like Orientals."

"Dave, does everything have to be a race thing with you?"

"Geez, Goofball, it was only a joke. Grab a sense of humour, will you?" He started telling me about how he met a girl over e-mail the other day.

"You're kidding, Dave," I scoffed in disbelief. "You picked up a girl over e-mail? God, you're such a geek."

"Aren't I, though? She's this physiology student at U of T. She was responding to my ad in *The Star* about my old laptop."

"What was she like?"

"Well, I found out she was Chinese."

"Were you disappointed?"

He blinked. "Huh? What do you exactly mean, 'disappointed'? I mean, I'd be disappointed if I found out she was, like, a *man* or something…" I guffawed loudly, and he continued. "No, not disappointed, but there's really nothing there, man. She studies too much, and she doesn't drink."

"You mean she's not TJ."

"I mean she doesn't drink," he said, a little too forcefully, so I let it drop. "She also has the idea of finding a Nice Chinese Boy to settle down with, and god knows I'm not *that*. I also found out that her last three boyfriends were these Caucasian frat-boy types, and her parents were pressuring her to get married or something. Now I know why Banana chicks start off as wild party animals but end up marrying Nice Chinese Boys – they know for a fact that unless they conform, their parents will be bugging them about it forever."

"Forever? Come *on*, Dave…"

"Chinese parents never die, my friend, unless someone stuffs garlic in their mouths and drives a stake through their collective hearts."

"And that's why you divorced your parents, right?" I said jokingly, and then immediately wished I hadn't.

"Let's not go there," Dave warned, and took another pull at his mug. He shrugged it off, and changed the subject again. "How are things with the ball and chain?"

"Kathy's fine, Dave."

"So, does she give head?"

"Shit, man, you're cut off!"

"Just asking, no need to answer. Yet." Dave refilled his glass, emptying the pitcher. "Serving wench! More wine, by Jupiter!" The waitress frowned.

By the time we were through the third pitcher, we were both completely wasted. Dave just looked like he was having so much fun, so, that one time, I said what the hell. It was just like old times, only my tolerance was a fraction of what it used to be.

"It's like being happy ninety-five per cent of the time," I slurred, pouring myself another beer and missing the glass.

"Happy, eh?" he said, wavering in front of me (I didn't know if that was my brain or his body).

"Yup. Happy and content and wanting for nothing."

"What about drinking?"

"What *about* drinking? You don't need to drink because you're so happy."

"I don't drink to feel happy," he explained, "I drink because I like drinking."

"Hmmm. I dunno then," I said, unsure of myself. I scratched my head. "Well, maybe drinking while being in love makes you even more happy."

"What about hangovers? They make me sad."

"I guess being happy in love negates feeling bad with a hangover, so you just feel, you know, normal."

"Now *that* sounds *great*."

We checked out some girls playing pool.

"*All The Pretty Chicks With Crimson Lips,*" Dave mused, stealing a furtive glance.

"You dig the blonde, don't you?"

"Dibs on the blonde," he agreed, bobbing his head. "Snug turtleneck, hip-hugging jeans, Fuck Me Boots. I tell you, dude, naked women just don't turn me on."

"Shit, man, you are *really* cut off!"

" 'Strue," he said, pokerfaced.

"So what…naked men, then?"

"Oh, shut up."

Before we knew it, it was last call.

"Well what do you know, the girls *do* look prettier at closing time," said Dave loudly, quoting some obscure country-and-western song and earning these wickedly evil stares from the girls at the pool table. Dave just doffed his ball cap and staggered out with me into the night.

The next day, Dave was laid low by a combination of the cold and a hangover. "Egad," he wheezed, "you should never, *ever*, drink when you have a cold. You're just asking for a two-week extension."

"Ain't it the truth," I said, feeding him Sudafed and another steaming cup of Kathy's Chinese remedy.

We spent the rest of the weekend hanging out at the house, talking, getting on each others nerves. Best friends we may be, but we do irritate each other sometimes. For example, there was this thing he said that always totally pissed me off. Whenever he got all hot and nasty, if someone (me included) ever said anything that he thought was really stupid, he'd give out one word that grated on me and made me want to punch his lights out...

"*Jeeeeeeeezus!*"

Maybe it's the Catholic upbringing. Or maybe it's the way he says it: he starts off the first consonant, spitting it out like venom, then hanging the word all long and drawn out, ending it off with a hiss. It makes my blood boil.

Sometimes it's just his general attitude that gets to me. For as long as I've known him, I've felt he's never taken me seriously – I'm merely The Goofball, and not much else. Just a stupid, bumbling Goofball.

"Thanks, sweetheart," Dave smirked condescendingly when I gave him some more cold medicine. And I just exploded.

"Don't *ever* call me a sweetheart! I'm *not* a sweetheart, got that?"

Dave recoiled in shock. I didn't get mad all that often, but when I did, people definitely paid attention.

People think I'm simple, innocent, stupid. And sometimes I am…sometimes intentionally, especially when things get tense, and I behave like a clown to lighten up the mood. But overall, it's just not true. I am *not* a clown for everybody's amusement. I deserve to be taken seriously like anyone else in this world.

I guess that's why I love Kathy so much. She takes me seriously. I was a *man* to her. Not a clown, a little kid. Not a Goofball.

And it feels *good*.

"See ya, Shel," Dave said, shuffling his feet uncomfortably at the door. His eyes didn't meet mine. "I'm, uh…sorry about the 'sweetheart' thing…I really…"

"It's okay, Dave, buddy. Don't worry about it. Have a good drive home." We shook hands. And then we hugged.

Wait for it…

"*Fag!*"

I'm glad Luke wasn't here this weekend. He'd shoot us both.

I took the next Tuesday off of work so that I could pick up Kathy at the Greyhound terminal. Problem was, she came in at six in the morning. If *that* ain't love, I don't know what is.

"How were your folks?" I asked, on the bus home.

"They were okay, but a week with them…" She shuddered. "I think I've kind of passed the point where I can actually, like, *live* with them for an extended period of time without getting into fights regularly. Do you know what I mean?"

"Yeah…yeah. I do." *Not really…*

"Anyway, it's good to be back. How was Dave?"

"Oh, super great. I love that guy."

"Did you sleep with him?"

"*Kath!*"

"Just kidding, Shelly." She put her arm around my shoulders and planted a large kiss on my lips in front of the crowd of morning commuters. Some smiled and averted their gazes.

We went back to her place for a nap, and I woke up at about two in the afternoon. Or whenever. It's so hard to tell during the winter in Ottawa – everything is so dark by the early afternoon.

> **Side A, Tape 1:** I wake up beside Kathy (which puzzles me because I thought she had classes), but then her other roommates bust into the room and start to Vogue for no apparent reason. I must be dreaming this…
>
> **Side B, Tape 1:** It's difficult to open my eyes because I'm so tired, but I roll out of bed, crawl to the door, and start loping toward the washroom. Hmmm, if my eyes are still closed, how can I be seeing? I enter the washroom and start splashing my face with water, but then I notice that Kathy's taking a shower – wearing only my hardhat. Oh, I'm dreaming this…
>
> **Side C, Tape 2:** I roll out of bed again with a thud and start slapping my face, desperate to wake up. I can't feel it even when I thwack myself with a big one, so of course I'm dreaming and I try again…

Fig. 12. Is it Real, or is it Memorex?

Eventually, I'm able to wake up into near-darkness, and after a few seconds of convincing myself that I'm not dreaming this time, I heft myself out of bed to fix some coffee. Winter in Ottawa was a real drag.

It's 3:45 in the afternoon – Kath should be back from classes in about an hour or so. We're going to a classical music concert tonight, somewhere downtown. I don't know a blessed thing about classical music, but Kathy's an expert. She's so much more cultured than I am. She's grown up with Beethoven and Bach and a lot of those German Broke *(Barak? Baruch?)* music guys. I think that's really neat. I've learned so much from her.

So I headed home to take a shower and change into a suit (my only suit, the one I wear for job interviews, weddings, and funerals – haven't done that one yet). After a dinner of leftovers, I walked back to Kathy's. It was six o'clock, and she was only a half hour late getting ready this time.

"You look marvelous," I said, honestly. She was wearing a

long black dress, and had her hair up in an interesting way.

"Thank you, kind sir. Well, here's your ticket. Did you eat yet?"

"In a manner of speaking, yes."

"Good. We should catch the 6:40 bus downtown."

The Ottawa Chamber Music Society concert featured a trio – violin, cello and piano (Kathy's specialty). It was almost three-hours long with the intermission: Beethoven Trio in E-flat, Op. 1, No. 1; Copland "Vitebsk: A Study in Jewish Theme"; Dvorak "Dumky" Trio, Op. 90. Kathy gave me some background on all this beforehand; I, of course, didn't know what the hell she was talking about.

After the concert, we took a little walk through the Market. The weather seemed to be warming up, but only a little.

"Shel?"

"Ye-*ah*?"

"What did you think?"

"It was very nice."

"What part did you like the best?"

I was trying to think of an answer that wouldn't make me sound like a complete goofball. "I liked the Beethoven," I replied.

"Which part?"

"The fast part…Allegro. I liked the Allegro the best."

"Me, too." [*Insert thumbs up for good answer here*]. She grasped my arm a little tighter, leaning her head against my shoulder. I gave her a small peck on the cheek.

We were undoubtedly different. Sometimes I felt like such a freak, a cultureless buffoon, but I think that's what she liked about me. Sometimes, she may wish that I could take part more in her world of culture, and sometimes, I wished that she could play a game of foosball with me, or watch hockey without falling totally asleep. Love is a little complicated…but it was, overall, very right.

On Friday, we had a retirement party for Mr. McFadden. When we all got in that morning, we were greeted with bottles of Glen-fiddich, placed in strategic areas around the office. I blanched. I hate scotch. I got sick on it once. So did Dave. During the Bad Times™.

I remember things were already kind of rocky between Jeanette and Dave even before they broke up. So I wasn't all that surprised when Rick brought over a bottle of Glen-something to my house to help ease Dave out of the girlfriend-blues. I guess the scotch alone wasn't all that bad, but the sixers of Guinness (*"The Beer That Eats Like a Meal"*) that washed it down didn't help much.

"I don't think it's a good idea to mix, Rick," I said, after the first bottle.

"We'll finish off the scotch first, then the Guinness. You know what they say: *Liquor then Beer, Never Fear…*"

"*…Beer then Liquor, Never Sicker,*" I chimed in, wearily.

"A song as old as the hills," Rick smiled.

And so we drank.

Later that night, after a bunch of hardcore drinking and complaining (and drunken phone calls, evidently), Jeanette swung by on her bike and Dave stepped outside to talk to her. I sat there drinking with Rick for about a half-hour, and it was really quiet when, all of a sudden, we heard some high-powered shouting, and then this big crash. We went outside to see what the hell was going on, and saw Dave, lying on the street, completely immobile.

It turned out Jeanette had run over him with her bike.

Rick and I totally *freaked* – we thought he was dead or something. Fortunately, Dave only had the wind knocked out of him, so we shuttled him back to the house, patched up a few nasty cuts and bruises, and finished off the booze. To this day, Dave refuses to talk about what happened that night.

Soon thereafter, Dave broke with his parents, and then there was The-Mother-of-All-Arguments. And that's when Dave's dam broke.

A few nights later, Dave and I ended up at the Bomber

again. We'd soared through a half-dozen pitchers and had just gotten kicked out after a failed attempt at stealing a beer sign from the patio fence. We stopped outside the Math building to take a breather, listening to the raucous chatter from the patio when the song changed and wafted towards us, echoing off the large concrete walls we were leaning against. *Pink Floyd*, I think.

Dave's face contorted in obvious pain. Suddenly, his eyes were bulging, red and streaming with fierce tears, trying to claw their way out of the ducts. I'd never seen him like this, and I don't think anyone else ever had, either – not Rick, not Mike or Luke. No harsh language or flip jokes or a pitcher to hide behind. Just *pain.*

"*Shel…*" he whispered.

I leaned over, a little closer.

"*Shel…I just can't take this anymore. Help me, Shel…kill me please.*"

He was whispering this to me, and crying and shaking and something had to be done. He needed my help. So I guess I hugged him. I hugged him as he sobbed and whispered his desperation to me, and I dried his eyes with my jacket.

"*Shel just help me get through this I don't know if I can make it I loved her so much you gotta believe me it hurts a lot how could she do this to me how could she fuck me over like this now I'm all alone don't let me be alone so fucked up no one with me no Jeanette no friends no family what am I gonna do? Shel, what am I gonna do?*"

And I didn't say a word. What was there to say?

Shakespeare said something about problems not coming in single soldiers but in armies. Or something. Man, he got that right. This had all come on the heels of The-Mother-of-All-Arguments.

We were at the Bomber celebrating the end of midterms. Luke, having freshly dropped out of school a month before, joined us, and we all grabbed a table by the stage and ordered a huge number of pitchers of Rickards Red. In the middle of getting good and stewed, Daphne came up to Rick and propositioned him. Rick was the only Asian guy on who Daphne plied her many charms. The bastard.

"Hey, Rick. Looking for a good time tonight?"

"Always looking for a good time, Daph," Rick said blithely. Rick always treated Daphne with a mixture of playfulness and disdain. "You know the rest of the guys, don't you, lambchop?"

She greeted the rest of us (purposely skipping over Dave) as if we were loaves of bread. Luke and I nodded; Mike averted his eyes. Dave looked like he wanted to hit someone.

"So, Rick, I heard you're going down to New York City. How are you going to live without me, baby-cakes?"

"With infinite difficulty, sugar-pop, with infinite difficulty."

"How 'bout a farewell dance? They're playing our song."

"I've got a better idea," Rick smirked, good-naturedly tapping his drink with Luke's red plastic drink sword. "Why don't you dance with bitter-boy over here?" He motioned to Dave, who immediately became livid. "He needs a good fuck to get over his problems."

"No thanks." She turned on her heel and went to prowl elsewhere.

Dave did a fast burn. "Rick, of all the motherfucking *nerve...*"

Rick just smiled, and left the table.

"Relax, Dave," Luke chided. "You're acting like a loser." This earned a psycho-look from Dave, who just blew up.

"You arrogant *prick!* I am fucking *sick* and *tired* of your needling! You never fucking lay off, do you, with you're useless comments – what the *fuck* do you know about me, anyway?"

"Now where the *hell* did that come from?" demanded Luke. "For god's sake, yell at Rick! Or better yet, Dave, just *deal* with your goddamn problems, okay? I mean, *surprise!* You're not the only one who's ever been hurt..."

"Don't you *dare* lay your pop-psychology on me!"

"Then don't lay your frustrations and your pathetic inadequacies on us, okay?"

"Guys guys guys," Mike motioned calmly, "come on come on come on…"

"*Jeeeeeeeezus christ*! [*Dave stretched out that curse like only he could*] You don't just *lay* pop-psychology! You *are* pop-psychology!"

"And *you're* friggin' substance, right?" shouted Luke, pounding his hands on the table and sending the last pitcher flying. "Render unto me a fucking *break*…"

"Settle down, guys," I pleaded.

Dave and Luke were standing nose-to-nose. Rick was now-here to be seen.

A bouncer strode up, eighteen-inch pythons flexing and ready for action. "Take it outside – *NOW*!" He marched all of us to the waitress, forced Dave to cough up ten bucks for the last pitcher, and filed us neatly out the door.

After a few more choice insults, Dave and Luke parted. Mike and me were left standing by the patio, feeling foolish. And no sign of Rick. He just disappeared.

I believe that people are basically good on the inside. They can be a real jerks sometimes, and mean, and bitter, but I know they're not really like that deep down. They're just hurting, in pain on some level, reacting like a wounded animal does, because they don't know how to deal with it. I'm not sure how I would have fared if the Bad Times™ happened to *me*. Perhaps better. Perhaps worse.

Of course, Luke and Dave made up in time – Dave apologized quite readily after the summer, and Luke understood that Dave needed to blow off steam, while admitting he wasn't a pillar of control, either. Hugs and drinks all around. Guilt works amazingly well for the Banana generation, too.

But that's what I don't get about Rick. He just disappeared. We were friends, and true friends don't do that. Through thick or thin, Dave and me will be best friends forever. Of that I am certain. I recall this one time during the Bad Times™, I was washing my dishes while he was lying on my couch, staring at the ceiling, completely miserable about having broken up with Jeannette. I told him my life's philosophy: "*Dave, if you ever remember anything I say, remember this: Women come and go, but good friends last forever.*" And you know what? I still believe this with all my heart.

I am now sitting in front of my TV, watching a rented testosterone-filled action movie starring Stallone and that hunky Latino dude that Kath actually finds somewhat repulsive. She got bored of the movie halfway, and was now slumbering quietly on my chest, my hands wrapped in her dark raven hair. We'd just ordered a pizza with a few Dr. Peppers, just relaxing.

Perfection.

Because I know now what it's about. The longing, the wide-eyed searching, The Quest™...all this was over, for me, at least. And I've got to find some way to tell the other guys: Dave, Mike, Luke, even Rick, if I ever talked to him again in this lifetime. Because we all deserve a taste of perfection in our lives. I think everyone does, really...if only a little taste.

Lights.

The highest denomination of American currency a member of the public can obtain is a ten-thousand-dollar bill. For the longest time, I was obsessed with possessing one. A crisp, new ten-thousand dollar bill.

"Why?" asked Shel, perplexed. "Why would *anyone* ask for ten-thousand dollars in a single bill? What would you do with it, anyway?"

"I'd scare the hell out of a variety store owner," I replied.

Money holds a remarkable allure. In all its forms. There's the physical aspect, for example. Coins: freshly minted discs, glittering golds and silvers, the milling, the engraving, a weightiness implying value. Banknotes: crisp new ones, green, engraved, freshly printed, numbered serially. Cheques, bonds, and other representational devices: it's incredible the amount of power a simple printed, watermarked note can be endowed with. Credit cards: brightly coloured, embossed with holograms, your electronic key to a universe of pleasure. Even something as purely conceptual as electronic fund transfers: the idea that encoded sequences of zeros and ones, spinning electrons greasing the wheels of economy, enough to make or break ventures, deals, human beings, sends shivers up my spine. Money. It's a beautiful fucking thing.

I'm driving my rental car across the Bay Bridge, heading back to San Francisco after wrapping up a five-hour meeting with my first potential client in Emeryville. It's a nice, sunny day, settling into a warm Pacific evening, even though it's mid-March and the suckers in Toronto are probably sick, freezing, or both. Apparently, San Francisco has only seen snow once in the past half-century or something ridiculous like that. Hmm. I should really consider relocating. Maybe I'll just buy the place.

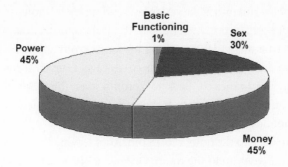

Fig. 13. Rick's Brain Chart™ (as of Mar. 16th).

Seeing the setting sun reflecting on the water, the lights from downtown SF flickering on across the bridge, the lyrics to an old *Journey* song come to mind, something I haven't heard in a long time...

> *"When the Lights go down in the city,*
> *And the sun shines on the bay,*
> *Oooh I wanna be there...in my city (oh-whoa!)...*
> *So you think you're lonely?*
> *Well my friend, I'm lonely too..."*

Grade 8 dances. Eighties fashions – upturned collars, fluorescent clothes, George Michael haircuts. Steve Perry's airy vocals echoing across the gym. Hanging with Lance and Kevin until they picked up. Going behind the lockers by the admin offices with Becky Anderson and...I shake my head. It's a clue to start taking the pills a lot more regularly. Need to call Shirley. I take out my cell phone and hit the speed dial.

I officially broke with the firm three weeks ago. As we speak, a top lawyer is working on contracts that should transfer a few key clients over to my practice with minimal difficulties. *Richard T. Wong and Associates, Management Consultants* – it has a very nice ring to it, looked impressive on the brass plaque beside the heavy oak doors of my new thirtieth-floor office at Richmond and Bay. I am strangely…tense. Maybe even a little apprehensive. I'm not sure what it is. Like when Shirley mentioned she'd run into Mike yesterday, sending a jolt through me. Well, not a jolt, it was a…weird *jolt*. Atypical response, to say the least. Maybe the jet lag's catching up to me from all the flying I've been doing for the past few days: Chicago. Denver. Toronto. London. San Francisco. Back to Toronto after this. First class may be an acceptable way to travel, but it's still a confined space that amplifies the effects of time.

I got back to the hotel at 6:18 pm. After leaving the car with the valet, I went up to the room. Ordered a bite while checking and returning messages from the East Coast. Changed shirts and put on a pair of Dockers. Had two drinks from the mini-bar. Filled out some cheques for Shirley, to be dropped off for FedEx at the front desk. Started on some paperwork. Hmmm, it's still nice out – how about a coffee? I grabbed my briefcase and headed down to Cannery Row. Might as well catch some local scenery before I leave tomorrow, Air Canada Flight 637 at 12:03 pm. The sun was still hanging like a molten peach on the horizon, and the bars and restaurants in the Row were teeming with yuppies, just off work, having drinks and trying pick-up lines on each other. Tourists were still browsing the shops and stands. A Jamaican steel-drum band was playing on a stage near the open area of the square, brothers wearing the colours jumping in time with the beats. I rounded the corner, studiously avoiding a shop specializing in stereograms of all shapes and sizes. I never look at stereograms. There is something disturbing about those swirling shapes, the twisted patterns. I believe they're the tools of the devil. I fear one day that I will stare at one and suddenly be faced with a huge, dancing 3-D pentagram surrounded by triple sixes. It will then consume my soul and suck me into the picture, where I will spend eternity as one of those little repetitive elements within. If you look closely enough at a stereogram, I'm sure you see the screaming, contorted faces of the damned…

I never look at stereograms.

Maybe there's something wrong with me.

I walked into a corporate-type coffee shop and ordered a tall Coffee of the Day (never did get into espresso drinks) and sat down at a small table by the window overlooking the Row. As I sorted through some files, I noticed three Japanese tourist girls at the table next to me. Two of them were pretty ugly, but the third one – hmm. Tall. Slim. Tanned. Long, luscious black hair with red streaks. Wearing a revealing black top, white "skort" (one of those odd combination skirt-shorts) and a pair of ridiculously cutesy silver shoes that only Japanese tourist girls would wear. *She'll do.* They were stealing looks at me over steaming cups of Colombian and almond biscotti, sharing rapid polysyllables amongst themselves. My Japanese is limited, but I was fairly sure they were talking about yours truly. I looked over, giving them roguish smiles between pages of a report I was skimming through, and sent them into small spasms of giggling. I wasn't really in the mood, but it was force of habit. Sexloverelationships is such an easy game. The key? Treating it exactly as you'd treat technical or professional matters. You see, in technical matters, there's only competence. You identify what needs to be done, and do it; what you want, and you get it. In technical matters, it's your business to control variables. In love, it's *my* business.

"Controlling variables. In Love." Mike repeated, as he drove me home from a bar in downtown Kitchener.

"Yup." I unscrewed the cap of my flask and took a leisurely pull. "Traditional thinking places a disproportionate amount of value on the romantic aspects of love. What they don't understand is that romance is just an artificial, psychologically-induced lack of control that eats at your ROR."

"ROR?"

"Rate-of-Return."

"Rate-of-*Return*?"

"A lot of people have the misconception that this sort of methodology doesn't work in Sexloverelationships. Or rather, they don't *want* it to work that way. Lovely, sentimental, ultimately useless. Let's be frank: love is a system. A system modifies an input to produce an output. To control the output, you modify the variables within the function representing the system." I drained the flask. "Simplicity itself."

"I don't know, Rick…"

"Geez Mike, *you* of all people have to start getting practical with Sexloverelationships. You've got a godawful track record."

A sarcastic laugh. "Thanks for reminding me. It's just not that easy. Love isn't practical by nature. You can't just treat it like an engineering problem…it's crazy, wacky, romantic…"

"That's sap thinking. You'll never get maximum value with that sort of mentality. Now, I'm not one to toot my own horn *[insert another sarcastic laugh here]* but if anyone knows value, it'd be me." I saw the skepticism in his face, so I tried to soften my philosophy a little. "Well, then you make up for it by being impractical in other parts of your relationship. Like random acts of romance, for example. Or public displays of affection. Or maybe even more – try having sex with your partner in public places or something."

Mike raised his eyes at that one, obviously interested.

"What?"

"Sure. In a parade, in the middle of class, or out a balcony hanging with your legs tied to bungee cords." I scratched my head. "Although all the blood would rush to your head…"

"So why not tie the cord around your neck?" Mike suggested, smiling just a little.

"Nah. That's sexual asphyxiation. I don't do that weird shit."

"Ah, but what a way to go."

"What a way, indeed."

"You've done this sort of thing, have you?"

"Not as such," I admitted.

Mike clucked his tongue in mock disappointment. "Man, Rick, I thought you were a player."

"Whatever."

After a solid half hour of giggling and furtive glances, the tall tourist-babe eventually comes over and speaks to me in Japanese. "*Nihon-jin desu?* (Are you Japanese?)"

"*Iie,*" I reply in pidgin Japanese, "*Ca-na-da-jin.*" I motion to my Canadian passport in my briefcase, which incidentally is beside a money clip, thick with C-Notes. She's hooked and asks me to dinner in a rather forward manner. I accept.

Three hours later we are back in my hotel room. She crawls over me, lithely, like a kitten, licking my chest, stroking my thigh, purring sexy polysyllables. And despite the pleasantness of her smell, the earnestness of her touch, I am feeling empty and tense. I crave relief. I ask her to perform acts on me, and she complies, but it is too easy. It's always too easy. In the morning, I wake up a 6:09 am and go out, wearing only a trench coat and loafers. I buy various tools to modify variables of this hot little system. Flowers. Tea. Paper. Freshly baked blueberry muffins. I bring them upstairs, and greet her with them, the sun shining through the window. She squeals in delight and bounds over the sheets naked, enveloping me in a starfish-like embrace. As I drive her back to the hotel where her tour group is staying, marginally listening to her happy burbles about future visits, meeting her parents, coming to Toronto…

I am still feeling tense.

I return to my hotel to pack, and then drive to the airport three hours ahead of my flight. Fortunately, airport bars open pretty early. I, of course, take advantage. I need to be absolved.

Two-and-a-half hours later, I pay the elevated bar bill and head for my flight. Beside the gate, there was a glassed-off pen for smokers (it isn't big enough to be a room.) The ceiling is stained a sick shade of brown, which contrasts starkly with the crisp-white ceilings outside. The ostracism is complete with a smallish air purifier at the centre of the room, groaning like an old man with the stomach flu.

Damn granola-eating health-conscious Californians, I think to myself. I drop my suit bag outside the pen and shuffle in, joining an unhappy-looking middle-aged woman in lighting up.

"Death Stick, Rick?" Dave said. We are driving down to San Francisco.

"Sure." I took a smoke and accepted his light.

"Good gravy!" he exclaimed. "We're married, and we're going on a family trip together!" Dave was on an internship with Microsoft, and I decided to swing out here on the tail end of my own job in New York City for a vacation of sorts. We rented a car and left a grey and rainy Seattle, travelling south for about twelve hours, making our way through the snow-blown Cascades into northern California, popping out the other side like gophers, sometime in the middle of the night.

A few hours later, right after sunrise, we approached the Bay. Shit, it was gorgeous – eighteen degrees Celsius, windows rolled down, arms hanging off the car doors, Wayfarers on, sun shining. I could see the imported palm trees, convertibles, beautiful blonde women. Cali-*fucking*-fornia. I can see why Mike treats it as The Promised Land.

The weather wasn't really warm enough for the beach, but Dave insisted on going, anyway. We dropped our luggage at the Travelodge, and headed straight for North Beach, still un-changed and unshaven, two of six people there. While Dave was skipping stones, I approached an attractive older woman, a thirty-four-year-old who was also from a cold place. She was sitting in a lawn chair facing the ocean, wearing dark glasses and a scarf around her head like Jackie O, blanket on her lap, reading a Harlequin romance.

"*Love On The Beach*?" I asked.

"Pardon me?"

"The book title."

We talked at length. She turned out to be a special education teacher who taught hearing-impaired children English in sign language. Almost reflexively, I smiled engagingly and signed out "*Hello, my name is Rick,*" which shocked and pleased her to no end – I could practically *see* the little cartoon hearts popping out of her head at that point.

As I recall, Dave spent that night in the hotel room watching *Die Hard 3* on SpectraVision while I was getting it on with Mrs. Robinson, *koo koo kitchoo*. I've led a semi-charmed kind of life, I suppose.

The flight passes quickly, a blur of little bottled scotches. We land at Pearson at around seven Eastern Standard and I drive home in yet another storm. According to the pilot, it had snowed heavily last night, which changed to rain during the morning, changing to freezing rain at noon, followed by more snow. The ground was sheathed like a newly polished bay window. Cars were strewn about the roads and ditches like Matchboxes after a Japanese-monster-movie-scenario. Gamera was *not* the friend of all children, this time around. Back at the apartment, I drop my bags and hit the gargantuan pile of mail and messages left by Shirley. There it is – the Pyloxodin™. Tasmin calls on the cell and tells me that she'd made arrangements to go *sik siu yeh* (a midnight snack) at the *Mandarin* at half-past eleven. That gives me some time to unwind. I pop open a bottle of California Red and down it along with my dosage. *Yeah…that's the stuff.*

Time…*8:13 pm.*

I heave myself off the couch and unwrap a fresh video cassette from the stack behind the big-screen TV. I pop it in a camera on a tripod beside the stereo and set it up in front of the couch. Good – the cables are still in place. So I set my wineglass on the table and turn on the camera and the TV with the universal remote. My face fills the screen. Goddamn, I'm handsome.

"*Baseline video number…number…*" I rack my brain for the previous tape number. "*Twenty-two. Baseline video number twenty-two, the date is Saturday, March 18th, the time is 8:18 pm. Hi there, Rick.*" I give myself a tired smile. "*You just came back from San Francisco…tied up a deal with Gene Speers of the Indigo Corporation, for a hundred thousand dollars. Or was that two hundred? You made a hell of a lot of money, in any case. Your status: three weeks out of Jones and Lavoie. You need results from lawyer by April 16th at the latest, or you can kiss a quarter-million dollars of potential billing goodbye. You need to get the details from your Palm Pilot..*" Whoo-eee…drugs are kicking in.

"*Last night, while I was with Naoko, I had a very strange dream. I dreamt I was Harrison Ford. Someone had stolen my mother's purse, some blonde thirteen-year-old, who escaped into a maze of cubicle office dividers. As she was selling the purse to a judge, I confronted her and ended up having sex with her in a dressing-room cubicle on top of a bed with a Popeye bedspread. Weird. Means anything? I don't know – I just wanted to tell you.*" I jog the wineglass, but catch it before it spills. I drain it in case anything else happens.

"*Your status with Tasmin: strained because of the travelling. You need to remind her father to talk with her – he needs to make her understand that the trips are for the good of the practice, and, therefore, all of us.*" I clumsily fish a small velvet box from my briefcase. "*The ring…nice rock, set you back eight grand. American. You should pop the question tonight. Should set the date for spring of next year – you're not finished sowing oats yet.*" I looked at the ring, shut the box and tossed it onto the coffee table with a clatter. "*Not that you're going to stop, in any case. You need to remember to set up a slush fund with the latest cheque sent by Mr. Lee…not sure where. Maybe a Swiss bank account. Neat to have. Things are going pretty well, overall. Log this as the start of something good. Baseline video twenty-two, over and out.*"

Time…8:36 pm.

I fumble for the remote and switched off TV, leaving myself in relative darkness. I'll file the tape away later. I got in the habit of making baseline videos after university. Every month, I'd set up the video camera and report on the status of my plans for World Domination. That's very narcissistic, isn't it? But useful. I review old baselines, make improvements on personal productivity. I charted the progress of certain key life variables on an Excel spreadsheet until it got a little too time-consuming. So I scrapped it.

Time…9:22 pm.

I had another personal recording system back in school.

His name was Michael Chao.

I'd known Mike through my parents when we were kids, but I didn't like him much back then – he seemed to me the stereotypically geeky and surly Chinese son: face full of acne, dorky haircut with a part too far to the left, med-school ambitions that were so obviously not his own. But once we got to university and I got to know him better, he seemed all right, if still kind of nerdy.

One thing I immediately recognized in Mike was his potential as a writer. He *was* a writer, pure and simple; the way he thought, observed, recorded. That he did not realize this fully, or refused to, was a personal failing on his part. Mike was always fond of making people think, presumably because he thought rather a lot himself, so I entertained him by saying all sorts of interesting things whenever I was with him drunk. Truths. Lies. Fears. Reality. Fantasy. All pretty random. I suppose we all have ways of inspiring, saving, creating. Mike wrote. I drank. I talked, and Mike wrote about it. It was my way of relaxing and opening up. Part of it was like enacting a covenant. In various bars, in various restaurants, we would sit down and enter a private, confessional state. I would turn my head downwards towards the drink, Mike, downwards towards his notebook. In penitence. It ceased being a simple, isolated act – it became more like a concept, a higher ideal, achieving an elevated domain. But to what end, even *I* didn't know. I think I thought of him as a "time capsule" of sorts, my black box, the emergency flight recorder.

Time…*9:08* pm.

I realize with a bit of shock that I've finished the bottle of wine. But I'm still sober. I'm feeling – something else. What? Upset? Morose? A little self-destructive. Bizarre, unexpected. The makers of Pyloxodin™ should have a warranty: *"Feel good, or your money back!"* I walk over to the bar and pull out a bottle of high-octane duty-free vodka from Chicago-O'Hare. Ain't Kettel One, but it'll do. A magnum of diet cola…mix it together roughly equal parts in a wide tumbler…*thaaat's it*. The drink is called a Battery Acid by Steve back at The Firm – a favourite punishment of his every time he broke up with Mistress

Barbara. Haven't eaten since the tiny Chicken Kiev on the plane. The Battery Acid tastes watery, so I have a second, and then a fourth. Strange feelings are wafting over me now. I feel compelled to punish myself. Punish, and then repent and purge myself the next day. I've been having semi-chronic stomach pains for the past six months. No one knows about them. I had a doctor's appointment to find out why, but I've been too busy to follow through. But I think I now know what is causing them. There is an alien in my stomach. *Well that's great, that's just fuckin' great man, now what the fuck are we supposed to do? We're in some real pretty shit now man…that's it man, game over man,* GAME OVER*! What the fuck are we gonna do now? What are we gonna do?*

That is how the pain feels, on and off. There is an alien in my stomach. I'm quite sure of this. I've been trying to make friends with it, though. I have grown to love my alien. In many ways we are very alike. He likes getting drunk, as do I. So we drink together, and he is soothed for another night, only to awaken and howl at me the next day. Or the day after.

Time… *10:66 pm.*

I'm staring at the black TV screen, Battery Acid stocks depleting rapidly. I need absolution. Mike was my absolution at one time. He is the only person besides Shirley who knows I augment my superpowers with pharmaceuticals. He warned me against it.

"Rick," he says, choosing his words carefully. We are sitting at a 'townie' bar in southern Waterloo – no students. "Drugs are kind of…unpredictable. Pharmacology differs across physiologies. Even experienced pharmacists and physicians are still technically in the dark ages when it comes to predicting the effects of certain medication."

"Interesting."

"A person who is not clinically depressed may engender what is called a 'serotonegenetic response': over-stimulation of the brain, too much serotonin. At that point, all bets are off – who knows what could happen?"

I nodded my head then. I nod my head now.

Who knows what could happen? Especially if you took it in a staggered, uneven schedule. Especially if you took it in irregular doses. Especially if you took it with large quantities of alcohol.

Back at the bar, Mike watches me drain another rye-and-ginger. "Not to mention the possible effects of anti-depressants when mixed with alcohol. I read some studies that show alcohol magnifies the effects of certain medications tenfold."

"Doesn't sound like a good idea," I lied.

*Time…11:16 pm…**Shit!** I'm going to be late!* I thrash around, picking up my jacket, wallet, keys. At this point, I've had three-quarters of a bottle of vodka, a bottle of red wine and the shot bottles of scotch on the plane. Oh, and a few at the airport before my flight. Oh, and a few lines here and there. I debate calling a taxi, but realize I'll have to wait for it, then I'd definitely be screwed. I'd *definitely* be screwed. So I go down to the garage to get the Beemer. It is a Saturday night, and there were a lot of cops out. But I am lucky.

Do I feel lucky? Now do you punk?

I get to the restaurant a half-hour late. Tasmin is waiting at our table, pouting.

"**Reet-chut-ah!** Yau moh **gau** choh-ah, nei **gum** ngan! (You've got to be kidding, you're so late!)"

I'm not in the mood to soothe her right now.

Do I feel lucky? Now do you punk…?

She looks at me and scrunches up her forehead. "Have you been drinking?" she asks quietly in Cantonese.

I give her a half-nod.

"How much?"

I shrug.

Do I feel lucky? Now do you…?

She doesn't say anything, obviously angry, and orders some food.

After an awkward ten-minute silence, she starts to pepper me with criticism. About being late, about drinking, about leaving her alone too often. She says she's been out with Thomas, an HK friend of hers, in an obvious ploy to get me jealous. Silly bitch, do I fucking care? I sit looking away from her, passively sipping my tea.

Do I feel lucky…?

The rice comes, and that's when I make the mistake of looking up.

"Good *God…*" I gasp in English.

Tasmin was no longer Tasmin…she was…

The image lasts only a few seconds, and I am not entirely sure what happened afterwards…

Next thing I know, I'm in bed curled up with a bottle of Crown Royal. Pyloxodin™ scattered all over the pillow. I am quickly losing control, a cartoon fight cloud spinning completely out of control, spinning into nothingness, dissonance, oblivion. I am beginning to hate myself. I am beginning to hate what I am. I am beginning to hate the ideal.

She has been trying to call me all night.

The phone rings.

I unplug the phone.

Cogito Ergo Suck.

"He who despises himself esteems himself as a self-despiser."
– Fred Nietzsche, 'Fun Guy'

It's a crisp, bitterly cold Friday morning. The sun rises over the buildings like a lone lightbulb in a basement storeroom, casting the city in a cold, passionless glare. There is snow and slush and concrete. And salt-stained cars. And very little else. This is Canada in the winter. The cold stings your eyelids and freezes the mucus in your nasal passages. Walking outside, you can practically feel the warmth draining out of this city, like heat draining out of the Eaton Centre's glassed-in atrium, millions and millions of dollars-worth.

For God's sake, does it ever stop snowing in this country? Once again, city maintenance has plowed in our driveway, and guess who pulls the winter shit duty around here? I had to clear the damn thing before heading to the bus stop – *happy* **happy**. They say that the city of Barrie, located about an hour north of Toronto, could save at least six million in snow-removal costs if it were a mere five minutes south of its present location. I look around at this weather and I don't believe it for one moment.

I exit the St. George subway station into the grey-black drifts encapsulating the cars parked on Bedford Rd. I'm a half-hour early for my meeting with Allenberg. Perfect time for a coffee. As I trudge over to the Second Cup, I dream of California.

California. Cal-i-for-nai-eh. I'm goin' back to Cali. Good weather, nice cars, beautiful women, choice careers. With the exception of earthquakes and property taxes, I figure that life in the California Republic must be perfect – tranquil yet stimulating, relaxing yet motivating. The Promised Land. A place where you step outside and the sun puts a smile on your face instead of a frozen scowl. A place where you can seek out a gently waving palm tree on a sandy beach to veg out, nap, have sex, write The Book™. A place where the howling roar outside your window is not an eighty-kilometre-an-hour blizzard that threatens to encase your house in a block of ice. It's the ocean. The beautiful, wide, warm ocean.

Mental note: check driver's license to see if name isn't Gauguin.

I step through the condensation-frosted doors of the coffee shop, showering the floor with salty slush. "Holy *shit*!" I exclaim, perhaps a little more loudly than I should have, engendering the stares of patrons at the front of the store.

Ingrid is there, all smiles. "Hey there," she says, automatically reaching for a cup. "Irish Cream?"

"Oh God, yes. You're an angel."

She laughs, brushing back her hair and tying it up with a black scrunchie, like she always does.

I also pick up a package of chocolate-covered espresso beans, anticipating a late night at the office. Six of those little fuckers and you'll be wired as a telio-phone pole. I hate the things, but they're like chips – you can't eat just one, and six just turn your brains into a pulsating mass of goo.

I sit down with my precious payload at my usual spot, the wobbly, round table by the washroom. I fish around my bag for my walkman, finding out that the battery has been bled dry because the radio switch had accidentally been jogged on. Curses. I spend a minor mint on double-A batteries every month. You can't have coffee without music.

"Life is full of little disappointments," I say aloud, attracting a strange look from a girl on her way out of the store.

Today? I'm registering for my next semester in this hellhole pit. Course calendar, chequebook, registration form (in triplicate), No. 2 mechanical pencil, primed to sign five more months of my life away to the Grad School Monster. I fill out my cheque, secretly hoping I don't have enough funds: maybe a bounced cheque'll be enough to get me the hell out of this place, my personal Emancipation Proclamation. Unfortunately, I'm confident my folks've deposited the right amount in my account. You can always count on the Chaos to Do The Right Thing, whether it be support an offspring in school, make him take piano lessons, or force him to eat all the *bok choy* on his plate.

Spoiled ungratefulness aside, I suppose I've come to realize that the evil Chinese tortures my folks inflicted on me in my youth were all about Doing The Right Thing. Sure, I hated the multitude of things forced at me, like grad school, piano le-sions, the freaky foods like ducks feet that sometimes made it to our dinner table, but I connected all of those as a rather desper-ate attempt to…infuse? Is that the right word? Infuse their children with their idea of what was "right." Chinese-style.

Dave says that most Bananas are messed up in one way or another, but the thing he tends to ignore is that our parents, the first-generation Chinese Canadians, are probably just as messed up, only in a different way. Funny thing is that it was the food that made me realize this. Like a lot of other Bananas I know, I used to hate Chinese food with a passion, and I'd get into these huge fights with my parents about it. The absolute worst was *jook* (Chinese porridge) on Sundays. After suffering several hours of fire-and-brimstone-talk at church, the last thing I wanted to come home to was a large bowl of grey and unhappy looking gruel. I can remember Jen and I cheering like idiots every time my mom forgot to put the *jook* in the slow-cooker the night before, and resigning themselves (with identical grimaces) to go to McDonalds, "just this Sunday only."

But that was before I went off to University. In Waterloo, after days of Kraft Dinner, canned ravioli and English muffins, I found myself longing for a decent pre-meal soup, steamed fish, *dim sum*, and yes, even a bowl of *jook*. The first Sunday after I graduated, while watching my mom dole out the *jook* and complaining how she needed a new stove, I suddenly realized that my parents were right about this one all along. And once I understood *that*, I grudgingly admitted that all their pressuring, their concerns about *mien ji*, their psychotic and unwavering devotion to med school – it all came from the best of intentions.

Although I was in a supreme world of hurt right now, it gave me some sort of satisfaction that the reason why I was here was because they loved me. That was for sure. Besides, any parents willing to put a piano in the hands of a surly eight-year old, and forcing themselves to listen to him practise every single day for seven years – come *on*, now. Even though most Chinese households were into the *yeet **low*** thing (you know, TV in the background, sink going full blast, pots boiling, piano banging), I still figured that the skull-splitting cacophony must have been as awful for them as the experience was for me. If I ever have kids, I think I'll teach them to play the dog whistle.

The next day, I came back to the Second Cup to meet both Dave and Luke for a group coffee break – Dave was in the area picking up some resumés from the U of T Computer Engineering department, and Luke was going to meet me anyway after his morning show. We sat around over cups of Irish Cream, staring at the wisps of breath from passersby outside.

"Michael, I have no idea why you put up with this Second Cup swill." Luke shook his head and tossed his cup aside in disgust. "It's so oily, and it tastes like Styrofoam."

"Grab a clue, Luke. Mikey comes here because of yonder coffee-babe." Dave grinned, motioning toward Ingrid and shaking his hand in a rude jerking motion.

"Oh Dave, do shut up." I yawned, caffeine not hitting me yet. "It's better than Starbucks. For a chain that opens a new store every hour, they sure have lousy coffee."

"You're an idiot," smirked Dave. "Starbucks is great coffee. Couldn't get enough of that stuff out on the West Coast. I'd commit murder for a Starbucks in my building."

"I can't believe you jokers," said Luke, snapping off his rubber band and letting his hair down. "You brainwashed louts have bought into the corporate coffee propaganda without firing a single neuron. Starbucks is just like the Second Cup… mediocre. You can't trust any shop with more than two outlets."

"Blasphemer!" gasped Dave, making a cross with his fingers.

"Well, I like the consistency," I said. "You know exactly what you're getting every time you walk in – no sudden or surprising deviation in quality."

"It's hard to deviate in the field of serving crap, Mike." Luke tapped the empty thermos in his bag. "The only coffee I swear by in this town is JetFuel™ Java, Parliament St. One man op, quality brew – even though the owner is a pot-head."

"You and your fancy shmancy artsy-guy coffee!" snorted Dave. "*Every* red-blooded Canuck knows that Canadian dough-nut shop coffee is the best. Tim Horton's, man. Memories of house-league hockey games at six in the morning, munching on a maple nut with a Cuppacanuckjoe." Luke and I softened a little bit, basking in Dave's surprisingly eloquent nostalgia.

Coffee is certainly a central fixture in all our lives. Our live-lihoods depended on it: The Morning Show host, the computer programmer, the construction worker. The perpetual profes-sional student. The madness all started in school – all those late nights holed up in the library or an empty classroom or a com-puter lab, studying for tests, doing assignments until four o'clock in the morning.

Out of all the guys, I guess I was the one who bought into the "coffee-thing" the most – I'm a total sucker for the feel, the environment, you know? *Perfect moments.* I figure if they ever developed a combination record store/bookstore/coffee shop, I would probably live, age and die there.

Speaking of dying, I figured I could do some serious damage to myself if I continued to log the time I did in this place. I have a friend who was riding a bike after five cups of coffee and ended up planting his face into the concrete. Cost: three teeth. So I usually limited myself to about two cups – three max – followed by some Swiss-processed Decaf, or tea.

"*Tea. Earl Grey. Hot,*" I said, doing a terrible Picard imita-tion while ordering from Ingrid. Ingrid smiled at me, not really getting the joke.

Two hours and four beverages later, I left the place com-pletely caffed up. My head was spinning, the air shimmered, and it felt like I was floating on a cushion of air – or something – as I made my way back to the office. At least I got my fix. Ride the snake, man.

I am walking down the eerily quiet halls of Ramsay Wright just before 11 pm, still working on a lab report for Allenberg, due in three days. The undergrads have gone for Reading Week – vacations to Florida or the Dominican Republic, lying on the beach, playing volleyball, drinking Mai-Tais and Daquiris. Having a life.

I walk over to the vending machine to get a cup of that awful coffee from Happy Elephant Catering (or whatever). It's far too cold to go outside. At seventy-five cents a cup, the Happy Elephant isn't too much of a bargain, but it's still coffee. Company on a cold, dark winter's evening. When I get back to the office, an e-mail message from Dave is the only thing saving me with a date with some rat poison…

> From: Dave Lowe <dlowe@Praxus.ca>
> To: "Malaise Guy" <mchao@neuro.utoronto.ca>
> Subject: Boy, You're a Loser!
>
> It's 11:03pm! What the *hell* are you doing still logged on? Love, Dave.

> From: Michael C.C. Chao mchao@neuro.utoronto.ca>
> To: Dave Lowe <dlowe@Praxus.ca>
> Subject: Re: Boy, You're a Loser!
>
> Dave Lowe <dlowe@Praxus.ca> wrote:
> >It's 11:03pm! What the *hell* are you doing still logged on?
> Lab report due Monday. It's dead quiet in here…unless you count the sound of my eyes looking at the clock every5min. MC.

> From: Dave Lowe <dlowe@Praxus.ca>
> To: "Malaise Guy" <mchao@neuro.utoronto.ca>
> Subject: RE: Re: Boy, You're a Loser!
>
> "Malaise Guy" <mchao@neuro.utoronto.ca> blathered:
> >>sound of my eyes looking over at the clock every 5 min

"Sound of my eyes???" Dude, I'm no doctor, but I suspect you should get that checked. Or at least call "Ripley's: Believe it or Not." GO HOME! Davey Dave.

I wander aimlessly. I pass the hallway where they hang the composites of past graduates. I move from the crisp new pictures from the nineties and the eighties to the yellowing images from the sixties and seventies. Man, did they ever look ugly – longhair, porkchop sideburns, polyester, butterfly collars – so greasy and unkempt.

What am I doing? Where am I going? Did I take a wrong turn at Albuquerque? It seems like I'm asking myself these questions every single day. I must be going mad. It's been known to happen to my ilk: while I was using the facilities in the Waterloo Sciences library, I came across a set of teeth marks in the wall plaster right beside the toilet. That's right, teeth marks. That pretty much summarizes what university is to me – a place of madness and pain and despair and…odd dietary habits.

On Monday, I was barely able to drag myself out of bed after a late night of panicking and procrastinating over the lab report. But it got done. Thank God for thesauri and a propensity for meaningless verbiage.

After slipping the lab report under Allenberg's office door, I stopped off by my office to check mail. Todd wasn't in (yet again), so tuned into *can.community.asian* for a bit. I'm so stupid. I'll never learn.

> From: Jack McGraw
> <jmcgraw@ottawa.freenet.ca>
> To: can.community.asian
>
> <<socialist whining deleted>>
> You socialists really are something. You lay out these laws such that any slant-eye can get on a boat and land in Nanaimo to soak up on the social welfare programs and give nothing in return, and you accuse any neo-con of being racist when we're trying to save this country. Look around you –

these people are the racists. They continue to
speak their chink-talk in public! Wake up. This is
Canada, we speak English here. They play us like
suckers when we're the ones good enough to let
them in. We should shoot all you socialists and
vote in a real government to ship all of these
slant-eyes all back to the shitty rice paddies
where they belong.
J/M
****
 The goal of socialism is to make everyone equally poor
****

Ya gotta love McAngus – besides castigating everyone who
disagreed with him as 'socialist' with a pathological-and-near-
sexual-obsessiveness, he likes to throw around the word "racist"
as if he wasn't the poster boy for Practitioner of the Year.

It turns out that McAngus had forged his UserID, the brave
patriot he was. The thing was that using a fake UserID resulted
in any e-mail sent to him (Her? It? You can never *tell* on the
Internet) to bounce back, message un-received. I went over to
Dave's office to ask him about the technical details behind this.

"Still addicted to Net news, eh?" he said, amused. "You should
kick it, man – that shit kills brain cells."

"This coming from an bonafide alcoholic. So, what about this
fake UserID business? Is there anything that can be done about it?"

"Not all that much. Here, lemme show you something…"
Dave turned to his Sun Sparc station and starting typing rapidly
at the prompt.

"Look at this," he said, swivelling his monitor and pointing
to a cryptic set of commands characteristic of UNIX. "I just tel-
netted to an empty port – in this case, 32 – on one of our server
machines downstairs. With a little tap-dancing, this enables me
to spoof any UserID I want." He typed in *mike@sucks.com*.

"Hardy har *har*, Dave."

"Liked that, eh? Anyway, I can use this forged UserID to
send e-mail to people, just like any other UserID – only nothing
can be sent to it because it doesn't really exist." He turned to me
and shrugged rather non-committally. "Yeller-bellied netters
pull this trick all the time – do you know how many white su-

premacist e-mails I've received from *white@power.fuck.you.chink* when I was still into this Usenet shit?"

"So you can't trace him or anything like that?"

"Sure you can…if you're a technical god like I am. But what's the point? Knock on his door and bitch-slap him? Bake him cookies?"

"No…but at least he'd be, you know, traceable."

"Mike, just give it up. You should treat e-mails sent like this as untraceable, at least by common schleps. I'll give you an example – what's the name of that hot chick you like down at the Second Cup?"

"Who, Ingrid?

"Yeah, her." He turned back to his keyboard. "Second Cup probably has a corporate e-mail address for comments about their lousy coffee and all that, right?"

"How should I know?"

"I'm very disappointed. You've been stalking her for months…here, let me check their web page." He opened up a browser, and then typed some more technical gobbledygook at the prompt. "There. You are now *mike@sucks.com* sending mail to Ingrid at *comments@2ndcup.com.*"

> From: mike@sucks.com
> To: Ingrid <comments@2ndcup.com>
> Subject: Message for Ingrid
>
> Dearest Ingrid: I think you are one hot momma…

"*Dave!*"

"Oh, all right."

> From: mike@sucks.com
> To: Ingrid <comments@2ndcup.com>
> Subject: Message for Ingrid
>
> Message for Ingrid: I really respect your coffee-serving skills. Sincerely, Gerald.

"Gerald?"

"I could sign *your* name if you want."

"Gerald is nice…"

He sent the e-mail. "Look, Mike, just forget about this Mc-Angus guy. He sounds like a sorry and twisted loser who ultimately has no real power, hence his whining on the Usenet. Poor bastard. Trust me, it's not worth it – that's why I swore it off years ago. I suggest you find healthier ways to interact with healthier people – hey, where are you going?"

I was heading for the door. "I'm going to log onto *can. community.asian* for a few hours, followed by a spirited round on *soc.culture.african.american* and *alt.sex.pitcures.binaries-erotica*," I grinned.

"Jesus, Mike, stop reading news and go learn how to scuba dive or something."

Actually, Dave's right. Getting the bends was healthier than fighting for social justice on a medium where your enemy could, for all intents and purposes, be a dog. A foaming, diseased, rabies-ridden racist Canadian dog.

Now, I wouldn't call myself an "activist" by any stretch of the imagination. As a Canadian, the thing they call Asian America is a strange and irrelevant place to me…not to mention way, way too American. We might share some common primordial roots somewhere back there, but beyond that, Ai-zhun 'Muricans are like any other crazed and dogmatic 'Murican, high on their own self-importance.

So where does that leave me and others of my ilk? In a political, Banana-creme vacuum. Where does the search for identity go when you're not sure you have one? Where can you find meaning in a space ruled by American cultural hegemony? It certainly doesn't help that I come from a relatively benign background. My childhood experiences were certainly not as epic as Shel's, as interesting as Luke's, as traumatic and psychologically-scarred as Dave's. It was, for the most part, pretty quiet. Most of my childhood friends were Jewish and South Asian…I balanced out the Chinese food in my diet with matzoh balls and samosas.

And then there's The Book™. Sure, it's my passion, but just what the hell am I trying to say? I don't even know what *juk sing* really means, beyond the literal translation. What makes a good "Chinese-Canadian" novel? A good immigrant story? Don't have that. The trials of growing up Chinese among whites? Don't really have that, either, really. Treatises on racism, Chinese history, rusty boats off the coast of BC? Nope. I even thought about embellishing The Book™ with a couple of dragons and phoenixes and such, but I know so little about stuff like this, that it always came out sounding contrived and stupid.

Rick cornered me on that one. "You should use Chinese myths in The Book™." he said, relaxing over a large vodka martini (three olives). It was two o'clock in the afternoon.

"Myths? Er, what do you mean? I don't know any myths."

"You *have* to have myths. They're are a hot commodity in Asian American-no-hyphen literature these days. Panders to a lucrative white book market – *Joy Luck* and all that. Myths will make The Book™, you know, more *exotic*."

"But I don't know any myths."

"What do you mean? Wasn't your mom a Chinese Lit major in Taiwan or something?"

"Yeah, but she never taught me much Chinese. I don't even know how to swear."

"Well, my mom used to tell me stories when I was smaller – that is, whenever she had the time. Loads of stories with emperors and sailors and warriors and stuff."

"Do you remember any of them?" I asked, pulling my notebook out.

"Nope. But the important thing I got out of them was the fact that my friends' parents always loved them. I repeated those stories to all sorts of white people – friends, girlfriends, teachers, that cute white chick in your Bio-Psy class who's majoring in East Asian Studies. All of them listened as raptly as you're listening to me now. That's the *point* – people *love* the exotic. Every year, rich westerners who perceive their own culture as empty, shell out tons of dough for rugs, replica vases, funky statues. And they'll shell out dough for The Book™ if it has myths." He took a large gulp from his drink and sat back, looking rather self-satisfied. *Call me butter 'cause I'm on a roll…* "But the myths they want have to be of one of two types. The first type is one that directly relates to their own background or experiences – something that fills their sense of historical void that generic modern life evidently creates. The second type of myth is one that *sounds* plausibly exotic and exciting. It doesn't have to be accurate or even grounded in fact, so long as it's heroic, shocking, filled with scandal maybe."

"But I don't know any…"

"Mike, man, you don't *have* to. You're a creative guy – make something up. That's my point; myths are insignificant grains of trivia embellished by imagination and proper branding. Give people what they expect. Like teachers, man. Most of them are these liberal-multicultural wavy-gravy types, misguidedly impressed by perspectives they don't know a lot about. The right myth'll give you A's across the board. Oh, and some girls go for that sort of stuff, too." He looked at his watch. "Oop. Gotta go. Bottom line; myths that reinforce general stereotypes *sell*, because they say 'Hey! Here's a historical story passed down from generation to generation – and whaddaya know; it says that *you are positively right in what you are thinking 'cuz you're a wise person!'* You got that?"

"I…er…uh…"

"*Thatta* boy. Just remember, when you make it big, I get a cut. Fifty-fifty sounds about right." He drained his glass, grabbed his briefcase and booked.

Hmm. It all sounded so reasonable. Vaguely offensive, but reasonable, nonetheless.

But the fact still remained: I don't know any myths. The closest thing to myths I have are those proverbs my mom shelled out wholesale whenever I did something wrong.

Dave dragged me down to the Second Cup the next day. He wanted to see if Ingrid would be acting funny about the e-mail, but she wasn't there.

"What a stupid country," I said to Dave, shaking my head. I'd just gotten off *can.community.asian* after a head-spinning flame-war with McJackass.

"What do you mean?" said Dave indignantly. "You live in the *best damn country in the world!* Sure beats the hell out of living in America!"

"I'm not so sure of that any more, Dave."

"*TREASON, TREASON, TREASON!*"

"Any red-blooded Canadian with two brain cells to rub together can rant against America," I explained, ignoring the histrionics. "They're an easy target. It takes a real patriot to mercilessly scrutinize their own nation and find further depth and meaning."

"Dude, we have it *all over* the US. Health care, social programs, violence, post-secondary education costs, beer…"

"That's all changing," I insisted. "Canadian compassion is in short supply these days. Just look around, Dave – turmoil, confrontation, stupid cruelty. We always assume that things are always worse in the States, as if the whole country is a cross between Watts, the Spanish Inquisition, and Alabama circa 1846, but that's a crock."

"Since when did you become pro-American?"

"God *knows* I'm not pro-American…I'm just a skeptical Canadian. In a lot of ways, it is a hell of a lot worse up here. It's a lot less…*honest.*"

"Bullshit, man."

"Look at race, for example. Race is this huge and festering wound on the face of America."

"America *sucks.*"

"They may suck, but you gotta admit, they've gone to race hell and back since the Civil War, right through the sixties, up to the LA riots after the Rodney King incident. They've grown up with it, they're dealing with it…and as a result, they have no pretenses about their prejudices – there's a whole counter-culture in the US that devotes itself to exposing the problems of their culture. Do we have an equivalent in Canada? Forget it –

all we have are 'patriotic' Internet personalities like McAngus."

"*That's* where your argument fails, Mike," Dave argued. "You can't extrapolate Canadian society from a few goose-stepping wackos on the Internet. Internet posters are usually fat, maladjusted cybermonkeys with no lives who need to validate their sorry existences through mindless flaming."

I shook my head. "It's not just the Internet. It's everywhere – the average, middle and upper-middle class Canadians with the house, white picket fence, two-point-two kids, minivan in the garage. In the States, you know your enemy. Up here, the backlash whips out at you from behind a smug, hypocritical, self-righteous superiority complex. *'Oh yeah, we're better than everybody else, more civilized, enlightened, 'cuz we're **not** American.'* Give me a fucking break."

"Sure, whatever." Dave was starting to get bored.

"We've just been spared the American race nightmare. Until now. There are patterns everywhere. Immigration has brought out the ugly, true face of Canada – didn't you just have a big fight in the supermarket? How about the BC-boat thing, the Reform Party, the New Red Scare? Fuck, man, how can you say with a straight face that Canadians are better than 'The Ugly American' when the average response around here is so mundane and pedestrian? How great can a Canadian truly be when he lets fear, anger and hatred overwhelm his common sense? It's just totally unbecoming of what I thought being 'Canadian' was all about." *Call me butter 'cause I'm on a roll…*

"And God help you if you try to argue with these idiots – their arrogant and over-privileged Anglo-Saxon logic brands you as a 'socialist' or a 'bleeding-heart liberal.' And if you even use the word 'racist' once, they lay that tired *'Oh, you're so politically-correct!'* mantra on you, or even worse: *'You can't accuse me of being racist. I married an Oriental wife.'* Sheesh."

"Yeah." Dave nodded thoughtfully. "Yeah, I guess." Then he frowned. "But sometimes, what with their cars and money and shit, ya gotta admit these FOBs can be pretty annoying." He drained his coffee. "Anyway, gotta run, ya pinko bastard."

As I watched Dave huff his way in the cold to the subway,

part of me agreed with him. Sort of. Because on the outside, we, as Banana Boys, are virtually indistinguishable from other Chinese. It isn't as if all the Chinese appreciated the sometimes-misguided Banana defenses of them…some are just jerks. Like the thoughtless relatives who criticize me, my choices, my failures. Like the ones who flash their money and whirring cell phones about like they were hot shit. Like the ones who snicker at my terrible Cantonese when I try to use it to buy some buns at the local cake shop. Divided we stand. Together we fall. Not being fully Chinese was only half the equation of Banana-hood, I guess. Was I Canadian? Was I Chinese? Or both? Or neither. The last one seemed the most appropriate. But the search continues, even though the country has become complacent, has stopped questioning itself. Canadians seemed to have lost their capacity as a people to question themselves. You should never stop questioning, you see. That's what makes it precious.

Before heading back home on the old Number 36A, I went back to the lab to tend to some samples. The Life of a Grad School Serf, Part 2046, Chapter 12, Verse 14. *And Ashkael begat Azrael begat Azzuberoth begat Joab from the flaming mount. And the counting of the Holy Hand Grenade will be to three* . I loaded up the freezers with a stock of monkey membranes and grabbed my coat, making my way down the main stairwell, anxious to leave the building. Absent-mindedly, I slipped on a patch of wet snow halfway down the second flight, grabbing the handrail just before I kissed the concrete.

Coulda broken my neck. Coulda died right there. Kind of wished I did, in some ways – I hear death makes life so much easier to handle. In my mind, I imagined my crumpled body at the bottom of the stairwell, discovered by two girls five minutes after my expiry. My soul floated above them, heading toward heaven – *no, wait* – I catch an escalator up there, just like in *The Simpsons*: *Please hold on to the handrail. Please do not spit over the side.*

In heaven, I am greeted by St. Peter/Krishna/Confucius/Sun-Ra/Ed McMahon/XY-4872. "How was your trip?" he asks benevolently.

"Lousy."

"Any regrets to voice before I process you?"

"Oh, you know. Family. Friends. Love. The Book™. That's it. Okay, could you please tell me what brand of brimstone we'll be repasting on today? I skipped breakfast this morning."

"You know better than that, my son. You weren't *that* bad an egg…you're going to Heaven."

"Yay." I twirl my finger in ecstasy.

"However, your end was premature and disappointingly quick – we'll have to fill out some paperwork before you get in, *and* [*geez, I knew there was a catch*] we have a small job for you to do that might make you sweat for your halo a little…"

"Sweat?" I exclaim incredulously. "Listen buddy – too much sweat already. Have you actually been down to that hellhole we call Earth lately? It blows chunks. Okay, okay, I know I'm in no position to complain here. I'll give it a shot. Any chance I can take a few eons off first? I need a breather."

"Time has no meaning here. Take as long as you want."

"Fine. So what, do you want me to trail my sister or something – make sure she graduates, gets married, raises a family, stuff like that?"

"No no no – too easy." He looks at the pair of stone tablets he is holding. "Hmmm…it says here that you are to go back as an African-American who loves blondes and Barry Manilow. Here's a V-neck sweater; good luck."

I laughed out loud. *Irony.*

"Michael, what's so funny?"

I was awakened from my stairwell reverie by Prof Allenberg, looking vaguely amused. I flushed red, embarrassed. "Nothing. Nothing's funny." I grinned. "Except for those tissue samples. Ha ha. Hilarious stuff, those wacky monkey membranes."

"Sarcasm's the lowest form of humour, Michael. See you tomorrow."

"Yeah. Sure."

✻

There was a time in my life when I thought about suicide at least twice a day. It was right after I broke up with Mina. I mean, it just seemed so much easier than going on with it all.

I'm much better now. *Honest.*

Now I think the answer to all my problems is far more mundane: *I need to have sex with lots of beautiful women.* But there's one slight problem.

"I don't have sex," I said to Sheldon over the phone. He called me to see how things were going, and ended up regaling me with his connubial bliss. I was so happy for him that I wanted to kill someone.

"Aw, c'mon, Mike. You're too hard on yourself. If a goofball like me can find someone as great as Kathy, then an egghead like you'll hook up in no time."

"But I don't have sex," I insisted.

"You know what the problem is? You think, like, way too much. You're a smart guy, Mike, but you have to think the way a woman does in order to connect. Oh yeah, and you gotta lose your latent homosexuality." Shel snorted at his own joke.

"I don't have sex."

"Well, talk to one of the other guys about it. Do you ever talk to Rick anymore? He had it all the time, evidently. Oops, someone's beeping me, it's probably Kathy, catch you later, okay Mike?" *Click.*

"I don't have sex," I said plaintively to no one in particular, still holding the receiver.

The truth is this: *I DON'T HAVE SEX.* Not because I do not want to, but because I am tired of it all. I've been to hell and back with Mina, and I fear that any emotional contact will bring me back to the bad place. I have heard all the obvious lies, and believed them, and I have paid dearly for them…

I promise never to hurt you.
I've always been honest with you.
I just want to make you happy.
I'll always remember you.
I can't live without you.
I'd do anything for you.
You can trust me.
I'm different.
It's not you, it's me.
I'll always be your friend.
I care about you.
I love you.

I do not want to hear these lies again, because I will believe them again. And it will hurt me. Again.

"You just haven't found the right one," Luke usually insisted, somewhat tenderly.

But who truly is The One?

I propose that The One is just a myth, a concept glamourized by movies and teenage fashion magazines and diamond commercials so that you buy more product. All those stories we hear from our parents – *if I hadn't stopped to tie my laces at that exact moment in front of the library when the sun was eclipsed, etc. etc.* – those are the *real* myths, more relevant to me than hackneyed Chinese tales of sailors and dragons and emperors. Real myths from a bygone era.

The One does not – *cannot* – exist in this time, this age, this era. We have the power to delude ourselves, to make anyone The One, but exercising that power ultimately hurts us through betrayal, deceit, lies, chaos, control.

So, how about this?

How about living life without the idea of finding The One? How about going through life and meeting, you know, people – just people. Some have relevance in your life, some will not. You associate with the good ones, avoid the bad ones. Maybe you'll attach yourself to someone, eventually, but he/she/it will not be The One. Merely *Someone*. Someone who's good enough. I know all this may sound too lackadaisical, but I think that the other option – becoming as cold and hard as all those bitches and bastards that hurt us, that continue to hurt us – is too damning, to dehumanizing a step. It just isn't worth it.

So I'm sitting with Todd and Jon, a Physics grad student, downstairs in the cafeteria. They were talking about women. Needless to say, I didn't have much to contribute.

"The best place to meet women," said Jon convincingly, "was back at undergraduate school. Past that, you have to work on it a hell of a lot more."

Todd agreed. "Man, I was really lucky to meet my girlfriend. I thought I was, like, totally sunk coming out of fourth-year without a girlfriend." That failed to cheer me up.

"So what to do if you do see a girl you like? I look at her. Okay?" Jon demonstrated by gazing at me with a neutral-positive expression on his face. "I look at her and convey my interest through meaningful eye contact. I mean, I just let her know that I'm interested, and I see where that goes." He turned to Todd. "How 'bout you, man?"

"Well, I approached my girlfriend by asking her for the time, and then I slid into a conversation about work and stuff. Then, after a bit of patter, I maneuvered the conversation to something a little more substantial…you know, life, love, aspirations, that sort of thing." He looked a little thoughtful. "I guess luck had something to do with it, too, but asking for the time was definitely my 'in.'"

"That sounds all right." Jon approved. And then he looked at me. "You, Mike?"

"I, erm…I…" I fumbled a bit with my words, clearly embarrassed. "Honestly? Do you guys *honestly* want to know what I do when I'm interested in a girl?"

They both nodded

"Well," I said slowly, "to start off, I guess I avoid her at all costs. I avoid eye contact, generally. And if I actually run into

her, I've been known to treat her, um, indifferently, maybe…
standoffish, even."

There was a slight pause from the other two as they stared
at me, somewhat shocked.

"What?" said Todd.

"Yeah, Mike, that'll reel'em right in," Jon cracked.

I smiled ruefully behind my cup. Hey, they wanted the
truth.

part 4
catharsis.

Roads.

Woke up this morning with violent German industrial on the brain. Looks like it's going to be a weird day.

I tossed out the playlist that Zeesh handed me yesterday, starting off the Mosh with some *Einsturzende Neubauten*, harsh take-no-prisoners-German proto-industrial. Sounds of pneumatic drills and quavering sheets of metal set to heavy, regular beats echoed through the station – very cool. I just love *Einsturzende Neubauten*. Sure, the music was excellent, but it's the *name* that makes them so great: Ein*sturz*ende *Neu*bauten. Ein*sturz*ende *Neu*bauten. Very cool – I just love saying the name. Apparently, it means "collapsing new buildings."

Zeesh was not pleased, but I shrugged it off.

I was feeling intellectually perverse – one of those days where I was dying to get into a good argument, get some entertaining reactions. So I called Dave up after work to see if he wanted to go for some drinks later that evening.

"Silly rabbit," he said. "What time and where?"

I told him to meet me at Grangers on Jarvis St., a scummy little dive, completely counter to the "cool" factor most T.O. clubs and bars try to shoot for. Grangers has absolutely no pretensions of being cool…or even any good. The place practically screams out the fact that it specializes in being lousy and grimy. It has bitchy bartenders, a tinny jukebox that plays the same music over and over, pictures of dogs playing poker on the walls (*"They're **dogs**! And they're playing **poker**! Haha… ahaha…ahahaha!"*). The beverage of choice is cheap, obscure beer like IPA and National Bohemian (served in cans, natch.)

"What the *fuck* is this place?" Dave exclaimed.

"You don't like it, Dave?" I batted my eyes innocently.

"The beer's lousy, and the music's even lousier. Patsy Cline? I'd prefer listening to your hip-hop shit over this stuff."

"Dave, for the last time you ignorant fool, Breakbeats is *not* Hip Hop."

"Whatever, Stick."

After a few cans of the featured Granger's Weird Beer of The Week (Old Milwaukee), I managed to get him entertainingly bitter and foaming.

"It's plain pathetic," he snarled into his beer. "We just seem to sit there, getting continually fucked up the ass by women, by whites, by the media, just smiling deferentially and kowtowing like the good little Orientals they expect us to be…"

"Dave," I said, mean streak revving up, "Have you ever considered the possibility that there really is no problem, and that you just want to be angry about something?"

"Nope."

"With you, it's always a distinct possibility…"

He ignored the bait. "The issue is that Asian men are merely *dismissed* in today's society, labeled like grinning monkey boys who do laundry or deliver Szechwan and program computers. At least Asian chicks get to do the weather or the news."

"But you *do* program computers, Dave."

Strike two…this was going to be harder than I thought. "I *test* them, honey. I'm just saying that if you try that labelling shit on blacks and women, see if they don't descend on you like a pack of piranhas and castrate you on the spot."

"That's 'school' of piranhas, Dave."

"Stick, why don't you shut up for once and listen to what I'm actually saying?" He's hovering around the worm, now. *Steady as she goes.* "The point is, we're dead in the water, status-wise. It's the way that The Man has planned it. We have to shout louder, say *something – anything*. Otherwise, how's it going to stop?"

I roll my eyes in contempt. "*What's* going to stop? Dude, get off of your Orwellian delusion and get into reality. We live in a pluralistic society. There's far too much information out there, and that makes people cynical. They don't just believe everything that is shovelled to them. People aren't these weak-minded buffoons…"

"The *hell* they aren't!" snorted Dave.

"The hell they are. The key is to get people – individuals – to know you, and that's more than enough to dispel any lame-assed typecasting cooked up by some Hollywood hack. And if these individuals get to know a bitter, whining loser, do you think that'll improve the lot of Asian men as a whole?"

Dave lapsed into a brief silence. And then he spoke quietly.

"I'd rather be typecast as an angry and bitter loser than as a weak-willed and deferential one."

Dave's getting a little too mellow to be fun any more.

Toronto is a pretty cosmopolitan city. Well, at least the corner of it I usually hung out in. Dave would dismiss the crowd I cavort with as "limp-wristed liberal artsie-types" – fanatically PC, purposely colour-blind. So the politics of that crowd – feminism and gay rights – were my politics, relegating racial discrimination to a status just below the homeless, but just above electric cars and soil erosion.

I guess I feel a little of his pain, though, Dave – and Michael. Only because they're my friends, not because of a common racial bond or anything like that. Maybe.

One of the reasons I hung around Michael was because I was fascinated by his pain. It was somewhat disturbing, his views on life, personal pain and suffering, and how it related to The Book™. Michael seemed to…*enjoy* his pain a little to much for his own good, you know? But that is the Power of Love, a Force from Above, Cleaning my Soul.

"Luke," Michael said softly two nights later after another drinking bout. He was lying in his usual spot – on the pad under the kitchen table.

"Yeah, Michael?"

"Let me tell you a story…

This is a true story.
A man – let's call him Dan – had loved this woman. Totally,

unabashedly loved. They had been going out for three years, and were engaged to be married within the next year. Happy as a clam, he was.

One day, due to some completely unforeseen circumstances, his fiancée decided she didn't love him any more. So she broke the engagement, broke up with him, with no explanation whatsoever.

Dan was devastated. He had loved and loved and loved, with all his heart, his mind, his soul – he was completely incapable of feeling otherwise. I dare say he was physically acculturated to being in Love with her, and simply could not physically function beyond those parameters. The trauma of the loss was devastating – he ended up losing his job, his friends, his ability to merely operate within the confines of the real world, and had to be hospitalized for six months.

Every single day, Dan, clad in hospital whites, would lie in bed, staring at the sterile white ceiling from morning until night, wondering what was the point of it all…why get out of bed, why get dressed, why find a job, go to work? Why go on living when the only reason for living had been ripped away from him?

To Dan, his love had been like a parasite on a pure and healthy organism – a tumor, if you like. The parasite entwined the vital areas of the organism with tendrils, feeding on it, growing exponentially until it became an integral, functional part of the organism, indistinguishable as a discrete entity.

*When extracted, when taken away, the entire organism broke down. It had grown to **need** the parasite, you see. Lacking the cynicism, the callousness of some of his peers, Dan, a pure soul at heart, had no natural defense mechanisms to deal with its extraction. What little defenses he did have rushed in to stanch the wound, and did not fully succeed; the organism, invaded by the parasite and now forced to do without it, died.*

But to his credit, Dan did not die. He almost did, was on the edge of it. He was totally incapacitated; it took ten, twenty, a hundred times the length of time for him to heal than other normal, well-adjusted organisms, and the process was excruciatingly painful.

He did not die.

Perhaps it was better if he did.

After six months, he finally got a semblance of a grip. He got out of the hospital, got a new job, a new life. After a little while, he was sitting in a bar, enjoying a drink, casually wondering how all this could have happened.

But then, like some bizarre joke, The Force From Above reappeared. It was her, walking through the door with another fellow. She had not noticed him as she sat down at the far end of the bar.

Dan felt a slight pang of pain in his heart, but he also felt that it was ultimately all right. Another woman came through the door, selling roses. Dan beckoned her over, purchased a rose and instructed that she send it over to his former fiancée…just for memories' sake.

She received it. She looked shocked. She glanced over, and whispered something to the fellow she was with. The fellow glanced over as well, and then proceeded to make his way across the room.

'Did you send this to her?' he asked, gently proffering Dan the rose.

Dan nodded. 'We used to be engaged. It's over now. Just for memories' sake.'

The fellow punched him in the face, sending Dan flying from his chair, his face a bloody mess. As he felt the rose thrown down on his prostrate form, the healing that Dan thought had taken place shattered into a billion icy shards, completely annihilated.

I lay there on my futon, pondering the story after Michael had fallen asleep.

Dan is not me. He may well have been me, had I fallen into the trap, had I not broke it off with Sonja.

Dan may well have been Dave, if a few things earlier on in his life had not turned him bitter, cynical, protected.

I could see Sheldon being Dan, the sweet guy that he is, so much in Love.

And of course, Dan could always be Michael, who in many ways is still a very pure person, was very much in Love.

"Michael," I said to him after feeding him coffee and bagels in the morning. I placed my hand on his shoulder. "*Healing* is the best revenge."

I firmly believe this.

After Michael left, I slipped on a new record I picked up from Metropolis Records the other day…thick, chunky Breaks, medium tempo, fat acid wobbles all over. Normally, I'd be bouncing around the apartment, dancing up a storm, but for some strange reason I found it tiresome today.

And I thought about the nature of pain, and how Michael eloquently but uselessly captured it in the pages of The Book™.

Perhaps healing *wasn't* always the best thing. Is conflict really a key to creativity? Is aggravation, suffering, or pain really essential to the creative process? Because all these things, quite frankly, sucked badly, which is why I avoided them at all costs.

But was it costing me anything?

Creativity? Vigour? Vitality?

Truth?

"*Wobblewobblewobblewobble,*" said the record. With an annoyed grunt, I slap the cross-fader over to the other turntable resume my session of Mental White Noise.

I'm going to tell you a secret: In many ways, I fear The Book™. I'm afraid that its pages, its stories, will tell me too much truth.

I do not want the truth. In many ways, I want to be clueless, empty, vacuous, "flaky" – one of Dave's favourite words for me.

Yes, I guess I am all that.

I like where I am. I guess.

Keep me here, please.

Woke up this morning with *REM* on the brain… 'It's the End of the World as We Know It (And I Feel Fine).'

Zeesh gave me my walking papers today as soon as I stepped out of the studio for the first news break. Two weeks notice. "You've been…*difficult*, lately," he said, peering at me through his horn-rimmed glasses.

"Mmmm."

"Nothing personal, pal, but it's more headaches than the station needs. You know?"

"Mmmm."

"Two weeks – you can gently wean yourself off The Morning Mosh during that time."

I nodded.

Five minutes later: *"It's the Morning Mosh, Luke Yeung here at 6 am…and soon not to be. I'm 'gently weaning' myself from this place because the **fucking** powers that be are canning the old Yeungster…well, that's just **fucking** dandy! Seems like old Zeesh Pardesh over here at the station **fucked** me over because of his personal problems – probably his aversion to pork. But personal bitterness aside, we all should help him in his time of need. So how about it, Moshers? Let's send the old boy a few more hundred pounds of the **fucking** stuff, all raw and bleeding – let's desensitize him to the shit, right? I seem to recall that tactic from a Psych class I took a long, long time ago…*

*"So I guess this is my signing off, as it were. There are going to be some production problems a little after this, so CMSH might be broadcasting some weird **fucking** shit far a half-hour or so, seeing as how I'm ditching this **fucking** place and just plain walking out. So why don't you nudge your tuner over to the right a little afterwards, and check out that **fucking** radical polka station next to our bandwidth?*

"Scab, man," I said over the mike, putting on a Pat Boone CD and breaking off the latch of the CD player with a satisfied grimace, "it's been great working with you. Good luck in all your future endeavours blah blah rhubarb…" I stepped out of the DJ booth and clapped him on the shoulder, wearing a large, artificial smile.

Scab grinned, despite the vitriol that had just poured out of his headphones. "Luke, you are one in a million. You'd better take off – Zel'll be in to rip your lungs out in one minute…"

I left the station feeling like a school kid whose supply teacher had suggested the class go outside and look at a solar eclipse.

I've been sitting at the Second Cup at the corner of John and Queen, with Death Sticks and a large Irish Cream Classic. It's a nice day for soaking in the first few rays of April, along with Second Cup-brand second-hand smoke. There are these large and cartoonish cumulo-nimbus clouds floating above a building with industrial-type smokestacks, in a very *Pink Floyd*-ish sort of way…lazy, ambient, tinged with colours. Sketchy kids line the streets with fun fur, floating past me the same way, idly passing the time before tonight's big rave, sipping frappucinos, practicing dance moves, selling each other vitamins.

An attractive woman walks by, wearing a sundress, even though it's still only thirteen degrees Celsius. I order another coffee, watching her glide by between the twin arms of smoke from my cigarette, winding their way from my fingers and dancing with each car that passes.

I think I have it figured out.

I think I grew up somewhere between then and now.

The cushion of brash confidence, the spinning cycle of fortune-electrons, induced and powered by youthful adrenaline and a bit of luck, had finally run out.

When I proceeded to adulthood, when I passed Go for the last time and found out there was no $200 to collect, I found out that it was just over. Played out. Finished.

The horse I rode in on just died.

I guess I need to find a new horse.

But I'm having doubts about this, too.

I stumbled into the 808 State a few hours later with a serious caffeine buzz. It was around dinnertime, but I wasn't particularly hungry.

I was alone in the apartment. I looked around for Seth. Nope, not here. I looked around for his stuff. Nothing. The only evidence of his visit was the brand-new Leaning Tower of Pisa in his stead, good for another forty CDs. I went over to the rack and started sliding some jewel cases into it, only to have them slide out again because – *surprise* – the tower leaned. Gonna have to set the tower by the wall at an 80 degree angle. That Seth, always the fucking joker.

After putting on some *Portishead,* I slid over to the kitchen-ette and reached for the top cupboard above the fridge, for the package of Totally Happy Crop I usually kept there – Northern Lights. *Empty.* Seth, again. Bastard. So I leaned slightly to the left, almost falling over, and grabbed a bottle of Southern Comfort, the next best thing, the only thing. Something.

I lumbered over to my futon and sat down, took a heavy pull from the bottle, and fell back artlessly, staring at the flock of posters on the ceiling blending together in a fuzz of caffeine particles. On the old milk crate night table was my old-fashioned wind-up alarm clock and a picture of my folks. It's a cool black-and-white picture, taken at an undetermined time. They're sitting on a bench beside a brand new Harley-Davidson. Pop looks suave, decked out in a slick single-breasted blazer, pressed slacks, crisp shirt, narrow tie, hair freshly Bryll-Creemed. Mom is a vision in a nice dress, hair up, looking very much like a Chinese Olivia-Newton John.

I turned my head and just stared at the picture. There they are, smiling, carefree, the classic bike in the background shining in all its glory. But on the edge of my eye, I thought I saw some-thing else I hadn't noticed before. What was it, I wasn't all that sure. *Look closer…*

Damn, I lost it once I started staring at it directly – hate when that happens. There he is, my father, eternally young, confident and rakish. Arm around mom, looking like he was King of the World. But what else was there? *Look closer…*

She is unstained by smoke or bitterness or the disap-pointments of marital failure, filial failure, emotional failure. My mother. She is happy, apparently with a lot in her life at that point. Who wouldn't be? A husband, a lifestyle, a fast bike. Rosy-cheeked and…what? *Closer…*

I looked at them both, focusing on it like a stereogram. The dots. They seemed different, dancing motes of black and white. Primitive technology of the sixties, couldn't hold a candle to the quality of pictures taken these days, yet beautifully appropriate, classical. Unmachined, natural. *Closer...*

Mom is cradling her stomach. Something precious, a purse, a treasure-trove, a valuable stone. *Me? Closer...*

My father, looking totally positive and unshakable, had his hand behind mom's shoulder, mom's lovely form obscuring an unidentified object. A gun? A pen? A cigar.

Me.

Closer...

And then I realized, the confidence wasn't for him.

It was for *me.*

Me.

I saw it.

The hopes, the desires, the expectations, completely devoid of fear because that's the way it was to be. The plans, the dreams, the pride. For me. For them. I had thought the confidence was just youthful cockiness. But it wasn't. It was pride. Pride in what they did, what they had, and what they...will have.

Then beyond the dots, I saw the disappointment, the pain of the future. The conflict between them, between us, even though I was a small boy, Janice a small girl. My father, and the conflict within himself. Regrets, perhaps, at the way he was, the way he could not be, the choices he made, people he involved.

But not children he had.

Me.

I looked at mom alone, at *her* disappointment, and the pain of her future. And it was a lot. It was unfair. She *was* purity, the original pure soul. Taken away for something greater, struck by something lesser. But she survived.

Despite **me.**

I removed myself from it all, just like my father had. The pain is not just a male pain, a romantic love-based pain. It is a pain for all seasons, caused whenever something of value was taken away — and what is more valuable than Hope?

My mother is strong. She kept functioning. Angrily, bitterly, of course…but she kept on functioning.

Is it too late? For me?

*For **us**.*

I must have stared at the picture for a full hour, absorbing every shade of grey, every contour of the images it held. I breathed deeply. I'm really not one to dwell on things. So I guess I'll just go on. I *must*, so I *will*. But not without my family. My culture. My faith. I want it back. I want back what I've sloughed away all these years, shrugging it off. I want the closure that I've scoffed at, the value in the ideals that family, culture, faith affords me.

I woke up fully clothed. It was almost 8 am, and my head was throbbing, the anvil for a Southern Comfort-induced hangover. There was a curious corner-shaped indent on my abdomen, from lying atop the picture of my folks.

I got up and forced myself to confront a carton of milk and a box of cereal. Lucky Charms. Rick's favourite. As I ate the oat morsels, leaving the marshmallows to discolour the milk, I started feeling better, despite the merciless pounding of my de-hydrated brain. It's funny, the tricks your brain plays on you. When you dwell on bad things, they get invariably worse. When you dwell on good things, they get invariably better. In psychology, it's called a *schema*, a collection of ideas your brain constructs, based in a limited amount of information. In Love, it can be translated into this homily: "*Absence makes the heart grow fonder.*" Or was that fungus? Any notable information you received from a romantic interest, good or bad, tends to play and replay itself, building itself up, or down. You think and think and think, and positive feelings grow even more positive. That's how you fall in Love, I suppose.

I am falling in Love. With what is to come next. Whatever it is.

Who knows? I think to myself. *Art…romance…travel… maybe even…ack! Finishing…you know…*

But Love can wait.

Gotta eat first.

The phone rang. I picked it up.

"Hello? Luke?"

I try to place the voice, not recognizing it for a second.

"Er…Shirley? Is that you?"

"Yes." She sounded curiously dispassionate.

"Hi." I pause, unsure of what to say. I hadn't spoken to her for a long time. "Um, long time no speak. What's up?"

She tells me.

Damn.

*What a **bummer**.*

Hard Memory.

My mind is gone, it's *gone*! *GONE*!"

It was 1:30 in the morning, and me, Jase, Eggman and the co-ops were grinding to get the UNIX port of our goddamn product out out the door. We were up to our collective eyeballs in bugs, and the thing was due in under eleven hours.

"Fuck, Jase! I can't take this anymore!" I groaned. His pale face was eerily lit by the multiple windows of Visual C++ shifting like an old-fashioned cartoon across his screen. I could tell by the intensity of the light that he had too many windows open, which meant he was fixing too many bugs at once.

"Peace, Dave, it's under control."

"This place is hell," I grumbled. "I swear, it's hell. It's always been hell. It's hell eternal. I'm sure that when people in biblical times did bad things, they were sent straight here when they died. In fact, I think I'm Moses."

"Part the water, then," called Eggman from down the hall. The descent into madness was not a pretty one.

"Bugs 1002 and 1003 done," chimed Markandandrew. They'd taken up residence in my office, but I almost couldn't see them from behind a fresh mountain of Jolt cans. I mumbled to them about twenty-odd bugs left in the log, and went back to setting up more software monkeys.

My mouth was sour from too much coffee. My throat was sore from too much swearing. My skin was parched and scaly from too much monitor radiation. It's common knowledge that monitor rays are quickly absorbed by your epidermis and conveyed to your mind, snapping it like kindling.

Except that my mind was in another place. It was in Vancouver on a warm summer's day. I am lying on the beach on English Bay, the sun beating down, haze off the sand shimmering like a freshly lit barbeque, wispy mirages traipsing erotically across the horizon. My back to a log, watching the tankers anchored off the coast. Walkman playing some good tunes, bottle of water in my hand, watching some rather nice bikini-clad females playing beach volleyball in the distance. Ah. The coarse sand feels damned good between my toes. English Bay has this interesting sand, coarse and grainy, but it still feels pretty good. I have these stubby, arch-less little feet, shaped like potatoes, and I am imagining that they are baking slowly, right there in the sand.

I want to be back there so badly, it hurt. I just want to relax and have a good time. Is that too much to ask for?

We finished the albatross a half-hour before noon, and, more importantly, just before Shogun came in. I completed burning the gold copies of the CDs, dropped them off in his office, and crashed on Jase's office futon for a few hours. Markandandrew were already brain dead, snoring in my office. They had brought sleeping bags last night – good co-ops. Jase and Eggman went home.

We woke up just after five, and after a slight lambasting from Shogun about cutting it close, I brought Markandandrew out for a big honking bowl of Vietnamese noodles at Pho Hoa, followed by beers at the Maddy, gleefully charging it all on the corporate card. Last Friday had officially been their last day before going back to Waterloo Engineering hell, but they were good enough to skip the first week of school to stick around for Shipping Hell.

"*I love you, man!*" I said, offering up a few sarcastic sniffles *à la* Bud Light commercial.

Then I shuffled them off and went home, collapsing into an uneven sleep. The next version starts in two days.

I wasted the last of my precious days off going to the doctor's office for a long-overdue checkup. Wasted because the results didn't surprise me one bit. But hearing it from Dr. Zhou was still a little disconcerting.

"Let me guess," I said, putting my shirt on after the series of needles, blood pressure tests, ice-cold stethoscopes. "Colon cancer? Low sperm count? It's my ovaries. Problems with my ovaries."

"Well," Dr. Zhou said, "Your weight is up. Blood pressure is, too."

"That's not good."

"There's wheeziness in the lungs – not sure about your cholesterol, I may need some more tests…"

"Oh come on, Doc, lay it on me. It can't be all that terrible."

"Let's put it this way, Mr. Lowe," he said, looking me straight in the eye. "At the rate you're going, if you were seventy or seventy-five years old, there's a chance you'd be dead by now."

A silence settled in his office. I scratched my three-day beard thoughtfully.

"Hum."

"How about a lifestyle change – better diet, quit smoking, start exercising…"

"I'll think about it."

"Now, Mr. Lowe…"

"I said I'll think about it." I grabbed my coat and headed for the door. "Thanks for your time." I quickly left the office. *Change my lifestyle?* I can't even change baseball caps.

After stopping by Tim Horton's for a maple nut and a coffee to go, I went back to the office. Apparently, I caught the tail end of a Free Stuff Bonanza – all the guys were happily wearing crisp white AspicWare T-shirts. AspicWare is an Independent Software Vendor (ISV) we recently signed a partnership agreement with.

"What do you think, Dave?" asked Eggman, who was (*surprise!*) wearing his new T-shirt.

"I think you look like a bunch of morons."

"Jealous!" teased Jase. "You're just bitter because you were offsite and you didn't get one."

I grunted, only in half-agreement. It was kind of silly, actually…all these grown men, almost thirty, still howling over promotional junk like a pack of cheetahs over a half-eaten can of tuna. I'd always suspected that working for a software company delayed your adulthood for five to ten years, just as I've always suspected working for regular, conservative corporation aged you by just as much.

And they were going to be wearing those damned shirts for days on end, looking like they were all cloned from the master cell. Gad. If a volcano erupted in the heart of downtown Toronto and the Praxus office was the first excavated by alien archeologists a thousand years later, I wonder what they would infer about our culture as a whole?

Report by: Star Gundark,
   Class-3 Star Archeologist, Zolgon Empire
Stardate: 7823.6
Mission: Explore strange new worlds, seek out life and new civilizations, communicate with green-haired starchicks, and (when possible) sleep with them.
Star Commander: Star Summary as follows:
Several star-measurements with various pieces of starequipment yielded the following star-results on 20th Century culture:
   • Subsisted on circular foods called "Dough-Nuts."
   • Addicted to caffeine-based products.
   • Bad eyesight and complexions.
   • Asexual [the Star-Sex-O-Matic detected no female specimens]
   • A seemingly peaceful society which solved problems using non-lethal weapons called "Nerfs."
   • Utilitarian in dress. Most star-specimens wore white, short-sleeved uniforms. (One humanoid, however, was found without a uniform; it is believed he was of the slave-beast class.)

"So how was your doctor's appointment?" asked Jase, idly rolling a trick ball over his knuckles.

"Lousy. He predicted a grisly, cholesterol-laden death for Davey-boy here." I brought up my e-mail, revealing a sick number of new messages. "Maybe he was doing me a favour."

"Bru*tal*." He eyed my doughnut.

"Jase, you know full well I cannot function without my daily doughnut and coffee. The fact that it's bad for me now just makes it doubly true."

"*Mmmm…forbidden doughnut*," Jase said, and I looked at

him sharply. I hate it when people steal my Homer Simpson lines.

Jase settled onto my doorframe like a nesting sloth. "By the way, Greg wants to see you about the next project. Pronto."

"Okay," I sighed. He flipped the ball over his shoulder, catching it deftly, then turned around and left. I looked at the doughnut in my hand, sighed again, and chucked the death-pastry through the Nerf-net into the garbage. Man, I *hate* this place.

From: Jason Lavalier <jlavalie@praxus.ca>
To: Dave Lowe <dlowe@praxus.ca>
cc: John Van Egmond <jvanegmo@praxus.ca>,
Gregory S. State <gsstate@praxus.ca>, Mark
Smythe III <mrsmythe@elecom.uwaterloo.ca>,
Andrew Whitehall <awhiteha@elecom.uwaterloo.ca>
Subject: What To Do When Confronted by a
Software Tester (fwd)

Yo Dave, you might appreciate this. JL.

<<forwards extinct>>
A friends' father just sent him a newspaper
clipping from the US Department of Fish and Game
that lists their tips for dealing with mountain lions.
Notice that if you substitute "software tester" for
"mountain lion" that most are still actionable...

What To Do When Confronted by a Software Tester:

1. Don't run from a software tester or turn you
back. Software testers usually attack from the
back. Instead, face toward the Software Tester.
2. Do not crouch or bend over. Instead, wave your
arms above your head. This helps make you look
bigger.
3. Shout or make some kind of noise.
4. Throw rocks.
5. Try to make eye contact with the software tester.
6. If attacked, fight back.
7. Don't hike or jog alone in Software Testing areas.
Go in pairs.
8. Avoid hiking or jogging at dawn or dusk when
Software Testers are looking for food.
9. Small children are especially vulnerable. Pick
them up to protect them.

"Har har," I snarled at Jase outside my door in the hallway . He grinned while he was taping up a copy to my door.

"Dave, man, you gotta admit you've been a beast lately. I mean, even for you."

"I think it's because he misses Markandandrew," teased Egg-man. As much as I hated to admit it, he was right. I miss those fucking geeks.

"*You'd* be bitching your ass off too if you got the raise that I got."

"Oh yeah? How much?"

I shook my head. "Let's put it this way. I thanked Greg for making my weekly pay phone ordeals much more bearable." That elicited a whistle from the two guys.

"Any plans for your cash bonanza? Buy us lunch?"

"I'd rather spend it on two bullets…one to put me out of my misery, and another one in case I missed the first time."

"And then will you buy us lunch?"

"Consumer electronics man," said Jase, "Gotta spend it on consumer electronics." He walked over to me and picked up my battered walkman of six-odd years. It was clearly falling apart, as evidenced by the elastic band wrapped around it so my *AC/DC* tape wouldn't fall out. "Maybe you should save your nickles and dimes and get a yourself a new phonograph machine."

"Guffaw guffaw. Go away guys, you're cramping my style." The two snickered and left.

Ah, what the hell am I doing here? Why aren't I working full-time out at Microsoft? What's the meaning of Life? What's the square root of 3478?

It's now Saturday afternoon. I woke up stupidly late, and I started off my day with a smoke, lounging on my bed, listening to some mellow *Robbie Robertson* on the ghetto blaster. Smoking in bed is bad news, I know, but it just felt right – one of Mike's Perfect Moments. Besides, I was careful enough to put a flame retardant foam pad underneath me, and had a glass of water close by. Good, responsible little Chinese boy.

The weather was getting better outside – early April, 13 degrees Celsius – but I rarely ventured outdoors by choice unless it reached a healthy 18 degrees. Still, there was nothing but a jar of olives and a six-pack of Blue in the fridge, and a half-block of cheese that apparently was moving of its own accord. Reminded me of university, where eating invariably ceased being anything other than a chore, and you only continued doing it only because it kept you alive (if only barely).

I toyed with the idea of driving to Mississauga, a half hour out of the way, for an Arby's roast beef sandwich, a splendid alternative to subs, burgers and 'za. The old hometown had an Arby's restaurant as its centerpiece, right on the corner of Murphy and London Rd. in front of the mall.

Although it takes more than a decent roast beef sandwich to conjure up pleasant memories of the old hometown – *Proust I ain't* – I was actually back in Sarnia fairly recently. Despite the racism, the thrashings, being excommunicated from the Lowe clan. I guess I wanted to show Shel around a little because a few summers ago I went to Saint John with *him*. That was kind of nice…he showed me all his childhood hangouts, the creeks where he fished, the fields that he laid in counting stars, the places where he got drunk. I listened respectfully to his stories about growing up. And I wanted to share the same thing with him.

After a bit of convincing, we set off from his house toward Sarnia. I guess I was a little apprehensive as I approached the outskirts, studiously avoiding the Golden Mile where my folks apparently still were. Vivid memories of mud and blood and cuts and bruises and jeering little white boys inflicting them on me, coupled with yelling teachers, landing choppers, rattling M-16s.

All that evaporated because of Shel. The jerk. I was pissed off at him because he was acting…well, like a *jerk*.

"What is this place again?" Sheldon asked, scratching his head as we passed into the town limits.

"Sarnia. Ontario. Canada." A pause. "North America."

"Looks like a hick town."

"Hey man, I came out with you to New Brunswick."

"But Saint John is a *city*."

"What the hell are you afraid of, a scene from *Deliverance*?"

And after a bit of a scolding, I pulled into the parking lot. He looked around and made a face. "This place *sucks*," he said.

Well, yeah, it did. The idea of visiting my hometown seemed a lot better on paper. Shel had regaled to me stories of playing in wide fields, shoals near rivers, blowing up graveyards with artillery shells. What could I tell him about, living in the Canadian equivalent of the Ozarks? *This is where I got beat up when I was 8. This is where I got beat up when I was 10. This is where the Craigs all ganged up on me and beat me up…*

But still, Shel was being such an insensitive jackass about it. "Sorry, Dave…I can't help it if you grew up in a boring town."

Jerk.

So after seeing the admittedly limited sights of hell on earth, we ended up at Arby's for Snapples and roast beef sandwiches. Shel then went into an arcade, and I went outside with a blue Mr. Freezie to grumble. Outside was the same as I left it…big Canadian Tire sign in the distance. Same wood-panelled benches, carved initials, cigarette burns. Slack-jawed yokels loading two-fours into a Chevette for a wild night of drinking.

And that's when I saw him.

Craig O'Brien – one of the triumvirate of Craigs who regularly administered trashings. This one in particular was a real retard. He had this Beavis-and-Butthead laugh that always grated on me. Like when I revealed that my mom's adopted anglicized name was Ethel: *Ethel…uh-huh-uh-huh-huh-huh-huh…what a stupid name.* Shut up, Beavis. I can remember my face flushing red, feeling helpless, wishing my mom didn't choose such a "stupid" name for herself. Bad Chinese Son.

Shaggy long hair, wearing a grimy jumpsuit with his name embroidered on the left breast, *Craig O.* He was listlessly pushing a pile of leaves and gravel with a broom to no apparent purpose. Same retarded look in his eyes, only…only *what*? A lot sadder, without the energy, the sometimes-cruel vigour of a hyperactive childhood behind them.

He looked up and stared dully at me for a moment, and then returned to his "work". He obviously didn't remember me – brain fried after some hard drugs, maybe? His body was no longer thick and muscled, as I idealized it to be when he made me kiss the pavement many times those long years ago. Shriveled by years of smokes and booze and baloney sandwiches bought with lousy paycheques. I frowned slightly and squished the freezie up some more. How about *that*.

He didn't remember me. And the way he looked, I thought I could have taken him down [*insert wave of Pavlovian-induced anxiety here, but quickly squelched by plain empirical proof*]. I thought about a dozen possible things I could do to "get back" at him – kicking him in the nuts, buying a milkshake and pouring it over him, or merely flicking the freezie down in front of his sorry form. But I didn't. *Dammit*. I only felt sorry for the son of a bitch. Jesus, even after years of torture, years of bitterness, shame, useless fantasizing about glorious revenge using hockey sticks, two-by-fours and flaming iodine-covered knives.

But all the fantasies involved a healthy, muscled and leering Craig O'Brien, not this poor minimum-wage earning schlep. I felt vaguely ashamed.

I finished the freezie and sheepishly pocketed the plastic wrapper as Craig was changing the garbage can in front of me. Some of the blue juice trickled out, making my pocket sticky, but it was an old pair of jeans, anyway. I went back inside.

In the arcade, Shel was struggling with the Gyruss joystick. "The thing started bunging up on me during the Bonus Stage," he whined. "I only got 2400…"

"Let's go."

"But I've still got one guy left…"

"I said now, Sheldon."

He looked at me with raised eyebrows, paused a bit, then nodded. "Sure, Dave, if you want." He backed away from the machine, leaving his 'guy' to bite it by ramming into one of those tri-pointed rotating ship-thingies.

I was pretty quiet on the way back to Toronto. Shel tried to ask what was wrong…I just shook my head, and he let it go.

314 • Terry Woo

Revenge is a dish best served cold. And nothing is colder than...*minimum wage*? In your late twenties?

I don't know. I really don't.

Life, I tells you.

Satisfaction is *not* guaranteed.

The only family connection I've maintained is with my sister Grace, who lives in Etobicoke. Being older, she already has a small family with her husband Jeff, a big mustachioed white guy, who is actually okay, although he reminds me a bit of the Stanley character in *A Streetcar Named Desire*. Grace and I got along only moderately during our childhood, but far better than me and Ellen, hence the connection. I visited her every couple of months, and she provides me with bits of news about mom and dad – not that I cared all that much.

She had invited me for dinner Sunday. So I went.

Pulling up to their modest split-level townhouse, I noted that she has what seems like a relatively normal, middle-class existence, if there was such a creature: overweight husband, a baby daughter, two hyperactive sons. Two compact cars, four square metres of lawn. Mortgage.

I shuffled into the house a little awkwardly and accepted a canned beer from Jeff, who was juggling little Katy and a beer of his own, watching the hockey game while waiting for dinner. Grace was in the kitchen cooking, and the boys were given away intermittently by the sounds of thumping, shrieking and smacked flesh from various sections of the household.

"Ki-*iiids*! DI-nerrrr!" Grace bellowed. The boys poured into the kitchen, followed by their roughhousing dad, Katy still dangling from him. Grace had cooked up a casual meal, a weird mixmash of Chinese and Western, like we always had when we were kids: *pau fan* (soupy rice) with fixings. Crunchy pickled cucumbers. Salami and other coldcuts. Fried Dace with salty black beans. Some left over KFC. Some things just don't change from generation to generation.

So…*eat.*

As we dug in, I felt comfortable familiarity mutate into a nauseous wave of nostalgia. It wasn't just the food – it was the environment, the mannerisms. TV squawking out the game, unattended in the next room. The kids whining about the selection of food, and then threatened by their mother into submission. Jeff slurping noisily (it had taken Grace years to teach him how to use chopsticks), inhaling his *pau fan,* stealing glances at the sports section of the newspaper.

"Daddy!" snapped Grace irritably. Geez, she even called her husband Daddy, like mom always did – you know you've been married far too long when that happens. "For goodness sake, quit eating so fast! You're making me nervous." Jeff just continued slurping.

I couldn't handle it anymore. My chopsticks clattered onto the table. "Sorry, sis…er, I'm feeling kind of sick. I…I gotta go." And I left them all, mouths agape. If I had been connected to the family, I would've caught serious hell for this. Kinda wished I was.

And, as I drove home in Jeepy, I came to a realization that I had not admitted for upwards of two years.

I want my mommy.

Jesus.

First thing Sunday morning, I hopped in Jeepy and headed back home to Sarnia to see les folks for the first time in a long time. Without showering, I popped on my well-worn Red Sox cap, slipped on a pair of fake Wayfarers, and just headed west.

It's an unbelievably dull four-hour drive from Toronto to Sarnia, past all those little hick towns with funny names… Drumbo. Ingersoll. Innerkip. Camlachie. I brought the usual snacks for the ride, of course, including the Fruit Loops. Memories are flooding back as I munch on them, dry, all the way home.

I can remember. Lining up at centre ice of the local hockey arena after getting creamed by a team sponsored by ScotiaBank,

taking our sweaty gloves off and shaking hands: *"G'game…
g'game…g'game…"* Mom and dad were there, as usual, waiting
with a Coke.

I can remember. Trying to get to sleep, while downstairs,
there was the crashing of pseudo-ivory Mah Jongg tiles – first
the mixing, and then the stacking. Dad sometimes got together
with some of the Chinese guys from the refinery for their weekly
game, drinking Labatt Blue and making with the *clackity clack
clack*. Cries of "*Pung!*" "*Seung!*" "*Aiya!*", along with a few other
Cantonese words I didn't recognize until mom yelled at my Dad
for swearing, floated up to my room.

I can remember. Driving with Paul and Timothy to some
rural fields by Modeland Rd. in Tim's pickup, indulging in pyro-
maniac games with Bic lighters, drinking smuggled two-fours
of watery American beer. Mom was livid because I came home
late and drunk. Cost: grounded for two weeks.

Mom loved me, you know. Wanted me to be "good people",
get a good job, have a family – but the problem was that she'd
never shut up. Not for a moment. She nagged me about my
eating habits, my chores, my schoolwork, my bouncing knee. I
could barely stand it, tried to hold it in, but it sometimes slipped out, my *Sei Ngau Gwok Jeem* (damned cow horns) against
her Iron Chicken's Beak (god knows I can't remember the Cantonese for *that.*) The Irresistable Force against the Immovable
Object, sharp, cutting, poking, fighting. Until I just up and left.
Until I came back.

I pulled into the Sarnia city limits, heading down the
dreaded Golden Mile. Changed a bit, actually – many of the
cheesy sixties and seventies-style plaza businesses were gone,
some replaced by warehouse outlets. A Costco, of course. And
then there was the restaurant. I almost didn't recognize it. It was
re-done in brighter, more modern colours. Gone was the old
yellow-and-black sign with the large crack on the left, replaced
by a large sign done in red, gold, and simulated jade, worthy of
a flashy Toronto-HK-style restaurant. Tien Wong, the Sky King
Restaurant. No longer Lowe's Canadian-Chinese Takeout
(Licensed).

It was a little late for lunch, but there were a fair number of cars outside. Frowning a little, I parked Jeepy beside a Mercedes-Benz with Michigan license plates, and went inside.

What the hell is this?

No more dingy, Neo-Chinese-Mish-Mosh. *Choi Sun Yeh* was still there, but he was a good-sized, fancy gold statue atop a fountain (crack pipe still in mouth, however). Mirrors made the place seem brighter, larger. Tables were different, as was the cutlery...geez, they even had these fancy pewter chopstick holders! The place was still filled with Caucasian patrons, but they were...hold on, they were mostly *Chinese*? Mom came out from behind the cashier's counter, which had been redone in marble, looking like a babe (*holy shit!*) in a silk *cheong sam*. She was sorting through some menus. "How many?" she asked before looking up and gasping, wide-eyed. I took off my grungy ballcap a little self-consciously.

"Erm, howdy Mom."

Silence.

"Just wanted to, uh...you know, stop by, see how things were. You know?"

Silence.

"Mom?"

Tears welled up in her eyes. "You stupid *stupid* boy *nei goh sei jei!*" she scolded, hugging me, burying her face in my chest. She virtually handcuffed me to the new brass fixtures and ran into the kitchen to get Dad. And there he was, in a suit, for Chrissake. He eyed me strangely.

"Um, hey dad."

Silence.

I shifted my weight to the other leg, uncomfortably, somehow feeling a sting in my left cheek and trying not to dwell on it.

"David." he said slowly. "David. You hungry? Sit down, and I'll get you some lunch."

"Sure."

I headed for the kitchen where I used to always take my meals, but he ushered me to one of the tables, pewter chopstick holders and all. I felt a little weird, being the only White Guy in the place, and also looking like a total slob compared to the yupsters and families seated around me.

Dad went back into the kitchen, and five minutes later I was eating like a horse. Hmm, not bad. I actually appreciated it now. Years of Kraft Dinner and hot dogs, I suppose.

"Want a beer?" Dad asked.

I shook my head, still feeling weird about drinking around my parents.

In short, it's all much better now. The weekend was loud and frenzied, punctuated with many gesticulations. A few harsh words were traded, but nothing more. Grace, and even Ellen came home to partake in my return – prodigal son, indeed. I skipped work Monday and went back to Toronto on Tuesday, again leaving various members of the Lowe clan angry about a few things. But I'll tell you something: we all stopped going at each other's throats at one point to watch the Leafs in a crucial playoff game against the Boston Bruins. Even mom. So it's not all bad.

A few days later, I was at work, complaining to Jase after orienting the new co-op students, who weren't half as geeky as Markand-andrew. I got a call from Shirley.

"*Shirley?*"

"Hi Dave."

Rick is dead.

I'll tell you about something I did after hearing about Rick's death. And I know it sounds sappy and silly and all that, but it really happened.

I found myself in The Maddy a few days after the phone call, alone with a beer on a sparse Wednesday night. Exams were finished at the university, so it was not busy at all.

And I thought about Rick. I ordered a few more beers and

thought some more – good times, Bad Times™. No times. The most prominent thing that floated in my brain, strangely enough, was the *Knight Rider* theme. Together, we could do the theme to the show perfectly – Rick was the tacky synth; I was the cool bass.

"Kind of lame, isn't it?" I said, offering Rick another beer as KITT jumped another bridge.

"Yeah. I mean, Hasselhoff doesn't really do shit, does he? He just gets the car to do it. '*KITT, jump the bridge.*' '*KITT, analyze this sample.*' '*KITT, get me closer to the plane.*' I mean, let's face it; the show was basically the car."

I nodded. "You could have Pee Wee Herman as Michael Knight, and it'd still be all about KITT. You know, when I was younger, I told friends that if I was rich, I'd buy a car like that *and* a midget with a red flashlight to simulate that flashing red-eyeball-thingy at the front of the car." I paused thoughtfully. "I guess I don't really need the midget…"

"Don't worry Dave. If you want the midget, you'll get the midget. When I get rich, I'll buy you that midget, I swear." We laughed and clinked bottles at that one.

Hmmm. *No midget.*

Beside me at the bar was a *Metallica* CD I'd picked up at HMV, and a baby tree. HMV was offering them for some environmental promotion or something. I didn't really know what to do with it until the sixth pint of Sam Adams Honey Porter hit the spot.

I settled up with Rod at the bar and staggered home to pick up some stuff – a soup spoon, shot bottles of Jack Daniels, some topsoil stolen from a flower box next door. Still extremely drunk, I made my way with my payload to this little natural area beside the pub and planted that tree with the help of the spoon and the soil. And then I sat down beside Rick's tree, and honoured him in my own dysfunctional way by toasting him with the JD.

It was a warm spring night.

I fell asleep beside his tree, and did not dream. For once.

I was woken up dawn by a bum asking for spare change. After giving him a loonie, I went home to sleep some more.

La Fuerza Del Amor.

I returned home to Brampton for a visit on Brent's birthday.

Brent, my youngest brother, is a difficult kid to buy gifts for – not that I'm any good at that stuff in the first place. Kevin's definitely easier to get stuff for…he's this typical teenage guy, into sports and video games. All I have to do is buy him Nike-type sportswear with some ultra-competitive basketball slogan (eg. WINNING IS EVERYTHING, LOSING IS NOT AN OPTION, PLAY HARD OR DIE, or I RULE, YOU SUCK, HAVE A NICE DAY), wrap it around a video game cartridge, and he's a happy camper.

Brent, on the other hand, is kind of like me in a way – not really into anything in particular. So I was stumped. I enlisted Kathy to help me pick something up, but that didn't work out so well. We ended up staying at the Rideau Centre three hours longer than I had intended, mostly because Kathy got, er, distracted…I followed her to four clothing shops, a book store, and a piano shop before we picked up a Discman for Brent. I wasn't all that happy about it, to tell you the honest truth – like most men, I'm a surgical strike mall-goer – I have a list of what I need, and I get it, then leave. By contrast, Kathy launched multiple warheads at every possible store.

Before that, we had gone out for *dim sum* with Kathy's parents, Mr. and Mrs. Tang. And her grandparents, and other assorted aunties, uncles and family friends, some of whom had come down from Sudbury to help move her stuff back for the summer. I'd only met her parents once before, and they seemed to take a real shine to me…it didn't take a sociologist to know it was because I was her first-ever Chinese boyfriend.

"You're probably right. Does that bother you?"

"No," I lied.

"Because it's not like I *only* went for Caucasian guys – for goodness sake, there were hardly any Orientals in Sudbury, or

Ottawa for that matter. What could I do about that?"

"No need to explain at all, hon-bun," I said, maybe a little too hastily, giving her a peck on the cheek.

Dim sum was utterly exhausting. Meals with large numbers of Chinese people at a single table are like miniature war zones, with people '*gahp*-ing' (selecting) food for each other, pouring tea for everyone else, and of course fighting for the bill as if it were one of their vital organs being ripped from their abdomen, the payers seeming on the verge of disowning if you aren't stuffed to the gills by the end of the whole ordeal. After thanking her grandparents six or seven times for picking up the tab, we retreated, collapsing with huge sighs by the elevator.

"You have to admit that it was better this time, Shel...last time, we were peppered with questions on when we were getting engaged and all."

I laughed. "Uh-huh. I also remember being stuffed with enough **cheung** *fun* [*shrimp rolls, expensive*] to turn my eyeballs orange." She giggled and kissed me on the eyeballs, and we went to the mall.

It's April now, and Kathy'll be back in Sudbury in a few days. And I've just returned to Toronto. I feel uneasy about it all. My contract in Toronto is only for two more months, and, after that, I have no idea where I would be. *Ba*'s even talking to relatives, looking into getting a job for me in Hong Kong.

The Long Distance Relationship thing. It worried me. A lot.

Even so, it feels really good being home. *Ba* yelling advice to the Blue Jays. Mom washing the dishes upstairs. Kevin blipping and bleeking his video games, Brent playing with Miller in the family room. Togetherness, family-style.

I met Luke at JetFuel™ Java. It's a pretty artsy place, and they don't have regular coffee.

"What the hell *is* this?"

"Latte."

"What's wrong with just regular coffee?"

"A latte is regular coffee," Luke said patiently, "it's just prepared differently."

"Everyone's into weird coffee these days. Have you seen the prices at some of these shops? Like, two bucks a cup? We get coffee for free at work. At the diner down from my last site, the coffee's only seventy-five cents. Good food, too – I always order the steak sandwich…"

"Sheldon, you're prattling."

"Oh, sorry."

"How's your girlfriend?"

"She's all right," I said, not entirely convincingly. Luke noticed it, too. "She's up in Sudbury right now. I think she's taking up jazz piano with a former Oscar Peterson prodigy at Laurentian University."

"Oscar Peterson, eh?"

"Kathy says he's the best."

"Don't tell that to Thelonius Monk."

"Who?"

"Never mind. She sounds nice."

"She's super nice. How's your love life, Luke?"

"Pretty much non-existent, dude." He let off a chuckle.

"Well, Mike was telling me that you were picked up by some girl at this club a few months ago or so."

"Oh, nothing happened there. We went out for dinner and drinks afterwards, and talked a little on the phone, but it never progressed beyond a certain stage. For one thing, she thought Breaks was the same thing as Hip Hop." Luke shrugged, and rolled his eyes thoughtfully. "There *was* this one girl I met at a party while I was down in Boston. She's a thirty-two-year-old PhD student in Poli-Sci or something."

"Thirty-two? Buddy, you're robbing the old-folks home."

"Sounds like you've got the nursery schools covered, bucko. Anyhoo, I've been down there once this month, and we talk on the phone sometimes." He scratched his chin and frowned. "I think we're 'in like', if you know what I mean, but I don't know."

"What do you mean?"

"I mean, I don't know. She treats things…kind of clinically. Like a political model, or something. Heaven knows I'm not the most expressive or aggressive person in the world, and there's the wall we're both hitting. It's like we're two Harriers, carefully hovering around in a circle…and one of us is bound to run out of gas. Or money." He patted his wallet. "Gas and phone bills ain't cheap you know."

"Yeah, I know what you mean." I sighed. "I talk to Kath every night, and even with these long distance plan-thingies, my mom is still on my case a lot. And I think I'm going to try to pop up there once a month, too."

"So what are you going to do when you leave for parts unknown, like after your contract is up?"

"I don't know. Have a long-distance relationship, I guess."

"No, you aren't. Dude, LDR's are fricken impossible – trust me on that one. Sonja and I kind of had one for a while, but, after a month, the misunderstandings that come with lack of eye contact and body language completely destroyed us. We fought and made up so many times over stupid stuff that I felt like I'd supplied Bell Canada with enough money to wire the entire Yukon Territory." He smiled ruefully. "Hate to break it to you, buddy, but when you're not 'there', you're *nowhere*…a soothing voice over the phone is only an inch compared to the mile a hug or a kiss provides."

"Geez, that's depressing."

"Well geez, that's life." Luke looked at his watch. "Oop, man, I gotta go…need to grab some *Einsturzende Neubaten* and a *Quad 349* album from Vortex before it closes. I have to piss off an authority figure. You understand." I nodded, not really understanding, and he booked.

*Einsturzen-**what**?*

Kathy and I are starting to fight. Just yesterday, I got angry when she said she was hanging out with Ryan, her old boyfriend, back in Sudbury.

"You're *what*?"

"We're just friends!" she insisted.

What's that supposed to mean?

"We just go out for regular stuff...you know, like movies. I mean, we *did* go out for two years. Out of everyone in this world, I feel that he knows me the best."

This is supposed to make me feel secure?

"Look, Shel," she said, trying to be reasonable but failing just, "if you wanted to hang out with an ex-girlfriend, *I* certainly wouldn't mind."

How do I know this? I thought. *I didn't have any ex-girl-friends.*

Depressed, I sought out Dave for some entertainment, company and, to a much lesser extent, advice. We met at his beloved Maddy that evening.

"How's work, Dave?"

"Good, actually," he said, a little too energetically. He looked like a mess – unshaven, and his eyes were slightly glassy from too much coffee. "Very good. Remarkably good. So good, in fact, that I'm almost finding it sexually arousing."

"Gad, Dave. You need to get laid."

"I need to lay off the caffeine. No worries – a few beers will counterbalance my nutzy demeanour. Wakka wakka wakka."

He then recounted a positively bizarre story of something that happened to him on the subway earlier that afternoon. "So's I was coming home from work, like, waiting at Queens Park station," he said, refreshing his pint glass of Canadian, "and admittedly, I wasn't in a great mood..."

"Since when are you ever?"

"I was kinda hyper, like I am now – three cups, and also I got into this stupid argument with Greg regarding the code name of a new project we're just starting..."

"Yeah yeah, whatever Dave, get on with the story 'cause you're boring me."

"Anyway, there was this scrawny white chick waiting at the platform, listening to her walkman, when this gaggle of black girls swarmed her and started pushing her around, trash talking and all that. One of them demanded some money and her walkman. Everyone else on the platform was doing the Big-

City-Apathetic thing – you know, stoically concentrating on their paper or looking elsewhere. Pretty sad, eh? This fucking city is going down the tubes.

"It didn't look like they had a gun or anything, and, like I said, I was feeling kind of weird and hyper, and I hadn't shaved or changed, so I looked like complete shit, like I do right now. Without really thinking, I walked up to them and just started screaming at them.

" '*AAAAAAAAH!* ' " He practically blew out my ears and drew some unfriendly stares from the other Maddy patrons.

" '*AAAAAAAAH!* '*Come on, Dr. Jones! Dr. Jones, come on!!! My girlfriend has just left me and my dog just died!!* ' " He laughed delightedly. "This is *exactly* what I said. I had no idea what I was talking about, and was vaguely aware that I was quoting some country-western song, but only vaguely.

"So here I was, jumping up and down, waving my fists like an escaped mental patient. I screamed again, '*AAAAAAAAH!*' And the black chicks just swore and beat it. I asked the white chick if she was all right, but she started gibbering and backed away from me like I was a lunatic, which, for all intents and purposes, was the effect I wanted." He chuckled, downing his beer. "It was fucking *hilarious.* I laughed and had to convince her I was just an actor who saw an opportunity to try out a part I was rehearsing for."

I looked at him, mouth slightly agape.

He chuckled again. "Sounds cool, eh? It's like the Good Cop-Bad Cop routine, only without the good cop. And I got three seats to myself on the train. Dang, I should have asked her for her number."

"Dave, this must be the *stupidest* thing you've ever done. You could have been *killed*, you know?"

And I could tell he was slightly hurt, and he cut our beer time short. Yeah, what he did took balls, but he could've gotten them blown off, for God's sake. That's just Dave, I guess. Ya gotta love him for being…well, Dave-ish.

Kath is coming down today. I'm kind of nervous. We've been going out officially for seven months, and it's been only three weeks since we parted, but we've had three pretty serious fights.

I talked to her a few nights ago about my Dad trying to get me a job in Hong Kong after my contract in TO expires. She just *flipped*.

"Why do you want to go to Hong Kong?" she said, obviously upset. "It's so far away – I'd never see you again!"

"That's silly, Kath, of course we'd see each other." *I think…*

"We'd be too far apart!"

"It's not a guaranteed thing, Kath," I soothed, trying a different tack. "I mean, it's only a possibility…"

"You can't go to Hong Kong! We'd never last – I *know* it. Why would you want to, anyway? I mean, you're like me…you can't speak Chinese worth a damn!" That pissed me off for some reason, but I didn't let on about it.

"Well, my contract in Toronto could always get renewed…"

"That's no help!"

"Fine." I said curtly. "Let's get married, and you can move down here. Or better yet, I'll move up there and you can support us both with the fortune you'll make as a Music major."

Zing. The conversation went downhill quickly.

Six hours later, as I waited in front of the Bay St. bus terminal, sipping a Tim Horton's coffee and staring out at the Red Lobster across the street, I felt tense. Anxious. Looking forward briefly, I caught of glimpse of something in the rear view…

An impending feeling of doom. My heart suddenly pounded, my hand grew sweaty, and I turned pale.

And then I saw her. *She is not smiling.*

Me and Kathy were doomed.

Our relationship. Millions of others like ours. Stunted by distance and time and misunderstanding.

"Atrophy," Mike said.

I couldn't believe how a relationship could atrophy in such a short period of time.

There was a time when my father, back in the seventies, got a temporary contract for eight months in Timmins, up in northern Ontario, doing mining support. Mom and him agreed that it was a lot of money, and he went. And they lasted. But that was over twenty years ago. Those stories filled with undying love and permanence and commitment had little application in Rick's vaunted modern economy.

I'd always thought that The Break-Up would be a lot more emotionally charged, like Mike's was. Instead, we just sat there at the Tim Horton's over coffee and French Crullers, calmly, even coldly, discussing it . Fatalistically. I felt detached as she explained to me that distance had changed her attitude towards me. Towards us. Surprisingly, I found myself idly calculating the expense (past, present, future) of the relationship with her – cost of maintaining it, the savings when it breaks off.

*Dear baby. Welcome to Dumpsville. Population: **You**.*

And then I knew: our relationship was too short to warrant a substantial commitment. But too long to not have developed an emotional bond.

And *that's* when the hurting begins.

I drove back to Brampton after dropping her off at her aunt's house in North York. She would return to Sudbury the next day, to her parents, her piano…to Ryan. She did not cheat on me, and I believed her when she told me this. She did the noble thing, in coming down, in telling me, in spouting the "Let's Be Friends" line.

But it still hurt. I am not bitter, but I am very sad. I arrive at my house, drop the keys in the ceramic chicken, push Miller away from me, and step into my room to look around a bit. Three weeks and I still haven't unpacked yet. It still feels like her love in here. I pick up some things from the boxes lying around. Her hair is still on my things, her scent on my clothing. She is still here.

"It pays to keep certain things in your life independent from your girlfriend," Rick once told me. "When you break up, you can maintain the same level of pleasure in those areas, free from emotional baggage, no biases, no attachments."

Because I am a sap, I put on a CD we both loved. Some sweet *Blue Rodeo* floats in the air, like syrup in water, nostalgic, sweet, sickening. I'm dancing now, slowly. Like we did in her room one cold winter night. I close my eyes, remembering bliss. A smile climbs across my face, fighting with the muscles in my jaw that have been set in stone for the past few days.

"Wounds heal, and bruises go away, but the scars still remain." Luke had said this to Mike after he had broken up with Mina. The memories are like scars. They hang off things like red tags at a sale – off of songs, places, people, phrases, food.

Well, thank God for good friends. After breaking the news to him, Dave dropped work like a hot potato and ushered me to The Maddy.

"I miss her, Dave," I said, simply.

"Well, Love *is* truly a drug," Dave sympathized. "Once you've had it, it's excruciatingly hard to kick the habit."

He was, of course, absolutely right. I thought about me and Kathy, and those small intangibles we had together, which made letting go the hardest – lying in bed with her legs draped over mine, renting a movie and snuggling up with a pizza and Dr. Peppers in front of the TV, that little peck on the cheek I gave her as I took off for work – all the things that you take for granted at the time exert some serious withdrawal symptoms on you when they are forcibly taken from you.

"You've got it, man," Dave said. "Lost Love is a hundred times worse than a nic fit – trust me, I'm in the know. I'm telling you, the person who invents Nicorette patches for broken hearts will be enshrined in history by millions."

And then I got to talking about myself, about how messed up I was. Not just because of this one incident, but just overall. I used to take umbrage with Dave's fundamental idea that all

Bananas were screwed up in one way or another – by racism, by their lack of culture, by Love. But at this point, I had to agree with him. Two relationships over the course of twenty-four years – one destroyed by genetics, and the other, well, because it was all screwed up.

Dave was right: we are all screwed up.

I am all screwed up.

He disagreed.

"When you think about it Shelly, everyone in this world is fucked up in one way or another. Most facades of normality hide some deep, dark secret of some sort: dysfunction, obsession, abuse, transvestitism. Alcoholism." He paused thoughtfully. "And the ones who *aren't* actually hiding something, well *hell*, they're the most abnormal of them all." He refilled our glasses. "Shel, out of all of us, I think you are the most well-adjusted, and totally destined for regular happy things, whether you like it or not. Just face it, dude. There's no way you can avoid it."

"Really, Dave?" I looked at him with wide eyes, needing what he was giving me.

"Swear to God – with a capital 'G' this time, which I don't do, usually." He raised his hand solemnly. "I, Sir David Lowest of the Lowe, do solemnly knight thee the least dysfunctional of the Banana Boys, destined for all the happy things a regular shmoe could ever hope for." He tapped my head and shoulders with an imaginary sword, and after looking at it and back at me, decapitated me with it. "C'mon. Enough of this depressing shit. Let me buy you another pitcher."

And I accepted. You always accept Dave's offers to buy you a pitcher, 'cause that's the ultimate sign of his friendship.

Yeah, life moves pretty fast. The next few weeks were a frenzy of depression, questioning, drinks, moping, heartfelt talks, more drinks, and drunken *"You're better off without her/You'll find someone else/I love you man!/Fag!"* comments.

Details are lost in a haze. Time stopped, then started, sped up and slowed down. I passed out on Dave's couch one night, whimpering about Kathy in dipsomaniacal despair. Luke staggered over and tried to console me a little: "Shel, you need to go on with your life…" was about as far as he got when he threw up on me. Dave laughed. Mike ripped off my freshly-stained shirt and threw it in the sink. It was a complete mess.

In the morning, I woke up with a pounding headache, and went into the kitchen (still shirtless) for a glass of water. I ran smack dab into a wall of tequila smell, which had me racing to the washroom to make a deposit, slipping on a pile of Kraft Dinner courtesy of Dave. *Yuck.* As I stumbled out of the washroom looking at Dave sprawled on the sofa bed, and Mike and Luke both snoring in sleeping bags on the floor, I knew it was going to be all right. For me. For all of us. Christ, with these idiots, how can it *not* be?

What does it mean to be in Love? Was I in it? Or was it something else? What *is* Love, anyway? Does anybody Love anybody, anyway? Too many questions, few forthcoming answers. The same as always. But the answers do come, not because they're there, but because you gain a certain acceptance of the things that happen to you, the reasons why, the roles you played, and will play in the future.

I am going to Vancouver in May for a month, and then to Hong Kong to find a job. And embark on a new Quest™.

Dave is going, too, if only temporarily. Just to goof around with me. He says he is going to try to find me a wife in Hong Kong. I don't know if that's going to work out, but I do believe what he turns up will be interesting.

The trip west will be fun. Lots of partying, vegging out, scamming on girls. Something will happen out in Vancouver. I'm going to meet this one, a cute girl, her long black hair wafting past her slim shoulders will walk by, decked out in a long skirt, suspenders, white blouse and combat boots. She will say something to her friends, and she will look over at me, and they will giggle. The games continue.

I will then be in Hong Kong, where another pretty girl, will probably say the same thing (whatever that was) to *her* friends, only in Cantonese.

And this will be the person I marry.

But this is the future. In the present, I am sad yet again. Rick has died. Shirley called me today, and suddenly my problems became trivial.

I wonder if he died accidentally, or if he actually killed himself. I wonder how anything in life, *anything*, can warrant killing yourself over.

I wonder if Kathy was worth it, and I answer with a resounding *no*. I would miss life too much – my friends, my work, quality time with the family.

I wonder if Rick lost sight of what 'quality' meant to him. I remember talking to Luke about him after he'd messed up his hand by punching out a car window at Oktoberfest.

"Rick *defines* quality. He knows what top quality is – nice cars, beautiful women, clothing, great restaurants, expensive wine. He's got a diamond cutter's eyes. He'd never be satisfied with second best." Then Luke frowned.

"What's the matter?"

He stirred his coffee a little, and shook his head. "I think that if Rick ever lost sight of what 'quality' actually meant, he'd be in big trouble." I was puzzled.

He elaborated. "I think that ultimately, everyone wants *satisfaction* in their lives. You know, needs fulfilled, Maslow and the whole bit. And, for some people, this comes really easily. If it doesn't, then you've got some sort of mental block or something." I immediately thought of Mike, looking depressed as hell, sitting in front of a Biochem textbook.

"For others, they can be satisfied – or at least fool themselves into thinking they're satisfied – with material and lifestyle quality. And there's nothing really wrong with that – everyone has their own definition of what 'real quality' means. And for still others, satisfaction comes from, you know, fulfillment and

self-actualization and stuff like that. Artistic stuff, spiritual stuff."
He paused to collect his thoughts.

"I think that if Rick ever lost sight of his adopted definition of quality – lots of sex, lots of money – if he ever began to doubt it, the shit could *really* hit the fan – he'll look back, see what he's lost and gained, look at his sacrifices and contributions, and probably regret them. All of them. Through that newly found, un-material, un-moneyed, un-sexy definition of quality, he'll feel like a total fuck-up. And what happens then is anyone's guess.

"I don't think Rick is shallow," he continued. "Actually, I think *that's* his problem: he's *not*. If he was, he'd be the happiest guy in the world and stay that way, probably forever."

I think I get it now.

I picked up the phone and dialed a number.

Baseline.

I roll myself off the bed on top of some discarded shot-bottles of JD. I'm still wearing my best suit, but I did not go to work today. All dressed up with nowhere to go. I haul myself into the washroom for a glass of water. And another. Then I head out the door, into the elevator, into the intense light of the day.

The next thing I know, I'm stumbling out of the elevator, clumsily fishing around my trench coat pocket for the keys to my apartment. It turned April a few days ago, somewhere. Wednesday, I think. I've lost track of the past week.

Something is wrong with me.

There is something wrong with me.

Something with me is wrong.

*Very **very** wrong.*

***Jesus**, I need a drink.*

My neighbour, Mrs. Brubaker, her arms full of books, her son Timothy in tow, passes by and looks at me, smiling and worrying.

"Are you all right, Richard? Need any help?" Timmy impatiently pulls at her leg, pulling her towards the elevators.

"No, Mrs. B...I'm fine...just tired, too much work, need some rest..."

She gave me another worried smile, not believing it for one moment, but, bowing to Timmy's impatience, moved on. Nice lady, Mrs. B, even though she always pulled Timmy closer to herself whenever I passed by.

Nice, smart lady.

After adding scratches number 641 and 642 to the lock on the door, I opened it and reeled into the apartment, turning on the switch to my big halogen light. You know, one of those tall skinny ones. The ones that collect flies and dust in the dish on the top like all get out. Them's good eatin'. Nyuk nyuk nyuk.

My voicemail, even before I unplugged the phone, was

crammed with messages, from Tasmin, Shirley, clients, potential clients, my folks, a woman with a sexy voice from the long distance company telling me about new rates for the spring. Sometimes, I would play these messages, until one day the tape screwed up and all the voices became sampled and distorted. But voicemail does not use a tape. So I guess the jokes on me *I looked 'em right in the eye said goodbye I was up above it now I'm down on it...*

Pills don't work any more. My mental circuitry is bunged up. I've tried double, triple, even quadruple doses, but it seems to have little or no effect, even if I mix them with a variety of other drugs and drinks and other drugs. And that doesn't really make any sense, does it? Because I remember Mike telling me once that alcohol amplifies the effects of this sort of drug...or maybe the *drug* was supposed to amplify the effects of alcohol. Have I taken the two in the wrong order, then? Something to try for tomorrow, I guess. And if that doesn't work, what to do? I don't know. Maybe I'll start drinking or something.

I think it's about 3 am or so. I stagger into my room and collapse into bed, trench coat and all, and fall into a fitful sleep, filled with wild and spectacular dreams.

I used to have crazy dreams before I started taking the pills. They disturbed me, somewhat, so I related most of them to Mike over a few drinks, just to get them off my chest. I think his little collection of notebooks was one-third me telling him my dreams.

But after the pills, all the dreams seemed to stop. It's as if my mental circuitry readjusted itself to make me disregard things so useless and unproductive as dreams. Because that's what they are, you know – useless and unproductive.

"When it comes down to it," Luke said, "dreams are merely manifestations of random files from your memory. While you're sleeping, your consciousness – the tight electrical net that organizes your mind, loosens up, resulting in the files popping up in a nonsensical order because while you were sleeping. Your brain picks up a lot of sensory input during your conscious hours, and it spills out in dreams that are ultimately random."

"Meaning?"

"We only give as much meaning as we want to give them."

I did not want to give them much meaning. So I was pleased after the first few doses killed them off. Stopped talking to Mike, and just ignored them all for the next four years. Only recently, I've had a renewed sense of interest in them because perhaps they can tell me certain things that have suddenly become confusing, suddenly shifted out of focus like a cheap camera in fast transit.

I roll myself off the bed on top of some discarded shot-bottles of JD. I'm still wearing my best suit, but I did not go to work today. All dressed up with nowhere to go. I haul myself into the washroom for a glass of water. And another. Then I go out into the living room and turn on the TV.

The *Twilight Zone* is on. Goddammit. I shiver involuntarily once more, feeling unfamiliar pinpricks of fear on my scalp. This show used to always frighten the bejeezus out of me when I was younger, more than anything else could. I used to hate the black-and-white eyeball that floated out at the beginning right after the doll's body, the broken window, the $E = MC^2$.

It is now about 1 am, Monday morning. But I show no signs of going back to sleep, preferring even the horrors of the *Twilight Zone* eyeball to the terrors of a subconscious, apparently warped beyond repair.

I gaze around the TV-lit room a little. The lake is dark and foreboding, the moon reflecting off various surfaces onto the wall in puzzling angles – the electronics, the framed prints, the pictures of Tasmin, before she changed, and off the glass American Music Award.

I pick it up, steaming it with my flushed hands, and look at the sculpture intently. It is quite beautiful, reflecting my face four times, and then four times again, infinitely spiraling inward. I sit fascinated by it until it reminds me a little too much of a stereogram, so I drop it with a clatter onto the glass coffee table. The table vibrates, metal parts shaking and squealing, but it does not break.

I switch on the big-screen TV over to the video camera. It's showing me a remarkably unappealing Richard Wong. Pale. Haggard. Sweating. Rings under eyes. Nails uncut. Suit still looks good.

"*Testing.*" I say, flicking on my stereo as well. "*Toast… toast …toast…*" My voice is raspy, coming out of the large tower speakers flanking the stereo, my words followed by grunting and groaning and giggling.

"*Baseline video number…number…Number 1. Baseline video number 1. Date is Saturday, January 1st, 2172, time 12:00 pm midnight. Hi Rick. You handsome devil you.*" More grunting and giggling. Good joke.

"*I need to say something to you, something I have been think-ing about for a long time. I am not sure if you will understand this, but you must listen to me.*

"*At this time, it is all like several divergent signals. Sine, cosine, secant waves, converging all at once in a single resonant frequency. I have received a temporary moment of clarity, and I must share it with you.*

"*I do not really think it's right, what I have done, and I would not still be doing it if I wasn't certain that they would put me in Double Jeopardy once I cross over the border, past the seraphim, into to the Holy Land. It is like a game of Monopoly gone com-pletely to hell…they possess Boardwalk, Park Place and all the railroads, and you have mortgaged all your properties twice. They have placed so much debt on your shoulders that the most reason-able option was to walk away and watch TV or something.*

"*So what can you do? Work fiercely, very hard, at the risk of wasting your limited resources, never ever getting back to where everything was 'normal'? Or stop playing the game entirely, start someplace new, with what I've learned. This is what I've learned to do. This is what I did. This is what I shall continue doing, until the day I die.*

"*Erased. Over. Out.*"

I roll myself off the bed on top of some discarded shot-bottles of JD. I'm still wearing my best suit, but I did not go to work today. All dressed up with nowhere to go. I haul myself into the washroom for a glass of water. And another. Then I go out into kitchen to mix myself a drink.

I do not know what time it is, except it is still dark outside. There is a strange grinding noise in the background, and it is eating my mind. Time is losing its meaning. As I am sitting here in the cold, in the darkness, the engines of time are revving up and going into overdrive. I am alternating back and forth, here then there. It is happening once again.

I am a young boy, walking along a dusty gravel trail from behind my house to school. The Vietnamese kids are surrounding me and sneering, speaking in their strange guttural language that I do not understand, although their intentions are clear enough. I stand there, waiting for Lance and Kevin to come along so that we can trash these bitches, only the sky turns red and they do not come. And soon the ground turns red, amidst their laughter and blades of silver, covered with my blood. I am dead.

I am in university, downing a variety of mixed drinks at a townie bar on the west side after a successful round of midterms. I have called Michael on my cellular phone a number of times, but he is not at home. After a few more rounds, I sigh and go to my Beemer parked outside. Five minutes later, I am bleeding and dying at the corner of Bridgeport and Erb St., as the fireman cuts me out of the twisted metal frame. I am dead.

I am in Los Angeles, coming home late from work. The night is warm and heady, but there's a tension in the air, or something else. I have been working for thirty-six straight hours and all I want to do is mix myself a drink and crash. All of a sudden, I sense a slight vibration. I see the palm trees in the distance sway slightly and then the horizon suddenly tilts and I am swallowed by the earth. Everything is dark. I am dead.

The scenes of what seemed to be my life are shifting with such frequency, a Ouija board gone completely insane. I am losing track of it all now, past, present, future. It's all a large, spherical, globular mass, no advantage, no disadvantage, no meaning at all. I have engineered my life too well. The idea of "problems" does not gel with the world I have created. They only see the "good" things in my life and become confused.

Everything has suddenly become so complicated, beyond

my control. What is wrong with me? I think I'm approaching a nervous breakdown. I can feel it in my bones. I feel lost and frustrated. I'm paranoid. My baselines are fluctuating too high, too low. My perspective has been expanded too far and too rapidly. I need to recover. I need a womb. Somebody give me a womb. I need a womb. No one can help me. I can't do anything about this. God is dead. I hate myself.

Success is becoming relative. There is anti-success. It is like anti-matter. Anti-success mixes with success and explodes in my brain, causing pieces of skull to pierce my body, my soul, my hands, which are bleeding from the nails on the cross I hang from. It's a cold, hard cross of silver. Roman soldiers are laughing at me. My head does not exist but for a tight field of electrons and neurons and they are all pulsing with hurt. Blood flows freely from me and nothing is coming back in return. I am a sick and violent person and I deserve to be destroyed. Everything is dark and crimson and on fire and it gives me no comfort. I need to drink more alcohol to keep the body parts preserved so I can do one last thing…

I tear my hands from the silver cross, losing bits of blood and bone, and grasp a bottle of alcohol. I pour the contents onto my wounded hands and the pain is ripping through my arms into my shattered skull but it is a good pain. Pain focuses you and cleanses you when you have nothing else. I have nothing else but my pain and my worthless thoughts spinning around the place where my head used to be. I am drinking from my hands and the liquor is mixed with my blood. Someone is stealing my blood and I need to steal it back. I can clean my arms and body as well. Alcohol is pure while I am dirty. Sterilize myself. Purified. Sanctified. Inside.

I suddenly feel a fear that I have never felt before, insulated in my tight, controlled world. It captures my spine and electrifies it. I become spastic And I know what I fear.

*I fear **her**.*

Blindly, I run to the sink and turn it on full, splashing water on my suit trousers.

I need to find…*rice.*

Rice is the key.

I sprawl over the kitchen counter to the cupboard, discovering there is none left. I howl, lunging toward the liquor cabinet in my wall unit and open a bottle of sake, rice wine, pouring some into my left hand and wildly sprinkling it in a circle, on the couch, on myself.

I collapse on the couch, adrenaline rush gone as fast as it came. Blinking away some tears, I look at the bottle of sake gripped tightly in my hand, and take a long pull, draining it completely.

The door opens slowly. There she is, the *Ching-shih*, the vampire, floating toward me on a cloud of fragrant green mist. She levitates across the floor with a single, smooth motion. Graceful. Elegant. Efficient. Sexual.

She is exquisitely beautiful, skin pale as the moonglow, lips red as wine and just as sweet, her hair a waterfall of black silk that blends softly with the night, taking her tresses into its fold. She is wearing an elegant set of red wedding robes done in the traditional Chinese style – conservative, but revealing enough to show her comely form, revealing herself to me because she loves me. I sense it, deeply, and am enticed. I fear, but she looks so beautiful and she loves me, I cannot resist. So I give in.

Her red silk scarf gently wraps around my abdomen, pulling me toward her pleading, outstretched arms. *Wo ei ni*, she says simply, *I love you*. Her voice is melodic and tranquil, her beautiful large eyes glistening in the dark, red lips quivering in the moonlight.

I am tired and drunk and lonely, so I do not struggle. I do not pray or make crosses with my hands, and submit passively. I feel her hot-cold embrace, sending messages of joy-terror up my spine into my wine-addled mind. *Oh baby*. We kiss briefly and gently, drinking of each other. I hear the soft peal of bells in the distance – wind chimes gently ringing in the night breeze. She smells clean and perfumed.

I am completely enraptured by her. She embraces me and leads me in a graceful, haunting dance. Across the floor, the moon, the sky. I cannot help but follow, I love her so much. *Wo ei ni*, she whispers again, gently undoing my tie and unbuttoning my shirt and running her long nails across my chest.

Glass shatters in the background. Blood is drawn. I am bleeding but I do not care. The blood is warm on my chest and seeps into my clothing, the red bleeds into the cold, fiery crimson of her robes. I am confused. I am in Love.

Her sweet scent wafts over me, overwhelming me, making me more drunk than the wine. I do not know what it is. I do not care. I am not in control, and that arouses me. My wounds are bleeding and arousing me. The pain blends into pleasure, and I cannot draw a line.

Wo ei ni, she says again, simply, her dark eyes still reflecting her innocence and hunger. She tears into my clothing with her claws, opening more wounds and drawing more blood. She starts to kiss them, lick them, sucking gently, drawing out my life, my essence. *Oh baby*. I am blissful and content and drunk. It has never been this good.

She kisses me, and her kiss, though soft and gentle, hits me like a blow to the forehead, knocking reason and fear out of me. Her hands grace over my body, drawing even more blood. *Wo ei ni*, she whispers, but she is much closer now and her plaintive, simple expression screams at me like a wind that does not stop.

She enters me. Suddenly, there is no sound, no pain. I have become the woman, she has become the man. She enters me, but there is no violence, no aggression, no violation. She enters me and life and vitality pours out of me in exchange for a tenderness I have never before known. *Wo ei ni*. It shouldn't be this way, this peaceful, but I do not know, I have always received, I have never given. I have always taken, I have always received.

Wo ei ni. There is no pain, and it is warm, but she enters me and all else is leaving me. Her love is inside me, it makes me whole.

Oh baby…

Get The Girl! Kill The Baddies!

There she stood in the doorway…I heard the mission bell…

I don't know her name. She is sitting here at the Second Cup, sun shining on her unevenly, through the window past the salt-and-slush streaks. There's some light jazz – Betty Carter – being piped in, and she is unconsciously bopping to the beat.

She looks about my age, maybe a little younger, although (and I hate myself for subscribing to the stereotype) you can never really tell when it comes to Asian women. She has long, lustrous black hair that caresses her green turtleneck sweater in a rich vein of black gold, Texas Tea. She has a pale, graceful, elfin look about her, one that alludes to interesting blood…descended from Manchurian princesses, perhaps, from days long past, nobility, aristocracy, royalty. She's an accountant, I think.

She dresses in smart, office-type clothing, set off by the commuter's brightly-coloured slouch socks and runners. She is concentrating on a dossier of some sort, a cup of Amaretto Almond cooling in front of her, sitting with her right leg crossed over left, idly flicking her pen over her thumb, brow slightly furrowed. She is truly an upwardly mobile vision.

I don't know her name.

She brings to mind one of my mother's Chinese proverbs: "*Chum **yue** lok ngan yung bei **yuet** sau fah jee mau.*" *The beauty of a woman causes the fish to sink in fear, the birds to drop from the sky, the moon to hide behind the clouds, the flowers to hide their faces in self-consciousness.* The beauty of a woman strikes fear in the hearts of men. Like me.

She only started to invade my Second Cup recently, obscuring even the beauty of Ingrid, and posing a particularly problematic concentration problem for me. I thought about approaching her, but how? There's a serious lack of precedent for me in that sort of thing. I started thinking about how my father met my mother. Apparently, dad courted mom for seven years, beginning at the age of sixteen. He would bike two hours to her house every day back in Hong Kong, just to sit at the curb for hours, staring at her house. Her father would look out the window and ask, "*Jee doh guh soh jei?* (Do you know that idiot?)" My mom would, of course, deny it.

But that wasn't particularly useful information for the here and now. That sort of thing may have once been considered devastatingly romantic, but these days, you'd be slapped with a stalking charge faster than you could say, "What's your sign?" A Sign of the Times.

Ironically, I was reading a textbook on the theorized chemistry of Love. The text laid out the process of Love very clinically: how initial attraction is a drug-induced reaction that prompts key physiological changes – release of hormones, increased blood flow, sweating palms. In plainer words, human beings are drug addicts. We are addicted to the endorphins and otoxins and other natural neurotransmitters created by strong emotions. Once we've had our fix, we need more…everything simply comes down to getting our hits, doing the shit, Riding the Snake. The rush of power, the rush of performing, the rush of Love…all of it is merely self-medication, chemicals playing with our minds.

How easy is it to change the chemical soups that make up our emotions? Easy. Too easy. We do it all the time, by drinking coffee, popping aspirin, watching a scary movie, having a beer. Taking the route Rick took. But most changes are much more subtle – under the hood, sub-atomic, spiritual. It may take some time, but once a change takes root, it's virtually unstoppable. Someone can love you, then suddenly hate you, very easily. Chemistry dictates that nothing is permanent. Nothing lasts forever. Especially Love. I guess it's this fact that makes me seem cold, distant and ineffectual to most. A protection mechanism. It became apparent to me that normal, human relationships just lead to pain when the chemistry inevitably changes. It ends up hurting and disappointing you, and God knows I don't handle that well.

There will come a time in a young boy's life when the freshness and innocence of youth is cruelly stripped away, by fate, by circumstance, by personal stupidity. After a tumultuous and often painful series of events, you may find yourself locked in a cold, clinical six by six room…plain white walls, oppressively clean, dull forty-watt bulb illuminating your sterile misery, twenty-four-hour Barney piped in through tinny speakers set up just beyond your puny reach. You are curled up naked in a fetal position, shivering, maybe sobbing a little because you are alone, but you get used to it because everyone gets used to everything, eventually.

*Suddenly, the Grace of God or The Gods delivers a window to the outside world in a fit of benevolence (strange, but it **could** happen). You gaze out into the sunlight streaming through this stereotypical cross-haired white-framed portal of salvation to a beautiful world of the outside – birds singing, green grass, teeming and pulsating with vitality, a scene straight from a picture drawn by a nursery-school kid. There's even a window box with bright red tulips.*

It's a nice day, isn't it? Freshly trimmed hedges, clear blue sky, birds chatting it up, flowers blooming. You, still curled up in a fetal position in the middle of this bland little room, reach your pale and sickly hand toward this freshness. Feels pretty good, doesn't it? The sun is warm and pleasant on your spindly little appendage. A light breeze blows through your fingers, you wiggle them around a little to let it through the grooves. You've forgotten how nice it is on the outside, so much nicer than this hospital-regulated cube of bleah.

So you slowly poke your forearm through the cross-hairs. The sun burns a little at first, but then it feels quite good. You had forgotten how nice vitamin D was. You extend the rest of your arm, your shoulder, and eventually your emaciated head, contentedly soaking in the sunshine and roses…if only for a little while.

No more clinically lit room, you think. It is now sunlight, warm breezes, summer tans, ice lollies and piña coladas on your parched tongue, long walks on hot moonbrunt nights on a tropical beach.

But then something's not quite right, hmmm? You didn't notice it at first, but there's a sinister shadow that makes your hackles twitch. You feel this shadow hovering over you, blocking the warmth, the sunshine, a jarring cut into the progressive symphony of beauty that was quietly playing in front of you. It's hard to make it out, but it looks suspiciously like a thousand-ton block of steel, similar to those that were regularly dropped on Wile E. Coyote, soooooper genius in Roadrunner cartoons.

It also has an Acme egg timer on it of course, clicking, filling your cubicle with an evil, oppressive rhythm. It is going to fall, and you are going to be killed.

Suddenly, that sterile room looks pretty good, doesn't it? In comparison to being crushed and walking around like an accordion. At least it is safe in there. IV-fed lunches weren't as appealing and as sexy as ice lollies and piña coladas, but at least it was easier than cooking as hamburger meat.

Have I stuck my neck out too far, you ask yourself? A mere babe in the woods, so soon after your mugging and stripping and humiliation in the fickle clutches of the modern relationship? Do I have a chance of making it to The Promised Land, or have I merely put myself in a precarious position, only to be maimed, even killed, once again? Do I retreat only with flesh wounds into the unbearably cold, clinical interior once again, or try to make the leap outside, only to risk complete annihilation? The uncertainty pierces your heart like a knitting needle through a balloon in a Beakman experiment…

Getting home that evening, I ran into my sister Jen, home for once. She was experimenting with different types of nail polish in front of the TV.

"Howdy, Jen." I dropped my schoolbag and sat heavily on the Ottoman in front of the family room coffee table.

"Hi Mike," she said without looking up. "I just got a new hairdo. Like it?"

"Looks very seventies."

She stuck out her tongue and flashed me the peace sign with her two fingers.

"That's the sixties, dear," I said, smiling slightly. Jen was pretty cool as far as sisters went…a little ditzy sometimes. Flipping through the channels, we talked a little about school – she's in first year Arts and Sciences at U of T – and, of course, her new boyfriend Omid, her new hunka-hunka burnin' love who mom hates. Jen goes through boyfriends like some people go through towels at the Holiday Inn. All of that good genetic stuff must've skipped over me.

"Oh Mike, turn it back to *Baywatch*."

"You actually like *Baywatch*?"

"The girls on the show look really gorgeous."

"I'm surprised *I'm* not the one saying that."

"Yeah. Kind of says something, Mike." She dropped her nail-painting paraphenalia and started fanning with her hands. "Maybe you can answer this: why is it that girls comment about how gorgeous other women are, but guys usually grunt and switch the topic to baseball when it comes to talking about handsome men?"

I shrugged. "It's just not done. Masculinity. Same reason why girls can always go out on the dance floor to cut a rug together, and guys end up backs to the wall, beers in hand, unless they have female friends with them."

"All guys or just you, Mike?" she teased.

"Just me." *I'm a loser, baby, so why don't you kill me…?*

(From the kitchen:) "*Mi-koh! Jen-i-fah! Sik yeh!* (Time to eat!)"

At the dinner table, Mom asked me about the guys. She'd heard that Shel broke up with Kathy.

"Did you have a good time at Dave's?" she asked me in Cantonese.

I winced. "It was okay."

"So how is Sheldon doing?"

"Not great. He's not handling the break up too well."

"Too bad. You should *gai siu* (set up) Sheldon with Jenny."

"*Mom!*" Jen protested.

"What's wrong with Sheldon? He's good-looking and he as a good job."

And he's Chinese, I thought. (Hunka-hunka was Persian.)

"I don't think Shel is ready for another relationship yet, Mom," I said tactfully.

"Too bad." She paused to smack my dad on the knee for eating too fast. "So, does Dave have a girlfriend yet?"

I snorted. "Nope."

"Luke?"

"Nope."

"*Cheah, gum kay gwai* (That's just weird)," she fumed, "why is it that you boys never seem to have girlfriends?"

"It's because we're losers, mom."

Later on that night, I headed downstairs to give Charisse another shot. Lately, I've been able to play her a little bit, but still not as much as I'd like to. I played some *Blue Rodeo*, some *Third Eye Blind*, some classic *Eagles*. I played some *Chris Isaak*, and some *U2*.

> *"And so she woke up, from where she was lying still,*
> *Said I, I gotta do something about where we're going.*
> *Step on a steam train…*
> *Step outta the driving rain, baby,*
> *Run from the darkness…in the night.*
> *Singing ah…ah la la la de day,*
> *Ah la la la de day…ah la la la de day."*

"*Mi-koh! Sik chang-ah!* (Eat your oranges!)" Mom had waited for me to finish the song. The folks'd long known I had a talent for this, but stopped complimenting me on it long ago.

"Coming," I sighed. I laid Charisse back carefully on her cradle and lumbered upstairs.

The guitar. I used to think it was the only thing that could save me, the only thing that truly loved me, unreservedly. The only thing that was pure and pleasurable in this cold, stupid, heartless world. But I recently realized that it's just a thing like anything else. And when I realized that, I was able to play a little again. And a little more magic was lost from my life. Dang, I'm sure glad I got such foolishness out of my system.

My mom is a pretty classy woman. Educated, attractive, and domestically impaired, she was the jewel of the Lee clan, sought after by legions of men when she was younger. Some mothers tended to get rather frumpy when they pushed the age of fifty, but not mom…she looks at least a decade younger than she really was, and is immaculately coiffed and dressed. She is also the classic high self-monitor, self-conscious, almost bordering on narcissistic.

"Do you think I look plain?" she asked me one day last summer when we were out for *dim sum*. It was a weekday after 2 pm (twenty per cent discount).

"What exactly do you mean, 'plain'?"

"I mean I'm not wearing make-up," she said in Cantonese. "So do you think I look plain?"

"Mom, you shouldn't give a *fig [I almost said 'fuck']* about how you look. I mean, look at me. I certainly don't care about my appearance." I was dressed like a slob, as usual – jeans, running shoes, shapeless oversized sweatshirt.

"But you're young," she said. "*Ching chun hei jue ho geh **bun chien**.*"

Another proverb. "Sorry, what does *that* mean?"

"'*Youth is the best makeup*'. You don't need to care about how you look because you're young – that's good enough."

I thought about that one for a bit, chewing on some *siu mai*. You know, she does come up with some pearls sometimes. "I'm the son of a Zen philosopher," I teased.

But these days, I've been getting into more fights with my mother. She can be pretty high-strung and hypersensitive, and her menopause isn't helping much. And, lately, I can't say I've been the paragon of tolerance, either – maybe because my life has been a lot less tolerable, my own frustrations and neuroses at an all-time high.

My mother has this habit which is the absolute *worst*: she always ends an argument by laying the blame solely on herself. After scolding the children with a choice selection of mortifying events from our checkered past, she'd then start flagellating herself, mercilessly and loudly – and always in front of us, of course. It's a devastating combination.

"It's all my fault," she'd lament. *"I haven't taught you properly. What did I do wrong? I was a bad mother. I just don't understand what I did wrong. What did I do wrong… ?"* God, I *hated* it when he blamed herself – it's far worse than when she yelled directly at me. It was as if generations of ancestors suddenly sat up from their graves and tisked. Bad Chinese son.

And so we fight. And it makes me sad when we fight, and sadder still to realize this fact: I do not think I can be here anymore. Our relationship can only be peacefully optimized by limiting contact to a weekly phone call and visits during Christmas and Easter. But where *can* I go? I'm trapped…I'm trapped. *I'm trapped I'm trapped I'm trapped I'm trapped…*

After yet another emotional slugfest in the Chao household, I grabbed the car and drove downtown to the school to do some work, thinking maybe it would take my mind off of things. How wrong I was – the ride down the Don Valley Parkway gave me time to amplify my problems, all the pain and misery in my so-called life melding into one huge pulsating tumour. A huge, pulsating tumour I wanted to extract using a twelve-gauge shotgun.

And as I parked the car in an alleyway behind the Sanford Fleming building, it all just came out. All the frustrations, the curses, the tears, the cries to God or gods in heaven. The lament at being so…*mundane.* I stopped the car in the middle of the alleyway and was crying and yelling and beating my head against the steering wheel of the family Honda, in a cathartic rage of despair.

It was all finished after a minute or so. I sat there, head resting on the steering wheel, hands tightly clutching a shredded ball of Kleenex, feeling drained and slightly foolish. I looked up and, through my filmy eyes, I saw a girl walking past, staring at me wide-eyed. She turned her head away quickly and scurried along.

I sighed. In books or movies, she would have been my

Angel In White, saving me from my personal hell, whisking me away to some tropical paradise with lots of sun and sex and word processing equipment. But this is Real Life, so of course that wasn't going to happen.

I started the car again, the sounds of *Kenny G* floating through the speakers beneath the Fasten Seatbelt bell; frowning, I slapped my tape back in and parked properly.

Working in the darkened halls of the Bio building, I thought about how nice it would be to have the ability to stop time. I've often fantasized about this – when you've been winded by several sharp blows to the stomach in succession, you want some time to recover, not to run the marathon you're scheduled for the next day. But life is obviously not like that. It keeps on coming, regardless of the multiple traumas you may have received the day before.

Life stops for no one…unless you stop **it**.

Hmmm.

I want life to stop. Just for a moment. So I can catch my breath. So I can sleep for a while. Collect myself. Grab a bite. Take a deep breath and plunge back into the grey chaos.

But that wasn't really it, was it?

All the anger, the despair, the bitterness, the depression, the pain, the suffering…after all of that, I can only come to these simple conclusions.

I am lonely.

I miss her.

"*Ah bao*," Mom said when I got home at around 1 am, tendering me sliced oranges as a peace offering. "You're late."

"Sorry mom," I mumbled weakly, unwilling to elaborate. Hell, would you?

It all comes back to chemistry.

I mean, look at Rick. The master of Better Living Though Chemistry. I saw Rick consistently ooze success and smoothness, strength and energy – all because he regulated and enhanced his chemistry.

"Think about it, Mike," he said. We were sitting at a 'townie' bar in southern Waterloo – no students. "What if you were offered a pill that helps you better conform to the norms that define success? Just think about it – confidence, independence, self-esteem – all if these can be *yours*, with few side-effects."

"You sound like a salesman for Sandoz Pharmaceuticals."

"Bud, in a few years I'll *own* Sandoz Pharmaceuticals. And all subsidiaries thereof."

"Rick," I said, choosing my words carefully. "Drugs are kind of…unpredictable. Pharmacology differs across physiologies. Even experienced pharmacists and physicians are still technically in the dark ages when it comes to predicting the effects of certain medication."

"Interesting."

"A person who is not clinically depressed may engender what is called a 'serotonegenetic response': over-stimulation of the brain, too much serotonin. At that point, all bets are off – who knows what could happen?"

He nodded. I nodded back. A few hours later, we were both wasted and he was telling me he was shifting into the future. That's when I started to worry.

The problem was that ninety-eight-point-nine per cent of the time, he conformed perfectly with the norms that define success. So perfectly that periodic revelations of what I assumed to be his real self, usually while I was picking him up from some bar where he was drinking heavily, hit like a shard of glass through the jugular. They seemed *that* deviant…most of the time, I half expected his head to start spinning and spewing green pea soup, or Mephisto himself popping up one day and saying "*Finished yet?*"

On occasion, Rick recommended I see a doctor about prescribing his wonder drug.

"Mike, you're a good writer – you know that, I know that," he said, downing his single-malt and ordering another one. "It's just that you lack focus. The drug'll give you that focus. It'll bring out your talent, and The Book™ – whatever it's about –

will get written, and we'll be rich and famous."

I didn't believe him – not about the drug, about the talent. Pretty soon, I didn't believe him about the drug either. Things were bad after Mina, but ultimately, one thought prevented me from being sedated to the gills, and that was this: *I need my pain.* Do you *hear* me, God, you flipping bastard? I am *stronger* than that. I *must* be. I *need* to be. It *can't* be any other way. Besides, The Book™ would never get written any other way.

Like it or not, and sometimes I did not like it, aggravation is extremely conducive to creativity. You can't imagine how many scribblings I've penned under the influence of angst – a lot of it is pretty good, I'd venture to say. The problem is, writing requires aggravation-free focus to actually organize all that raw data into a semblance of a novel. I guess I'll just have to get back to you on that one.

I woke up for no reason in the middle of the night and started sifting through the contents of my Campbell's Soup box.

My oh my. The contents of twenty-six years in these fragile pages – *that's my soul up there.* Pretty much all the things I hold precious about my life are in this simple corrugated container. It's slightly comforting to know that despite being an abject failure in almost everything else, at least I could still write.

Am I mystifying it too much? Maybe I'm mystifying it too much. But in a life that's so utterly devoid of magic, what else can I do? It's either that or taking a class on Wiccan sacrifices at the Learning Annex. The Chinese held the written word as sacred. Once. Looking at these slightly yellowing pages, I guess I can see why. For some strange reason, I take pleasure in the crispness of the pages of my notebooks. Thin, crisp pages, filled with blue, black, even green scrawls, crinkling between my fingers. The pages *do* feel ancient, even holy. Like wads of freshly-minted banknotes, or medieval parchment, so clean and mean- ingful and truthful.

Yeah, I guess I *am* mystifying it way too much. Maybe I

should grab a clue from Dave: '*Get a life and grow up.*'

*But, this **is** my life.*

I've "got" it all, right here.

And as unpleasant as it might get sometimes, it will continue to go here. And in The Book™.

I realized at that moment that those who are lucky enough to be able to fully realize their dreams are in the minority. Indeed, those who are *able* to have dreams are pretty darned lucky within themselves. And upon understanding that, I slept a little better. If only a little.

I woke up a little earlier today – 7 am – because I had to drive my mom to a doctor's appointment at the doctor's office by the Loblaws at Highway 7 and Warden Ave.

We got out the door late, so mom started nagging again. It wasn't my fault, though – bad hair day. I'd venture to say that a lot of Asians have bad hair days. My hair drives me crazy sometimes, especially in the morning. Chinese hair is flattish, stiff, susceptible to the ravages of bedhead and ball caps and toques, and it can get seriously spiky and unmanageable after a night of tossing and turning.

"Just think of it as a manifestation of our true inner-punk selves, rebelling against restrictive cultural norms imposed on us by parents and such," smiled Luke.

I got mom to the doctor's office on time, though, and, after an hour, we were walking back to the car, parked by the grocery store.

"Oh *baby!*" I exclaimed.

It was a beautiful red Porsche 911 – as smooth as a soap bar on wheels, and just as slick.

My mom peered in. "*Ah bao*, only two seats," she said in English.

I nodded. "Yup. Very neat."

"Do you know what they call a car like this? *Jee mm jee doh-ah?*" she asked in Cantonese.

I shook my head.

"*Gon jeut ngoy moh ying*," she said, chuckling a little.

"Meaning?"

"*Ngoy moh* means 'mother-in-law'," she continued. "*Gon jeut* means 'a dead end' – driving something or someone into a dead end. *Ying* means style. So this style of car is 'driving your mother-in-law to a dead end'. Two-seats, no room for her."

I laughed out loud. "I guess you want me to get a school bus then – plenty of room for you," I teased. I looked at the Porsche wistfully. "This must be a total babe machine. What a cool car."

She was still peering into the car, at the bucket seats and the Alpine sound system when its owner, a large blond fellow came out, carrying a bag full of Chunky soups and Special K. My mom looked up at him and nodded, smiling.

"Cool car," she said.

So I'm back at the Second Cup. Fearing. Fantasizing. Foolishly.

A moment of clarity. A shock of truth.

I am tired. Of being in a perpetual liminal state. Disconsolate for what seemed to be a ridiculously long time. I feel as though I am in this ridiculous situation, thinking these ridiculous thoughts, forced into these ridiculous quandaries. I feel simply…put-upon.

So this is what I've decided: I don't want the future.

*I want **now**.*

I put down my coffee and get off my chair, jaw squared, arms akimbo. *Damn it to hell, I'm going to get some resolve – any resolve.* Deep breath, here. *Fuzzy logic's got me down, man. Time to switch into binary.* Another deep breath. *It's heads or tails, man, raise or fold, spin the wheel, let's see what's behind Door Number One…*

"Excuse me."

She turns with mild surprise on her lovely face.

"Do you have any HB leads I could buy off of you? My pencil just ran out." (*Of course, my personal stock of leads was buried safely, under the spare batteries in my knapsack.*)

"As a matter of fact, I do," she says. Her voice is quite nice, too. She reaches into her bag and roots around a little.

"Thanks, you're a lifesaver." I lean against the opposing chair. "So, do you work around here? I've noticed you hanging out recently."

"Yup...I work for an accounting firm." *(Root **root**, root **root**.)* "I was recently transferred from Mississauga to the down-town office."

"That's interesting. How do you like it?"

"Very much." She flashed a smile, and I almost melted had I not held my resolve to be melt-free. "Here you go. Don't worry about it," she said, handing me a package of leads and deflecting the loonie I handed to her, "I steal them from the office, any-way." *(Cue laughter.)*

"Well, let me buy you a coffee, at least," I said, trying to be engaging. *(Seems like it's working so far.)* "My name's Mike... Mike Chao."

"Donna Yuen."

We shook hands. Her hand was remarkably cold – poor circulation. No ring on her finger, too, but I'd already noticed that. So I bought her another Amaretto Almond and I sat down, and we talked a little. She seemed bright, animated and not a little interesting. *(Uh oh. Strike One: No woman this great is unattached...at least, no one I've ever run into. Waiting for the next pitch...)*

"So Donna, what do you like about being downtown?"

"Oh, lots of things," she said, taking a small sip from her steaming mug and leaving a lipstick mark on it. "I like the con-venience, mostly. A lot of my friends are down here, too." *(Time out on that one...Strike Two: Nice women always refer to boy-friends as 'a friend' first, so as to not hurt your feelings. Third base coach signals Proceed With Caution...)*

"And what do you do, Mike?"

"I'm a grad student at U of T."

"Oh yes? What in?"

"Neurochemistry."

"You're kidding!" *(Insert overwhelming wave of anxiety here,*

Retreat, dammit! Retreat!) "Do you know Todd Brudner?"

(*Shit.*) "Yes…in fact, he's my office mate."

"Wow! He's my boyfriend!"

(*Silence.*)

Steeeeeeeeeeeeeeeeeeerike THREE!

YERRR OUTTA HERE MIKEY! SEE YA!

I nod dispassionately. "You don't say."

"Yes! This is just so weird!" she squeals.

And suddenly, the sun broke through the clouds. Not outside…in my mind, my heart. The sun broke through that six-by-six cubicle, melting it away like acid on cartilage, exposing my tender naked body to the rays. It hurt, it burned, but it got me yelping, running around, private parts bouncing, running off to where I wanted to be. It was freedom after a long, long time, and I am not looking a gift horse – you take the bitter with the sweet.

I give Donna my most engaging smile. Mister Nice Guy. Radiating the highest degree of benevolence. *Bitch.* "Yeah, what a coincidence!" I glance at my watch and fake shock. "Gracious! I'm late for a meeting with Prof Allenberg – I'm sure Todd has told you about how particular he is. I've really got to go." (*Nothing personal, my love…okay, so it is.*)

"Sure, Mike." She smiled too. Such a lovely smile. "Maybe you, Todd and me can get together for lunch later, or coffee or something."

(*As if.*) "I'd really like that, Donna."

"So would I."

"Well, Donna, it's been a pleasure meeting you. See you again sometime?" (*Not.*)

"See you, Mike."

I smile back and turn away, with lipstick on my collar and a song in my heart.

I guess that's *it.*

All *right.*

All RIGHT!

I'm *outta* here!

The Plot Thins.

*R*rrrriiiing.
Rrrrriiiing.
Rrrrriiiing.
Godammit, you're always in the middle of something…
Rrrrriiiing.
Fer Chris*sake*, where the hell is the receiver…?
Rrrrrii…
"Hello? Hello… ?" I dropped the receiver on the ground, so I dropped my ear to the ground beside it because my hands were full of T-shirts and sock rolls.
"Hello? Mmm. Mmm hmmm. Mmmm. Mmm hmmm.
"Right. Okay."
Click.
*Man, why can't people die **after** you've left…?*

part 5
kenosis.

Pattern Recognition.

I managed to borrow the car from my parents right after the funeral, for a trip to Waterloo. Dad said he'd take care of mom, and told me I was free to do whatever I needed to do.

That was good.

I pulled off of University Ave. onto the Ring Road, trying to find a parking lot that wasn't patrolled by the University Police. The campus was relatively deserted – exams were probably finished – so that wasn't much of a problem. I was relieved to find Jeepy and Luke's bike parked beside each other in the same lot.

I walked into the Campus Centre, a little self-conscious because I was still wearing the dress from the funeral. They didn't give me time to change…after a few murmured condolences, the guys just took off for a private wake at the Bombshelter Pub. I guess I was a little self-conscious as to what I was about to do as well. I had seen the videotape earlier this morning, and though the police did not allow me to take it because of the investigation, that was okay. It was not conclusive, it would not have helped much, anyway. Taking a deep breath and clutching the envelope in my left hand, I showed my ID to the bouncer and went inside.

The bar was populated with a relative sprinkling of students. The Banana Boys stood out like sore thumbs among the sandals and cutoff jean shorts, huddling around a wobbly wood table, several emptied pitchers in front of them, suit jackets slung behind their chairs.

"…total loser what kind of total loser freaking *drinks* himself to death?" Dave was exclaiming, motioning his hands in agitation. The others were sitting around in various states of dejection, not particularly responding. "Cripes, I've *never* lost control of myself when wasted, and I certainly would never fall and cut the hell out of myself. It's like all those newspaper articles about stupid frosh taking part in stupid hazing stuff, getting wasted, and falling off buildings and shit. Christ, man, you deserve it if you're that stupid." He was trying to sound off-handed, callous, but not quite succeeding.

"Eh, I don't even know why it's hitting me like this. We had some good times, but I haven't even talked to him in, like, two years or so – so why the hell should I care? *He* was the one who ditched *us* for the lifestyles of the rich and famous. Oh, hi Shirley."

The guys looked up from their drinks and grunted their respective greetings. Luke dragged an extra chair from a nearby table with his foot.

I sat down and smiled wanly. "How are you guys?" There was a disheartened chorus of 'okays' and 'all rights'. Shel snagged a chilled glass from the waitress, and I accepted a measure of beer.

There was a long silence.

"By the way, Dave," Shel suddenly asked. "What was in that paper bag you put into the, uh, coffin?"

Dave hung his head. "You don't want to know." He looked at me apologetically.

"Why do you say?" I asked gently.

"Because of the way it, you know, all happened…"

"Dave," said Mike slowly, "you didn't put liquor in the coffin, did you?"

"Yeah," he admitted, "Yeah, I did." He held up his hands. "I guess it seems…tasteless. It is, I guess. Yes, it is. But…" He was saying this haltingly. Were his eyes reddening a little? "But Christ, man, me and Rick…we just *loved* those things. It was the *idea*, you know? It was, like, 'our' special thing." He stuck out his lower lip, and then shrugged. "I'm not sure if I can even explain it. I can't really change it – the significance, you know? I just felt that …you know." He looked at me like a puppy dog that had just chewed through a pair of new shoes.

"I'm sorry, Shirl. Dumb thing to do, I guess."

I shook my head. "It's okay, Dave. It's between you and Rick."

Dave turned to Luke. "Are you gonna lecture me about this,

Stick?" he said, expectantly.

"I'll save it for the next time you do something else bone-headed."

"Thanks, jerk-off."

Another silence.

I took a deep breath. "Well…I just came by to see how you guys were doing. And to give you this." I put the white envelope onto the beer-drenched table. "I found it in the pile of Rick's stuff the police let us have back. Just some items they found on his body." I noticed the guys shuffling uncomfortably when I said that. "Mom didn't have the strength to sort through the box. So I did it." I sat back and waited.

The guys stared at the envelope on the table, seemingly entranced by it. And it just sat there for a while, soaking up beer. After what seemed like an eternity, Luke finally broke the stillness by picking it up. He read the smeared grease-pencilled inscription – *Right shirt pocket* – then opened it.

"It's a picture," he announced plainly.

He handed it to Shel, who scrutinized it and shrugged, and then to Mike, who barely glanced at it.

Dave looked over and spewed his beer back into his glass, gagging. "That's not a picture," he choked, so Sheldon whacked him on the back.

"That's *somebody's feet!*"

Mike looked at it again, furrowing his eyebrows. Nothing registered for a few seconds, and then he nodded in a so-so sort of way. "Yeah, so it is," he stated. "Dave, wasn't, uh…wasn't this taken that night? You know, *that night?*"

"What night?"

"No no no, *that* night," Mike insisted, snapping his fingers and smacking his forehead. "Ugh, Tequila Brain-Death Night."

"Oh, *riiiight*," agreed Dave.

I took back the picture. It showed a pair of feet stuck in a toilet bowl, the swirls of water flushing over them. There was a piece of the toilet cover showing, as well as an obscured bottle of Toilet Duck.

"Whose feet were those?" asked Shel.

Mike shrugged. "I don't know...could've been anyone's. We were all pretty wasted, as I recall. I know Rick brought along a camera that night to take pictures of us. He wanted to blackmail us for lunches or something. Always enterprising, that Rick." The guys all chuckled a little. "Boy, that was a rotten night."

"Shit man, I couldn't even *look* at a tequila shot for months afterward," added Dave. He turned to me. "So, what does this mean, like?"

"The picture was found with Rick the night he died," I said. They stared back blankly. "In his right shirt pocket. There's an inscription behind it." Luke took the picture and turned it over, revealing what looked like Rick's trademark professional script: *Tequila Sucks.*

Luke smiled wryly. "Simple, truthful, yet poignant. I like it."

"So, what does this mean, like?" Dave repeated.

I shook my head. "I don't know. I just thought you guys would...want it." I debated telling them about the videotape, but decided against it. For now, at least.

We all paused thoughtfully. The pool table across the room cracked as a trio of students broke and started playing Cut-throat.

Mike spoke up. "Regrets? Nostalgia, maybe?"

Dave snorted. "That boy had a mind focused like a diamond cutter. There's no way something as impractical as nostalgia could happen to him."

"Oh, I don't know, Dave," Shel said. "You always say that nostalgia is like an irresistible drug for some, right?"

"Yeah, but only for romantic losers like you, Shel." Shel immediately gave him the finger. "Trust me, dudes – Rick was not that sort of guy. He was way too practical for stuff like that."

"Have to disagree with you there, Dave," said Mike. He sighed. "I don't know about you guys, but I had some...some extremely strange conversations with Rick back in school. *Extremely* strange. I wouldn't really call them 'romantic' or 'deep' by any means, but they were definitely, you know, strange. About odd dreams he had, and what he thought they meant. He was way more introspective than we give him credit for, maybe."

Mike looked at me intently.

"Ah, come on," Dave smirked. "He dumped us like a case of empties. No regrets."

"These things have a funny way of re-surfacing after a while," Mike said quietly.

I shuffled my shoes underneath the table. We all didn't say anything for a long time, the guys pausing to take it all in. And then Luke pursed his lips and nodded lightly.

"Guys," he announced, "In absence of any other evidence, I'd be tempted to say that, well…"

We all looked at him.

"Well…I think he missed us." Dave and Mike shook their heads, but you could see the hope in their actions, a hope that needed to be coaxed out.

And then Sheldon did it. *Good old Shel.*

He *cheered.*

"That's *it*! That's it, I think. I believe he missed us. I really do believe that." He gave us all a broad grin.

"Shel, get off what you're smoking please," Dave said.

"But don't you *see* guys? You *have* to believe it," Shel continued. "I think that's all you have to do. And I *do*. I believe that Rick was this good person who got what he wanted, but it cost him a lot."

"What cost?" smirked Dave incredulously, "*Us*? That's being kind of…high on yourself, isn't it, Shelly?"

Shel shook his head. "Look. I *love* you guys," he said sincerely. "Really. And you might think I'm an idiot for saying it, but it's true. You're all very valuable to me, even though sometimes each of you can be just plain stupid." He waved his arms around, including all of us. "And that's the point. Even though we're all just a bunch of stupid morons, *you* are still valuable to *me*…maybe even more so because you *are* so stupid."

"Chee, tanks," Luke said, dryly.

"You know what I mean. And I know you guys feel the same way – or we wouldn't all be here, right? You guys think you're too cool to admit it. Well, so did Rick, I think, and he was way cooler than all of us combined. I think he *missed* us. I believe this."

He turned to me. "Shirley, do you believe that?"

I nodded. *That's why I am here.*

Shel then turned to Luke, who sighed. "Yeah. I guess." He gave us an rueful smile. "You know, dudes, despite it all, I really do think he loved life. We all complain about it all the time, and sometimes we do something about it to make a change. But it all comes back to the important things we start off with. He just got his priorities messed up along the way, maybe. You don't change your values like *that*, and expect everything is going to remain stable and peachy." He sighed again.

"Yeah, what the hell…I believe."

And me, Shel and Luke nodded together in confirmation, believing.

Then there was Mike.

"Yeah. Yeah. *Yeah!*" he pounded his fist into the table, causing beer to spatter all over my skirt. "Oop, sorry Shirl. You know, in a way, I think we *have* to believe. We *must*. It's…it's like we *have* to have faith. In Rick. In…*ourselves.* In the whole picture…" he waved his arms around vaguely. "You know? Otherwise, it's just too meaningless to bear. Meaningless and pointless and crushingly stupid. And it isn't, really.

"It can't be. We can't *let it* be."

Dave poured everyone another round. "So you're saying we have to have faith…maybe we even *owe* it to him to. Hmm. Sounds kinda dumb, really…it doesn't change anything. He's still dead as a doorknob. But you know what? Ultimately, I guess it's just the right thing to do." He raised his mug. "So here's to doing the Right Thing. Here's to having faith. In Rick. You motherfucking bastard. I miss you."

The guys toasted: *"To the motherfucking bastard. I miss you,"* and pulled heavily on their mugs.

And at that point, our spirits suddenly lifted like sheets to the wind. The dejection that hung over the table like a wet towel not moments before was speared by a little red plastic sword, and thrown far, far away, leaving a peculiar, somewhat illogical understanding of the deed, the events, the situation, that did not take away from its awfulness, but gave it a certain clarity that was rather comforting. Relieving. Decent. And ultimately acceptable.

Dave slammed down his empty mug with satisfied sigh. "Reaching my happy place. Yo, Mike."

"Yo."

"You brought your guitar, right?"

"Yeah. I did."

"Then get it and play something, dammit. This a *wake*, you know." Mike struggled out of his chair and went outside. Five minutes and half a pitcher later, he came in wielding Charisse.

"So what do you guys want me to play?"

"Your choice, Michael," said Luke. Mike nodded.

"Something sad, then. But something right." He thought for a moment, and then brightened.

"Okay."

Mike lumbered over to the stage, grabbed a stool, and started tuning Charisse, attracting the attention of the few patrons at the Bomber, including the bouncers, who were unsure of what to do.

And Mike started to play. And sing. Nothing fancy, but clear, his voice laden with a touch of sadness. Enough to do Bono Vox proud.

> We turn away to face the cold…enduring chill
> As day turns to night, for mercy, love.
> Your sun so bright, it leaves no shadows…only scars
> Carved into stone…on the face of earth.
> The moon is up…and over One Tree Hill
> We see the sun go down…in your eyes.
> You run like a river…on like the sea.
> You run like a river…to the sea.

Mike continued, exacting an impressed silence from the pub. Charisse sounded smooth and liquid in his hands, and Mike sang, oblivious to everything except his last paean to my brother. The bastard. I *miss* him.

I don't believe in painted roses…or bleeding hearts,
As bullets rape the night…of the merciful.
I'll see you again…when the stars fall from the sky
And the moon has turned red…over One Tree Hill.
We run like a river…on like the sea.
We run like a river…to the sea.

And the song ended, earning unsure scowls from the bouncers and applause from everyone else, including the enthusiastic hoots and hollers from our table.

"Mike, you're so *cool*!" yelled Luke.

"You the *man*!" bellowed Dave, raising his glass.

"Encore! *Encore*!" yelled Shel, doing the woofing motion with his right hand.

Mike flashed a smile and a thumbs-up sign, and started expertly plucking out the notes to a classic Celtic drinking jig by *Spirit of the West*: *"You'll have to excuse me, I'm not at my best/ I've been gone for a month, I've been drunk since I've left/These so-called vacations will soon be my death/I'm so sick from the drink I need Home For a Rest…"*

On cue, Luke, Dave and Shel scrambled up to the stage, singing robustly and off-key, ignoring the two bouncers who were about to throw the drunk Chinese guys out, once again. And I just sat there, glowing, smiling, a little tipsy, tearing up a little, because it seemed all right.

Okay, I cried. I cried for the first time, in a long time.

And at last – at long last – I think I understood these boys. They're just ordinary people. Ordinary and flawed. But their personal flaws, neuroses, idiosyncrasies, self-loathing, self-criticism, unrelentless…that's the fire than tempers them, purifies them, ushering the pure within them, making them better, vital, precious people. I guess some don't have the depth or subtlety to see this, and may ignore them, dismiss them. But in that case, they probably wouldn't have use for them, anyway, I gather. They've got themselves, and that's enough.

It's *got* to be enough.

I looked at them and smiled again. These boys. These *men*.

Milestone Zero.

Y ou know, it sounds overly sentimental, but I feel as if I've awakened from a deep, deep sleep to the purest of days. I'm feeling the warmth of the sun and cool of the breeze, and I'm starting to appreciate the possibilities of this world, the potential it holds for being good. Great, even. Unimaginably fantastic. Life as an endless stream of Cherry Cokes.

It's mid-May, and I'm finally going to California, The Promised Land.

There's bad but energetic seventies blaxploitation music blaring from the substandard car stereo – one of Luke's cassettes: "*Shaft, you is one bad **mutha**…*" I liberated an entire section of cassettes from his Wall o' Tapes for my trip – where he's going, he won't need them. The plastic cases are scattered all over the front seat of the car now, right beside some cold pizza and my precious Campbell's Soup box. It's a decent and wide-ranging selection: *Massive Attack, Supertramp, Faithless, Daniel Lanois, Matchbox 20.* Some DJ mixtapes. *America, Dire Straits, Rage Against the Machine, Ned's Atomic Dustbin.* Some Ska, some Acid Jazz, *Peter Gabriel's* best. Some weird industrial music, some *Beautiful South.* Ah, Paul Heaton's sweet, sweet, airy voice. Excellence.

I am somewhere between Toronto and San Francisco. I quit school, withdrew my student loan money, sold or gave away everything that wasn't nailed down, and just plain took off. Didn't even tell my folks. Got Shel and his dad to help me buy this old Subaru. Painted a deep green, bondo spots liberally dotting the left side, it looks like a large wedge of green Swiss cheese on wheels. *Ain't no Porsche, but it's mine, all mine…*

I also borrowed an old notebook computer from Dave with an aged version of Word and Solitaire. And a stack of floppies for backups.

And the tapes from Luke.

Man, I love those guys.

Before I left, I visited Rick. Yeah, I know it was kind of cornball, but it was nice. It was peaceful…the warm red of his gravestone, nicely carved Chinese and English inscriptions. The bushes, the flowers, the oranges by the site. I stayed there a little, not talking to Rick because that seemed a little too silly. Instead, I enjoyed the grass, the sun, the distant whir of a lawnmower, leaning on the warm stone, drinking bottled water.

I thought about the lazy bastard I had been. I thought about the shackles I slapped on myself because I thought my limbs were too weak to support me on their own, like the spook from *The Wizard of Id*, forever hanging in that dungeon. I thought, not without a twinge of sadness, how Rick didn't really have to buy it like this. But he did, and even though I was going to anyway, I am going to write about it. I'll launch that Message in the Bottle for him. *And for myself,* I smiled.

I got up, uselessly trying to slap off some of the grass stains from my freshly converted jean cutoffs. Before I left, I bowed three times in front of the grave. Cultural programming dies pretty hard, I suppose.

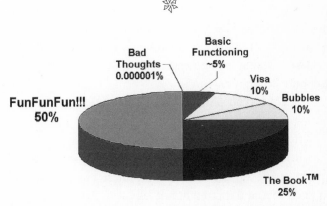

Fig. 14. Mike's BrainChart™ (what day was it again?)

Here's the deal: Luke is ditching Toronto and riding across the country to attend Sonja's wedding, and to finish up his Psych degree at the University of Victoria.

"You sure they're going to take you?" I asked.

"Nope."

"Uh."

He shrugged. "It'll be hell trying to get them to count some of my old Waterloo credits, but it's *Victoria*, man. The place for mellow granola-eating dudes like me. I mean, Victoria's probably the place Mahatma Gandhi would choose to live in if he were a suburbanite Canadian with a wife, two kids and a mountain bike, it's that mellow." And the best part is we're going to meet up on the West Coast and just hang out for a while.

He checked his watch. "Oop gotta go, dude. Dinner with Mom and Janice."

"So you're okay with your mom, now?"

Another shrug. "Yeah, I guess. Better than before. She even offered to set me up with some relatives in Vancouver. I dunno. It might be okay." From his tone, though, I knew he thought it was going to be better than okay.

Shel was going to Hong Kong to look for a job. "I'm young, I'm alive," he said, "Why not?"

"Aren't you worried about the Communists?"

"You shouldn't ask me if I'm afraid of *them*. You should ask them if they're afraid of *me*!"

"Yeah, what*ever*," said Dave, rolling his eyes. "Your ass is going to be popped by some Commie hickboy soldier with an AK when they eventually crush the common people, trust me."

Dave is taking a long vacation to keep Shel company, and raise some hell in Asia.

"Dude, can you picture *me*, of all people – in *Asia*?" he chortled.

"Actually, I sort of can." I smiled at him, oddly.

"Chyeah *right*, man! I'm lucky the company didn't fire me outright 'cuz it was the middle of a project, but I told them I had to do this, and that I'd quit if they wouldn't let me. Turns out I'm a little more valuable than they let on. Go figure. Jobs are a dime a dozen in my bid-ness. But good friends aren't. Shelly needs my help right now, and I owe that Goofball a serious debt."

"I love you, man!" said Shel.

"Fag!"

"You guys are idiots," I said.

Another "problem": Dave met Linda, a Masters student in Sociology from the U of T, at Rick's funeral (figures Dave would pick up at a *funeral*). She was intelligent, very hot, and also a practising witch, worshipper of sorcerous faiths.

"Lin was wearing more black than Rick's family combined," Dave said, bemused. "I met her for dinner the next day, and she tried to cast a spell on me. Weird shit, man." Dave's smitten – he's resolved to give up drinking (yet again) and get in shape.

"More for the Dark Mistress to feast on," he said.

"There's a change in the wind," he said.

"This might be The One," he said.

"It'll never last," said Luke to me, confidentially.

I've heard it said that everyone's lives can be converted into a decent book that could make it to at least No. 4 on the New York Times Best Seller list. With very few exceptions. I guess it's kind of hard to believe. Because in Real Life, the mundane and boring tends to overwhelm the exciting stuff (that is, if there is any). For every obligatory car chase, gunfight, or gratuitous sex scene, there's ten times feeding the cat, shopping for English muffins, cutting a cheque for rent and utilities.

Also, in Real Life, the ending's never there. Movies and books and plays may end neatly with a frilly *The End* where issues are resolved and the cows come home to roost, but we all know that Real Life isn't that way, because there's always the *And Then What?* factor.

The key, then, is to express it in the right voice.

Everyone has a story. All they need is the right voice.

And with it, we can start to see that the most beautiful

things in the world are simple, even boring, at least from the outside. Fabergé Eggs they are not, but they could hide something really special.

"I'm glad that you've finally realized the bottom line: you're a *writer*, dammit!" Luke trumpeted.

"Luke, I now know that I want – I need – to do *something* – *anything* – about it. Before I lose the passion." I took off my ball cap and brushed my fresh crew-cut. "I'm not stupid, man – I realize I can chalk up much of my angst and passion to the age factor. And I know this will fade away when I'm thirty-five, with kids, a white picket fence, and a minivan in the garage."

" 'Attaboy, Michael," he grinned, slapping me on the back. "Now you know, and knowing is half the battle…so they say. Be sure to show me whatever you've done when we meet up out west. Promise me that."

"I promise," I said, holding up my hand. "Scout's Honour."

"Well, at least you're doing something," Dave said over the speakerphone, keyboard clattering in the background, "and not just lying down and accepting it passively, like you used to, you wiener."

"Thanks, Dave."

"I mean, you know it, and I know it – there are just so many of us, these bruised Bananas, *juk sing* – miserable, frustrated, alone, branded dysfunctional geek-losers, by others or themselves." I could hear him pound his fist on his desk in frustration in the background, earning a yelp from Jase who was juggling beside him.

"Goddammit, why the hell *is* this? Is it genetic? Is it our own fault? Is it our destiny? I'd like very much not to think so. I think you can do us all a great service by finding out, exploring it, finding the roots of it all."

"And make lots of money doing it," I added.

"Damn straight. No point otherwise." He grunted. "Lately, I've seen a lot of crap being published – books by these yuppie-baby-boomer-types, or these Gen-X entrepreneurial types. And, oh God, if I read another dust cover describing a book about three generations of Chinese women escaping the shackles of bondslavery, I swear the oatmeal's gonna hit the wall."

"Cripes, Dave, you're such a pig!"

"Anyway, if *they* can get published, a loser like *you* can get published, no sweat. I got faith in you, buddy. Call me if you need anything."

Shel, of course, was a lot less cerebral about it, because he was Shel. "I swear to God, Mike," he warned jokingly, "if you make my character gay, I'm going to come to California and beat the crap out of you!"

"For the love of criminy, Shel, give it a rest. Seriously though, your character in The Book™ isn't really *you*, you can't take it as if it's a reflection of…"

"Yeah yeah, you're boring me already. If you have any problems with the car, call me, buddy."

"Thanks."

"No problem. Good luck, eh?"

I pulled into a service station with a Popeye's Chicken n' Biscuits. I parked the car under the shade of an apple tree in the crowded plaza. Geez, I looked like a slob – old T-shirt, torn cutoffs and a ball cap angled badly on my head. Scuffed Tevas, Velcro strip on the left ankle worn to the point that it always kept slipping off. I dropped my sunglasses in the car, because I wanted that damned light-sensitive gland at the back of my head to suck in as much as it could possibly consume.

I grabbed a basket of chicken and went outside to eat, while reviewing my financial status…

- Remaining student loan
- Cashing in RRSPS (at a severe tax disadvantage)
- Proceeds from personal fire sale
- Small loan from Jennifer
- Credit card cash advances (at a severe interest disadvantage)
- Last Chinese New Year's Lucky Money
- Beer bottle deposits from the basement
- Change from the fish bowl in the family room
- Money from selling my body to the night.

Let's see…carry the four…factor in food, fuel, tolls, the odd beer on the road. No motels, just a sleeping bag in the back of the Subaru in parking lots, towel and a bar of soap…

Hmm…

Not so good. Oh well. You have to sweat a little for your dreams. If you don't, it's not worth nearly as much. Don't you think?

In a dog-eared thesaurus I always carry around with me, I once discovered a very cool word: *kenosis*. The literal Greek translation means an emptying out, a distancing such that renewal, rebirth can take place. I think this is what is happening to me right now. I'm regaining vitality, exponentially. Newer material is filling up the hole in my heart, engulfing the emptiness. I…*feel* again. I want you to understand how *incredible* that is. How precious it is.

I *feel*. I *am*.

I am scripting a story that is mine and mine alone. And *that's* what makes it sacred. Vital. The truth, or at least my perception of such. Valuable in its own right.

I am creating it.

I've come to understand that experiencing the richness life has to offer is what makes it worthwhile. I've become a firm believer in the dual theory of emotion: the greater the pain you endure, the more it shows your capacity for appreciating pleasure, the heights you can achieve. Not necessarily *will*, mind you, but at least you know you'll be able to. If you try. And with a little luck, I suppose.

I am only twenty-six years old. There is still much time to see the world. That, I believe, is the main advantage of being young – being able to make fresh starts when they need to be made. And Lord, this one was long overdue.

I finished up my lunch and stepped over to the shop where they sold maps, chocolate bars and really bad tapes. I heard this country-western song on someone's radio waft by as they pulled out of the service area:

You're the love of my life…
But you ain't my truck.

Boy, you can't get more profound than *that*.

I slap the Visa down at the Internet kiosk to send off a quick and cryptic piece of e-mail. Something not very comprehensible. But something that needed to be said.

From: mike_travelling@yahoo.com
To: shirley.wong@artsci.utoronto.ca
Subject: I think I've got a handle on all this now…

It's all about equilibrium – good, solid equilibrium. It usually comes when you've tasted all the extremes. Extremism naturally doesn't sit too well with the majority of people – that's why it's called "extremism" – so when you figure it out and settle on a happy medium and *whammo*! There's it is.

You know Shirl, I've been to hell and back, I may have hit bottom some time ago back there, but do you know what? It's all *okay*. And it's *going* to be okay.
I am convinced of this.
Take care of yourself.
I'll see you soon.
I promise.

After getting some fruit from the store, I walked out into the New York sunshine…and I lifted my arms up to the sky, doing a little twirl as I headed to my car, basking in the warmth, drinking in the light. And I knew – I *knew* – standing out there, worshipping the sun-god in front of some incredulous tourists, that all the badness and the pain that coursed through my veins for years was draining out of me at that very moment, into the infinity of the big blue sky. I was purifying myself, cleansing my soul if you will. Just feeling happy to be alive.

I closed my eyes, and began spinning around. On mad impulse, I stuck a banana sticker on my forehead and started prancing. I stuck my fist out defiantly towards the sky and started jumping up and down, joyously.

I focused all the anger, all the bitterness, the discontent, the self-doubt, the self-loathing, into a solid beam of negative energy. And I launched this beam from my stomach with all the force I could muster to the east, 180 degrees away from where I was going.

And it will travel up through the stratosphere, through the ozone layer and plunge into the vacuum of space to the land of the dead, rocketing around the moon in a parabolic trajectory, returning, gaining in speed and acceleration, levelling out and passing around the world, picking up all the anger, bitterness, self-doubt, self-loathing it can, and trying to return it to me on a beach in California. But it cannot enter me again. It just can't, for I will have been internally fortified by vitamin D and piña coladas and far too much relaxation and fun.

*I deserve it. I do. I'm proud of how far I've come. Sure. Why not? I **have** come far. The old Michael is dead, his chronically-depressed corpse decomposing in the warm American sun. Well, okay, not dead…just very, very distant.*

And what if people still cling onto the idea of the old Michael? What if they expect the quiet, depressing, marginally-suicidal, empty shell they've come to know and love? I don't really care, I figure. The new Michael is here and now. It is who I am.

I collapsed on the ground, chest heaving. *Sigh.* I guess lengthy travel does that to you. I scrambled back on my feet, giving a jaunty salute to some people who were staring at me slack-jawed, and I got into the car. I felt like Dustin Hoffman sitting at the back of the bus, smiling vacuously like an idiot. And my Campbell's Soup box is my blushing bride.

Just minutes out of the service area, I see this girl trying to hitch a ride from a truck inspection area. She's thin, cute, her long brown hair tossing in the breeze like cornsilk. She's wearing a worn-out, oversized plaid shirt, cutoffs and scuffed Tretorns, and is carrying a camping knapsack. On impulse, I pull over and doff my ball cap.

"Carriage awaits."

She beams and gets in, launching her knapsack over the passenger seat on top of a pile of cassettes in the back. "Oops. Thanks for stopping. My name is Pam by the way." He voice has a peculiar twang to it – *Carolinian, perhaps*? She extends her hand, and we shake. I notice her hands are cold – poor circulation, again.

"Howdy, Pam. I'm Mike."

"Howdy Mike."

"Howdy."

I slide back into the thruway traffic. We don't speak for a while, and I start fantasizing a little. I smile. In my mind, she's commenting favourably on the music I'm playing.

In my mind, we're having an intricate conversation about the meaning of *Supertramp*.

In my mind, she's gushing over the guitar and asking me to play John Denver for her sometime.

In my mind, she's feeding me doughnut holes while I am trying to read a map.

She sees me grinning, and says something about it. "You're grinning," she says, amused. "Did I do something funny?"

"Oh no. I was just thinking about an old episode of *Gilligans Island*. Man, that Skipper."

"Ah."

A pause.

"So what's a nice girl like you doing on an interstate toll highway like this?"

She laughs. It was a nice, friendly laugh. "Do you always used tired old lines like that?"

"Not always. I'm a Capricorn, by the way, and I like camping, pasta, swing dancing, and long moonlit walks on the beach."

She laughs again. "Gemini, and I skeet shoot. Actually, I just graduated from fashion design at SUNY Buffalo, and I'm on my way to see some relatives in Chicago. I'm kind of short on cash, so here I am."

Chicago, eh? I can go to Chicago... "Don't you know it's kind of dangerous for a beautiful girl like you to hitch rides like this?"

"I know. That's why I'm *soooo* lucky to've caught you, the sun reflecting off your suit of shining armour and all." She winks at me, and it's my turn to laugh.

*Okay, this **might** be a good trip...*

A shot. A scream. A flickering candle.

Strange and wonderful shadows twist on the wall, magnified a hundred times, a thousand. They linger, taunting, inviting, mocking.

A hunger awakes inside this frail shell of a man, screaming and howling like ten thousand angels thundering from the mouth of salvation itself. They will not be denied. I will not be denied.

Creation is destruction. Destruction is purity. The misbegotten soul that is free confronts the millions of possibilities on a blank canvas. Clean, white, pristine. Unsullied by genetics or neurochemistry or DNA structures. Not all of these possibilities are pleasant...some even end up with me dead in a motel bathtub outside of Los Angeles, having taken a hundred Darvons or something.

But they are mine. All mine.

Not enslaved to crumbling institutions, ignorant people.

Not perturbed by dated values, a lack of understanding.

Not influenced by unsavoury politics, unreasonable norms.

Not captive to a person who can hold your heart atop a bed of nails...and drop it.

Compelled to do something meaningful, something prideful and with inherent value in this world. Compelled to shout and scream, to be heard, to make a difference. Something that is mine and mine alone. I am bathed in light. I am surrounded by spirit and goodness.

I am one with Brahman, Atman.

I am the walrus.

Goo goo g'joob.

Acknowledgements.

I owe a ton to some key people:

To my folks, Stephen and Winnie…for your love, faith, support, and tolerance over and above the genetic norm. Mom, thanks for the endless stockpile of Chinese proverbs and those pesky Cantonese and Mandarin translations. Dad, thanks for letting me live rent-free.

To my sister Vicky…for your love, sisterly encouragement, and future root canals (free).

To my publishers, John and Attila…for giving me a shot at this. John, thanks for your superior editing job, and for your compassionate attention to detail.

To Jim and Kathy Chang, my patrons…for hooking me up with John and Attila.

To my editor, John Herr…thanks for a quality editing job and drinks throughout.

To my good friend, Vince Ng…thanks a megaton for letting me stay at your pad in the Bay Area for those two months, where I eventually finished this #@$#%*$ thing!

To Erick Yoon…for your help with the web page, and for introducing me to the scene.

To Tom Lowe…I'm a lucky bastard for meeting you that one drunken night in New York.

To Jim Wong-Chu and Kenda Gee…thanks for your advice.

To Gabriel Wong, Gene Goykhman, Sam (Zeke) Lee, Sam Cheun, Dave Chu, Mauro Forcolin, Dustin Frank, Hau Lee, Scott Penton, Ethan Henry…for various quotes, assorted inspirational devices, and your friendship.

To Hector, Jesse, Angie, Steven, Tara, Willie, Androulla, Kevin, Jane, and the rest of the crew at the Markham-Unionville Second Cup…thanks for the endless cups of Irish Cream Classic, brewed to perfection.

And, finally, to Moe Jacobs, wise teacher to little grasshopper.

So casual it hurts: The author, circa 2000, having a brewski at the Maddy. Photo by Gene Goykhman.

Terry Woo is a Banana Boy. Born in 1971 somewhere in southern Ontario, he has lived in Toronto, Seattle, New York and San Francisco. He enjoys hockey, jazz, breaks and trance breaks, California, Black and Tans, racial equality, baking lasagna, candlelit dinners and long walks on beaches. This is his first novel.